UNGUARDED

Steel and Desire - Book Three

KENDRA GREENWOOD

Published by Blushing Books
An Imprint of
ABCD Graphics and Design, Inc.
A Virginia Corporation
977 Seminole Trail #233
Charlottesville, VA 22901

Kendra Greenwood
Unguarded

EBook ISBN: 978-1-64563-278-8
Print ISBN: 978-1-63954-040-2
v1

Chapter 1

March 30, 1993

Lightning flashed. Thunder crashed. A baby bawling. Her heart pounded, *thump-thump-thumping* in her ears. She rushed to the baby, wrapping her small hands around the crib slats and pressing her face into the space. "Shush, baby. Don't be scared. I'm here." Outside, an OPEN sign for the corner store pulsed, illuminating her brother's precious face in green flashes. He stopped crying the second he saw her, sitting up in that wobbly infant way.

"Mama." He smiled, snot smearing his face.

"Mommy will be home soon." Their mother had to go to work but promised she'd hurry home. "Are you hungry, baby?" She should make him a bottle. "I'll be right back. Don't cry." She ran to the small refrigerator. Lightning illuminated the tiny colorless room and thunder boomed again, but she wasn't afraid. It was the angels bowling—*strike!* She lifted the milk carton and sniffed. The smell made her gag. She'd have to go across the street and buy some. Her brother's cry made her stomach hurt. She needed to feed him. Now.

She slipped into her yellow raincoat and matching rubber boots, snapping the gold buckles, then opened the door to the pouring rain. From the side table, she pocketed the key with the big number five. Money, she needed money. She dragged a kitchen chair to the counter and climbed atop, searching the cabinet for the jar where her mother kept dollar bills. Standing tippy-toed, she reached near the back and grabbed a few dollars, tucking them inside her pocket.

The blinking green sign across the street beckoned. She pulled the hood over her tangled red curls, locked the door and stepped out into the damp darkness. The door to the mini-mart proved heavy. Using both hands, she managed to open it. She headed toward the glass case. Barely reaching the handle, she gave a tug.

"Can I help you?" came a soft voice from above.

She glanced up but the hood blocked her line of sight and she pushed it back. Blonde ponytail lady in a black pantsuit stood next to her... she froze... a gun hung on her belt.

The pretty lady crouched down, eye-to-eye. The bright silver star on her chest had the numbers 495 on it. She smelled nice, like vanilla cupcakes. "My name is Sarah. I'm a police officer. What's your name?"

She wasn't supposed to talk to strangers, but this was a police lady. She'd seen one on TV and police were nice, mostly. Didn't they help people? Haltingly, she said, "I'm Jamie."

"Nice to meet you. How old are you Jamie?"

She held up four fingers.

"Four years old?" Police Lady's eyes brightened.

"And a half."

"You have gorgeous red curls."

Everywhere Jamie went people said nice things about her hair, but she thought she had clown hair. She wished she could have Princess-y locks like Police Lady.

"Where's your mommy?"

"At work."

"Your daddy?"

"Mommy says he better be dead, if he knows what's good for him."

Police Lady's eyebrows lifted, eyes wide. "Oh my." She opened the refrigerated case. "Need some of this?" she asked, retrieving a milk carton from the shelf.

"My little brother is hungry."

"I see," Police Lady said. "I'll help you." She grasped Jamie's hand and escorted her to the checkout. Jamie fished out the crumpled bills and laid them on the counter.

Police Lady asked the clerk, "Do you know this child?"

The man with the black towel on his head leaned over the countertop and gazed down. "She's been in a few times with her mother and a baby. I think they're staying at the motel across the street."

The man accepted the money and offered Jamie a few coins, which she tucked into her pocket. "Thank you, Mister."

Outside, a policeman leaned against his black and white car. Moisture tickled the air, even though the rain had stopped. "What do we have here?"

"John, this is Jamie. I'm helping her get milk for her brother."

Officer John chuckled. "Protect and serve, protect and serve."

Police Lady said, "Do you live across the street, Jamie?"

She nodded.

Officer John clasped Jamie's other hand and they walked over the double yellow line together. Strange and nice having her hands held by the two police people. She felt… *safe*.

They entered the small room and Police Lady strode to the crib and picked up Jamie's screaming brother. She wiped the tears and snot off his face with a tissue and put him against her shoulder, patting his back. The baby calmed, a relief to Jamie's ears. She offered, "The bottles are in the sink."

Officer John asked, "Are you home alone, Jamie?"

Jamie nodded again. "But my mommy should be home any minute. She had to run to work."

The police officers glanced at Jamie and then at each other. "Call it in," Police Lady said.

Chapter 2

Monday, January 14, 2019

Acrid burning rubber seared her nostrils. Jamie floored the accelerator and glanced to the rearview mirror. He was gaining. The speedometer read eighty-five. Damn, she must escape. She eased off the gas and wrenched the steering wheel right and her gunmetal gray Dodge Charger went into a sideways skid. Tires squealed. She accelerated and he sped past her, but did a one-eighty, in pursuit again.

The speedometer neared ninety, the late afternoon sun unable to temper the subzero wind whipping her face. Adrenaline raced in her veins. Faster, faster. She drew the Glock from her holster, racked the slide and chambered a round. The next time he got close she'd take her shot. Slamming on the brakes, she did a one-eighty and advanced on him. A head-on collision imminent, way past playing chicken. He swerved at the last second yet lost control and the car did a three-sixty, coming to a complete stop about ten yards away. Smoke billowed around the supercharged Camaro. When a gap opened, she fired. The bullet slammed into the side of his head. A haze of red mist exploding.

She laughed.

They met at the entrance gate, both cars trailing tire smoke. Jamie jumped out and removed her helmet and aviator sunglasses, her shiny red locks tumbling to her shoulders. One booted foot on the doorframe, she leaned her forearm on the car's roof, her chin perched atop. Applause fueled her excitement.

"One of these days I'm gonna beat you," he said.

"In your dreams." They mirrored wide smiles. Jamie loved driving the TEVOC track. All of them. The serpentine path around the cones, the reverse drive out of an alley, and even the final exam that demanded all of those skills and more, mercilessly taking out the opponent. A true test of mettle. And after graduating the Naval Academy, the field training and physical fitness requirements at Quantico were like a sprint around Central Park. Easy peasy, at least for her. Now, some of the boys, on the other hand...

This was the seventh time they'd performed this demo for the new recruits at Quantico. Sal had been her TEVOC instructor back in the day and she was the only recruit to ever beat him. Each year he invited her back in hopes of trouncing her.

Sal wiped the red paint from the side of his head with a rag. "That motherfucker hurts, you know."

"Yeah, no, I wouldn't know." She beamed in triumph. Damn she loved this.

Sal addressed the gaggle of uniformed recruits. "That's how it's done, ladies and gents. Special Agent Jamie Gallagher still holds the undefeated record for TEVOC." More applause, along with some hoots and hollers.

Jamie's phone rang. "Excuse me. This might be important."

She stepped inside the training building and answered, "Hey Rob, what's up?" Rob Scarborough was her new boss. She'd recently transferred to the New York office from her post working with the Secret Service in D.C. She liked working for Rob; he was surefooted and direct, perhaps a bit too anal at times. And leaving the hysteria and dysfunction of Washington behind seemed almost joyous.

"Just making sure you'll be back in the office tomorrow morning."

"Yep. Catching a Marine transport in about an hour."

"Good. We've caught a case requiring your skillset. I'll fill you in when you arrive."

"Roger," she said. "See you first thing tomorrow morning."

Chapter 3

Colin MacKenzie rarely worked at the St. Andrews club on a Sunday night. Friday and Saturday were fine, even the occasional Thursday, never Sunday, yet Jack begged him. The cache of experienced Doms and Dungeon Masters had dwindled of late, coupled by an increase in membership. Jack worried that without sufficient monitoring something untoward might happen, his club's reputation vital to its success. Clients paid high dues to play, based on his establishment's stellar rep and upscale atmosphere. His Doms and Dungeon Masters had impeccable reputations and clients needed to feel safe and secure, especially since the unconventional sexual behaviors they'd experience kept most on edge. Fear was good, the right kind, and ideal amount.

Jack implored him, "We've got eleven submissive trainee applicants and interviews to complete. That's taking more supervision off the floor. Can you come in and meet the new trainees? We've got nine females and two males."

Colin pressed his phone to his forehead. He didn't take a salary, it was more for fun, plus he offered a very unique service to the like-minded, or curious. He'd been a member of the club for six years and he and his best buddy Steve Moretti had often trained the new submissives together. But Steve left the club after marrying

Laura Logan, who became pregnant with their first child. Steve and Laura occasionally attended parties at the club, yet not since Laura was expecting.

"Sure," he said. "Happy to help out." He'd spent his usual Friday and Saturday evenings acting in the capacity of Dungeon Master and working with a number of current submissives, but truth be told, he'd satisfied his sexual urges for the moment and would rather chill before starting his work week

Colin arrived at six, garbed in his black polo with the club insignia and slim black jeans, meeting Jack in his office. Jack informed him all eleven trainees would be in attendance and he'd scheduled them at half-hour intervals. Jack would interview four, including the two men and Colin could take the other five.

"You can use private suite number five upstairs and I'll use my office." He handed Colin five files and Colin grabbed the key. He entered the luxurious bedchamber festooned in olive green with gold accents, the wall sconces bathing the atmosphere in romantic light. He settled into the faux-velvet recliner, recalling how many times he'd fucked a new submissive in this exact spot.

Perusing the files, he noted important details, and memorized photos of women with abusive sexual pasts. They'd require special attention.

A soft rap on the door and Colin checked the schedule. Alyssa Thayer. Twenty-nine, five foot seven, short tousled black hair and blue eyes, no abuse. He opened the door, pleased by her attractive facade. She stared at the floor, her hands behind her brown leather miniskirt, her ample breasts barely covered by a silky, copper-hued cami. "Eyes on me," he ordered.

Alyssa complied slowly, pale blue orbs meeting his. "Welcome, Ms. Thayer. My name is Colin but you will address me as Sir or Master. Come in."

She took a step toward him, yet he didn't move. He'd wait and see what she did. She stopped, her nose almost touching his shirt, and her chin dropped, eyelashes down. "Eyes up, little subbie."

Their gazes met again and he continued walking backward, reseating himself on the recliner. "Take a seat on the bed," he instructed.

Alyssa surveyed the room, then set her petite backside on the foot of the bed, hands folded in her lap, eyes pinned to the black and gold flowered rug. He flipped open her file and reread the pertinent details. "Why do you want to play at my club?"

She spoke to the carpet. "I-I work a lot of hours and don't have time to meet men. And the men I have met are boring and more concerned about their own pleasure. I usually have to fake an orgasm."

"A common lament," Colin said, crossing his legs. "What kind of work do you do?"

"I'm a physicist. I work at Brookhaven Lab in Upton, on the particle accelerator." She bit a fingernail. "This is all confidential, right?"

"Absolutely. The privacy of our clientele is vital to the success of our club. And if you do meet someone you recognize, be that a person you know or a famous persona, you are not to react and you must keep it to yourself per the NDA you will sign."

"Very smart. That makes me feel better."

"Good. We want you to feel great while you're here. No anxiety and guilt. It's all about erotic play and we want you to leave happy, with countless endorphins saturating every part of you." Alyssa managed a grin. Colin scanned her application. "Do you have any experience with the BDSM lifestyle?"

"I do not."

"I see that you're interested in bondage, blindfolds, spanking, mild pain and sexual intercourse. No whipping, caning, masks or extreme pain. Are you good with oral sex, both given and received?"

Alyssa nodded.

"Use your words, please."

"Yes."

"Yes, what?"

Alyssa frowned.

"Include my title."

Alyssa swallowed hard. "Yes, Sir."

"Better." He uncrossed his legs and put the files on the floor. "Come here."

Alyssa rose, walked closer and faced him. He stood, a good head taller, and secured her upper arm and marched her to the room's center, directly below the chains bolted to the ceiling. He tapped the hem of her cami. "Remove this, please." She didn't hesitate and pulled the flimsy garment over her head, casting it on the floor. He focused on her beautiful breasts, rosy nipples taut, already aroused. "Very pretty. Are you wearing underwear?"

"No, Sir. I was instructed not to."

"Good girl." He brushed his fingers over her shoulders and the soft curves of her breasts, struggling not to smile, to keep his expression stoic, lethal even. This was the best part. Exploring a new body. Introducing a newbie to protocol.

Circling her body, inspecting her, he continued the interview. "You understand what a safe word is?"

"Yes, Sir."

"Have you selected one?"

"I'll go with the traditional red, yellow, green."

"Fine, so if I make you uncomfortable you warn me with 'yellow'. Red means stop, no questions asked and we're done for the night. We will discuss how to avoid it in the future."

He pulled a pair of fur-lined, red leather handcuffs from his back pocket and fastened one to each of her wrists. He detected shivers. "Are you cold?"

"No, Sir, just a bit nervous."

"Good." He chuckled. "It's important for a submissive to always be truthful with her Dom. Otherwise, you could get hurt." He raised one of her arms and buckled the handcuff to the chain dangling above, then repeated with the other. He yanked the opposite ends to pull her arms taut. She gasped. "You okay? Green?"

"Yes, Sir, green. You just startled me."

"Feet apart." He watched as she widened her stance by about a foot. "A little more." She complied and he questioned, "How are you with other Doms touching you, taking you? Or women? Members can request a trainee for a scene, which might involve anything from light pain to bondage and sex. You'll be exploring your limits."

"Except for the women, all good, Sir."

"Excellent, pet." Colin slid his fingers under her skirt and touched her bare pussy. She gasped again and closed her eyes. Even in this low lighting he saw the flush creep over her porcelain skin. "Very wet, I like that." Alyssa opened her mouth to respond yet he clasped his other hand over her lips. "You are not to speak unless I ask you a question. And you must obey my orders without hesitation or I will punish you."

He ran his fingers over her clit. He stroked it rhythmically, and she moaned, then bit her lip. "Like that, pet?"

"Yes, Sir. Very much, Sir."

Colin's fingers retreated, afraid she might orgasm too quickly. "You're well suited to the submissive lifestyle and I would be happy to let one of our experienced Doms work with you tonight. You game?"

"Not you?"

"Not tonight, but soon. I have other prospective clients to interview. Perhaps next week."

"Yes, Sir. I would love to work with you."

Colin smiled. "I know."

COLIN EXITED his chauffeur-driven silver Porsche Cayenne and stepped onto the Manhattan sidewalk in pursuit of caffeine. He never wavered from this ritual, unless he was out of town, neither rain nor snow nor clingy one-night stand. His office suite featured a fancy machine that made espresso, cappuccino, lattes and nearly every possible coffee permutation invented since Eve bit into the apple. But he preferred plain old Columbian from his corner barista.

He desperately needed a java boost this Tuesday morning since he'd been at the club Sunday night and hadn't returned home until nearly midnight, and then Monday was an extremely busy day and he had worked late.

Colin reached the coffee shop door about two seconds after an attractive redhead, clad in a tan trench coat over a simple black pantsuit and crisp white shirt. He held the door for her.

JAMIE WAS RUNNING LATE, not late for the time she usually arrived but for the earlier time she'd mentally committed to. Tossing and turning most of the night, she fell into a deep sleep sometime before dawn and slept through her alarm. She often stopped for coffee before she got on the subway but since she was in a rush, she thought better of it. The office brew would have to do this morning. Then she remembered that quaint café near her office where she'd met fellow agents and friends, Alyx Cameron and Laura Logan, for lunch one day. Now that they were both married – something she never saw coming – she wondered if they'd taken their husband's names. She doubted it, they'd had this discussion back in the day and vowed never to take a man's name as their own. She planned a quick stop, hoping it wasn't mobbed. Glancing at her watch: 7:46. Doubtful.

Her phone pinged an incoming text message. She drew her phone from the pocket of her tan trench coat. Rob: *How soon will you be here? Big case.*

"Asshole," she said. Already an hour ahead of her usual reporting time and he was busting her chops?

"MOST PEOPLE JUST SAY THANK YOU," Colin said, holding the door ajar.

The woman glanced up and he could see himself reflected in her mirrored aviators. He removed his Persol shades and placed them in the pocket of his black cashmere overcoat.

Her pretty pink lips parted. "Oh, sorry, not you. It's my boss."

"Your boss is an asshole?"

"No, he's just a bit… anal." She entered ahead of Colin. "Thank you," she said over her shoulder then took her place in line.

Anal wasn't a word Colin used outside the St. Andrews club.

She turned toward him. "I didn't mean that the way it sounded. I guess it's a control thing, you know?"

"I'm not sure I do." Colin wasn't being truthful. Control *was* his thing, not only in business but as a Dom at the club.

"Probably compensating for a small dick," she said. She slapped a hand across her mouth before uttering, "Oh my God. I don't know what's wrong with me." Except then belly-laughter erupted from her.

Colin smiled. How fucking adorable. Probably a spitfire in the sack. And he'd love to teach her a thing or four about control. At the club.

She couldn't seem to stop herself. "Besides, you probably have a great boss and *I* sound like the asshole."

Colin struggled to keep a straight face. "I do have a great boss and I know for a fact that he has a rather impressive endowment." He could barely contain himself and pressed his lips together to stifle a smirk.

"Don't stop. Do tell."

"That will cost you," he said as they inched closer to the counter.

Her gaze narrowed, but then her eyes widened. "Let me guess. The boss is you."

"Ah, smart *and* sexy."

They'd reached the counter and she said, "Large, regular milk and one sugar, please."

Colin clapped three times, the same way he took his coffee. The clerk placed two coffees in front of them. "Put it on my tab, Jeff."

"What? No, I should pay for yours to apologize for my inappropriate commentary."

"Too late," Colin said, handing her the covered paper cup.

She hesitated but eventually took the fresh brew. "Thank you, and I apologize again."

"No problem." This time, she held the door for him. "Thank you," he nearly tacked on *pet*...a term often used at the club. Recently, someone had called him out on it stating she wasn't a dog and he was trying to drop it from his vernacular when outside the club. Maybe he should drop it inside the club too.

They exited onto the sun-drenched city sidewalk, the chill breeze swirling her long red mane around her face. She ran her fingers through it, moving strands off her perfect porcelain skin.

"Bye, and thanks for the java," she said, walking backward.

Colin grabbed her upper arm and pulled her into his chest.

"What the…?" She tensed up.

His pulse quickened. She emitted warm fragrances, cinnamon and vanilla. So sweet. Close enough to kiss. He desperately wanted a taste.

Colin held her gaze for a few seconds, mesmerized by her emerald irises, then pointed over her shoulder with his chin. A fast-moving rack of clothing maneuvered by a garment worker sped by. "You almost took a serious hit."

"Jesus," she said, rubbing her forehead.

"Can I give you a ride? My car is right here."

"Ah, no. Thank you. My office is just around the corner."

"You're sure? I don't mind."

"I said no." She donned her sunglasses and melted into the crowd of busy Manhattanites bustling off to work.

JAMIE'S FACE burned even with below freezing temps. What had come over her? She'd acted like a total jerk in front of that guy. A really *hot* guy. Her law enforcement and profile training pegged him as a man of means. The coat and suit alone must've cost ten grand, and she was reasonably sure his shoes were Testoni. His watch, Hublot. The guy shouted serious dough and probably an ego to match his self-proclaimed giant dick. She laughed, which eased her anxiety. At least she'd never have to see him again.

Chapter 4

Jamie trekked the three blocks to 26 Federal Plaza. She lived in Chelsea and took the subway to work, which deposited her within walking range. She rarely drove her government-issued white Chevy Impala home, content to leave it parked in the garage at headquarters. Driving around Manhattan was tedious on a good day and she only relied on vehicular transportation for work-related activities, a blaring siren and flashing lights helped immensely.

She sipped her coffee, her mind lingering on the encounter with the handsome stranger. His eyes radiated a stunning shade of blue, and oh that wavy dark brown hair that nipped his collar. When he'd pulled her into his chest to save her from impending doom, their eyes locked for a split-second and she thought maybe she'd never breathe again. Yeah, that was the perfect adjective for him—breath-taking. Her pulse still beat a little too fast.

Entering the massive building, she swiped her ID card through the scanner and headed for the elevator to the 17th floor. She nodded hello to the familiar personnel, not knowing everyone's name yet. Her desk sat across from Matt Holloway, and they often worked cases together. Matt had frequently partnered with Alyx Cameron before Alyx got assigned to lead the new task force on human trafficking. Roommates with Alyx at Quantico, they recently met for lunch. Laura Logan joined them, along with Molly Masterson, Laura's roommate at Quantico. Molly had a three-year-old daughter and Alyx and Laura were both expecting babies, their due dates on the same day—Incredible. What were the chances?

Their fellow recruits at Quantico nicknamed them the Four Horsemen of the Apocalypse because they'd graduated at the top of their class and were considered lethal weapons—their class-mates decided if the end was coming, they'd want one of them at their side.

Jamie ranked number one in her class at the Naval Academy and her excellent grades allowed her admission to NYU, where she'd earned her law degree. She'd considered going into the JAG corps but stayed in naval Intel until the FBI came calling and she decided against re-enlisting.

"Morning," Matt said as he shuffled papers on his desk.

"Hey," Jamie said. "How'd the baby fare last night? Get any sleep?" Matt and his wife just welcomed a second baby into their home.

"I thought the first one was a terrible sleeper, but this guy has her beat by a mile. I think I'm getting a vasectomy ASAP. I've only got enough stamina for two."

He laughed but Jamie didn't think he was ha-ha laughing, it was more of a nervous laugh. "What does Jillian say?"

"She's fully on board. We're both exhausted and she was anxious to get back to work." Matt's wife was a radiologist.

Jamie hung her coat on the rack in the corner then rested her purse on her desk and sat to sift through new paperwork. "Rob said we caught a new case. Any idea what's up?" Before Matt could answer, a coat-clad Rob approached her desk.

"Forget what I said yesterday. Something else has come in that's top priority." Rob Scarborough proved an imposing figure, tall and strapping with fiery red hair, not like hers, over the years her hair turned more auburn. He resembled a Scottish warlord. And he was demanding, expecting fast, thorough and disciplined work. You didn't want to screw up on Rob Scarborough's watch. But he also had a good sense of humor and could disarm the most recalcitrant witnesses and perps. And he always had your back.

"A bomb was detected at MacKenzie Industries. The CEO is a big deal. On the mayor's advisement board and he's very philanthropic with the city. PD and FD are on the scene. The building is evacuated. Only one device detected so far. Matt you're coming too. I'll drive myself and you two drive together because I'm not sure how this will play out. It's in mid-town, 1700 Park Avenue between Broadway and Park."

Jamie retrieved her coat and purse. Matt jumped up and slipped on the pea coat hanging on the back of his chair. He pulled his keys from his pocket, "Okay if I drive?"

"Sure." They headed toward the parking garage.

They arrived at the crime scene behind Rob, flashing lights and sirens clearing their path. The road was already cordoned off and they left their cruisers outside the yellow crime scene tape. The bomb squad's remote-controlled robot loaded the device into the total containment vehicle, departing with a police escort, to be hauled off to their safe site for examination and if necessary, detonation. Crime lab techs would be on scene for forensics.

Several hundred people filled the streets and Jamie suspected most had exited with the fire alarm, which still blared, but a good number were probably onlookers waiting for something spectacular. And not necessarily *good* spectacular. The press was everywhere. The entire incident would be plastered over the airwaves in less than a nanosecond.

The building epitomized modern New York City architecture. Futuristic, all glass, panoramic reflections, sharp edges. Jamie gazed up, had to be thirty floors. They showed their credentials to the officers posted at the door. "They're allowing everyone back in the building. The Commissioner is upstairs with the CEO," an NYPD officer said. "30th floor. He's expecting you. See the receptionist."

The doors opened to a large lobby, the walls festooned in bright blue paint. Photographic renderings of waterscapes filled the blank space: oceans, rivers, waterfalls, ponds and creeks, even a stunning shot of a glacier surrounded by icy cerulean water. Some depicted sunrises and sunsets over their respective bodies. Giant ornate script over the elevators read the lyrics of *"America the Beautiful"* :

O beautiful for spacious skies,

For amber waves of grain,

For purple mountain majesties

Above the fruited plain.

America! America! God shed His grace on thee,

And crown thy good with brotherhood

From sea to shining sea.

Sounded like MacKenzie industries was on board with saving the planet from climate change.

A young man clad in a blue suit sat primly at a reception desk. Jamie wondered if he was dressed to match the décor. Alongside were unarmed security guards tandem to turnstiles with scanners for IDs.

Rob displayed his credentials and announced, "Special Agent in Charge Rob Scarborough. And these are Special Agents Jamie Gallagher and Matt Holloway. We're here to see Mr. MacKenzie."

"Yes, sir," he said. "I was told to bring you right up. Follow me." The receptionist pushed a buzzer and one of the turnstiles opened. They trailed him to the elevator banks and rode to the top floor. As they exited, he said, "Right this way, sir."

The man opened one side of frosted glass doors. Both the police and fire commissioners approached. "Morning, Rob," the police commissioner said. Both officials shook Rob's hand. "The device has been removed by the FD bomb squad and we're taking it to the safe site. We've got photos." He handed his phone to Rob Scarborough who perused the images.

"Looks pretty primitive," Rob said. Jamie and Matt took their turn viewing the pictures, which consisted of a square package tied with white string. The addressee was C MacKenzie, 1700 Park Avenue, NY, NY, no zip code. The parcel had been partially opened to reveal wires and a timer.

The fire commissioner added, "Not sure if it was viable. We'll know something soon."

Several plain-clothes detectives were speaking to a tall gentleman with his back to them. Jamie recognized NYPD Deputy Inspector Scott Winfree, Major Case Squad. "Rob," he said, "I assume the FBI will be taking lead on this."

"Yes."

"Glad to assist any way you need. Just say the word."

"Thanks, Scott. What do we have so far?"

"We're interviewing Mr. MacKenzie, the CEO, since the package was addressed to him it appears he was the intended target."

The tall man turned. Jamie's heart stopped, the breath frozen in her chest.

Mr. MacKenzie approached, introductions made and hands shook in greeting. He moved closer to Jamie, taking her hand. His eyes lit up. "You?"

Chapter 5

Her mouth suddenly dry, Jamie didn't respond. No words came. Was she destined to act like an idiot in front of this guy forever? Men rarely intimidated her, yet something was unsettling about this man. As if his blue eyes had their own light source, from inside. And a certain mischievousness, a sparkle, made him even more attractive. He held her hand in greeting too long, the warmth – no, the heat – overwhelming.

Rob Scarborough penetrated the silent interlude. "You two know each other?"

"Not exactly," Mr. MacKenzie said. "We bumped into each other this morning at the coffee shop." His eyes never left Jamie's face. "Although the circumstances are unfortunate, it's a pleasure to officially meet you, Agent Gallagher."

Say something. Anything. Jamie swallowed, then mumbled, "Same here." He released her hand. *Thank God.*

His wide smile made her forget the crime scene. "I take it you made it to work safely?"

"Yes."

"I wasn't quite sure there for a minute." He addressed Rob and Matt. "Agent Gallagher nearly had a head-on collision with a rack of evening gowns." Mr. MacKenzie smirked. "Is this your boss?" he asked Jamie.

Jamie winced. If she could crawl under the gray-checkered carpeting she would. "It is," she said, struggling to regain her equilibrium. She bit her lip imagining her handsome stranger musing about Rob's dick, while she couldn't help thinking about *his* dick.

Rob cleared his throat and retrieved a small notebook from his inside jacket pocket. "We will need some information from you regarding the device left at your office."

"Why don't we sit," Mr. MacKenzie said, ushering the cadre of police and fire officials to a large conference table opposite his massive mahogany desk. Mr. MacKenzie held a chair out for Jamie then seated himself at the helm.

Rob Scarborough began, "The parcel was left at your assistant's desk, is that right?"

"Yes, it was there when he arrived. He gets here at eight and I arrive around nine. Today was no exception."

"Where is your assistant now? What's his name?"

"Luke Desden. He started to open the package but became alarmed when he saw wires and alerted security. They evacuated the building as a precaution. He exited with the alarm."

Rob turned to Scott Winfree. "Get someone to find him so we can take his statement."

"Sure thing," Inspector Winfree said, leaving the table.

"Do you normally screen your mail?" Rob asked.

"We do, but this didn't come through the mailroom. Someone left it on the desk after hours." Jamie and Matt scribbled notes as Mr. MacKenzie detailed the incident.

Mr. MacKenzie leaned against his chair back and crossed one long leg over the other, his hands folded on his lap. Jamie thought him entirely too relaxed for a man who'd nearly had his building blown up. "You'll have to speak with my security chief for further details. By the time I arrived everyone was on the street."

"The package was addressed to you?" Jamie interjected.

"Yes."

"And security called the NYPD?" she said.

"That's correct."

"We'll need to speak to that employee," Rob said.

"Of course."

Matt asked, "What about video surveillance? Is there CCTV?"

"Only outside the building and in the general areas: hallways, elevators, entrances to offices. We strive for more privacy inside the actual office space and of course in the breakrooms where people let down their guard."

"Who has access to the building after hours?" Matt said.

"Anyone with identification whose chip allows it."

Matt followed with, "We'll need a list of those employees."

"Of course. Either Luke or my security chief can get that for you."

Rob flipped a page in his notepad before asking, "I'm wondering why, if you were the intended target, the package wasn't placed in your office?"

"My inner office can only be opened by me, my security chief and Luke. There's a good deal of sensitive information in my office."

"Then the perp might have general building access but your office would require other authorization?"

"By design."

"What about enemies? Is there anyone who wishes to do you harm?"

Mr. MacKenzie chuckled. "Agent Scarborough, in my business there is a host of people who would be elated at my demise. I garner a large share of the tech market in the northern corridor of the country. I'm only rivaled by my West Coast competitors and we've worked together on many projects but do not have an adversarial relationship."

"What about your personal life? Ex-wife? Disgruntled employees? Jilted lovers?"

"I believe my employees are treated and compensated well. There are no pending grievances I'm aware of." He leaned in, his hands intertwined on the table. "Never married. No family troubles. I'm an only child. My parents live on the north shore of Long Island. They're both attorneys." Colin hesitated before continuing, "I don't date much. Work is my mistress."

Rob closed his notebook and stowed it in the inside pocket of his suit jacket. "We have forensics examining the device. Hopefully, we will get a lead off that. In the meantime, we'll run down the list of employees having access to the building after hours and review any video you have. Who can we see about that?"

The office door opened and in walked a bald man in a black suit. Judging by his build and the way he carried himself, Jamie was pretty confident the guy had a military background.

"Speak of the devil," Mr. MacKenzie said. "This is Brett Forrester, my head of security." The agents stood, each introducing themselves and shaking Mr. Forrester's hand. "Brett, the FBI will need to view video surveillance files from last night and this morning. Also, give them a list of all employees who have access after-hours since the device showed up sometime between when you left last night and your arrival this morning."

"No problem, Boss. I'm here to serve."

Rob Scarborough said, "If you give me a minute to speak with my agents, I'll tell you how we need to proceed."

"Of course," Mr. MacKenzie and Brett Forrester said at the same time.

Rob Scarborough escorted Jamie and Matt toward the door, out of earshot. "Matt, you get the list of employees back to the office and have every available agent determine where each was last night. I'll get copies of the surveillance video and bring them back to the office as well." He turned to Jamie. "You're on body-guard detail. I want you sticking to this guy like glue."

"What?" Jamie said too loudly. "Babysitting duty?" Protection detail… playing bodyguard. Nobody likes that assignment… waiting around for something to happen and actually hoping it doesn't.

Rob grimaced. "This guy is a huge deal and if anything happens to him it will be a giant black eye for the Bureau."

"But he has his own security detail."

"I don't give a crap. You're an expert in the field. I didn't pull you from Secret Service without good reason."

"You recruited me? I thought I was the one who initiated the transfer?"

"I made sure the vacancy came across your desk."

Jamie huffed. "Fine. I'm on him twenty-four seven until we're sure he's out of danger."

"Excellent," Rob said. "We'll keep you posted on our progress."

"Great," Jamie said, shoving her hands inside her trench coat's pockets.

Rob returned to Mr. MacKenzie. "Agent Gallagher will work with your security team to assure your safety."

The security chief frowned. "That won't be necessary, Agent, we are perfectly capable of protecting Mr. MacKenzie."

"Not an option," Scarborough said.

Mr. Forrester pressed his lips together, then finally said, "Of course."

Rob continued. "Mr. Forrester, we'll meet you in your office after we interview Mr. MacKenzie's assistant."

"Of course," Mr. Forrester said again. "It's on the first floor."

Rob and Matt exited the office to interview Luke, and the remaining FDNY and NYPD personnel followed.

"Babysitting?" Mr. MacKenzie said to Jamie.

Jamie fumed, apparently they hadn't been out of earshot. "I prefer to be out in the field chasing down leads. That's all. Just a preference."

Mr. MacKenzie scrutinized her and she suddenly felt naked. The man unnerved her. She had no idea why. Mr. Forrester said, "I appreciate your desire to protect Mr. MacKenzie, Agent Gallagher, but we have him covered. Don't get in our way."

Jamie bristled. "I will be at Mr. MacKenzie's side every minute and I'll let you know if I need assistance. I've guarded both POTUS AND FLOTUS. I can handle this just fine."

Mr. Forrester relented. "Of course. We both want to ensure Mr. MacKenzie's safety." Brett Forrester exited, pulling the door closed a little too forcefully.

She was alone with Mr. MacKenzie.

"Since we're going to be spending a good deal of time together, please, call me Colin."

Jamie worked bodyguard duty many times, but never to the point where she inhabited the residence of her mark. She'd be living with the guy until the Bureau pulled her out.

"Okay, *Col*-in. But if we're going to be spending all our time together, I'll need to stop by my place and pick up a few things."

"Of course. I've canceled the rest of my day, but I have to make some phone calls first."

"I'll stay out of your way until then."

"Where do you live?"

"Chelsea."

Chapter 6

J amie sat alongside Colin in the back of his Porsche Cayenne. His driver's name was James and Colin joked about being together in the car with J-squared. They arrived at her 5th floor walk-up around 2 p.m. hoping to return to Colin's Tribeca apartment before getting slammed by rush hour traffic. Colin's phone rang but he declined the call.

"This won't take long," Jamie said. "I'll be right back."

"I'll go with you," Colin said.

"What? No, I don't need any help."

"I insist," he said, exiting behind her.

She stood facing him, arms crossed over her chest. "I take it nobody ever says no to you."

He smirked but didn't respond.

"Let's be clear. I'm the boss until this is over. You do as I say and do not question me."

"I'm just being polite. I'll carry your bag," Colin said. He knew she was onto him, he gave the orders and people jumped. She didn't know that at the club, he was a strict Dom and a woman would never speak to him like that. Yet they weren't at the club and she didn't work for him. Perhaps she had the same propensity. As a federal agent she gave an order and people immediately complied.

"I'm perfectly capable of carrying my own duffle."

"I'm just curious. I like seeing where someone lives, it tells a lot about a person. You're going to see mine so I think I should see yours."

Jamie harrumphed, then turned on her heels. Fine, she thought, he could follow her if he wanted. She hadn't been expecting company but she was a neat-nick, always making her bed as soon as she rose. At the Naval Academy she'd never made her bed because students never actually got *in* their beds. All midshipman slept on top of their covers for the entire four years so they'd be ready for inspection in a split-second. She was used to living in tight quarters. At New York University she inhabited a small dorm room her first year, then moved into a studio apartment near the campus. When you lived in small spaces clutter wasn't an acceptable lifestyle.

They trekked up the five flights and Colin followed her inside. "Jesus, what is this like six hundred square feet?"

"Six fifty."

"What's the rent?"

"Thirty-two hundred."

"That's highway robbery. Although Chelsea is hopping these days."

"It's a good neighborhood, lots of interesting people and great restaurants." Not that she met her neighbors or ate in local eateries very often. Work was her entire life.

Colin gravitated to the far wall where her ceremonial sword awarded at graduation hung over the gas fireplace. He ran his finger over the sleek metal. "This is beautiful, is it yours?"

"Yeah, we get them when we graduate."

Colin leaned in and studied the stunning blade engraved with her name and rank. "You went to the Naval Academy?"

"Guilty."

"Wow." He turned and said, "Why do I get the feeling you kicked some Navy ass while you were there?"

Jamie couldn't imagine why he'd think that. She'd been a bumbling idiot at their initial meeting and figured he thought her some bubble-brained carrot-top. Being a redhead was one step above a stereotypical blonde, or maybe one step below. Brains were not expected.

Jamie entered the tiny bedroom, just big enough to fit a twin bed and a small nightstand, however it had a huge closet complete with built in shelves so no need for a dresser. She grabbed her duffle and gathered mostly casual stuff since she'd blend into the background while she was with Colin, her intent to be unobtrusive. His security guys could play the intimidating bodyguard persona while she'd be the unassuming secret weapon lurking in the shadows. "Do you have access to a gym?" she asked.

"I have one in my apartment."

"Great, then I'll bring workout clothes."

Colin slouched against the doorframe watching Jamie pack when his eyes landed on it. She never let anyone see it. Besides her parents, only Alyx, Laura and Molly knew she had it and she planned on keeping it that way. He stood erect and headed right for it. His fingers clasped the gold medallion hanging on the red, white and blue lanyard, his thumb stroking the engraving.

"This yours?"

"Yes."

He faced her, the memento still in his hand. "You're a gold medal Olympian?"

She focused on her underwear, stowing it in the duffle. "Guilty again."

"What event?"

Jamie sighed. "Winter Biathlon: skiing and shooting."

"How old were you?"

"Seventeen, I was a senior in high school."

He let go of the medal and walked toward her.

Jamie threw her yoga pants and a tank top into her bag, snatched her e-reader from her nightstand—not that she'd probably have much time to read, although surveillance detail often required long boring hours. She went to her closet to grab her running shoes. She huffed.

"Wow again. Now I'm really glad I insisted I come in here. You never fail to amaze."

Jamie glanced up. "You've only known me like ten minutes."

Colin crossed his arms over his broad chest. "And that terrifies me. Imagine what other secrets you're hiding."

"I'm not hiding anything. I just don't advertise."

"I'm utterly captivated with your talents and abilities."

Jamie exhaled. She wished they could start over, never having made their acquaintance at the coffee shop where she trashed her boss, a boss she really liked. "It's makes me uncomfortable to talk about this stuff. Let me finish packing so we can get out of here."

She walked past him but the narrow space forced her to brush his arm. Touching him, even slightly, made her pulse quicken. Why did he have this effect on her? She entered the tiny bathroom and collected her toiletries and birth control pills, shoving them into her make-up bag, then gathered her hair dryer and shower cap. Zipping the bag closed she turned, bumping into Colin. His smile disarmed her, what did he have to smile about?

He secured a strand of her hair and slid his fingers down it. "You're adorable, you know."

Jamie blushed. No one ever called her adorable. Formidable, bossy, lethal even, but adorable? Never. She chuckled. "And you're crazy." She shook her head. "Let's go."

She slung her duffle over her shoulder but Colin stole it away and exited ahead of her. She locked the door and followed him down the stairs.

The thought of sleeping at Colin's house made her uneasy. Maybe she should call Rob and ask for someone else to take over this detail. No chance of that happening. She'd just have to remind herself this was a professional gig and not a relationship. At all.

Chapter 7

S leeting rain turned the city streets into a living hell. Driving in mid-town was a nightmare on a good day but when bad weather hit, Manhattan became one giant parking lot. Why did a little ice or snow turn drivers into idiots?

Jamie's phone rang. She glanced at Colin. "My boss, maybe they have some news."

"Hope so," Colin said. Although he sort of didn't. He was looking forward to having the little spitfire around for a while. Bringing her home had him pumped. Although he doubted anything would happen between them because technically, she was on the job, but he did want to know her better. He'd never met such an accomplished woman.

Part of the reason he didn't date much was women only saw his money and even the rich ones were looking for status, after his last steady girlfriend and he split he became a confirmed bachelor, like his best friend Steve Moretti used to be. He met Steve in kindergarten. Colin was an only child and Steve had two older sisters, and they quickly became the brothers each didn't have. They were an unlikely pair in many ways. Colin's family had money whereas Steve's family was more middle-class. Steve's mother was a local high school principal and his father the town attorney. He and Steve spent summers entertaining girls on Colin's boat, showing off their water-skiing skills and hanging out on Fire Island where they drank too much and broke curfew on a regular basis.

Steve's family treated Colin like one of their own and he ate dinner with them more often than not. Steve's parents were great cooks and watching them in the kitchen together was a thing of joy. He developed a fondness for Northern Italian cuisine, especially what they called 'Grandma Tina's sauce' over linguine with freshly grated Parmesan. Colin never tasted anything like it, as his mother was more of the no-fuss, no muss and *no calories* kind of meal preparer. Although they had domestic help in his household, his mother insisted on doing the evening meal preparation, but she could never compare to the Morettis' cooking. No way, no how. Steve and his family were a large part of why Colin rejected going off to some snooty all-boys prep school.

"Nothing? No prints?" Jamie said into the phone, dragging Colin from memory lane. "Yeah, we're on our way back to his place. I'll make sure to do a sweep upon arrival. Keep me posted."

"No leads yet," Jamie said, returning her phone to her coat pocket.

"I gathered," Colin said.

They sat together in the back seat of Colin's car, separated by about a foot. Jamie glanced out the window as busy Manhattanites braved the relentless sleet.

"We should probably pick up something for dinner. Or we could eat out. My housekeeper leaves me something but I had a dinner meeting scheduled for tonight so I told her not to bother."

"You're not going to your meeting?"

"I thought in light of today's events I'd take a step back. I gave my employees tomorrow off too so they could gather their wits."

"That was honorable of you. Did you pay them?"

"Of course."

"So, you're a good guy, a good boss." Jamie cringed, recalling her ridiculous conversation with the handsome CEO this morning.

"I try," Colin said.

"Sorry again about sounding like a complete ass this morning at the coffee shop." Jamie gave a sideways glance at the handsome billionaire to judge his expression. He smiled.

"Nah, don't give it a second thought. You were venting."

"Because Rob is also a great boss, a great guy, and I'm lucky to be working with him."

"Back to dinner," Colin suggested.

"Don't fuss. I don't plan dinner on work nights because I never know how the day will break. I either get take-out or pull something out of the freezer."

"Should we order a pizza?"

Thrilled, she rarely let herself indulge in pizza, she said, "Perfect. I love pizza."

"What kind do you like?"

"I like anchovy pizza but no one on the planet agrees with me."

Colin winced. "I'll try anything once." He hoped she might too. The things he'd like to do to her… although the leap from anchovy pizza to kinky shit in the bedroom might be a stretch.

They pulled into the entrance of the underground garage in Colin's building, a high-rise, the tallest structure on the block. The salient quality of tinted blue glass like giant votive candles to the altars of commerce and power, mirroring other buildings, cars and people hustling past—a comely disguise.

Colin's phone rang and again he declined the call. James steered the car into a humongous elevator and punched in some numbers on a keypad. The door shut behind them and the car jerked upward, rising to what Jamie assumed would be the penthouse. James drove the car out the front of the elevator and parked it in one of five spots between a red convertible Mercedes and a jade-green Porsche 911 Carrera. Apparently, Mr. MacKenzie liked cars. She couldn't blame him, she was sort of a car buff herself. She still owned her vintage Aston Martin, a graduation gift from her father, garaged at her parents' place for the time being. It didn't make sense to have it in the city.

JAMES RETRIEVED Jamie's duffel from the trunk and Colin grabbed it before she could. "Good night, James," Colin said. "Not sure what I'm doing tomorrow. I'll let you know if I need you. As of now, plan on taking the day off."

"Sure thing, Boss. Holler if you need me." James walked to a smaller elevator and punched in a code, disappearing into the night.

Uneasiness niggled at Colin. He never brought women to his apartment. On the rare occasion he might go back to a woman's place but as soon as the festivities ended, he was gone with the wind. His parents stayed over now and again when they were in town for a play or other event, or for the holidays.

With Jamie's bag secured on his shoulder he headed toward a set of double glass doors where another keypad awaited. "The code is 1225," he said. "In case you need it."

"Got it," Jamie said as the doors swung open. She turned toward him and said, "You're a tech guru, I would have thought you'd have more advanced technology, like a fingerprint or optical reader."

"Working on it. In light of recent developments, I probably need to speed that up." Colin swept a hand out in front of him. "After you."

She entered a small anteroom with black marble tile and glorious golden walls. Colin stopped, his hand on the doorknob of the French doors leading to the inner rooms. A round wooden table topped with a large vase of white daisies stood in the center. Jamie stared at the giant bouquet of flowers thinking it a rather feminine touch for a guy's house.

"They're my mother's favorite and I always have them on hand."

"Do you see your mother a lot?"

"Every few months or so. My parents were here for the holidays. We saw a few plays and did the usual Christmas activities like good city dwellers." He opened one door and Jamie followed.

"Do you have any siblings?" Jamie said.

"Nope. An only child. You?"

"I had a brother, but he died."

"Oh, I'm sorry."

"It was a long time ago. I still feel him near me, sometimes."

"Must have been rough on your parents."

Jamie studied his handsome face, marred by a frown. "My mom is dead too. No idea who my dad was."

"Please forgive me," Colin said. "I didn't mean to pry."

"No worries. I knocked around the foster care system for a while before getting adopted by the Gallaghers. They're great."

"You still see them?"

"Yeah, I consider them my real family. My dad and I are close. He's the one who taught me how to ski and shoot. And ta-da... Gold Medal in my pocket."

"Cool, very cool. Where do they live?"

"Upstate, Lake Placid. My dad is a local detective and works the ski patrol on the weekends. He also gives lessons."

Jamie glanced around the large room of white walls and dark oak floors. A circular chocolate brown couch framed the granite fireplace with a rectangular glass coffee table nested in a shaggy white rug.

"Nice digs," she said.

Chapter 8

J amie noted they'd accessed Colin's residence via the back entrance, directly from the garage. A second door, quite grand and featuring ornate molding, stood at the opposite end of a massive living room, more like a great hall, the space expanding into the cavernous kitchen. She scanned the twelve-foot ceilings trimmed in off-white paint, which complemented the textured, honey-hued walls. How the other half, or rather one percent, lived.

"This is a second egress?" she asked, pointing toward the large wooden door.

"It's the front door leading to the lobby elevators."

"Does it require a code also?"

"Yes. The panel says PH and you press the button and it prompts you to enter six digits. The elevator won't move without the code. And you enter it again when you arrive at the PH floor."

"I'll need that code."

"775645."

"I will perform a thorough search before you settle in," Jamie said, shrugging out of her coat and hanging it over the back of the couch. She dropped her purse on a half-moon table nestled between two closets. Adorning the tabletop, she recognized a 15th Century statue of Adonis – similar to the piece by Duquesnoy in the Louvre – having immersed herself in art history as an elective at NYU.

Colin scrunched his eyebrows together. "You think someone could have gotten in here?"

"I have no idea how sophisticated these guys are so we'll play it safe. Okay if I snoop around?"

"Have at it."

She opened the door to the left, a coat closet and rummaged around before declaring it safe. The other closet housed electronics.

Colin answered before she could ask. "Controls my audio and security systems. Climate, TV. Everything's so damn smart nowadays."

Yeah, including criminals. Jamie inspected the blinking panels. "Look normal to you?"

Colin peered over her shoulder. "Yup. But I don't know shit about this system."

"I thought you were a tech guru."

"I hire tech specialists, I'm more a business guy."

Colin slipped out of his coat. "I can hang up my coat then?"

"You can."

He held out his hand, "Give me yours." Jamie snatched her raincoat and handed it over. Colin removed the cell phone from his pocket and laid it on the nearby table, then hung both in the closet.

Jamie sauntered around the enormous room flowing into a kitchen with a granite-topped island surrounded by eight high-backed white leather chairs, shiny pots and pans hanging from the ceiling. She opened cabinets and closets looking for anything suspicious, the double-doored stainless-steel refrigerator stocked with organic groceries, high-end brands she wasn't familiar with. Her lonely fridge held yogurt, salad and almond milk.

An arched entryway led to a spacious formal dining area, simple yet elegant in its furnishings: an eight-foot-long beechwood table and twelve dining chairs with seats covered in a black, brown and ivory fabric. A golden glass bowl in the table's center held gleaming marble spheres and a sparkly chandelier hovered over-head. No breakfront or other furniture. A floor-to-ceiling window highlighted the magnificent Manhattan skyline as sunlight faded into stunning colors. Orange, apricot, shimmery steel, indigo. No matter how many times she viewed it, the city sunset always amazed her. Different from the Aurora Borealis she'd often witnessed in the night sky of her hometown, but just as magnificent.

She imagined Colin holding fancy dinner parties with tuxedoed waitstaff passing hors d'oeuvres, martinis and champagne in cut-crystal glasses to beautiful gowned women wearing diamonds and emeralds. A life she knew nothing about.

The Gallaghers were down-home folk, pot roast with mashed potatoes or chicken and dumplings their traditional fare. Her mother made the best-mulled wine at the holidays and her hot apple cider was no slouch either. And she often baked her way to a blue ribbon at the county fair. Mom's pies voted 'Best In The Land'.

"Upstairs next?" he said.

"After you," she said, clutching her duffle.

Again, Colin absconded with her bag. She trod behind him up the carpeted circular staircase guarded by a black iron rail. A long hallway broke right and left. They stood in front of an open door to a bedroom decorated in shades of gray, a king-sized bed with an intricate brass headboard and footboard pulling focus. "This is the master."

"How many bedrooms do you have?"

"Four more, to the left. You can take the one next to mine." He walked down the hallway and opened the door. Jamie trailed him into the adjacent bedroom. Colin rested her bag on the four-poster canopy bed in a room adorned with violet motifs and a flowered quilt matching the canopy, plus pristine white furniture boasting gilded trim. A mosaic-rimmed oval mirror hung over a vanity with a small stool upholstered in lavender. A *very* feminine vibe and she wondered who had stayed in such a room. "You have your own bathroom," he said, nodding toward a white door.

"I was planning to crash on the couch," she said. "I should position myself somewhere between you and the exits."

"Sleep wherever you want." Colin returned to his boudoir's entrance, and she followed.

Hesitating, Jamie peered to the right. The hallway led to a dead end? Odd. Inside the master suite, she said, "I know this probably feels intrusive."

"NO WORRIES. JUST DOING YOUR JOB." He almost said he had no secrets yet he did, a whopper just ten feet away. Though only Tuesday, he thought he'd have more time to explain his weekend plans. He hadn't considered she'd search his premises and didn't think he'd have to show her, or even admit, he had an XXX play-room in his house. No woman had crossed that threshold in months. Not after Ellen and he broke up. And she hadn't been into the lifestyle anyway, which was surely the reason she'd dumped him.

There wasn't much to inspect in the master as most of his belongings were stowed in the walk-in closet. Jamie circled the space, opening his nightstand drawer where he kept a flashlight, dental floss, a small bottle of mouthwash and condoms—mostly out of habit since he'd limited his sexual activities to the club these days. Of course, anyone he took into the playroom must sign an NDA, that in itself sent most of them scurrying before they even knew what he had in mind. Consequently, he doubted he'd find a woman with his proclivities outside the club. There'd been a few interesting women at the St. Andrews club, except never one he felt inclined to date. Like a boss employee relationship, it just felt *off*.

His dilemma? To find a woman with the same sexual appetite who wasn't scheming to tap his fortune. Did she exist?

Jamie perused the bathroom, rifling through the cabinets before exiting. "That a closet?" She nodded toward the closed door.

"Yep, help yourself," Colin said, standing aside.

Before entering, she closed in on the wall-sized window, savoring the mottled sunset. The full moon had risen, muting the stars around it. The shadow on its face took on human qualities, like an old man warning her that something ominous lay on the horizon. "Nice view. Not very private."

Colin smiled and pressed the button on his nightstand. The windowpane frosted over.

Jamie grinned. "Smooth."

Colin pushed the door open and flattering amber light illuminated the closet. Even the giant full-length mirror was lined with tiny bulbs, like you'd see in a movie star's dressing room. Jamie gasped. "Jesus, this is twice the size of my apartment." An exaggeration, yet not by much.

She took a few steps in and scanned the racks of suits and shirts, the built-in shelves like hers, where jeans and casual shirts were neatly folded and stacked. A large upholstered bench filled the center where she imagined the handsome billionaire, clad in one of his Armani suits and a crisp white shirt, tying the laces of his polished russet Brunellos. Colin lingered alongside her.

A loud bang startled them. The door! It had shut itself.

"What the hell?" she said, Spidey-sense tingling. "You got ghosts?"

Deep lines creased Colin's forehead. "No, absolutely not."

Jamie's law enforcement radar blew a gasket. A device hooked to the door hinge by a red wire snaked along the floor molding. She maneuvered around the gray cushioned bench in the center, and followed the wire until she arrived at its conclusion.

"Stay put, don't move," Jamie said as she approached the suspicious parcel.

"What is it?"

"Nothing good."

"You think it's another bomb?

"In living color. And the door is booby-trapped and will trip the wire if we try to open it." Damn, damn, damn. Trapped. She fished in her pocket for her phone. "Jesus. I left my phone in my coat. Do you have yours?"

"No, it's on the table by the downstairs closet."

"Shit," Jamie said, huffing a long sigh. "Looks like we're going to have to figure this out ourselves." Surveying the space, she noted a blanket on the top shelf and went to retrieve it. "Hunker down in the corner and cover yourself with the blanket. I'll see what I can do." Jamie's stomach knotted. A blanket wouldn't protect against C-4 explosives. Even if it could keep his body intact, blast waves would melt his insides. Hers, too.

Colin stared at her, the white wool blanket draped over his arm. "You know how to defuse a bomb?"

"Depends on what type, and how it's connected to the detonator. And if there's somebody watching then they know we're in here and could trigger it remotely. I'm thinking that's not the case or we'd already be ash." She squatted and studied the package.

"Not a comforting thought," Colin said.

Chapter 9

Jamie studied the wire. "The blast cap is embedded in the C-4. Too risky to open the project box to see what kind of circuit it is."

Colin peered over her shoulder. "Is it that little black box?"

"Yeah. And cutting the wires could be the exact wrong move. Besides, we don't have any wire cutters. And there may be a dead man's switch."

"What's that?"

"A backup detonator. In the event the first one is deactivated, it kicks in." Jamie combed the area for more clues. "Here," she said, pointing toward a pair of Colin's red Nikes. She knelt again and carefully removed another detonator attached to an old-fashioned timer.

A crackling sound. The lights went out. The closet plunged into darkness.

"Peek-a-boo. I see you! Peek-a-boo." A disembodied voice – synthesized, high-pitched and creepy – came out of nowhere. So loud, too loud. The decibel actually hurt her eardrums.

Jamie covered her ears. Listening. Nothing. Silence, the worst kind of quiet. Dread. She uncovered her ears and yelled, "Who's there?"

"Someone must have gained control of my system," Colin whispered in the pitch blackness.

"Tick-tock, tick-tock," the vocoder voice shrieked. "Blow your world up, you trust fund fuck." Maniacal laughter bellowed.

"Who's speaking!" Jamie demanded.

"Peek-a-boo. I see you! Peek-a-boo."

Jamie rose, assuming Colin was still to her right. "I think it's on a loop, a recording."

"I'm holding my breath here," Colin said.

"Defusing the device is tricky when you can see perfectly, but in the dark?" she said, ignoring the nefarious robotic voice that kept booming the same threats over and over. She reflexively reached for her cell again, she needed light. Yeah, no phone, no flashlight.

And what had triggered the power outage? Had she misjudged? Was somebody watching live?

"There is a God," Colin exclaimed. "And her name is Jennifer. If I get out of this alive, I'll thank her big time."

"What are you talking about?"

"Several years ago my housekeeper gave me some LED lanterns for Christmas to use in case of a blackout. They're in the bench. I'll get them!"

Sudden movement. Colin's foot twisted around her ankle, tripping her, leveling them both. His hard body like a slab of cement pinning her to the ground. She felt his heart beating the same staccato rhythm as hers.

"Oh God, sorry." His face close, his breath on her lips. "Hey, is that a gun or are you just happy to see me?"

Seriously? She pushed him off and sat up. "You're a terrible comedian. Get the lanterns." Jamie pictured him crawling toward the bench, hopeful he'd come to the rescue. If not, they were fucked.

"Bingo!" Several seconds later the room filled with abrasive light. "Man, these suckers give off some serious wattage."

"I'll say." Jamie dropped the hand protecting her eyes.

She held her breath as she faced the explosive device again, wondering if she'd ever taste her mom's key lime pie again. Or hug her dad.

"This detonator isn't live until the other one is disengaged," Jamie said. She disconnected the wire from the timing device.

Colin slid both hands down his face and let out a painfully slow exhale. She studied him carefully, beads of sweat covering his forehead and upper lip. "I'm gonna get us out of here. Don't worry."

Jamie wasn't certain of anything, but confidence was her game and it hadn't failed her. Yet. Besides, if the device blew, she and Colin wouldn't know. They'd be incinerated.

"I think I should tell you I'm not ready to meet my Maker."

"Makes two of us." Tick, tick, tick. The sound pinged her ears. She rested the defused timer and wires on the gray bench and ran to the IED. Holy mother and all the saints. The main timer had started. Red numerals announced fifteen seconds, fourteen, thirteen... "I'll pull the detonator wire, then we wrap it up and run like hell."

Their eyes locked and Colin swallowed hard. He picked up the blanket and held it open to accept the formidable package.

Seven, six, five...

She yanked the wire free. Colin threw the blanket into her hand. She wrapped the project box in soft layers and rushed the door, grasping the knob. Two steps out, *pop-pop-pop*. The sparks zapped her chest and acrid smoke seared her nostrils. *Phew.*

She glanced up into Colin's face. So pale, phantom-like. He wasn't so much raking his fingers through his hair again as he was yanking the strands. "Jesus fucking Christ."

"All clear," Jamie said. "I need to call this in." She placed the blanket on the ground and took Colin's hand, leading him down the stairs. "Does your security system have a fire alarm?"

"Yeah, but it evacuates the whole building."

"Pull it," Jamie said.

She grabbed her phone from her coat pocket as Colin opened the door to the electronics closet, watching as he pressed a red button. The alarm sounded. She dialed Rob Scarborough's number. "Come on," she said to Colin as he took his phone from the table and pocketed it.

They rode the elevator down, although technically it wasn't supposed to be used in a fire emergency. A crowd formed outside the building, people clad in casual clothing as they wound down from the day. *Shit. The press was already here?*

"Rob," Jamie shouted into her phone, "there's a second device in Colin's place. The closet was rigged. I defused it but six blocks of C-4 are still in his apartment. I've evacuated the building and NYFD is on the way."

"You did what?" Rob said. "You were able to defuse the IED yourself?"

"It wasn't that complicated even with the backup detonator."

"Nice," Rob said. "On our way."

With a fire station a block away, the response time was practically instant. Firetrucks littered the roadway, screeching sirens plus the pounding alarm made Jamie's head hurt, or perhaps it was the after-effects of nearly getting blown to smithereens. She sought out a firefighter who directed her to the Incident Commander.

"Special Agent Jamie Gallagher," she said, presenting her credentials.

"Captain Anthony Speck."

"I discovered an IED in Mr. MacKenzie's apartment. I defused it but six blocks of commercial C-4 remain. We evacuated the building as a precautionary measure."

"You defused it?" Captain Speck's brows lifted.

"Yes, sir. It was a simple device with a backup detonator. I disabled that first then pulled the wire from the explosives."

"Why didn't you call it in rather than risking your and everyone else's safety? Are you a trained bomb expert?"

"Irrelevant. The closet was rigged with us trapped inside, the detonator attached to the door. Too risky to cut the wires. No cell phone either, but the signal could've set it off anyway."

"You know your stuff, Agent Gallagher. I'll give you that."

CAPTAIN SPECK FOCUSED ON COLIN. "I recognize you from the call this morning. You're Mr. MacKenzie."

"I am, sir." Colin extended his hand and Captain Speck shook it.

"Second attempt to cremate you?"

"Apparently," Colin said.

"Lucky to have Special Agent Gallagher come to your rescue."

"You have no idea," Colin said, glancing at Jamie. "She's my hero." The impact of the day's events closed in on Colin. He'd nearly died. Twice. A man who led a safe and predictable life. He couldn't imagine anyone plotting his demise.

The captain said, "Let's hope there isn't a part three to this."

Colin prayed the man was right. Would he have to hole up in his apartment until the guy was apprehended? Should he drop off the grid for a while, maybe a long while? No way. He wasn't a coward. He wouldn't give some dirtbag control over him.

Jamie interrupted his musing and said, "Right now, we've got to get the explosive out of the building."

"I can cover that. Excuse me," Captain Speck said as he marched away.

"Jamie," Rob said, as he and Matt approached. "Everyone okay?" He scanned Colin with narrowed eyes.

"I'm fine," Colin said. "Your girl here is quite the tour de force."

GIRL, Jamie thought. Seriously? But she decided to let the remark slide and told Rob, "The fire chief is managing the removal of explosives. We can have our forensics team coordinate." Jamie tucked her hands into her armpits. Literally freezing out here and she was anxious to move this along and return inside. "Something else…"

"Spill," Rob said.

"A voice spoke to us while in the closet. Mechanical, probably on a loop, taunting us with 'Peek-a-boo, I see you, and tick tock, I'll blow you up.'"

"You sure it wasn't live?" Matt asked.

"Pretty sure."

"If it was live you could have been…"

Jamie raised both hands. "I know but I had to go with my gut and turns out I was right."

Rob ran his fingers through his gray and red locks and sighed.

"Right." To Matt he said, "You handle the forensics and get someone over to check his security system. Make sure no one can hack it again."

"On it, sir," Matt said and he sought out Captain Speck.

"Mr. MacKenzie, we are doing everything in our power to apprehend this perp. We'll work around the clock," Rob assured Colin.

Colin turned up the collar of his suit coat and shoved his cold hands in his trouser pockets. The wind picked up and the temperature plummeted. Snow was predicted tonight, just a dusting, but the air already held that *wintery scent*.

Rob removed one glove and plucked his notebook and pen from his coat pocket. "Does anyone have access to your apartment while you are out?"

"Just my housekeeper. She comes around nine and leaves by one or two. And of course, my security team has access but they would check with me before entering my private residence."

"Was your housekeeper here today?"

"Yes."

"We need a name and address. Telephone number."

"Jennifer Rose," Colin said as he pulled his phone from his pocket. He displayed the housekeeper's contact information. Rob scribbled in his notebook. "I don't know her address offhand. I can get it when I'm back in my apartment. She only lives a few blocks away. She walks here."

"No need," Rob said. "We can track her down from her phone number."

Matt returned and said, "Our guys are on their way to coordinate with the FD on the bomb forensics. As soon as the C-4 is removed, we'll gather any remaining evidence and ensure the place is safe. And Jason from tech will be over to check out his security system within the hour."

"Anyone else who could have been in your apartment?" Rob said. "Repairman?"

Colin frowned, pinching his chin with his thumb and forefinger. "Actually, now that I think about it, Max was supposed to come over and check out my cable, I've been having spotty service."

"How well do you know this guy?" Rob asked.

"Very. He works for me and he installed the system. It couldn't be him."

"You sure? Everyone has a price," Matt said. "The housekeeper too."

"No way. They're both loyal employees and Max is a friend. We play hoops together and his kids are on the youth basketball team we sponsor."

"How would he get in? Does he have access to your security code? He did install it."

"True, but he wouldn't have to, Jennifer would let him in."

"Mr. MacKenzie!" Colin saw Jennifer rushing toward him. "How are you? I saw it on the news. I ran right over. Was there really a bomb in your apartment?" She gasped, covering her mouth with her mitten-clad hand.

Colin grabbed her upper arms. "It's fine, Jennifer. We got out without a scratch." He nodded toward Jamie. "Special Agent Gallagher here saved my ass. Both our asses." Colin released Jennifer.

"Thank God," Jennifer said.

"And those LED lights you bought me saved the day. I think I'll be sending your kids to college."

Jennifer gasped. "Seriously?"

"Deadly. I'll even put it in my will."

"Thank you, sir. I don't know what to say."

"Ms. Rose," Jamie said. "Mr. MacKenzie indicated Max was expected today to work on the cable system. What time did he arrive?"

"Actually, it wasn't Max. The guy said Max was sick so he came instead."

Chapter 10

Jennifer's saucer eyes signaled her anguish at having made a grave error.

Jamie approached the woman. "So, you've never seen this guy before?"

"No, but he gave me his card. I left it in the basket on the kitchen counter." She shifted toward Colin. "Did I screw up, sir?"

Before Colin could respond Jamie continued her interrogation. "Can you identify this guy?"

Focusing on Jamie again, Jennifer said, "Sure. He was here for about an hour."

"Did he only access the electronics closet?" Jamie said.

"At first, but then he said he had to go upstairs to check something in the attic."

Colin frowned. "Jennifer, there is no attic."

Jennifer pressed her lips tightly together before speaking, clasping her hands prayer-like under her chin. "I-I didn't know that, sir."

Colin placed his reassuring hands on her shoulders. "I understand. Not your fault."

Rob announced, "Ms. Rose, you'll need to come with us to give a statement and look at some pictures." To Jamie, he said, "We've got pics of all the employees. We'll have Ms. Rose review them. If nothing matches, we'll do a sketch."

Colin fretted. Jennifer's frown seemed permanently etched into her forehead. "Don't worry, Jen. The FBI will catch this guy."

But Colin sensed she was still distressed. Before he could ask, she said, "I-I'm a little freaked out there could have been a bomb set to go off while I was still there."

Colin comprehended. Jennifer had two small children and the thought of them growing up without their mother caused his stomach to churn. He squeezed her shoulders before releasing her, his ire welled. It was one thing to put his life in jeopardy but to place others in danger just added to his fury. *Bastard.* When they got this guy, or woman, he wanted pounds and pounds of flesh.

Fire department personnel cleared a wide berth as the remote-control robot exited the building carrying the container of C-4. Colin sighed. This was the second time today he'd watched a bomb being removed from his proximity. Who could be targeting him? He searched his memory for someone who'd wish him dead. No one. Not one person, Goddammit. He might be rich as a king, but he was also one of the good guys, he paid his employees well and treated them like family. He was a loyal friend, a good son. Right? His mantra was the Golden Fucking Rule.

He pondered the club. Sure, he was a strict Dom and levied more than his share of punishments to willing submissives. But, consensual adults. So that couldn't be it. None of this fit.

Wait. Hold on a minute. Could it be someone close to him who was the actual target?

CAPTAIN SPECK APPROACHED. "You guys can head back in. We'll keep you posted on the forensics."

"Thanks," Jamie said.

Rob asked Colin, "What's Max's last name? I need his number too."

"Max Harper." Colin pulled out his phone. He showed the contact info to Rob who noted it on his pad. His phone rang but Colin ignored the call.

"Matt, track down this guy and get a statement."

"Done," Matt said.

"We'll keep you updated," Rob told Jamie and Colin, and Matt and Rob left with Ms. Rose in temporary custody.

Colin stared off into the distance and Jamie wondered if he was okay. "Colin," Jamie said. He didn't answer. "Colin?"

He jerked his head toward her. "What?"

"Seemed like you checked out there for a minute. I know the stress of something like this can sneak up on you."

Colin massaged his temples. "I'm wracking my brain as to who would want me dead."

Jamie slipped a reassuring arm through his, leaning into his rock-hard body. The guy sure was built. An image of him naked flashed in her mind and her pulse throbbed. It took a few seconds to banish the carnal image. What was wrong with her? This was work. She shouldn't be having lascivious thoughts. She swallowed, hard. "We'll figure it out. We'll catch this perp."

"Lock the bastard up until he rots."

JAMIE'S ARM entwined with his gave him a sense of security. A warmth even. Like a silken tether anchoring him to the ground. Yet sturdy, unbreakable—a lifeline. He needed it desperately, feeling off-balance, unsteady, a new sensation.

Colin glanced over Jamie's shoulder. Fire trucks departed and people re-entered the building. Rob and Matt were gone, as was Jennifer. Colin pictured Jennifer in an interrogation room and cringed. "They'll treat Jennifer with kid gloves, right? She's not involved. I know it."

"Of course. Don't worry about her. Promise."

Colin exhaled into his hands. "I'm freezing, exhausted and starving."

Jamie released his arm and mimicked Colin, blowing breath into her hands. She pumped up and down on her toes a few times. "Me too. Come on, let's head back to your apartment."

They followed the crowd into the lobby and waited their turn at the elevator. Colin said, "I doubt anyone will want to deliver a pizza here now. I don't know if I have any food in the house."

The doors opened and they entered along with a crowd of others pressing buttons for their respective floors. Colin hit the PH button and entered the code, blocking the keypad with his body, then robotically facing the front of the elevator, like everyone else, garnering the usual stares from other residents. Jamie was scrunched into Colin's side in the crowded elevator, her warmth continuing to assuage his frazzled nerves.

"Your fridge is well stocked," she assured him. "I'll whip something up."

"You can cook?"

Jamie winked. "Of course."

"I didn't think women cooked anymore."

She shoved her body into his side. "That's a gross generalization."

Colin grinned. "Sorry. I didn't mean it that way. I think people in general would rather order take-out than cook these days."

"Yeah, however, I'm still a small-town upstate girl. That trend hasn't migrated to my house yet." The elevator stopped frequently until they were finally alone, nearing the penthouse. With the freed space, Jamie moved away from Colin's side, leaving him feeling bereft. He liked her by his side, pressed against him.

He shoved his hands in his pockets. "Sounds like my friend Steve's family. Growing up, the Morettis were my second family. His parents are amazing cooks and I ate there more often than home. I'm surprised they didn't ask my parents for a food stipend."

"Steve Moretti? Laura Logan's husband?"

"You know Laura?"

"We were at Quantico at the same time."

"Then you know Alyx Cameron too?"

"Sure. She was my roommate."

"Wow, small world. I know Alyx's husband Daniel."

Jamie's jaw slackened. "Don't tell me you work at that... club."

Shit.

The elevator stopped and Colin entered the six-digit code again. He hadn't planned on mentioning the club until it was necessary. However, if she were going to be by his side twenty-four-seven then she'd have to accompany him to the club this weekend. He doubted that would go over well. Or maybe she'd be into it... and maybe she'd be interested in playing there with him. Someday. After this entire debacle concluded.

They stood in the foyer of his penthouse and Jamie stopped short, her forehead crinkled. Colin dragged his hands down his face. "Why don't we get changed into more comfortable clothes and open a bottle of wine. Then we can go over my calendar for the week in the event this situation isn't resolved by then."

Jamie's stunned silence threw him off-balance again. He liked her. He liked her a lot, bodyguard or not. He didn't want to screw this up.

Chapter 11

J amie wanted an answer. Well, she did and she didn't. She liked Colin, but the thought of him working at a sex club threw her off-kilter. Whips, gags, masks, and all that cum-soaked leather. Yikes. Bondage and spanking? Did people really need that kind of stuff to get off? Geez. But then Alyx and Laura confessed they'd both married guys – Doms – who were regulars at this club out east. Which meant Laura and Alyx were *submissives.* She found the whole idea unsettling. Laura and Alyx were both confidant, assertive women, in control, aggressive on the job. How could they possibly find a relationship like that satisfying? Jamie only saw them recently, that one time for lunch and now both women were home awaiting the stork's delivery. They hadn't gone into much detail about all this BDSM stuff and Jamie hadn't been inclined to probe the particulars.

And why would Colin need to get laid at a club? He was rich and gorgeous and seemed like a genuine soul. He could have as much sex as he wanted and probably any woman he desired. Was he really one of those Doms? A man who needed to dominate women. That wouldn't work in her world. But the image of Colin tying her up and doing wicked things kind of made her moist.

"Did you hear me?" Colin prompted.

"Hmm?"

"Why don't we get changed and make a toast to not being dead."

"I'm on duty. Can't drink," she said, crossing her arms over her chest.

Colin peered into her eyes, his gaze intimidating. "A little wine won't compromise you. I have a strong suspicion you can handle your alcohol."

Jamie struggled not to smile. Colin was right on the money. She had a high tolerance for spirits and never met a guy she couldn't drink under the table. She'd escorted many a date home over the years and tucked him into bed before disappearing into the night. Most guys didn't remember, or perhaps their egos wouldn't allow them to admit they'd wussed out. Usually, she never heard from the guy again. Consequently, her dating life proved dismal, convinced she was too intimidating for most men and those who were more alpha than she were giant toads. She'd never had a serious relationship and resigned herself that Mr. Right wasn't out there.

"All right," she finally said. "I'll meet you in the kitchen in five. We need to eat something."

"Great," Colin said and he headed for the stairs.

Jamie followed and veered left to the beautifully appointed bedroom Colin assigned her. She unclipped the Kydex holster securing her .40 caliber Glock from her waistband and laid it on the bed. Being a petite woman, it took months to find the right holster. The Kydex, made of a molded synthetic, held up in all weather conditions. It kept your weapon accessible while running, seated in your car and even upside down or while rolling around in a fight. And it was faster on the draw than leather. She removed her black suede boots and placed her right foot on the bed and unbuckled her ankle holster carrying her compact 9 mm. She placed it alongside the Glock, then undressed, hanging her black suit and white blouse in the closet and stowed her boots there too. Donning a pair of ankle-length yoga pants and her favorite oversized gray NYU sweatshirt, she grabbed her toiletry bag and trod into the bathroom to freshen up. She winced at her reflection in the beveled oval mirror over the sink. What little make up she wore had evaporated. What a long fucker of a day. She wished she was home in her tiny apartment with her feet propped on the coffee table watching the nightly news.

The news… poor Colin, he was probably plastered all over it. She wondered how this might affect his business, never mind his life. He'd been holding up fairly well. Maybe that Dom thing… a guy who practiced total control more easily maintained his sanity. She thought of the sex club again. He mentioned his calendar. Was he planning on going there soon? Oh God, she'd have to accompany him.

What would the Bureau say about that? Although she knew Alyx went there to prepare for her undercover assignment, which eventually resulted in cracking a big sex trafficking ring. Apparently, the Bureau was capable of looking the other way on certain occasions. Hmm…

She washed her face, added a touch of blush, and brushed her hair securing it with an elastic into a messy bun. She toed into a pair of white lace-less sneakers, stood, and inhaled deeply. Pulling the 9 mm. from its holster, she thought what to do with it. She tucked it into her waistband at her back.

The clock on the nightstand displayed 9:57 p.m. She needed food and descended the staircase.

COLIN STARED at his open closet door. A shudder slithered down his spine as he recalled being trapped inside with six blocks of C-4. If Jamie hadn't been here? Jesus. He broke out in a cold sweat. A fast shower might be in order, scalding water banishing the chill from his bones.

Colin entered the kitchen, barefoot, clad in sweatpants and a black t-shirt, to view Jamie's delectable ass protruding from the refrigerator. "I'm liking the view."

Jamie stood too quickly and banged her head on the shelf. "Ow," she said, rubbing the painful spot. She faced him holding a carton of eggs and an array of vegetables. "Careful, dude. This is a business relationship and you're bordering on sexual harassment."

"Duly noted, Agent Gallagher. Won't happen again." But damn, she was adorable in casual clothes, her hair pulled back in a knot. Although he liked her hair down better. He'd love to run his fingers through those ginger locks, then hold her tight against his chest while his tongue plundered her mouth. He felt a tightening between his legs.

Jamie placed the items on the center island. "I thought I'd make a frittata and a salad." Colin knew he was staring but he couldn't help himself. Her fresh-faced beauty awed him. Jamie obviously noticed. "What's wrong?"

Colin leaned his hip against the marbled counter and crossed his arms over his chest. "I'm not used to having a woman in my kitchen. It's weird."

"Come on, a hot, rich guy like you? Women probably throw themselves at you."

Colin lifted an eyebrow. "You think I'm hot?"

Shit. She couldn't believe she'd said that.

"What I meant is your incredibly good-looking. You have to know that."

"Careful, Agent Gallagher, you might be guilty of some sexual harassment yourself."

Jamie tightened her lips. Best to change the subject. "Duly noted, Mr. MacKenzie." They mirrored smiles. "So, frittata and salad?"

"Sounds great, how can I help?"

"You can set out the dishes and silverware."

"Will do, ma'am. But first I'm opening a bottle of wine. Red or white?"

"I like both. Whatever you want." She claimed a bowl from an overhead cabinet.

"I have a 2016 Caymus Napa Valley cabernet I've been anxious to try. How's that?"

"I know nothing about wine, Colin. I couldn't tell a hundred-dollar bottle from a ten-dollar bottle. So don't waste anything good on me." She set the oven to 400. "Where's your pot closet?"

"I have no idea."

"I take it you don't cook much."

"Never."

Jamie chuckled. Obviously, the shiny ones hanging from the ceiling rack were for show. Having searched his kitchen earlier she thought she remembered pots stowed under the center island and found the cache of cookware as expected. "Wow, you've got Langostina. Impressive. My dad gave my mother a set for Christmas one year. It took him a year to save up the money." Jamie selected a skillet and laid it on the countertop.

"Back at'cha. I wouldn't know good cookware from the cheap stuff."

"Why do you have it then?"

"I got Jennifer a credit card and told her to buy whatever she needed."

"Then she knows her stuff."

Colin busied himself opening the bottle and decanting the claret liquid into a glass carafe, then plucked two stemless wine glasses from the cabinet next to the refrigerator. "It needs to breathe a bit," he said resting the glasses on the center island.

Jamie finely chopped a red pepper and a shallot, and some ham, whisking it with six eggs and a handful of shredded cheddar and a splash of milk. She poured the mixture in the pan as the oven timer announced it was ready. She slid the skillet into the oven and set the timer for ten minutes, then searched the pantry and refrigerator until she found all the ingredients to make a green salad with a simple vinaigrette.

Colin arranged place settings on the center island and poured the wine, handing Jamie a glass. "Here's to my hero."

They clinked glasses. "I have to admit you're holding up better than expected."

"Never let them see you sweat."

"Good for you."

"Honestly, I don't think it's hit me yet."

"I get it. On the occasion when things get sketchy on the job, the reality doesn't set in until I get into bed at night. Then I have my 'holy shit' moment."

"If I freak out in the middle of the night will you come in and comfort me, tell me it's all going to be all right?"

Jamie tilted her head, squinted. "I think we need someone from HR to supervise us or give us a refresher course. We seem to keep venturing into dangerous territory." Her phone rang. "Hi Jason, all right." To Colin she said, "Our tech guy is here, can you buzz him up?"

Colin grabbed his phone and hit a button. "Done."

Chapter 12

Jamie cut the omelet into six wedges and served Colin two and herself one. They added salad to their plates and sipped more wine while Jason worked in the electronics cabinet. "I have to admit this wine is scrumptious."

"Told ya," Colin said. "I'll agree a lot of it depends on your taste, and just because a wine is expensive doesn't mean you'll love it."

"Maybe I don't appreciate it because I know nothing about wine." Jamie ate a bite of frittata, the savory concoction of veggies, ham and cheese one of her faves.

"I'll teach you," Colin said. "Maybe after this is over and we're both still alive I could take you out for dinner."

A laugh erupted and Jamie felt uneasy. Why would Colin want to take a simple girl like her on a date? Colin stuffed salad into his mouth, his sumptuous lips distracting her. She refocused on her food. "I doubt I'd be an appropriate date for you. You need a fancy lady. I don't even own a pair of heels."

"A fancy lady? Isn't that a euphemism for a prostitute? I'm pretty sure I heard it on TV or something."

"What?" Jamie said. "You know that's not what I meant." Their eyes locked and neither broke the connection. Colin laughed and Jamie joined him.

They finished their meal and cleaned up. Colin stopped short, his gaze fixed on the counter where Jamie had rested her weapon, flush to the backsplash.

"Sorry," she said standing alongside him. "I'm required to keep a weapon in proximity at all times."

"Of course."

She placed a hand on his forearm. "Is it making you uncomfortable?"

He studied her with serious blue eyes. "I'm not much of a gun advocate. For civilians, that is. I expect law enforcement and military to have them." Jamie picked up the small 9 mm. and returned it to the waistband behind her back. He added, "Do you really think someone could break in?"

"I don't. But better safe than sorry, right?"

"Yeah."

They loaded the dishwasher and Jamie put a soap pod into the compartment and pressed the start button.

"I'm embarrassed to admit I've never seen the inside of my dishwasher."

"You're pathetic," Jamie said. "Or maybe you're a spoiled brat."

Colin stood in front of her, only inches between them. His scent all citrus and woodsy. She gazed into his azure eyes. "I'm not. I'm just not domestically inclined. And I'm not home much. My work keeps me out late most nights."

Jamie swallowed hard, her mouth dry. His physical presence too much for her.

Jason entered the kitchen. Jamie cleared her throat and stepped back.

"All clear, Agent Gallagher. I reset the system so no one can hack into it again. If you have any more problems give a ring."

"Thanks, Jason. Appreciate your help."

"Glad to be of service." And Jason left without further comment.

"So, back to work," she sputtered. "You said we should go over your calendar for the remainder of the week."

"Right. Let's take our wine into the living room."

He exited and Jamie followed, fully cognizant a discussion about *the club* was imminent. She vowed to keep her opinions to herself. *Do your job and keep your mouth shut.*

Colin flipped a switch and the gas fireplace ignited. He used his phone to lower the overhead lights, and a lilting piano sonata wafted from hidden speakers. The room shouted romance.

Jamie opted for a side chair, avoiding the proximity of sitting on the couch alongside Colin and deposited her weapon on the nearby table. She stepped out of her sneakers and curled her feet under her. On her second glass of wine, she reminded herself to sip it slowly and then she was done. Colin settled on the couch and focused on his phone. "As I said earlier, I've given everyone the day off tomorrow so I don't have to go to the office. But I have a fundraiser tomorrow evening at the Plaza Hotel. Did you know Laura started a foundation for educating impoverished children? I've partnered with her."

Jamie frowned. "No, I didn't know. I haven't seen Laura in years. I lost touch with her and Alyx after Quantico. I did meet up with them for lunch when I first arrived."

"She's doing amazing work and I couldn't help but jump in. By the way, I didn't see you at Steve and Laura's wedding, or at Alyx and Daniel's either."

"For Alyx's wedding I was out of the country and for Laura's wedding I couldn't get time off. I was involved in a highly sensitive counterintelligence op."

Colin smirked. "Intriguing. Something to do with the recent election?"

Jamie dragged her fingers across her lips and mimicked the key turning.

Colin laughed. "I get it. But you'll be able to hang out with Laura and Alyx at the fundraiser. That should convince you to come as my date."

She'd like to see Laura and Alyx and meet their new husbands. "I'll think about it."

"Good, we're making progress. Moving on... Thursday, I planned to visit my parents to finalize our plans for our ski trip next week. Probably take them out to dinner." He clasped his chin between his thumb and forefinger. "Hmm, I should probably call them, my mother has phoned several times."

"Is that who you've been ignoring all day?"

"Yeah, but I'm sure it's all over the news and internet by now so I should probably confirm I'm still alive."

"Yes, please call your mother and put her mind at ease."

"I will, as soon as we're done. So, Friday and Saturday, I'm at the club in the evenings and I stay at my Hampton Shores place."

Jamie steadied her voice and concentrated on sounding professional. "Don't worry, I'm good at blending into the background. You'll hardly know I'm there."

"Doubtful," Colin said. "You're too attractive not to be noticed by every man in the general vicinity. And probably a large contingent of women."

He peered at her again, and this time she had no words. She'd never been good at taking a compliment. Even when she won her medal at the Olympics, the accolades made her uncomfortable. "It's my job. I've guarded POTUS and FLOTUS and no one even knew I was there. I try to be invisible and I can do that for you."

"The fundraiser is easy. I'm not sure what to do with you at the club. I don't want you to be uncomfortable, but I doubt you want to blend in there." His eyes enlarged, his grin grew mischievous. "You'd have to be in a state of undress and although everyone would most likely be appreciative, including me, I wouldn't ask that of you."

The silence extended before Jamie finally spoke. "Let's be rational about this, Colin. One, I don't own any evening wear and two, nor do I own any fetish wear."

"I think wardrobe is the least of our worries."

Jamie sighed. "Besides, don't you have a date for the fundraiser? It seems a guy like you would have women clamoring to show up on his arm."

"You mean a *hot* guy like me?" They smiled and Jamie felt a little more at ease. He did have a way of disarming her.

"Yes, sir, a hot guy like you."

"Did you call me sir? You've taken your first step into protocol for the club."

"What? No way, I was teasing."

"I enjoy a good tease." Colin's lips quirked upward. "But seriously, Jamie, I don't date. Most women in my world are overly concerned with status and money and that type of woman doesn't interest me. And I'm too busy to date."

"I'm sure there are women in Manhattan who aren't looking for that. You need to give someone a chance."

"Perhaps, but not this week. So, tomorrow we'll go and get you something to wear to the fundraiser. I need to think about the club."

Jamie chewed on a fingernail. She needed to think about the club too. Think very, very hard.

COLIN'S MIND WHIRLED. Imagining Special Agent Jamie Gallagher in glamorous evening wear was one thing, but a vision of her at the club gave him a serious hard-on. He crossed his legs to conceal his burgeoning erection. He cleared his throat. "I have a personal shopper at Saks. I'll arrange an appointment for tomorrow."

"Colin, really, it's unnecessary. I mean, don't you always have security with you? I'm sure those guys don't dress up while they're guarding you."

"I don't travel with security other than my driver. He's armed and a former special services guy, but for the most part I can take care of myself." Until recently. His phone rang and he glanced at the readout. "My mother. I should take this."

"Of course," Jamie said.

"Hi, Mom."

"Colin, I've been out of my mind. You couldn't take five seconds to call and tell me what's going on? I had to see it on the news?"

"Sorry, Mom. It's been an insane day. Don't worry. I'm fine. The FBI has me under wraps. They've assigned an agent to be at my side twenty-four-seven."

"But honey, were there two bombs? One at the office and one at your apartment?"

"Yes."

"How did they get into your apartment? Is Jennifer okay?"

"She's fine. It's complicated, Mom, and the FBI hasn't come up with any intelligence yet. Hopefully, we'll know something soon."

"Is there an FBI agent there with you now?"

"Yes," Colin said again.

"I feel better knowing that. You'll let me know something as soon as you do?"

"I will, Mom."

"Promise?"

"Promise."

"I can't imagine who would want to do this to you, Colin. Do you think it has something to do with your business?"

"That's the likely scenario. My personal life is pretty mundane. I can't imagine I've pissed anyone off in my inner circle. It has to be some misunderstanding with my company."

"All right, darling. Will we still see you tomorrow at the Plaza?"

"That's the plan. If anything changes, I'll let you know."

"Night, darling. Stay safe and we'll see you tomorrow."

"Night, Mom. Love you." Colin hit the red button.

"You should have called your mother before this," Jamie said.

"I know," he said, "no excuse."

JAMIE SIPPED the last of her wine and settled the glass on the side table. She pulled her knees up and wrapped her arms around them. She needed to talk Colin out of all this ridiculousness. No evening gown was needed. And the club, hmmm, what to do about that? She still couldn't fathom why a guy like Colin went to a sex club. Was he that shallow? There couldn't be any feelings involved in that kind of sex. Although, she should talk. She'd never been emotionally involved with any guy she'd slept with. Then it hit. BDSM. God, he had to be either a sadist or a masochist. Was he into pain? Did he whip women? Or maybe he was a masochist and got off on people flogging him. Egad. Her mind traveled down a dark path. And yet, he seemed so, normal.

"You're thinking too much. What's marring your pretty face?"

A long silence ensued until she finally said, "I don't get it. Why do you need to go to a sex club?" Then the words emptied out of her. "Do you whip women? Are you a sadist? You're into BDSM, right?"

"Whoa." Colin put up two hands. "Let's slow this down."

Jamie put a hand over her mouth. She'd overstepped. Big time.

"Come over here and sit next to me." He reached over and grabbed her hand, tugging her toward him.

Chapter 13

Colin wasn't in the habit of having to explain his involvement in the BDSM scene. It wasn't something he shared with anyone. An old high school buddy introduced Steve and him to the scene in Tampa while on vacation during spring break their senior year. That club hooked them up with the Long Island venue, where they met Daniel.

It was getting lonely with Steve and Daniel gone. It was more fun when they worked the submissives together. However, it was the only place where sex was good for him. He liked control and he especially enjoyed showing an inexperienced or wounded woman how to reach a mind-blowing orgasm. And when a woman surrendered to him, there was nothing better.

Close enough to touch the adorable FBI agent, he kept a respectable distance between them on the couch. "Jamie, I have no intention of subjecting you to anything that will make you uncomfortable. I don't recruit people into the lifestyle. They come of their own accord and for a variety of reasons. I'm happy to answer any questions you may have, but it is not my intent to convince you of anything."

Jamie's eyes cast downward and she fiddled with the hem of her sweatshirt. "I'm sorry. I said too much. It's none of my business."

She settled against the couch back. "On the other hand, I'm not a wimp. And naked bodies don't faze me. I've seen plenty of abuse in my life, I can handle it."

"There's your first mistake. It's not abuse. Do you really think I would abuse a woman?" Colin tilted his head and raised his eyebrows.

Jamie smiled. "No, but then again I've only known you one day."

Colin huffed. "Put your mind at ease. I'm not a sadist or a masochist. And I'm not into pain. If a woman wants that I hand her off to someone else. Flogging is popular, as is spanking, but I would call that more stimulating than painful. It's all fun and games. Adult playtime. Most women enjoy things like bondage and blindfolds, they increase excitement and your other senses are intensified."

"I'll take you at your word."

"Good. Try to refrain from judgment until you see it for yourself. I'm happy to answer any questions you have then."

"Deal," she said.

"I have to explain your presence. There are several options. We can be upfront and say you're my bodyguard and you can sit in the corner in your boring black suit, or we can say you're there for the tour as an interested participant. If we choose the latter, you will be under my protection and you can keep your clothes."

Jamie's eyebrows lifted and she shook her head. "I'm definitely keeping my clothes."

Colin laughed. "Well, there will be plenty of people picturing you naked."

"Oh? Like you?"

"Absolutely not. I'm a gentleman. Even at the club."

"Yeah, right. You're a guy. I doubt that."

Colin couldn't help himself and he laughed again. She was right, guilty as charged. "No comment," he said. "It's late, we should probably get some sleep."

"It has been a long day. If you can get me a pillow and a blanket I'll camp out on the couch. I need to be between you and both egresses."

"I don't want you to be uncomfortable."

"The couch is fine."

"All right, be right back with some bedding."

COLIN TOOK the stairs two at a time, disappearing down the hallway. Jamie chastised herself for being so difficult. He was her mark and she just needed to follow him around until this crime was solved. Maybe she'd luck out and they'd find the guy soon and she could get back to work on another case. Sitting around waiting for something to happen was pure torture. She preferred action, investigating, apprehending the bad guys. Although, the thought of never seeing Colin MacKenzie again dismayed her and she *was* curious to observe him at the club. Would *he* be in a state of undress? She wouldn't mind seeing him naked. From what little she knew, a sexual dominant sounded scary, but sort of good scary. And she bet he had some skills between the sheets. Laura and Alyx both hinted as much about their men.

Colin returned with an armful of linens. "Will these do?"

"I only need the flat sheet, the pillow, and the quilt. I'll fold the sheet in half."

"I'll help you make up the bed." He removed the back cushions on the couch and tossed them on the floor. Together they covered the sofa with the sheet, tucking the fold into the crease. Jamie plopped the pillow on the armrest and Colin spread out the quilt.

"I'm going to go upstairs and get ready for bed," Jamie said.

"Do you want to leave the fireplace on?"

"No, shut it off."

Colin flipped the switch and plucked the TV remote off the coffee table. "This controls the cable, the sound system, and the overhead lights. The readout should be self-explanatory."

Jamie took the remote and studied it before dropping it on the couch-bed. "I'm sure I can figure it out."

"And if you need anything, holler or you can text or call me."

"Will do. Oh, and don't sneak up on me in the middle of the night. I have a weapon."

Colin frowned playfully. "Good to know."

Jamie climbed the stairs ahead of Colin, then turned and said, "Good night."

"Night," he said. "Thanks again for saving my ass today. I'll never be able to repay you."

"No worries. Glad I was here."

"I could get used to having a full-time bodyguard, especially such a beautiful one."

Jamie wagged a finger at him. "Unh-uh... HR is listening."

Colin laughed, then entered his room and shut the door.

COLIN FELL crosswise onto his bed, hands clasped behind his head, his feet on the floor. What a fucking day. He'd nearly died, twice. Then, this magnificent woman entered his life and he secretly hoped she would be around for a few more days. Even if they found the guy tomorrow, he'd still want to take her to the fundraiser and fully intended to see her again after this whole debacle ended. Man, he'd love to get her into the club, or into his playroom, a hope for the future. Sure, he could take her to the club under the guise of his bodyguard, but he'd like to get her there for fun. It might take some time. Could kinky sex be in her repertoire?

He shrugged out of his clothes, tossing them on the nearby chair and readied himself for bed, slipping naked under the covers. Thoughts of Special Agent Jamie Gallagher in the throes of desire, screaming her release, danced an erotic jig in his brain. An erection. Again.

JAMIE SETTLED between the covers on her makeshift bed. She shut off the overhead lights and flicked on the couch-side lamp. Exhausted, maybe too exhausted to fall asleep, she powered on the TV and found the Hallmark Channel, a decadent pleasure she'd never admit to. Her teenaged niece nagged her into watching it during Christmas last year, the holiday romances nostalgic and heartwarming. Jamie was thankful the Gallaghers adopted her at the tender age of nine. She'd never experienced a real Christmas. And she often thought of the two police officers who'd rescued her from the awful motel room and drug-addicted mother. They were a major factor in her joining the Navy and subsequently, the FBI, bolstered by John Gallagher also being in law enforcement. She definitely suffered from sheepdog syndrome, explained to her early on at Quantico. Both sheep and wolves roamed this world and the sheepdog too, who protected the sheep from the wolves. Protecting sheep was her calling.

The four years in foster care was rough, five different families, none she wanted to become permanent. She never suffered any sexual abuse, although it had been close once. Fourteen-year-old Evan Smits grabbed her on the way out of the shower. Twice her size and five years older, his crotch was eye level and she punched him in the nuts. He collapsed and she jumped on his chest and knocked the snot out of the pimply-faced teen. He told his parents the black eye was a result of football practice and never touched her again.

When John Gallagher walked into the social services office that rainy afternoon Jamie knew he was the one. A tall, strapping man, with matching red hair, his smile could light up a football stadium. She'd been through this drill a half dozen times without success but that time she got her man… or rather family.

Sally Gallagher was beautiful, soft, and smelled like baby powder. John Gallagher used his law enforcement connections to track down her brother and offered a shoulder to cry on when she learned of his death. *She'd* endured a rough few years in foster care and could only imagine how a two-year-old with cerebral palsy fared. John reassured her that he'd been with a loving family until he died at age four, but Jamie still felt pangs of guilt at not being able to take care of him. She shut off the side lamp but left the TV on for company.

A minute or an hour later, a man's voice startled her awake.

Chapter 14

J amie seized the remote and switched off the TV, plunging the room into total darkness. A thump followed by, "Ouch! Fuck me. I'm coming down. Don't shoot."

"Shit, Colin. What's going on?"

"I can't see a thing. Are *you* trying to kill me?"

She reached over and flicked on the lamp. "Sorry, I wasn't thinking."

Colin hopped on one foot, holding his big toe. "Jesus, that hurt. I thought I was out of steps." He limped over to the couch. "I was coming down to get a drink. Why would you turn off the television so suddenly?"

"No reason. You startled me and I got confused. I wasn't sure where I was."

"Or… you were watching something you didn't want me to see? The Playboy Channel?"

"What? No."

He grabbed the remote and flicked on the TV where two lovers were smooching, followed by the credits. "The Hallmark Channel? Seriously?"

"I wasn't, it just came on."

"No way would I have the Hallmark Channel on. That shit will give you emotional diabetes."

"You're a regular riot, but how would you know? You said you've never seen it."

"It's a cliché. People talk about it all the time."

"Maybe your housekeeper was watching it."

Colin squinted one eye shut. "*May*be..." He stared at her for an interminable moment then headed toward the kitchen, and quickly returned with two bottles of water. "Want one?"

"Sure," Jamie said, taking the plastic bottle.

"Can't sleep?" Colin asked.

"Over-tired. I must have dozed off."

"Sorry I woke you." Colin pivoted, one bare foot on the step. "Good night again." He trod up the stairs and Jamie wanted to follow. God, what was she thinking? Well, she was thinking about sleeping beside the handsome billionaire, and maybe not doing all that much sleeping.

COLIN CHUGGED some water and returned to bed, the enigmatic redhead on his mind. Fearless and lethal, juxtaposed—her feminine physique and pretty face. Her soft pink lips and huge emerald eyes. If he met her on the street, he'd never sense her command, her control. Did he dare consider it? *Dominance.* Although he *had* met her on the street and totally misread her. She'd almost seemed ditsy, and he doubted she had a submissive bone in her body. The club might freak her out, or worse, disgust her.

The feelings she aroused in him were like nothing he'd ever felt and yet he feared they might not be sexually compatible. The notion of pursuing her in a relationship dominating his thoughts, his attraction irrefutable. He didn't think having sex with such a strong woman would work, not for him. A conundrum.

Colin closed his eyes, seeking sleep.

JAMIE WOKE to a man's screams. Disoriented for a split second, she realized it was coming from Colin's room. She grabbed her gun and bolted up the stairs. No way could someone have gotten to him. She flung open the door and rooted around on the wall for the light switch, illuminating the room. Colin writhed on the bed, flailing his arms, his muscular chest on display. "Jamie, be careful. Are you sure you know what you're doing?" he screamed.

She laid her weapon on the adjacent table and sat on the bedside, securing his wrists and shouting his name. "Colin, wake up. You're having a nightmare."

Colin's eyes flew open, his head off the pillow, and yelled, "The bomb. Is it defused? Are we safe?"

"No danger, it's passed."

Jamie released his wrists and Colin relaxed, his head falling back on the gray pillowcase. Sweat dotted his brow, the tousled hair on his forehead damp. "Jesus," he said, "I'm sorry. I don't often have nightmares. I was back in the closet watching you defuse that C-4."

"No worries. I told you earlier, when things are bad they can sneak up on you at night, even though you think you've processed it already." Colin scrubbed his face with his hands, then fingered his hair off his forehead. Jamie grabbed the water bottle from the nightstand. "Here, drink."

Colin chugged the remaining water. "I warned you I might need you to comfort me in the middle of the night."

Jamie laughed. "You did."

"I was joking at the time but I guess this is taking more of a toll on me than I thought. Stressed to infinity."

"It's to be expected. Don't be too hard on yourself." She tucked him back in bed, folding the top of the sheet around his shoulders and smoothed out the covers, then stood.

Colin said, "A little PTSD, I'm afraid."

"We'll catch this guy and lock him up and your worries will banish. Trust."

"Thanks for coming to my rescue. It's becoming a habit."

"That's what I'm here for. After this is over, I'll be part of a bad memory."

"I doubt it," Colin said.

"Night," she said.

"Night."

She retrieved her 9mm, switched off the light and padded down the stairs.

She slept poorly, haunted by images of Colin in the throes of a nightmare… his dark tousled hair, piercing blue eyes, the sharp edge of his jaw. A perilous air about him. Those ferocious eyes. Like he could eat her alive.

THE SUN SHONE through the window of Colin's bedroom. Too bright. He'd forgotten to switch it to frost mode. He checked his phone, 7:20 a.m. Normally he'd be getting dressed for work. He couldn't believe he'd wimped out last night and Jamie played the white knight, again. He'd never been a scaredy-cat as a kid but now he acted like a ten-year-old crying bogeyman. However, this bogeyman was real.

He rose and showered, donning a pair of jeans and a two-button dark blue pullover, combed his hair and headed for the stairs barefoot, boots and socks in hand. He usually worked out in the morning but decided to take today off. His entire routine was shot to hell anyway.

He announced, "Jamie, you awake? I'm coming down."

"Yes, safe to approach." He entered the living room as Jamie's phone rang. "Hey Matt, what's the latest?"

Colin sat on the side chair and listened to the one-sided conversation, suffering a long silence, Jamie's forehead scrunched together. Finally, she said, "So no prints, no forensics, no suspects. What about CCTV?" Another pause. "What about the housekeeper, could she identify the guy or do a sketch?" More damnable silence. "Send it to my phone and I'll show it to him." Jamie listened intently. "I'm fine. He's actually nice for a snobby billionaire." She glanced at Colin and smiled. Colin narrowed his eyes in response. "We're going to do a few errands today and he has an event tonight at the Plaza so I'll be with him there. I spoke to Brett Forrester early this morning. He posted guys outside both entrances and they will continue until the threat's neutralized."

Colin wished he could hear the other end of the conversation which eventually ended with, "Let me know the minute you hear something," then, "talk later."

"You forgot hot," Colin said.

"What?"

"You called me a snobby billionaire, but you forgot hot."

Jamie threw her pillow at him, which he intercepted.

"You're an ass," she said.

They laughed. Jamie's phone pinged and she crooked her finger at him. "This is the sketch they made with your housekeeper. Any chance you recognize him?"

Colin sat beside Jamie on the couch-bed and studied the picture, then shook his head. "Nope. But I have a lot of employees and even some temps so I can't say for sure."

"We compared it to all the ID pics of your employees and no match. We also showed all the photos to Jennifer and she couldn't identify the guy either."

"No leads at all?"

"No prints on the devices, and no traces on the equipment or where any of the items were purchased." Jamie narrowed her eyes. "The CCTV cameras didn't reveal anyone near your assistant's desk. Either he hacked the cameras or had some other way to conceal his image."

"There's something you're not telling me," Colin said.

"Matt, Rob, and I agree, if this guy wanted to kill you he'd have been successful. Either he's not that sophisticated or his intention is to get your attention, to scare you. Maybe he plans to shake you down for money, threaten your family."

"You think my parents are in danger?"

"I don't know but we're assigning agents to them to be on the safe side."

Colin ran his fingers through his hair and sighed. "Jesus, this is fucked."

"I didn't mean to cause you worry, try and put it out of your mind for now. We'll figure it out."

"Soon, I hope. I'm not sure how much longer I can keep a stiff upper lip." Colin inhaled and let the breath out, slowly. "Sorry about last night. Nightmares aren't normally in my repertoire. And I'm not in the habit of acting like a ten-year-old."

Jamie placed her hand on his knee. "You're being way too hard on yourself."

Colin covered her hand with his. "Thanks."

Jamie smiled and their eyes lingered on each other. "And speaking of nightmares, you get to take me shopping for a dress. That will be a serious challenge. I hate dresses."

"I love a good challenge."

Jamie slipped her hand out from under his and stood.

"You want coffee?" he said. "That's one dish I can make."

"Sure. I'm going to grab a quick shower." She gathered the bedding but Colin reached over and took the sheets, and grasped the pillow.

"I've got this. You go."

Chapter 15

Jamie entered the kitchen dressed in skinny jeans and a taupe angora sweater, her hair wet from the shower hanging loose down her back. A minimalist with makeup, she used a tinted moisturizer, a dab of blush, some mascara and pale pink lip gloss. Her black puffy coat in hand, she hung it over one of the high-back chairs at the island.

A delightful aroma perfumed the air. Colin placed a steamy mug of Joe on the center island counter in front of her. He'd already added cream and sugar.

"As I recall from yesterday, we take our coffee the same way."

"Was that yesterday? Seems like a lifetime ago."

"Considering I nearly died, *twice*, it seems like *two* lifetimes ago."

Jamie smiled, then sipped her coffee. Ah... the first mouthful was always the best.

"Andrea is expecting us at ten, then I thought we could grab some lunch."

"Andrea?"

"At Saks."

"Oh yeah, the dress adventure. Gird your loins, mister. I guarantee I'll be a giant pain in the ass. And it feels a little too much like a scene from *Pretty Woman*."

"So, we're back to the hooker analogy?"

"Ha, very funny."

"I promise I'm up to the task, Special Agent Gallagher. I'll make you a fancy lady yet."

Jamie wrinkled her adorable nose as if a foul stench wafted into the kitchen.

"Do you want something for breakfast?" Colin asked. "I don't have much. Mostly cereal, and not the healthy kind. My mother ran a no-sugar, no-fat household. When I got to college, I binged on any sugary cereal I could get my hands on. Do you have any idea how many varieties are out there? I nearly went into a coma."

Jamie laughed. "I imagine you would. But I don't eat breakfast. Coffee is fine."

"Me either," Colin said. They sat at the center island, venting over the previous day and Colin wracked his brain for who might be doing this to him. What did they want? And what would he do if they demanded money? Were his parents in danger? Hostages? He'd pay anything to keep them safe. He summoned the suspect's image Jamie showed him and wondered who it could be.

Colin donned a red parka, a ski-lift ticket dangling from the zipper. He pulled it free and tossed it into the kitchen trashcan while Jamie slipped on her jacket, securing her Glock on her waistband.

"Since I gave James the day off, I thought I'd drive," Colin announced.

"Sure," Jamie said. "I told Brett Forrester to have someone keep an eye on the cars after we searched them yesterday."

"I still can't believe I have to live like this. I sure took my freedom for granted."

"It's not like this guy can bomb every place you go. It has to be somewhere he knows you will be and he has to plan. Saks shouldn't be a problem."

"You're the expert. I'll take your word for it."

Colin opened the back door leading to the garage, disarming the alarm, resetting it after they exited. A man with a buzz cut and pocked complexion stood guard outside. "Morning, sir," he said. He nodded at Jamie, "Ma'am."

"Morning," they said.

"I'll be taking the Porsche," he instructed the guard.

"Yes, sir."

Colin pulled the fob from his pocket and the car chirped to life. He opened the door for Jamie and she slipped into the passenger seat. He shut her in and took his place beside her. They exited the parking garage via the car elevator and turned right onto Park Avenue. "Hopefully, the traffic won't be horrible," Colin said.

THE WEATHER HAD IMPROVED since yesterday, the sun bright in a cloudless azure sky. Jamie checked the weather app on her phone, the temp predicted to hit a high of fifty-five. Not bad for January in New York. The Porsche's heated seats warmed up nicely, embracing her body in soft russet leather.

A half-hour later they entered an underground parking garage and Colin handed the keys to a valet. "How much cash do you have?" Jamie asked Colin.

"I don't know, maybe $500."

"Give me a hundred."

Jamie flashed the hundred-dollar bill to the valet. "Is this enough for you to stay by the car and make sure no one tampers with it?" The dark-haired Hispanic held her gaze. "It'll only be for an hour or two."

"Sure," the man said with that sexy accent. "No problem."

"Thanks." She handed him the money.

"Good thinking," Colin said.

They walked the block to the legendary store and rode the elevator to the women's department where Andrea awaited, her teeth too big, her smile too wide for her face. The bright cerise lipstick jarring to Jamie's eye.

She clapped her hands together when she saw Colin. "Mr. MacKenzie. Good morning. Wonderful to see you again." She extended her hand in greeting and they shook. Her liner-rimmed, hazel eyes focused on Jamie. "Is this your special lady?"

More like Special Agent. Colin cleared his throat. "This is Jamie Gallagher and she's a colleague. She will be accompanying me to a formal gala tonight and didn't bring any evening wear with her. I'm counting on you to help her out."

"My pleasure. Follow me, Ms. Gallagher." Andrea pivoted, her wide skirt swishing as she walked, her swaying hips exaggerating her gait. *Talk about a fancy lady…*

They entered a private area with a pale blue couch, two flowered upholstered chairs, and an oversized tri-fold mirror. A white slatted door to the right, likely the dressing room. "Make yourself comfortable, Mr. MacKenzie. What can I get you? Coffee? Water? Champagne?"

"No thanks, I'm fine," Colin said.

"Ms. Gallagher?"

"Nothing for me, thank you."

"Let me know if you change your mind. Hopefully, this won't take too long."

"A size six, Ms. Gallagher?"

Uncanny. "Usually."

Andrea clasped her hands together at her waist. "I assume a full-length gown. Do you have anything in mind regarding style? Color?"

"No," Jamie said. "I'm not much of a…" She almost said fancy lady and glanced over at Colin. He smirked, cognizant of her near slip. "I mean, I don't dress up much so I'll rely on your expertise."

"Excellent," Andrea exclaimed, clapping her hands together again.

"Why don't you go into the dressing room and undress." Colin settled onto the couch and pulled out his phone. Andrea walked to the white slatted door and opened it, ushering Jamie inside with a wave of her hand. "I'll be back in a jiffy."

Jamie undressed, hiding her Glock and 9mm under her clothing. The sight of which would give little Miss Andrea apoplexy. The large chamber, about the size of her apartment, was mirrored on all sides and Jamie's visage reminded her she wore a sports bra. Truth be told, she didn't own any fancy stuff. Ugh. There was that word again.

Andrea knocked twice. "Come in," Jamie said, her arms folded over her breasts. The salesgirl entered with a rainbow of dresses on a rack not unlike the one that nearly knocked her on her ass when she'd bumped into Colin at the coffee shop. An omen, perhaps? Andrea pulled the door shut behind her, and stopped short. She pointed her index finger and made tiny circles. "Oh dear, that bra will never do." She pressed her lips together before adding, "34 C?"

Jamie blanched. The woman had magical powers. "I'll be right back." With a swish here, a swish there, Andrea vanished.

A chill shivered down Jamie's spine and she wasn't sure if she was cold or horribly uncomfortable at this whole charade. Why did she agree to this?

Andrea returned with two lacy bras, one nude and one black. "Try the nude one first. If we decide on a black dress, we'll change it up."

Jamie stayed silent, pulling the elastic undergarment over her head and dropping it on the nearby chair. She tucked herself into the lacey bra and closed the clasp at her back. She viewed her image in the full-length mirror. Wow, it did make her breasts alluring.

"I'm focusing on your skin tone and lovely auburn hair. You've got a fabulous body. I take it you work out a lot."

"My work has a physical component to it and keeps me in good shape." She expected Andrea to ask what line of work she was in, and wasn't sure if she should tell the truth, yet guessed the sales-girl had been trained to not be too nosey with elite clientele.

Andrea rifled through the gowns. "The recommended palette for redheads is green, purple, blue and white. Of course, black works on everyone. Apricot and lavender work too, and pink is awesome. But something tells me you're not a fan of pink."

"I've spent a good deal of time in a uniform so I don't give a lot of thought to my wardrobe. Most of my stuff is practical and neutral. I'll follow your lead."

Andrea studied her and Jamie figured she was curious about the uniform so she informed her, "I went to the Naval Academy. In Annapolis."

"Oh, are you still in the Navy?"

"I'm not."

"Thank you for your service," Andrea added.

"It was my pleasure and privilege to serve." Jamie decided to leave the discussion there.

"How about this one?" Andrea said presenting a fitted emerald green dress with a low neckline and a smidgeon of sleeve at each shoulder. A translucent fabric lay atop the darker one, flaring a little around the ankles. "It matches your eyes."

"It's beautiful," Jamie said. Never, ever, had she pictured herself in such a dress. "What kind of material is it?"

"It's jersey underneath with a voile overlay." Greek to me, Jamie thought.

The clerk helped her into the gown and stood behind her as they gazed at the mirrored image. Who was this woman?

Andrea draped her long locks over her chest, the overhead lights highlighting her shiny strands. Dare she think it? She felt unnervingly—*feminine.*

"I think the length will be fine once you don a pair of heels. A six?"

More magic. "Correct."

"Back in a flash."

Jamie called after her, "Nothing too high, I'm not used to wearing heels." She didn't want to fall on her face at the gala.

The dress was actually comfortable. Jamie circled, viewing it from all sides. She searched for a price tag, to no avail. Hmm. Guess rich people didn't consider the cost when buying most things.

"Here you go," Andrea said. "I brought a matching evening bag too." Jamie studied the handbag. Good, it was big enough for her 9mm, because she must be carrying at the gala.

Andrea knelt Prince Charming style and offered a pair of pale satin pumps. Jamie slipped into the shoes. They fit perfectly.

Andrea stood and forced Jamie to face the mirror again. "Do you like?"

"Very much," Jamie said, although she was definitely out of her element.

"Shall we show Mr. MacKenzie?"

Jamie squirmed. Parading in front of the handsome billionaire felt cheesy. And yet she must play the part. It was her job, right? Although, not like any previous job. She thought of Alyx, her friend and fellow agent, and the lengths she went to on her special assignment to nail those sex traffickers. Alyx actually had sex with that guy and performed at the club. However, she did wind up marrying the man. By comparison, Jamie was getting away easy. So far.

Chapter 16

Jamie inhaled and blew out a long slow breath. "Let's see what he thinks," Andrea said.

Andrea held the door open and Jamie found her way to Colin. He glanced at her and gasped. "Incredible! Turn around." Jamie did a three-sixty. "Feel like Cinderella?" Colin asked.

"When I find out the price, I'll probably turn into a pumpkin."

Colin narrowed his eyes. "Price isn't a consideration."

"But, Colin… I don't…"

"Not another word. After what we've been through, I'd buy you anything."

Jamie glanced at Andrea out of the corner of her eye, Andrea's eyebrows raised high. She could only imagine what Andrea surmised from Colin's comment.

"We have a few more to try before you decide. Come," she said to Jamie.

Next up was a lavender number festooned with silver sequins. Andrea zipped it up, the high hat lighting bedazzling the gown in miniscule shooting rainbows. "Just lovely," Andrea exclaimed, "it's a great color on you."

"Maybe a little too flashy," Jamie said.

"Let's let Mr. MacKenzie decide." Andrea put a hand against her back and nudged her through the slatted white doors.

Jamie's anger flared. She could decide on a dress for her goddamned self and didn't need a guy to tell her what to do. She bit her lip and kept her ire in check. Just suck it up, girlfriend.

She faced Colin, wobbled on her spikey heels, righted herself and then her ankle turned, plunging her right into Colin's lap. Her breasts smooshed into his face. Oh God. She could maneuver an obstacle course in record time, sure-footed and fast, yet these heels were turning her into someone who literally couldn't put one foot in front of another.

Colin righted her and stayed silent. Two points for being a gentleman. Her pulse raced and her cheeks flushed, the heat radiating from deep inside. No chance of hiding it. He studied her, smothering a smile. She smoothed the skirt and righted a spaghetti strap that had drifted off her shoulder.

"I think it's too fancy," she said.

Colin twirled his finger again and she turned in a circle. "Maybe, the color is good, but I like the green one better.'

"Agreed," Jamie said.

The next dress was black, fitted to the ankles, then flared into something Andrea called a tulip. It was strapless and Jamie felt uncomfortable, not geared to any kind of action should she need to interact with a perp, however unlikely it would be that the bomber was in attendance at the gala. Matt said they screened the guest list and all IDs would be checked at the door.

Jamie managed to perform the same ritual and not fall on her face, or more aptly, on Colin's face. "It looks great on you, but everyone wears black. So far, I like the green best."

They tried on several more gowns, some unbearably uncomfortable and others needed alteration, but there wasn't time. The green one it was. All told, they were out in an hour and a half, dress, shoes and underwear wrapped for transport. She never saw Colin pay and assumed he had an account where purchases were processed without discussion of price. She was tempted to ask how much the bill came to but on second thought, who wanted to become a pumpkin?

THE VISION of Jamie decked out in the spectacular gowns took Colin's breath away, literally. The way they caressed her voluptuous breasts, necklines plunging just enough to reveal a hint of cleavage, her narrow waist and slim hips caressed by luxurious fabrics. His pulse still buzzed a little too fast.

He placed his hand against Jamie's lower back, escorting her out the front doors, the wrapped gown slung over his arm. Jamie carried the other parcels. They returned to the parking garage to stow the packages when the attendant approached. He spoke to Colin, handing him the key fob. "Sir, there was a man near your car. I was behind the car and he didn't see me at first. When he did, he walked away like he was in a hurry."

Jamie answered. "He didn't touch it?"

"No, miss, I did what you told me. I protected the car."

Jamie pulled out her phone and showed the attendant the suspect's sketch. "Is this him?"

"I think so. Yeah, looks like the same guy."

"How long ago was he here?"

"Right after you left."

Jamie pressed her lips together. "Hmm… He could be anywhere by now. You got video surveillance?"

"We're supposed to have it for insurance, but it doesn't always work. You can see the shift supervisor."

"Thanks. I appreciate your diligence." She dialed Matt. "Get a warrant for video surveillance at the garage on W 49th and Park Avenue. The guy was in the vicinity of Mr. MacKenzie's car."

Colin watched as Jamie's sharp and well-trained mind dissected the situation, her powers of deduction acute. She should work for him. Ah, yeah, no… that would be a terrible idea and the dynamic between them would shift into uncomfortable territory.

"Let me know when you've got it. We'll want to show it to Mr. MacKenzie," she told Matt. Colin couldn't hear Matt's response and Jamie ended the call with, "We should be back at the residence in an hour or so. You can send the video to my cell."

"I hope I can identify this guy," Colin said.

"It would be a huge break."

"Do you still want to get lunch?" Colin asked Jamie.

"Might as well. Nothing we can do until we get our hands on the footage. It will take a good hour to get the warrant."

"You got another hundred?" Jamie asked. Colin forked over the bill. She asked the attendant, "One more time? And if the guy shows up again call me. Here's my card."

The attendant's eyes widened. "You FBI?

"Yes, sir."

"Is this guy dangerous?"

"Not to you," Jamie said. "Unless you're filthy rich."

"If you keep handing me hundreds I might be soon."

"Thanks," Jamie said. "We'll be another hour."

THEY LOCKED the packages in the car and Colin followed Jamie out of the garage, nudging her right onto Park Avenue. "Shit," he said, "this guy is getting too close. I don't like it."

"Maybe we should secure you in a safe house."

Colin stopped on the Manhattan sidewalk, halting Jamie in her tracks. "No way. What would people think if I disappeared like some scaredy-cat?"

"That's absurd. Keeping you safe isn't being a chicken. It's just good sense."

Colin put his hand behind Jamie's back and they continued their forward progress. "Besides, it's bad for business. My clients need to know I'm around and available."

"I know. He's getting sloppy and that's good. Eventually, he'll make a mistake and we'll catch him. Don't worry. But a safe house isn't off the table yet."

"If you insist." Colin slipped an arm through hers. "There's a great Pan Asian place around the corner. Want to go there for lunch?"

"Sounds good," Jamie said.

The restaurant was crowded but a booth opened and they followed the hostess to their seats. They ordered Pad Thai, a plate of potstickers and iced tea. "By your own admission, you're a small-town girl. Do you like living in the city?" Colin asked.

"I do. I like it much better than D.C. I think there's something evil in the water there. You're always looking over your shoulder. The press is relentless. I know they need to do their job and a free press is necessary for democracy to work, but you hope you're never their target."

"I hear you. I keep a low profile. Although now that this shit has hit a turbo fan, I think that ship has sailed."

Their drinks arrived and Jamie sipped the icy liquid. "So, you grew up on Long Island?"

"Yeah, my parents are both attorneys and I'm an only child. Steve Moretti and I were inseparable in high school. He's got two sisters so we were like brothers."

"I was pretty much an only child too. I was separated from my brother when I was four and he was just a baby. I barely remember him."

Colin studied her with serious blue eyes. Anytime she brought up her sordid background people got uncomfortable. She knew they wanted to be sympathetic but often felt uneasy, not knowing what to say. "Don't pity me," Jamie said. "I had a tough start but the Gallaghers saved me. You know how you caught me watching the Hallmark Channel last night?"

Colin smirked. "As I recall, you denied it."

Jamie chuckled. "Yeah. Truth is I never thought I'd have that kind of life. A real Christmas. A kind, generous, family who loves me." The food arrived and Jamie picked up her chopsticks, then hesitated. "So, I got my happily-ever-after and those sappy movies remind me that I was damn lucky." She fumbled a potsticker before getting it on her plate. "Tricky little devils."

Colin shoveled some Pad Thai onto his plate then added two dumplings and doused them with soy sauce.

"And," Jamie continued, "I'm convinced I wound up in the military, and law enforcement because of the two police officers who found me. I was buying milk to feed my brother when a female officer spotted me. She and her partner brought me back to the motel and discovered my mother was out turning tricks and I was outta there in a flash. Plus, my dad is a local detective." She laughed. "I'd say law enforcement is in my blood, however, no DNA involved."

"Interesting theory," Colin said, popping a dumpling into his mouth.

"What about you? How did you wind up where you are?"

"My parents have money. Not exactly honest money. My great grandfather was a bootlegger." Colin raised his eyebrows. "Statute of limitations?"

"Yeah, you're safe."

"They went to Harvard and wanted me to attend a private boarding school. I refused, mostly because of Steve and his family. My mom is a little tight… emotionally, and a big health nut. As I mentioned, no sweets in the MacKenzie household. But the Morettis were awesome. A big, warm, Italian family and I spent more time at their house than my own. No way was I going off to some snooty private school with a bunch of elitists."

"And your parents agreed?"

"It took some time but they could see how happy I was. Steve and I played sports together, spent all summer at Fire Island, boating, surfing, and drinking too much. The best years of my life."

"I went to Fire Island once. My parents rented a house at Davis Park. Got the worst sunburn in the history of mankind." Jamie grimaced. "But it is beautiful there."

"We graduated and Steve went to Holy Cross on a football scholarship and I acquiesced and went to Harvard like my parents."

"So, your money is from your parents?"

"No, a college buddy and I wrote an app and made several million dollars. I used my share to start my own company. I buy ailing software and data companies, revitalize and absorb them. Sometimes I grow them, then sell them."

"Tech flipping. Hmm. Are you on the stock exchange?"

"No. I stayed private which means I don't have to answer to a board of directors and stockholders. Plus, I can be as philanthropic as I want. Nobody tells me what to do with my money. I think people who have more money than they could spend in a hundred lifetimes have a responsibility to do some good. No one needs a zillion dollars."

Jamie stared. "Wow, that's a pretty awesome way of looking at the world."

"Nah, just basic humanity to me."

They talked and ate, like two friends hanging out, or dare she say it? A date? A bona-fide, in the flesh, in glorious technicolor warm-blooded... *Date*!

Chapter 17

The perp never returned to the car and Jamie and Colin drove back to Colin's Tribeca apartment without incident. Jamie unsheathed the glamorous gown and deposited it in the closet of her assigned bedroom, running her fingers over the shiny fabric before closing the door. Stowing the sexy bras in the empty top dresser drawer, she placed the shoes on the floor at the end of the bed. An odd mixture of emotions flooded her. Acting the part of a glamorous socialite made her uneasy and yet an unwelcomed surge of adrenaline spiked. She never played dress-up as a kid, opting for cops and robbers with the boys in the neighborhood, building ramps for their bikes, climbing trees and stealing apples from Farmer Jessup's orchard. Once he came after them with a shotgun. It wasn't loaded, as she later learned when her father paid the ornery farmer a visit, but it did scare the living shit out of them.

COLIN KNOCKED on Jamie's door. She opened it and he tamped down the overwhelming urge to kiss her. Again.

Jamie's phone rang and she fished it out of her purse. "Matt, what's up?"

Colin hoped for a break in the case. He wanted this over. And he wanted Jamie. Preferably on her back, blindfolded, legs kicked up. Which was an impossibility until she was done bodyguarding him.

"Great, send it over." Jamie faced Colin. "We've got the guy on video. I need you to take a look." She focused on her phone waiting for the ping. "Got it," she said, sitting on the bed and patting the space next to her.

Colin sat and studied the images. "Play it again," he asked. Thinking, thinking… a connection formed. "I know him. It's Dave Planchet. He's the college buddy I told you about, the one who made the app with me. He's got a beard and he's lost some hair, but I'm pretty sure it's him."

"When's the last time you had contact with him?"

"Not since college. We sold the app and both started tech companies. He went into business with his dad and his brother. He lives on the West Coast. San Diego, I think."

"And you haven't seen him since?"

Colin rubbed his forehead. "*I* didn't, but my attorney did. His company didn't do well and I bought it sometime last year. My attorney handled the deal. I never got involved. We got it for a steal."

"This is huge," Jamie said. She stood and called Matt back, giving him the details. "What's your attorney's name," she asked Colin.

"Jeb Sampson."

"What's his number?"

Colin left the bedroom to retrieve his phone and returned. He held the contact info out for Jamie to read to Matt. "Let me know what you find out." The call ended and she said to Colin. "Big break. We'll find him, don't worry."

Colin sunk onto the bed and sighed, running his hands down his face. He propped his elbows on his knees and hung his head in his hands, focusing his eyes on the floor. "This might actually be over soon?"

"Let's hope."

He raised his chin and held Jamie's gaze. "What a relief. I don't know how much longer I can keep my shit together."

"From my experience, you're holding up well and there's a good chance I'll be out of your hair soon. And you can have your life back."

"I'll be glad when it's over but I have no intention of letting you walk out of my life."

Jamie frowned, tilting her head to one side. "That's ridiculous, Colin. You don't know me. We aren't friends. We're barely acquaintances. You're a high value target I've pledged to protect with my life. I have no place in your real life."

"I disagree. I think you're an incredible woman, no, an incredible human being. I think I'm falling for you."

Jamie paced, then stopped in front of Colin. He gazed up at her. "Have you ever heard of transference?" she said.

"You mean like falling in love with your therapist?"

"Exactly. It can also happen when someone saves your life, like when firefighters rescue someone from a burning building or a car wreck. The feelings are difficult to sort out and are often mistaken for love. It passes with time and distance from the rescuer."

Colin stood. "This isn't that."

"You can't know that."

"I felt it the minute I saw you at the coffee shop yesterday."

"What? When I was acting like a blithering idiot?"

"I didn't think you an idiot. I thought you were incredibly attractive and adorable. And now that I know more about you, I find you even more… More, more. More."

"YOU'RE OUT OF YOUR MIND." Jamie walked to the window and gazed down onto the busy Manhattan street. The sun sat low in the sky, peeking through the massive skyscrapers, orange and purple snippets lacing the horizon. She crossed her arms over her chest. She liked Colin, how could she not? He was funny, sweet, and a genuinely kind and generous man. Not to mention sexy as hell. Any woman would jump at the chance to ensnare the handsome billionaire. But then, the club and his need for kink. BDSM. Oh God, she could never—

She sensed him behind her. "I'm sorry if I overstepped," he said, "but I wanted you to know how I feel." He was close enough that his breath came like fire on her neck, something more subtle tingling her skin.

"Let's put this back in the bottle." She faced him. His azure eyes seemed bottomless as if she could see into his soul. God, she was waxing romantic, in her own little Hallmark daydream. *Wake. Wake up.* "We need to hold tight until this is over, then we go back to our lives and this will become a distant memory."

"I disagree. Daniel and Alyx and Steve and Laura are important in my life and I think you'd fit in fine with us. Although I am often forced to live the high life, I also enjoy the simple things: the outdoors—skiing and boating, swimming in the ocean, walks on the beach."

"An obscene collection of automobiles parked in your private garage in the clouds suggests otherwise."

They smiled. "I do like nice things, good food and wine, and cars. Is it that bad?"

"The jury is still out." Jamie desperately needed to change the subject. "What time do I have to be ready for the fundraiser?"

"It starts at seven but you never know about the traffic so we'll leave at six. One of the guards on duty will drive us."

"Fine. I need to take a shower, so scoot," she said, turning him toward the door and giving a nudge. I'll see you downstairs in an hour."

Colin turned before exiting. "I'm not giving up."

Chapter 18

Colin detested wearing a tuxedo, give him jeans and a t-shirt any old day. He tugged on the white bowtie, centering it under the starched white collar. His suit jacket followed and he regarded his image in the full-length mirror. Not too shabby. Or not shabby enough.

Colin entered his closet and opened the cabinet door concealing his safe. He hesitated, contemplating the long velvet box inside, then dialed the numbers. His mind wandered for several seconds before claiming the package and slipping it into his pocket. *She'll probably be pissed.* He smirked.

Pacing the living room, he decided on a drink and poured himself two fingers of scotch. He sipped the last drops as Jamie appeared. He'd never been to a flashy fashion show, although Anna Wintour had invited him several times. He imagined this is what a model making her runway debut would look like. He envisioned dramatic music and flashing lights overhead. Applause, hooting and hollering. He wasn't sure that was how people responded at a fashion show, and he'd probably never know. "Wow, you look absolutely amazing," he whispered before going speechless.

Jamie folded her hands at her waist, fiddling her thumbs, eyes lingering on the floor before she raised them to meet his. "Stop being so dramatic."

Her sparkling green irises ignited a flame deep in his gut. He'd give anything to kiss her. Tongue her mouth all the way into her throat until she couldn't remember her name. Colin swallowed hard, hoping to banish the image from his mind. He walked toward her, pulling the box from his pocket. Seeing the velvet package, Jamie's jaw dropped and Colin feared her wrath. Or pity.

"These are my grandmother's. She left them to me. I would be honored if you wore them tonight." He popped the cover and displayed the diamond solitaire and matching teardrop earrings.

"Oh, Colin, I couldn't. It's too much."

"Nonsense," he said, handing her the earrings, then unfastening the clasp on the silver chain. "Turn around." Jamie complied, pulling her long locks to one side. He slid the chain around her nape and closed the clasp. Jamie faced him, then donned the diamond earrings and tucked her auburn hair behind her ears.

That went better than expected. "Perfect," Colin said. "They suit you."

"I doubt it," Jamie said, yet her eyes stayed focused on him. "Fancy jewelry isn't my thing."

Colin chuckled. "Come on, work with me. I'm trying to make you a fancy lady."

They grinned. "You're an idiot," Jamie said.

"Yeah, but tonight I'm *your* idiot."

She slapped his lapels and shook her head. "You're incorrigible."

"Guilty as sin."

JAMIE DECIDED to forgo wearing her tan trench coat, which even for her would be a fashion faux pas. Besides, she'd be getting into a heated car and it would be a short walk into the venue. They settled into the backseat of Colin's Porsche Cayenne and the driver maneuvered the vehicle onto Park Avenue. Jamie's phone rang. "Hey, Matt."

"You've got the all clear for the Plaza."

"Great, thanks. Any leads on the perp?"

"Nothing yet. There's a good chance the guy erased his entire existence. He's qualified to hack anything."

"Makes sense."

"We did track down the father, sort of. He committed suicide about a year ago. After the business sold. We're interviewing witnesses now. The brother also seems to have vanished. Pretty good idea they swapped out identities."

"Which will make them possibly impossible to find."

"Afraid so," Matt said.

"Keep me informed if anything breaks."

"Will do. By the way, two wishes for the night. Have yourself a ball. And stay vigilant."

"Story of my life."

Matt laughed. "Later."

Jamie ended the call. "They swept the Plaza and we've got guys posted throughout."

"Great," Colin said. "What else did Matt say?"

"It seems the father committed suicide after the business sold. There's no trace of either son. I assume they're capable of adopting new identities?"

Colin frowned. "Yeah, Dave could manage that in his sleep."

Traffic was reasonable, considering the hour, and they arrived at the famed Plaza Hotel at seven, taking their place in the line of stylish cars and limos waiting for their famous passengers to disembark.

Jamie blanched. A red carpet? Press? Gawkers? "You're kidding, right? This is like a Hollywood awards show. I can't."

"I'll admit Anna Wintour and I have a friendly little competition as to whose event is bigger." He wagged his eyebrows.

"The Met Ball is a huge event," Jamie said. "You could have warned me." Panic choked Jamie's throat. "Colin, they're going to think I'm your date. They'll want to know who I am and why I'm here with you." She gulped. "This is bad."

"Don't be ridiculous. And you are my date."

The driver opened Colin's side first, then Jamie's. A cold blast of air fanned her heated face. She inhaled deeply, focusing on Colin's beckoning hand. His firm, warm grasp grounded her, tugging her from the seat as she placed one beige pump onto the crimson carpet. *Oh God, what had she gotten herself into?*

Strobe lights flashed, blinding her and she slipped her arm through Colin's so she wouldn't fall on her face. Reporters shouted Colin's name: "Who's trying to kill you? Do you have enemies? Who's your date?" Jamie gazed up at him, his brilliant white smile like a beacon above a valley of darkness. He waved to the adoring fans but remained silent. "Almost there," he murmured to Jamie.

They entered the crowd of attendees, many stopping along the way to be interviewed by entertainment reporters, but Colin ignored their pleas and ventured forward. Jamie's arm was still tucked under Colin's, his other hand atop hers. "Daniel," Colin shouted.

A tall dark-haired man turned, his hand entwined with a stunning brunette in a black gown. *A very pregnant brunette.* Alyx. Relief swamped her.

"Colin," Daniel said as the couple approached. Jamie recognized Laura Logan behind them, attached to another handsome chestnut-haired man.

"Jamie," Alyx said. "Oh my God, what are you doing here?" They embraced around Alyx's enormous belly.

Laura moved in next and hugged Jamie. "It's so good to see you, Jamie."

Alyx and Laura introduced their husbands and Jamie wondered if all *Doms* were this good looking. Both men hugged her as if they hadn't just met and Jamie felt as though she was submerged in a sea of testosterone.

"So? Spill," Alyx said. "How do you know Colin?"

Colin and Jamie exchanged glances. No way was Colin walking into that landmine so he left the response for Jamie. Before she could answer, Daniel said, "Hey, man, how're you doing? We saw the story on the news."

"Yeah," Steve said. "I tried to call but got voicemail."

Colin sighed. "I'm holding on. The whole thing pretty much sucks."

"Any idea who's targeting you?" Alyx said.

"We got a lead today, hopefully, it leads to an arrest," Jamie offered.

"You on the case?" Laura said.

"Bodyguard duty?" Alyx added.

"Yes, on both counts."

"Colin," came a voice behind them.

Colin shifted. "Mom, Dad." He leaned in and kissed his mother's cheek and his father embraced him in a bear hug.

His father scowled. "What's going on, son. Any idea who's doing this?"

"Maybe," Colin said. "I'll let you know as soon as I do."

"Where's your FBI bodyguard?" his mother asked. "Shouldn't he be here beside you?"

Colin smiled. "She is." He clasped Jamie's hand and pulled her close. "This is Special Agent Jamie Gallagher."

"Pleased to meet you," Jamie said, extending her hand.

His mother gaped at the diamond around Jamie's neck. He hadn't thought about having to explain this to his mother and he had no intention of doing so now, hoping she'd be discreet. And thankfully, she was. "Oh," she muttered. "I was expecting…"

"A man?" Colin said.

"Yes, I suppose so. Times change."

Colin's parents shook her hand.

"Trust me, Mother, she's quite lethal. I'm lucky to have her by my side. She saved my life once already."

"What?" his mother shrieked, landing her fingers on her expertly applied pink lipstick.

"Details later, Mom, I'd like to forget about it for a few hours and just relax."

His father said, "Thank you for protecting our son."

"Two agents have been assigned to us too," his mother added. "They searched the house first and then parked out front. I guess they'll be there until this is resolved."

"Absolutely they will, Mrs. MacKenzie," Jamie said.

A waiter offered a tray of champagne and Colin took two, handing one to Jamie, who smiled when she recognized Matt working undercover. Colin whispered near Jamie's ear, "Is that…?" Jamie shushed him with her finger.

"This is so James Bond," he whispered.

Colin said to his friends, "Let's find our table."

Jamie lagged behind, chatting with her friends about getting together again soon. "Colin's pretty hot," Alyx said. "As soon as this is over you need to jump him."

Laura laughed. "He's a Dom, a Master at the club, I doubt he'll tolerate Jamie topping him."

Jamie huffed. "Yeah, and what if he doesn't want me to jump him."

"You crazy? You're gorgeous and hot. He'd be nuts not to jump in with two feet… or with…"

Jamie put one hand up yet Laura continued. "All the guys at the office say you're like an eleven. Trust me."

Jamie placed a hand on her chest. Was it getting hot in here?

Alyx gasped, one hand atop her gigantic belly. She doubled over. "Oh God," she said, "I think I'm going into labor."

Chapter 19

The puddle between Alyx's black three-inch heels confirmed the diagnosis. Daniel snatched his phone from his pocket and called his driver. "I'm so sorry," Alyx said. "I can't believe this."

"We have another two weeks," Laura said. "You're early."

"Discuss this later," Daniel said. "Let's get to the hospital." Then he told everyone, "We'll keep you posted." Wrapping an arm around his wife's shoulders, he escorted her to the waiting car.

"Damn," Laura said, "now I'm nervous. I can't miss tonight, been planning it for months."

"You feeling okay?" Steve said.

She placed a hand on her belly, making small circles. "I think so, sort of having sympathy pains."

"But not *real* pains, right?" Steve said.

"I'm fine. Let's find our table. I'm probably just hungry."

On the way to their table, a tall gray-haired man, clad in the obligatory tuxedo, intercepted Colin. "Colin, my man. Excellent turnout. I think you and Mrs. Moretti have outdone yourselves."

He pointed an accusing finger at Colin. "Anna is looking for you. Gird your loins."

Colin smacked the mayor on the back and they shared a laugh. "I'm unafraid."

"Well, I'm not," the mayor said. Laughter filled the air as onlookers listened to the exchange. He regarded Jamie. "And who is this magnificent woman?"

"Jamie Gallagher," Colin said, omitting her special agent moniker.

"Pleasure, Ms. Gallagher," the mayor said, taking her hand.

"Nice to meet you, Mr. Mayor," Jamie said.

"My wife," he said of the petite black woman beside him. "Chirlane."

"An honor," Jamie said, shaking her small hand.

"You're at my table," the mayor instructed Colin. "Table one, along with the Morettis." The mayor hugged Laura and shook Steve Moretti's hand. "Shall we?" He extended an arm, pointing the way to their table.

Place cards identified their seats, Colin's parents to his left and Laura and Steve to Jamie's right. The mayor and his wife across from them. Alyx and Daniel's seats vacant. The party settled and Jamie put down her purse and champagne glass and proceeded to pull out her chair. Colin stopped her. "Let's dance," he said, clasping her hand and whisking her onto the marble floor.

Oh God. The idea of being wrapped in Colin's arms threw her off center. He smelled good enough to eat at arm's distance, any closer and she'd swoon. What was wrong with her? She was acting like a hormonal teenager. Before she could answer, one arm surrounded her waist and her hand slipped into his. The orchestra played a melodic ballad, nothing Jamie recognized, yet definitely *romantic*. A song to make love to.

Her chin rested on his shoulder, her forehead against his cheek. His scent divine and she breathed in his exotic essence.

"I've been dying to get my arms around you since we met," Colin whispered in her ear. Jamie didn't answer, her mouth dry.

They danced to two songs, the rhythmic rocking soothing her mind, body, soul.

COLIN INHALED SLOWLY, relishing the scent of her hair, the brush of her skin against his cheek. Breath to breath, heartbeat to heartbeat, a melding of their bodies. He could stay like this forever.

The song ended and their bodies stilled, but their eyes searched each other. Looking for—

The orchestra conductor broke the spell, "Ladies and gentlemen, please take your seats. The Honorable Mayor will say a few words."

Colin released Jamie, clasping her hand and drawing her toward their seats. He pulled out the chair and pushed it closer as she sat, then took the adjacent seat. The mayor ascended the stage and spoke into the microphone. "Welcome one and all to our first annual gala in support of the Sarah Chamber's Fund, named after the mother of one of our generous benefactors, Laura Moretti. As most of you know, the fund's objective is twofold: to help children thrive by making sure they have enough to eat and to provide tuition assistance for teens who cannot afford higher education. Laura Moretti's dream has come to fruition this year and doubled its contributions, not only by your generous donations but with her recent partnership with one of our most benevolent benefactors, Colin MacKenzie. I've often said that there's no better combo than great wealth blended with great wisdom, and these two prominent New Yorkers are the embodiment of this. I commend them on their generosity and empathy for our oft-forgotten citizens, many of whom have no voice. I am pleased to announce this year we raised $7.3 million for the Sarah Chamber's Fund and through the ministrations of Mrs. Moretti and Mr. MacKenzie will feed thousands of children and allow hundreds to realize their dream of a college education, and beyond."

The crowd applauded and gave a standing ovation. The mayor urged Colin and Laura to stand, which they did, and the adulation continued for a full minute. The crowd quieted and the mayor urged, "Now please enjoy this spectacular evening of dancing and dining under the auspices of Chef Oliver Cheng. And on behalf of the Sarah Chamber's Fund, thank you for your support of our most vital resource. Our children."

Applause for the mayor reached a crescendo as he exited the stage to return to his seat.

JAMIE PLACED her hand on Colin's leg. "I'm glad I came, even if it was under peculiar circumstances. The work you do is important. I wish someone knew my brother and I were starving all those years."

Colin scowled. "It saddens me to think you suffered at such a young age. No one should live like that."

Jamie squeezed his thigh and smiled. "I made it out. I think that's what bonded Alyx, Laura and me. We had rough starts, for different reasons. None of us fared well in the parent department and our pain was the same." Jamie removed her hand and grabbed the menu card at her place. "Wow, some menu," she said, changing the subject. She picked up the gold embossed card and read it aloud.

"Lobster with wild herbs and saffron radish with edible 23-carat gold flake

Baby lamb chops with fresh mint and almond pesto

Branzino with lemon caper brown butter.

Gold dusted truffles and chocolate dipped cape gooseberries... I don't think I've ever eaten anything so fancy."

Colin laughed. "If you're going to learn to be a fancy lady..." He winked.

Jamie smirked. "Wise guy."

"This is a pretty elite crowd and they expect exotic cuisine, so we aim to deliver. Personally, I'd prefer a good steak and French fries."

"I'm with you," Jamie said, "however, it doesn't hurt to try new things, right?"

COLIN HOPED Jamie might extend that thinking to the bedroom. He desperately wanted to expand her horizons in his world. He wondered if he could exist on vanilla sex for the rest of his life. With Jamie, he just might.

They ate, drank, and boogied the night away, Jamie having limited herself to two glasses of champagne, and arrived home after midnight.

Colin removed his suit jacket and tossed it over the couch back and loosened his tie. "So, you survived your night as a fancy lady."

Jamie opened her purse and retrieved her 9 mm, placing it on the side table. "It wasn't so bad and you were right, it was good to see Alyx and Laura again. I plan on seeing more of them." She kicked off her shoes and placed them on the bottom step leading to the second floor. "No word yet on Alyx?"

He pulled his phone from his suit coat pocket and checked. "Nothing yet."

"Maybe we can stop and see the baby if it's here by morning."

"I'd like that. I still can't fathom the idea Daniel and Steve are going to be fathers."

"I could say the same about Alyx and Laura being mothers. I didn't think it was on their radar… on any of our radars."

"A good lesson. Your life can take an unexpected turn at any moment." Colin envisioned the gears in Jamie's head grinding. Their meeting had been unexpected on two counts. First, in the coffee shop and now this. He hoped the universe was telling him something profound. Something delicious. "Do you want kids?" Colin asked.

"No, I didn't get the maternal gene. I'm not even wife material."

"Why would you say that? You already confessed to being a sheepdog… taking care of people is your calling, right?"

"That's different. It's not personal."

"What's wrong with personal?"

"Nothing. I don't think I'd be good at it."

"I think you're selling yourself short. You have a family now. You love them and would do anything for them, right?"

"Yeah, except…"

"So, you know what good parents look like. You're not destined to become your birth mother." Jamie rubbed her forehead and Colin worried he'd pushed her too far. He came close, holding her by her upper arms. "You're too hard on yourself, Agent Gallagher. You need to let your guard down. Maybe let someone take care of you once in a while."

Jamie reached up and touched his cheek. "You're sweet, really. And I know you mean well, but I doubt being *unguarded* is in my nature. I *am* a bodyguard."

Colin laughed, wrapping his fingers around her hand on his face. "I'm persistent, Agent Gallagher and I'm not giving up on you."

Jamie extricated herself from Colin's near embrace. "I guess we should turn in."

Colin wanted to smother her in kisses, his lips everywhere, but he acquiesced. "I guess…"

Releasing the clasp on the diamond pendant, she removed the dazzling earrings and took Colin's open hand and nestled the jewels in his palm, closing his fingers over them for safe keeping. "Thank you for these. They're beautiful."

"You are most welcome." Colin wanted her to keep them, but it would be inappropriate. Maybe someday. He slipped the gems into his pants pocket.

"What's your plan for tomorrow?" she said.

"I've decided to take the rest of the week off and plan on sleeping in, something I never do. I didn't work out this morning so maybe we could hit the gym. And we're having dinner with my parents."

"Sounds good. You said you have a gym in your apartment, but I assume I never got that far after the closet incident."

"No. It's at the end of the hall after your bedroom." Colin thought of the other room he hadn't shown Jamie. The playroom. His pulse spiked at the idea of taking Jamie in there. The vision of her sprawled across the spanking bench, feet and hands bound, aroused him and he prayed his trousers hid his excitement.

Chapter 20

S nuggled in her couch-bed, Colin called her from his bedroom at 8:30 and said Alyx and Daniel had a baby boy, 7 pounds, 6 ounces. They named him Michael, after Alyx's father. They agreed to meet in the gym in ten minutes.

Jamie tied her sneakers, clad in yoga pants and a blue tank top over her sports bra. She brushed her teeth and combed her hair into a sleek pony. She needed this workout. Sleep had been torturous as she and Colin had fucked like animals all night... *in her dreams*. She wasn't sure she'd be able to look him in the eye without picturing him naked.

A knock at her door. She opened it to find Colin dressed in a gray tank top and black gym shorts. She gulped. Dressed in a t-shirt and jeans the other night hinted at a smoking hot body, then his naked chest in the throes of his nightmare and now this... her blood might scald her insides. "Morning," she sputtered.

"Ready to get your ass kicked?"

"I'm ready to kick my own ass, you need not apply."

"As you wish, Special Agent Gallagher." He bowed and swept a hand into the hallway. She stepped out and waited. Colin led the way to the door at the hallway's end and opened it, allowing

Jamie to enter first. "I suppose you're familiar with all the equipment."

"Yup."

"There are water bottles in that fridge over there," he said, pointing to the far wall, "and towels in the adjacent cabinet. Help yourself."

"Thanks." Impressed by the array of apparatus, she headed for the red rubber mat to stretch.

Colin stood near the mat's edge, hands on his hips. "I'm liking the view. I don't have anything interesting to occupy me while I'm grinding out reps."

"Tsk, tsk," Jamie said. Inappropriate.

"Technically you don't work for me. *You're* actually the boss of me, so I think I'm on solid ground."

"Hmm…" Jamie said, scrunching her eyebrows together.

"So, you better not be ogling me," Colin said, wagging his finger.

Colin went to the leg press, adding four one-hundred-pound plates, then settled onto the black leather seat. He completed three sets of fifteen without breaking much of a sweat. They took turns on the squat rack, switching the weights between sets, three sets each again doing a full body workout, the final piece of equipment being chest presses on the inclined bench requiring them to spot each other. Twenty minutes on the elliptical served as a cool down.

"Good workout," Jamie said, wiping her face with a towel. "Thanks."

"I like you all sweaty," Colin said.

Jamie was sure she blushed, luckily her face was already red from working out. Her mind traveled back to her tortured night of sleep and those unconscious sexual escapades. Cold shower, here she came.

THE TEPID WATER attempted to cool Colin's overheated flesh. Working out with Jamie had him pumped and it wasn't his *muscles* that needed a chill-down. Not the usual ones. He feared he would be in a permanent state of arousal as long as the little scarlet spit-fire was around. Her body reminded him of a panther—sleek, taut, lithe… strong. She could move some serious weight for her body size and he considered her a likely fierce combatant. Yet, she was feminine, more feminine than she knew. He liked her dressed in the beautiful evening gown and heels, and his grandmother's diamonds suited her.

Dressed in a white button-down shirt and jeans, no tie, and a navy-blue blazer, Colin slipped his socked feet into his Grenson suede topsiders. He entered his closet, which still gave him the heebie-jeebies, and selected his dark blue cashmere overcoat. Nearly noon, he and Jamie agreed to grab coffee on the way to the hospital before making their way to his parents' house.

Colin stood beside the kitchen island, scrolling through emails and texts on his phone. Her footsteps on the tile floor made him gaze up. She wore her skinny jeans and a white pullover cable knit sweater. Her hair hung long and sleek, one side falling across a breast, the other down her back. The overhead lights reflected tiny rainbows on the soft strands. There was a sparkle to her, both inside and out. He wanted to comment on her glow but refrained. "All set?"

"I am. I can't wait to see the baby."

"Yeah, I haven't been around many babies and not in a really long time. I think the last baby I saw belonged to one of Steve's sisters and those kids are like ten now."

"Me either. No babies in my purview."

"Then neither of us should attempt to hold the little bugger. We might drop him."

"Agreed." Jamie retrieved her coat from the closet and Colin helped her into it. Her phone rang. "Matt..." After a lengthy response from Matt, Jamie said, "I'll tell him. We're going to see Alyx's baby and then heading to his parents' house for dinner. I'll keep in touch."

"Tell me what?" Colin asked.

"Matt interviewed your attorney and is going over the paperwork for the purchase of your former roommate's company. His gut tells him something is off but doesn't have anything to back it up right now. He'll get back to me."

"You suspect my attorney might be involved?"

"Not sure. How well do you know this guy? Do you trust him?"

"Implicitly. He handles all my business, personal and for the company. I pay him well. I can't imagine he'd be compromised in any way."

"Let's wait and see if Matt comes up with anything to the contrary."

COLIN OPTED for the Porsche 911 and secured the fob from the garage security sentry. They stopped at the same coffee shop where they first met and Jamie remained in the car while Colin acquired coffee. The video in her mind replayed their initial encounter. She hadn't noticed Colin holding the door for her when she made that awful comment about Rob. Then she buried herself deeper talking about the size of everyone's dick. Oh God. What an ass. And yet, he'd seen past her inappropriate behavior, at least he claimed as much. A wave of heat rippled through her and she realized her breath sat frozen in her chest. Colin exited the coffee shop and at the sight of him, she still couldn't release her breath. Breathtaking... her original assessment still held.

"Thanks," she said, accepting the paper cup of aromatic brew.

Colin scrutinized her face. "You look a little flushed."

"Yeah, maybe the heat is too high."

"It's set at sixty-eight. Most women I know find that too cold."

"I'm not most women."

"I'll drink to that," Colin said, pressing his cup against hers. He adjusted the thermostat down a few degrees and pulled away from the curb.

They arrived at New York Presbyterian hospital around one and stopped at the gift shop to purchase flowers and a onesie printed with, "Birth Nailed It," then maneuvered their way to the maternity ward. Alyx sat propped against her pillows, her hair up in a messy bun. A clear plastic bassinette sat adjacent to her bed and Daniel stood over it, eyes fixed on his new son. "Hey," Alyx said, "so cool that you're here." Jamie placed the flowers on the side table alongside two dozen red roses, which she assumed came from Daniel. "Thank you for the flowers, Jamie. They're a welcome breath of spring."

Jamie gave Alyx the bag with the baby gift. Alyx pulled it from the paper and howled. "Oh my God, this is hysterical."

Daniel leaned in and laughed. "What a hoot. Thanks, you guys."

Colin embraced Daniel in a brotherly hug, then pecked Alyx on the cheek. "Congratulations. So happy for you."

"Yeah, congrats," Jamie echoed, hugging Alyx, then Daniel. She walked to the clear baby crate. "Hey, little guy."

Colin joined her. "Wow. You guys made this?"

"A miracle, isn't it?" Daniel said.

"For sure. Hey, little man, welcome," Colin said. "You picked great parents."

Jamie considered Colin's remark. How did a baby pick its parents? She wasn't the religious type and considered most things to be random luck, both good and bad. She'd witnessed terrible things happening to good people and good things happening to terrible people. Maybe karma played a role, but it seemed a stretch. She often considered the plight of a child born in a country where food, clean water, and sanitation were not a given, as opposed to someone like Daniel, Steve, and Colin who were fortunate enough to get wonderful parents. Whereas, she, Alyx and Laura hadn't been so lucky. Was it just luck?

Jamie touched the newborn's hand. His fingers curled around her index finger. "Wow, he's strong, good grip."

Alyx chuckled. "Tell me. When he latches onto my nipple, I have to bite my lip so I don't yelp."

"Hey guys, congratulations," a female voice said. Laura and Steve entered the small private room, flowers in hand.

Alyx said, "It's starting to look like a nursery in here. The flower kind not the baby kind."

Daniel raised his eyebrows. "Let's hope you're better at taking care of a kid because you've killed all the house plants."

"Very *not* funny," Alyx quipped.

Chapter 21

Colin accelerated the Porsche onto the Cross Island Parkway... every New Yorker's nightmare, only the Belt Parkway was worse. The chances of avoiding traffic, nil. He encountered clear sailing only once in his thirty-four years and that was at 3 a.m.

They averaged thirty miles per hour, stopping and starting, and avoiding drivers who should never have been granted a license.

"This road is a nightmare," Jamie said. "I travel to Long Island for work, and sirens and flashing lights are a major advantage."

"Tell me. I avoid it at all costs. I either use a driver so I can get some work done or I helicopter in."

Jamie studied the handsome billionaire's profile. "Helicopter?"

Colin turned, his eyes shielded from view by his sunglasses. He didn't say anything and Jamie wondered if she'd insulted him. Finally, he said, "Are we back to the spoiled brat meme?"

Shit. She'd stepped in it, again. "There's a case to be made that any man with a helicopter is spoiled. Not that there's anything wrong with that."

Colin hit the brakes as a tan Subaru drifted into his lane. "It's a matter of convenience," he said. "I need to get back and forth from the East End of Long Island on a regular basis and time is of the essence. Traffic back to the city can be impossible on a Sunday, especially in the summer. I have people counting on me to pay them big salaries. Can't do it sitting in traffic for three hours."

"Makes sense. Do you pilot it yourself?" Jamie pulled gum from her pocket and offered some to Colin. He nodded, and she dropped a tab into his outstretched hand, then popped one herself.

"Nope. I have a pilot on standby."

Jamie thought of the club again, located on Long Island's far east end. Colin said he had a beach house nearby and spent nights there after his festivities at the sex venue, returning to Manhattan sometime Sunday.

Tomorrow. She'd be with him at the club tomorrow. Would they be taking the helicopter?

SILENCE RULED FOR SEVERAL MINUTES, until Colin asked, "Dollar for your thoughts?" He'd mentioned traveling to the East End and wondered if she was thinking about the club or maybe uneasy about the helicopter. Although he doubted she was afraid of anything.

"I was recalling the helo drill at the academy. They strap you into an inverted helo in the middle of nowhere and you have to extricate yourself and find your way back to base. Took me hours."

Helo? Not wanting to sound stupid, he didn't ask her to explain and assumed it was navy lingo for a helicopter. "Sounds rough."

"Some didn't make it and needed a rescue."

"I take it you made it?"

"Luckily."

"Knowing what I know about you, luck wasn't involved."

Jamie chuckled. "Still wasn't as bad as NOLS."

"NOLS?"

"Survival training. We were assigned the Alaskan Mountain adventure. Six weeks in the wilderness with no bathroom and no showers. Fourteen of us. You can bring one pack, two walking sticks, and you can't leave a footprint. No paper, which meant no toilet paper and don't even ask me how we managed our periods. They air drop food in once a day, but you have to find the location of the drop using your compass and map. We were divided into smaller groups and were assigned a task each day. The first night, one group didn't arrive. They showed up the next day in time for breakfast. We slept under the stars."

"Not sure I'd survive under those conditions. Can't imagine not showering for six weeks."

"The first week was awful, we all looked like grease balls and smelled bad, but by the second week it all disappeared."

"Weird."

"I got stuck in quicksand. Wedged in up to my thighs for a good half hour."

"Quicksand? I thought that only existed in cowboy movies."

"Oh, it's real. The group before us radioed a helo to pull the guy out, but it nearly ripped him apart."

"Jesus. How did you get out?"

"My team used their walking sticks. It turns out it's sort of like an ocean rip current. You can't maneuver straight out, you have to move parallel to the ground."

"Geez, that's some crazy shit."

"Tell me."

"Was it winter?"

"Summer, thankfully. Beautiful country, amazing sights."

"I'd love to see Alaska, but give me a boat and hotel."

"Oh, so you're a fancy man? You need toilet paper and a feather pillow?"

"Deodorant and moisturizing soap, please. I'm *spoiled*."

They laughed. "I'm glad I did it, but I'd rather not do it again."

Colin pulled into his parents' driveway and threw the car in park. The white clapboard colonial with black shutters and two-story pillars, reminded Jamie of a smaller version of Tara, from *"Gone with the Wind."*

Colin killed the ignition switch. "I wanted to go out for dinner but my mother insisted on cooking. Be forewarned, she isn't the greatest cook."

"No worries. I eat anything."

A dark sedan parked at the curb. As they exited the car, the passenger window rolled down and a man said, "Hey, Gallagher."

"Omar, how are you?" Jamie said.

"Good, you?"

"Great. All quiet here?"

"As a church. Next shift due at five."

"Sounds good."

"That my parents' protection?" Colin asked Jamie.

"It is."

The front door opened before they knocked. "Darling," his mother said. "How lucky am I? I get to see you twice in one week." She glanced at Jamie. "Glad you've brought your body-guard with you."

"Hi, Mom." Colin kissed his mother on the cheek, then held the door for Jamie to enter. "I see you've got your own protection detail."

"Luckily, they just watch the house and the cars and are incon-spicuous following us around. Although they do enter before us wherever we go."

"Nice to see you again, Mrs. MacKenzie," Jamie said.

"Wonderful to have you, dear. And please, call me Carol."

Colin's dad joined the group and apparently Mr. MacKenzie was a hugger. He wrapped his arms around her and squeezed... hard. He reminded Jamie of her father. A big man, gregarious, full of life.

"Let me take your coats," Mr. MacKenzie said.

"I've made Chicken Marsala, quinoa, and a kale salad for dinner. Would anyone care for a drink?"

"We'll skip the drink, we have to drive back to the city tonight and I didn't use my driver."

"Dinner will be ready in a half hour," Mrs. MacKenzie added.

"Good, enough time to go over our plans for the trip."

They sat at the dining room table and Colin laid out the itinerary. Jamie said, "I'll sit in the living room while you review your plans."

"I think not," Colin said. "Unless you've got that lunatic locked up by Monday, you're coming with."

Jamie hadn't considered accompanying Colin and his family on their ski trip. But he was probably right. If they hadn't arrested a suspect by then she was bound to stay at his side.

"I'VE RENTED a four-bedroom chalet on the mountain," Colin said. Then to Jamie, "We're going to Telluride. Have you ever been there?"

"I have. The skiing is great and I love the town."

"It's our first time there," Mrs. MacKenzie said. "But online it looks amazing. The scenery is breathtaking and the town is so quaint."

Colin pushed a typed piece of paper toward his father. "I've scheduled the jet for 11 a.m. A car will pick you up at nine."

"Agreed," Mr. MacKenzie said."

"Don't worry if you arrive late, the itinerary is flexible." Colin opened a folder and laid out a series of brochures. "Familiarize yourself with the trails and the amenities. They have a spa and the restaurants are world class."

"Do you ski or snowboard?" Jamie asked Colin.

"Both, but this week I'll probably ski."

"We only ski," Mrs. MacKenzie said. "No way am I strapping both my feet to one board." She laughed.

"I hear you," Jamie said.

"Do you board?" Colin asked.

"I do both. But my first love is skiing."

Colin told his parents, "Jamie won an Olympic Gold medal for the biathlon, skiing and shooting. She was only seventeen."

Awe transformed the MacKenzies, as if invisible wires pulled their facial skin back into exaggerated versions.

"Impressive," Colin's father said.

"Your parents must be so proud," Mrs. MacKenzie added.

Jamie gave him the evil eye, but he didn't care. The kitchen timer beeped and Mrs. MacKenzie said, "Dinner is ready. Colin will you set the table?"

Colin closed his folder and laid it on the coffee table in the living room, then pulled plates and silverware from the nearby break-front. Jamie set the silverware while Colin folded dark green napkins and laid them on the plates. He retrieved crystal glasses from the cabinet for wine and water. "Maybe we can have one glass of wine," he said. "It will make eating the food less painful."

Jamie slapped his arm. "You're terrible. And you should talk, you can't cook either."

"I'm refraining from commenting because whatever I say will be deemed sexist."

"Good thinking."

They ate and talked, Mrs. MacKenzie quizzing her son on the suspected perpetrator. Colin explained what he knew but couldn't quite justify why his old pal could be trying to kill him. He hoped the FBI was mistaken.

Later, Jamie stood at the dishwasher loading plates when Mrs. MacKenzie said, "I noticed you were wearing my mother's diamonds last night. I'll admit it surprised me."

Before Jamie could respond, Colin said, "Mom, don't." He rinsed the last wine glass and placed it upside down on the toweled counter, then faced his mother. "I insisted Jamie wear them and they're spectacular on her."

"I agree," Mrs. MacKenzie said. "I was just startled. I haven't seen them in years."

Colin held his mother's gaze for several seconds until she finally glanced away. "I'm glad they're getting some use. I thought they might stay buried in your closet for eternity. I wish you'd find…"

And she was off! Trying to settle him down and get him married.

THEY HOPPED on the Northern State Parkway, and once again traveled the Cross Island Parkway back to Manhattan in the usual stop-and-go traffic. "Your mother is a fine cook," Jamie said. "You're too hard on her."

"I'll admit she's improved since my high school years. She always jumped on the latest diet advice: no fat, no carbs, organic. The worst was the fat-free tuna noodle casserole. My dad and I drew the line there, we dumped it and went out for pizza. I think we hurt her feelings but she got the message. She's evened out it seems, no crazy stuff." He honked his horn as a guy veered into his lane. "Asshole." He let out a slow breath.

Chapter 22

A rriving home around nine, they machinated through the usual routine: greeting the sentries on duty, handing over the car to be monitored, entering the apartment past the front door guard.

"I know I said I was taking the rest of the week off but I need to stop by the office tomorrow before we leave for Long Island. We can grab some dinner and then head to the club. Need to be there by six." Colin extended his hand and Jamie surrendered her coat. She wondered what pretense Colin would use about her attendance at the sex venue. She didn't have to wait long.

"I've decided to say you're coming for the newcomer's tour. You'll be under my protection so no one will bother you."

Jamie's throat tightened as her imagination ran wild. She'd seen plenty of sordid behaviors in her years at the FBI but somehow this seemed more stressful. Painful, and… *personal.* Plus, she still wondered if Colin relied on the club for all his sexual encounters.

"Exactly what does that entail?"

"Zack monitors the front door. You'll have to fill out the NDA and agree to the terms of service. Then you'll be at my side for the night. I'll show you around the premises and introduce you to other Masters. Currently there aren't any new clients who need constant supervision and training, but I do have to inspect the submissive trainees and assign them Doms for the evening. That shouldn't take long and then we can have a drink and hang out, as if we were at a regular bar. I do act in the capacity of Dungeon Master. I give instruction or discipline as needed, or rescue a sub who is in over her, or his, head."

"There's an actual dungeon?"

"There is. But its use is highly restricted. It's pretty hardcore play. Not something I'd advise for you to witness. If I do have to leave you for a short period, I'll either park you in the submissive's pen or put you under the supervision of another Master."

"Submissive's pen?"

"It's a cordoned off area where submissives wait to be approached by a Dom. But you'll be wearing red handcuffs without charms, signifying you're a non-participant."

"No way."

"All submissives wear handcuffs with specific color-coding charms. It indicates what behaviors they are willing to participate in: Green for intercourse, red for pain…"

Jamie took a big swallow. *Yikes.* Still, no way would she incapacitate herself. "Never gonna happen. First, I must have you in sight at all times. And my hands have to be free in order to keep you safe."

They stared at each other for an endless moment. Dominant to Dominant. Jamie gritted her teeth. Who would give in?

Colin pressed his lips together then spoke. "You have to wear the handcuffs but we'll keep them unattached. It's just a symbol of your submissiveness."

"Fine." That settled, she tried to picture what she was about to experience.

Colin smiled. "For such a tough guy, you look terrified."

"I am not."

"Yeah, sure… Come on, let's have a glass of wine. Maybe a snack, my mother's cooking isn't exactly filling. I think there's ice cream in the freezer."

Colin headed for the kitchen and Jamie slipped off her shoes and followed him. She took a seat at the kitchen island. "Maybe it's none of my business but, do you have sex outside the club?"

"Are you propositioning me?" Colin asked, popping the cork on a bottle of chardonnay.

Jamie rolled her eyes.

"Don't get me wrong, I like a woman who's in charge of her life, successful, happy. A woman who knows what she wants and isn't afraid to go for it. But I'm also a control freak. I like total control in the bedroom and most women I've met in the vanilla world aren't into that." He poured two glasses and passed one to Jamie.

"So, you're bossy in the bedroom? Why? So you can get what you want?"

Colin laughed. "That's not it at all. It's for the woman. To take her places she'd didn't even know existed. Where she might be too afraid to journey."

Jamie sipped her wine while Colin opened the freezer. "I still don't get why someone would need to go to a sex club to get off. I can get there in under a minute with my vibrator."

Colin pivoted, wide-eyed, and laughed. "And you call that good?"

"That's the point, isn't it? To orgasm?"

"It's not a race. It's like eating fast food, sates your hunger but it's not particularly satisfying. I wouldn't call quickies satisfying. Maybe when I was thirteen, but not as a man."

"I've had plenty of sex and not orgasmed."

"Then you haven't been with the right person."

Jamie studied her clasped hands on the granite countertop yet didn't respond.

Colin came close, a pint of mint chocolate chip ice cream in hand. He placed it on the counter. "Haven't you ever heard the expression: It's all about the journey? Half the fun is getting there. The longer you stimulate and delay orgasm the better the orgasm."

"I don't get that. The end is still the same."

Colin shook his head. "Oh darling, that is so not true. You need some restraint, some discipline. Once you go tantric…"

Jamie blanched at Colin's use of those words. "So, what, you need to spank a woman to get off?"

"It's not for me, it's for you. The man should get excitement from pleasing the woman." Again, Jamie remained silent. Colin continued. "You must have fantasies. What's your most secret desire?"

"I don't have one."

"Everyone has them."

"What's yours?" Jamie countered.

"I live my fantasies. I take what I want from a willing woman. And in the BDSM lifestyle it's the woman who really has all the control. There are safe words and 'no' always means stop."

"But then he dumps her, right?"

"Depends. They discuss what happened and decide if they want to continue. It's about finding someone with similar likes. The problem with most women, and plenty of men too, is they're stuck in the mundane, the routine. What's exciting the first few times doesn't hold the same level of thrill after months or years. You have to keep it fresh. It's playtime. You don't see kids always playing the same game. They're creative, they use their imagination, they change it up."

Heat traveled up Jamie's neck flushing her cheeks. Perhaps the cold ice cream could provide an antidote. She opened the cupboard and secured two bowls, then two spoons and returned to her seat. "Dish it up," she ordered, mopping her forehead with a paper napkin.

Colin gave a lopsided grin as he scooped the icy confection into bowls. "Can't stand the heat in the kitchen?" he quipped. "Since we're not cooking anything, I think just talking about sex is getting you hot. Remember at the fundraiser the other night when you said it doesn't hurt to try new things?" He handed Jamie a bowl and spoon.

"I was talking about food." She shoveled in a large spoonful, the coolness tamping down the flames igniting within. Colin was right, talking about sex with him was arousing.

Colin swallowed a mouthful, then said, "Sex is food for the soul."

"Now you're waxing a little too poetic." Their eyes met and his hooded gaze wasn't doing much to quell the heat rising between her legs.

"You'll see at the club. Something you've never tried before might interest you."

Jamie put down the spoon and sighed. He was wearing her down. "All right, some of what you're saying makes sense, except don't you want to have a sex life with a woman who's your equal? Not a submissive?"

Colin peered at her brilliant green irises. "I'm not sure she exists. At least I haven't met her yet." Or maybe, *he had.*

Chapter 23

Jamie donned her uniform... black suit, white blouse and boots in preparation for accompanying Colin to his office. Last evening, he'd lamented about the number of emails and other correspondence he needed to attend to before leaving for the weekend. Apparently, some important clients had the jitters and he needed to soothe nerves. Luke, his personal assistant, agreed to meet him at the office and facilitate the sending of said correspondence.

They'd completed a thorough workout in Colin's gym earlier and Jamie felt pumped and ready for the day. She'd slept reasonably well, although their conversation about the club and Colin's sexual preferences crept into her dreams – or were they night-mares? – more than once. Jamie shook her head. Why did she interrogate Colin about sex? None of her damn business. And she'd confessed way too much about her own, or lack thereof.

Assessing her image in the mirror, she felt like her usual self... professional... businesslike. Yeah, out in the world, back on the job. The aroma of freshly brewed coffee wafted past her. For having no culinary skills whatsoever, Colin made a damn good cup.

She packed her things, made the bed, and scanned the beautiful bedchamber for signs of disarray. With any luck, this case would be over by the weekend and she'd be back in her cozy apartment. A twinge of disappointment nudged her. Skiing Telluride would have been a blast. Maybe she and her dad could hit the slopes for a few days. She made a mental note to call him this weekend and set something up.

COLIN ADDED milk and sugar to two travel mugs and stirred. Jamie walked into the kitchen beaming. She'd been a great workout partner this morning, cheery and witty. Something about her calmed him. And considering the dire circumstance of late, he should be anything but.

"I figured we'd save time and get caffeine here." He handed her a mug.

"Thank you," she said, inhaling the steaming brew, then taking a sip. "Yum, well done, barista."

"Why, thank you, madam. You can leave a tip on the counter." Colin took a sip from his mug, then handed her the cover and sealed his own. "Ready to hit the road?"

"All packed. Let's do this."

They exited the kitchen area, donned their coats and Colin picked up Jamie's duffel.

"No suitcase for you?" she asked.

"Everything I need is at the beach house. Makes things easy. James will drive us to the office and then we'll take the helicopter out to the house."

"Where do you take off from?"

"The office building roof."

Colin put a hand against Jamie's back and escorted her to the waiting car.

LUKE SAT PRIMLY at his desk and stood as Colin approached. "Morning, sir. How are you holding up?"

"Morning, Luke. Considering the circumstances, I'm fine. Agent Gallagher here has a unique ability to keep me sane and my nerves in check."

"Morning, Agent Gallagher. Glad you've got things under control. I can't say I've fared as well. This whole thing is rather unsettling." Luke exhaled noisily. "Now that was a stupid thing to say."

"No problem," Jamie said. "We're making progress on the investigation and hopefully this will all be over soon." She slipped off her gloves and stowed them in her coat pocket, then deposited her trench coat on a nearby chair. "Colin, I'm going to check in with the office and see if there are any new leads while you and Luke work. I'll wait for you out here."

"Great, but feel free to interrupt if you have any news."

"Will do."

Colin and Luke disappeared behind the frosted glass and Jamie sat on an upholstered loveseat and dialed Matt. "Tell me you have some amazing news."

"I'm going over the paperwork from the deal to buy the company from Mr. MacKenzie's old buddy. I interviewed the attorney and got a bad vibe. Like he wasn't telling me everything. I ran his bank statements and he made a million-dollar deposit shortly after the sale. He claimed it was his commission on the transaction, but twenty percent is a pretty big percentage. They bought the company for five million and he got a cool mill?"

"I assume it was a private company, not on the stock exchange?"

"Exactly. But these guys have disappeared from the planet as far as bank accounts. There's no record of anyone except the father. He committed suicide the week after the deal closed and was cremated. No burial site and his records are gone. I did find health records. He'd been ill for several years. Cancer, and the medical bills piled up. But the debt vanished. Not sure if it was paid off or they hacked it and made it disappear."

"Huh. I don't understand why this guy would target Colin. What grievance does he have against him? He got paid five million for the company, was there something underhanded about the deal? Did he undercut him on the price?"

"That's my sense. What if the attorney lied about the price? Say he pays the guy only a million for the company but tells MacKenzie they paid five million. Then he cooks the books to give himself the million as his commission but the other four million goes into some offshore account. I get the feeling MacKenzie trusts this guy implicitly and doesn't check his work."

"Is there any way to determine the company's value before the sale?"

"I'm working on it. There's no doubt the company was in trouble. I don't know to what end. Something else… he'd made some big withdrawals. All cash."

"Maybe he was in financial trouble."

"That's my take."

"Any CCTV footage after the guy left the parking garage the other day?"

"None. The guy's good at disappearing. And for a guy with his expertise, I'm surprised he showed up at the garage in the first place. He had to know we were keeping an eye on the car."

"That's why I paid the attendant. I figured the perp would assume the security detail would be with Colin, not the car and it might draw him out."

"It worked, at least we have a suspect, but we're not any closer to finding him."

"Doesn't do us much good if we can't find him."

"I know."

"Thanks for the update. Colin and I are taking the helicopter out to his place in Hampton Shores after he finishes at the office."

"Must be nice. Perks galore."

"Yeah, but they're not all good. Guess where he goes on weekend nights?"

"Don't tell me he's friends with Alyx and Laura's husbands? You mean that sex club?"

"Bingo."

Matt laughed too hard and too long. "I can't believe all three of you have been dragged into that place."

"Tell me. Have you ever been there?"

"Yeah, I was there the night Alyx got abducted. A total cluster-fuck. It was her first night undercover and we lost her. Daniel lurked in the background in case she needed him. He lost his shit when she disappeared. He clocked Rob. Knocked him on his ass."

Jamie's jaw dropped. "No way."

Matt chuckled. "Yeah, way." He paused then added, "It's a wild scene. You've got to see it to believe it. Although Alyx and Laura weren't put off. And then they upped and married the dudes."

"I don't get it."

"Rumor has it they're adept between the sheets. Maybe I should become a member. Learn some new tricks. Jillian might like it."

Heat flushed Jamie's cheeks. Again. She shouldn't be talking or thinking about that damned club. "Shut up."

"Let me know what you think."

"We'll see. Not sure I won't be traumatized."

"I doubt it. You're a pretty tough cookie. Who knows, you might like it and end up marrying the dude, just like your pals."

"I don't think so."

Colin and Luke emerged from the frosted glass doors. "If you need me for anything, or if a client needs me personally, text." He handed a few files to Luke.

"Absolutely, sir. I'll keep my fingers on everyone's pulse. Hand-holding is my superpower."

"I know." Colin smiled, then turned to Jamie. "Any news on the case?"

"Nothing that's broken the case. I'll fill you in on the ride."

"Sounds good. Ready?"

"As I'll ever be," she said, her mind focused on where she'd be tonight. But she wasn't sure she was prepared at all for the sordid undertakings of a sex club. Not prepared at all.

Chapter 24

The elevator doors opened and they stepped onto the roof where Brett Forrester waited. "We've combed the aircraft, sir. You're good to go."

"Excellent. Thanks, Brett."

The rotors whirled and Jamie fastened her coat's top button to ward off the January chill. She couldn't decide if the freezing wind was due to the whirling blades or because they were thirty stories up. Probably both. She twisted her hair into a makeshift ponytail to prevent it from whipping her face.

Colin held the door open and she hoisted herself inside, taking the far seat and buckling the harness. He slid in beside her and strapped in. The pilot pulled his headset off one ear. "Ready, sir?"

"Ready," Colin said. "Fred, this is Special Agent Jamie Gallagher."

"Nice to meet you, ma'am."

"Pleasure," Jamie said.

"You ever ride in a chopper?"

Colin answered for her. "She's a Navy vet, she's fine."

"Yes, sir," Fred said. "Marines, ma'am. Served until 2012."

Before Jamie could comment, Colin added, "She went to the Naval Academy. And she's an Olympian."

Jamie glared. "Really, Colin? I don't like to lead with that stuff."

"Sorry. I'm just so proud of your accomplishments."

"I don't like to advertise. It's pretentious."

Thankfully, Fred focused on take-off and let Colin's boasting of her skills lay fallow.

The city vista vanished and Jamie focused on the shoreline as they cruised the ocean coast, the frothy white waves breaking on the pristine sandy beaches. A few fishing boats dotted the cerulean water, not like in the summer where pleasure crafts and sunbathers populated the coastline. "Too bad it's winter. I wouldn't mind working on my tan while we're at your beach house."

Colin smiled. "Then you'll have to spend a weekend with me this summer. I wouldn't mind seeing you in a bikini."

Jamie offered her best *faux* frown. "Careful, mister. We're still on the job."

"Speaking of which… I'm hoping this ends soon and I'm still alive so I can take you on a date."

Jamie didn't respond. The handsome billionaire was wearing her down. Maybe she'd go on one date.

"So, fill me in on the latest news," Colin said, interrupting her musings.

The noisy chopper made it difficult to hear so Jamie only shared the highlights of her conversation with Matt.

"You still think my attorney might be involved?"

"It's an angle we're exploring."

"No way. I can't believe Jeb would steal from me and then get me killed."

Conversation became too difficult and Jamie concentrated on the spectacular view until the helicopter alighted on the asphalt of East Hampton's private airport.

COLIN EXITED FIRST, then reached up and grabbed Jamie by the waist. She landed her hands on his shoulders. He deposited her on the macadam, his hands lingering on her hips longer than they should have. They wore sunglasses on this cold sunny day so he couldn't assess her expression. Releasing her, he pressed his hand against the small of her back and ushered her to the waiting forest green Range Rover. His driver held the door for them and Jamie slid into the backseat and he alongside her.

"Did you enjoy the ride?" Colin asked.

"The view of the ocean is spectacular. And the ride is much smoother than a military helo."

They arrived at the house in under ten minutes. The car ambled along the lengthy gravel driveway stopping at the front door rather than entering the garage.

Jamie peered out the side window, her mouth agape. "You call this a beach house? I'd call it a seaside compound."

Jamie did a three-sixty, trying not to gawk at the immensity and grandeur of the two-story great room. Glass windows made up the entire back wall and offered a spectacular ocean view. She strode across the beechwood floor and gazed out at the waves crashing on the sandy beach. A giant stone fire pit sat center stage on a massive slate patio. She imagined sunning herself on a spacious lounger then running into the water to cool down. At night they'd sit around the fire pit and toast marshmallows. Jesus. She'd already moved herself in.

"You have a pool too?"

"Yup. Salt water."

"Very cool, mister." She drank in the expertly bedecked room. "You decorate this yourself?"

"No. When I bought it the real estate agent hooked me up with a caretaker. I gave her carte blanche to hire a decorator. She consulted me on some things but mostly I left it to her. She takes care of the place when I'm not here and stocks it when I'm coming to town."

"She has good taste, whoever she is." The half-circle seafoam sectional faced the back windows and could probably seat fifteen. A glass coffee table occupied most of the inner space. The see-through top revealed a miniature beach bedecked with seashells, sand dollars and starfish skeletons. The coffee-hued walls were lined with built-in shelves filled with the mandatory cache of books and knick-knacks, and an array of beach-glass filled jars. Sunlight pierced the bevy of glass shards, scattering rainbow rays onto the gray wood floor.

"I'm glad you like it." Colin placed her duffle on the bottom step leading to the upper level. "Make yourself at home. *Mi casa es su casa.*"

Jamie walked toward him, stopping about a foot away. "You're wearing me down, Mr. MacKenzie. I just might take you up on your offer to visit this summer."

Colin smiled broadly, revealing his perfect white teeth. "I told you I'm tenacious, Agent Gallagher. And I haven't even shown you the good stuff yet."

And what the hell did that portend?

Chapter 25

Colin escorted Jamie upstairs and into a large bedroom festooned in shades of yellow. A four-poster bed with a buttery-colored quilt – and enough pillows for a serious pillow fight – centered the chamber. The white wicker furniture had knobs fashioned as scallop shells. A floor-to-ceiling window on the far wall veiled the magnificent ocean view in gauzy ivory cloth. Jamie parted the curtains and leaned her hands on the white wooden frame, feasting her eyes on the distant blue and orange horizon.

"I think you'll find everything you need. If not, let me know. My room is to the right."

She faced Colin. "It's weird. Being here feels like I'm on vacation, not in the middle of a big case."

"I wish. Nothing would make me happier than to turn this into a romantic weekend."

Jamie wanted to protest, but she kind of felt the same. "Honestly, Colin, the thought is tempting, but…" She shook her head. "Never mind. Let's keep focused on the case."

Colin came close, close enough to touch. "What about the future?" He took her hands in his and laced his fingers through hers. She gazed down at their joined hands. She wanted those hands… everywhere.

Jamie sputtered, "The future will always be there, waiting."

He released one hand and pressed a finger against her lips. "Don't say another word. Let me bask in the possibility you might say yes one day."

Jamie smiled beneath his finger and he finally released her. He bent down and gave her a sweet kiss, then strode away. "We're going out for an early dinner. Change out of that damned black suit into something more casual. Meet you downstairs in ten."

Jamie touched her mouth, the warmth of his lips lingered, her pulse launched somewhere into the stratosphere. If it wasn't for that damned club.

COLIN ENTERED HIS BEDROOM, hurling a victorious fist in the air. Jamie had opened her heart a crack and he planned on making his way in. All the way in. He stripped out of his suit and shirt, kicked off his topsiders and sought out jeans and a sweater from his closet. He laughed at the juxtaposition of his situation. He'd nearly been killed twice, someone likely still after him, and yet he'd never been happier in his life. If this bad thing hadn't happened, he'd never have met Jamie.

He dressed, combed his hair and bounded down the stairs.

Jamie sat crossed-legged on the couch, dressed in her white sweater but exchanged her jeans for a short black flouncy skirt. "I'm liking the skirt," he said.

"You're welcome."

The afternoon sunlight pierced the window glass and illuminated her crimson hair as if tiny rainbows encased each strand. She'd glossed her lips, making them even more enticing than usual.

"You beat me," Colin said. "I thought girls were always late."

Jamie frowned. "Again, with the stereotypes?"

"Every girl I've ever dated was, including my mother."

"Then you haven't been with the right girl."

Egad, she just used the same line Colin did during her interrogation about his sex life. A conversation where she revealed way too much about her own.

"Apparently, I am now," Colin said.

Jamie ignored his insinuation. "I'm always early, which is why I was annoyed with Rob the morning I bumped into you. I was already gonna be an hour early and he was busting my chops."

"Makes sense, but I didn't judge you, not even about the dick comment. I thought it was hysterical. And when I fessed up about being the boss, well, the expression on your face was priceless."

And there she was again, musing over Colin's dick. She shook her head but remained mute. "Let's eat. I'm starving." She stood and reached for her jacket, but Colin beat her to it and helped her into it. "Thank you."

"At your service, madam, for all your needs."

Jamie shook her head again and smiled. But she couldn't stop thinking about Colin as a lover. An expert lover? Well, Alyx and Laura had certainly hit the jackpot.

Colin clasped her hand and tugged her toward the front door. Jamie nodded at the FBI agents posted outside as they approached Colin's Range Rover. No driver so Colin held the door open and she slipped into the seat. He exited the driveway, accompanied by their FBI tail.

"There's a great little farm-to-table restaurant in town. I thought we'd eat there. They make an amazing butternut squash soup and the bread is baked on premises. Oh, and the pies are award-winning."

"Sounds scrumptious."

Colin angled the car into a parking space in front of East End Farmstead. "In the summer it's impossible to find parking in town and especially this close. Sometimes I ride my bike."

Jamie laughed. "No hot air balloon?"

"Funny."

They sat at a table near the front window surrounded by the delicious smells of foodstuffs, both sweet and savory. The waitress handed them a menu and Colin ordered a bottle of pinot Grigio. Jamie ordered the squash soup and a cranberry, blue cheese, walnut salad, committed to ordering a slice of pie for dessert. Something she rarely indulged in. Colin ordered the soup and a slice of quiche. In between bites of food and conversation, his foot kept touch or sliding past hers under the tablecloth. Stealthy but nice and she chose to not acknowledge anything, even when his foot ventured upward and caressed her calves.

Soon they'd finished their repast, rhubarb pie on the way, when Jamie's phone rang. Several minutes later, she said, "We may have a lead on the brother's whereabouts."

"Where?"

"Colorado. Facial recognition picked him up at Telluride airport."

"Do you have him in custody?"

"Not yet."

"What's the brother's name?"

"Noah."

"How the hell does he know about Telluride?"

Jamie frowned. "The five-million-dollar question."

Colin laced his fingers together and landed his elbows on the table. "Maybe we should cancel the trip."

"I think that's wise."

"On second thought." Colin reached across the table and snatched Jamie's phone. "Use me as bait," he barked into the phone."

"Absolutely not," Jamie said, pulling her cell from his grip.

"Ignore that, Matt."

"I want this over and I'm fully prepared to take a risk to catch this guy."

"We still have several days and we hope to have him in custody before then."

"You two done?" Matt said in her ear.

"Yeah, done. Talk later."

Jamie ended the conversation as two slices of warm rhubarb pie landed in front of them. "Thank you," Colin told the waitress. He stabbed his fork into the gooey fragrant yumminess. "I'm not afraid. I know the FBI will protect us. But I damn well should have a say in this."

"There are no guarantees, Colin. Sometimes things go awry, despite our best efforts. We're not talking any more about using you as bait. And you weren't so brave in the throes of a nightmare. Maybe you should listen to the voice in your head."

"But—"

"End of discussion."

Colin watched as a morsel of pie passed Jamie's lips. She closed her eyes and moaned, then chewed slowly and swallowed. "My God, this is divine."

"Told ya."

Colin paid the check and they took a walking tour through the quaint village of Hampton Shores.

"So, Daniel and Alyx have a home here too?"

"They do. Daniel has a practice in the city but also has privileges at our local hospital. They have an apartment in the city as well. Have you been there?"

"No. I haven't had much free time to hang out with either Alyx or Laura since I moved here. I went to the baby shower last month but it was at a restaurant."

They returned to the car and headed back to the house, followed by the dark government sedan. Uneasiness prickled Colin's insides. He almost thought himself nervous. Bringing Jamie to the club might not be the right move. Both Daniel and Steve abandoned the club after they met the love of their lives, although now that he thought about it, Daniel stopped coming long before he met Alyx. Could he find sexual satisfaction outside the club too? Vanilla sex for the rest of his life… and with *one* woman? He was overthinking this. Jamie hadn't even agreed to go on a real date.

"What should I wear to the club tonight?" Jamie said, pulling him from his musings.

"What you're wearing is fine."

"Good. I was afraid you'd make me wear something slutty."

"Don't tempt me. There's a fetish-wear shop at the club and I could whip you into something in a nanosecond." He lifted his eyebrows.

Chapter 26

En route to the club, Jamie's imagination ran feral. Her heart fluttered and she couldn't decipher it… trepidation, for sure. Excitement too? She'd engaged in violent gruesome shootouts with the most notorious criminals on the planet, and hadn't blinked. How could a high-class sex club instill such terror?

Especially since she'd simply be an observer. Yet then she worried about *observing* Colin. What would he be wearing? Would he wear anything? Would he fuck some woman right in front of Jamie, or many women (or men?) one after the other, and she'd be forced to watch? Egad.

The car stopped in front of a stone edifice with a massive wooden door. Colin ushered Jamie from the car and slipped an arm around her waist. "Remember if anyone asks, you're here for the newcomer's tour."

"Regardless of your Dom position, I am in charge—"

"That's not going to work in there."

"Here's the deal. Your life is in my hands. This is serious, Colin. As long as we do not, I repeat, do *not* separate, there will be no problem. That's an order. Other than that, I can act as submissive as you need me to."

His sea blue eyes searched her face. "Fine, but you look anxious." His index finger tucked her hair behind one ear.

"I killed two of El Chapo's men in a joint raid with American and Mexican law enforcement. I've nearly been strangled to death by a serial killer who'd evaded capture for three decades. I am not scared of a bunch of rich people spanking each other for kicks."

"She doth protest too much."

"Stop projecting."

He smiled, then helped her up the steps. "Welcome to St. Andrew's."

Jamie focused on the large brass doorknocker. The façade of the place radiated a medieval vibe, but she took her own advice and tried not to *project*. She followed Colin into the sizable foyer. A huge man dressed in a simple black suit, white shirt and no tie, sat behind a mahogany Queen Ann desk. He rose upon seeing Colin.

"Master Colin," he said with a respectful chin nod.

"Evening, Zach, how's it hanging?"

"All good in the hood, Sir."

Zach paused before saying, "I saw you on the news, Sir. Is it true, somebody tried to blow up your place?"

"Afraid so, Zach. But I have every confidence the FBI will catch the perp quickly. In fact, this is Special Agent Jamie Gallagher. She's my bodyguard."

"Wow, where does the FBI go to recruit all these beautiful girls?" Colin frowned, and Zach added, "Sorry, Sir… Miss. Didn't mean nothing. It's just that the other two agents I saw here were hotties, too."

Colin cleared his throat. "As far as anyone knows she's here for the newcomer's tour. No need to announce her status to everyone."

"Of course, Sir. Your secret is safe."

"She'll still need to fill out the appropriate paperwork as an observer. No play."

"Of course. Let me take your coats and I'll lock them in the Masters' Lounge."

Colin helped Jamie off with hers and handed both coats over to Zach who disappeared behind a locked door. He returned and opened the top desk drawer and retrieved a three-page document, setting it on the tabletop. He plucked a feathered pen from the holder and placed it alongside the papers.

Colin turned Jamie toward him. "Read and sign the disclaimer and wait for me. I'll be back in ten minutes." He said to Zach, "Do not let her in without me. Understood?"

"Absolutely, Sir."

What was it with Colin? Did his Dom nature need to exert control in every situation? Jamie said, "We just went through this. I am not leaving you alone. Not even for a second."

Colin's brow furrowed. "All right, I'll wait here while you sign the disclaimer and we can go in together."

"Have a seat," Zach instructed. A crooked smile softened his acne-scarred face, which on first impression made him rather scary. Poor guy. His nose had definitely been broken more than once.

Jamie settled into the dark upholstered chair beside Zach's desk. The shiny black marble floor paired with the onyx and white striped wallpaper evoked a certain elegance, the complete opposite of her imaginings.

Zach said, "Make sure you read carefully. There are punishments for breaking the rules and take my word for it, it's something you want to avoid."

Jamie read, yet found it difficult to concentrate as her mind wandered to what happened on the other side of the black door. Coat-clad young adults drifted in, plus middle-aged and a few elderly too, all signing the registry before entering the carnal chamber, the mood festive, each acknowledging Colin's presence, calling him Sir or Master. Everyone wore concealing coats and she imagined what fetish wear, if any, adorned the new arrivals. She caught glimpses, six-inch leather collars with large brass rings, black fishnet stockings merged into high boots with spikey heels. Finished, she signed her name.

"Great," Zach said, taking the document and scanning it into the computer on his desk.

She rose and Colin took her hand, leading her into the inner sanctum of ecstasy and pain. Heavy metal music played over the sound system, not so loud you couldn't hear yourself think. Human musk permeated the air. A salty sweaty aroma mixed with something heavy and almost sweet. Bodies scantily clad in leather and latex, or nothing at all, moved to the pounding beat of a classic Guns N' Roses song. Flesh pressed flesh in erotic gyrations. Studded collars attached to leashes surrounded both men's and women's necks, many had piercings in places that made Jamie cringe.

She gawked at the size of the place. Cavern-like. A second floor guarded by black wrought-iron railings with lighted display windows lined the far wall. What was on exhibition? They crossed the crowded dance floor and came upon a bar constructed entirely of glass, which lent the impression of being sculpted from ice. Faint blue lights embedded inside gave the countertop a slick eerie glow.

A large man stood at the counter's end sipping a drink. He wore a black polo shirt with an insignia, and she realized it matched the one Colin wore. He must be what Colin called a Master. The guy was built and maybe fifty. He exuded power and strength. Did she dare think it? *Dominance.*

"Jamie, this is Jack, the club owner," Colin said.

Jack extended his hand and Jamie took it. "Pleasure, pet. Welcome."

He studied Colin. "Some bad shit came your way this week. How you doing?"

"We should talk in your office."

"Sure thing." Jack slugged the rest of his drink and placed the glass on the counter a little too forcefully.

———

JACK IGNORED his desk and settled onto one of two red velvet loveseats. Jamie and Colin sat opposite him. "I was told you'd be escorted by a bodyguard. Where is he?"

"You're looking at *her*. This is Special Agent Jamie Gallagher. The FBI assigned her to protect me until this guy is caught."

"I apologize for the affectionate moniker, Agent Gallagher. I assumed you were a new client."

"I've been called worse."

Jack scowled, hesitating before speaking. "I don't like this, it's giving me a migraine. Nothing against you, Agent Gallagher, it's the fact that every time you FBI chicks come here you steal one of my club's best Masters."

Jamie remained silent. True, both Alyx and Laura had lured their husbands away from their roles as club Dominants. She had no idea the difficulty in finding new personnel.

"Do you have any leads?" Jack said, moving on from his lament.

Jamie answered. "Yes, but I'm not at liberty to discuss the case.

I'm here to assure Mr. MacKenzie's safety and since he needed to be here tonight, I am obliged to accompany him. I won't get in the way."

Colin said, "We'll say she's here for the tour. I'll keep her near me at all times."

"Of course. I'll get a pair of red handcuffs to signify her status." Jack retrieved fur-lined crimson manacles from the armoire behind his desk and handed them to Colin, then returned to his seat.

"Wrists, please," Colin said. Jamie gave him the evil eye. "You need to embrace a tad more submissiveness if we're going to pull this off, Agent Gallagher."

She extended her wrists and Colin snapped a cuff around each, then hesitated. "Don't even think about it," Jamie exclaimed. "I need my hands free."

"Fine. You're the boss." *For now.* Colin had never said that to a woman before. "Besides they're mostly symbolic, as a way of identifying you. You can get out of them easily if you need to."

Jamie didn't drop her glare.

"Are you armed?" Colin asked.

"Of course."

"Where?"

"None of your business."

"Doubt you'll need your gun," Jack said, shrugging. "Don't mean to second-guess you, my dear, but I don't think the bomber is on premises. Colin's private security team and the FBI swept the club this afternoon before anyone entered. And we won't allow anyone we don't know in tonight."

"Let's be clear. I'm in charge here."

"But we do require members to lock their guns in my safe. I do have a lot of law enforcement personnel on my roster."

"Bullshit," Jamie said. "I'm on duty and I must have access to my weapon at all times." To Colin she took an even firmer tone. "We should have discussed this in more detail *beforehand*."

Jack cleared his throat. "I guess that's settled then. By the way," he said to Colin, "we have a new Master. His name is Ian Turner, he's from Detroit. Came highly recommended by the owner, an old pal from my military days. I want to introduce you. Remind me." He gave Jamie a sideways glance. "If you Feeb girls keep stealing my dungeon masters, I'm going to have to close up shop."

"We could use some new blood, Jack. Guys we can trust."

Jack glowered at Jamie, yet the corners of his mouth curved up. "I'd watch myself if I were you, Master Colin." His scowl morphed into a wink.

Chapter 27

"**D**o you want to check in with the trainees?" Jack asked Colin. "They're in the spa area waiting to be inspected."

"I do," Colin said.

"I'll send Ian down to meet you. You can advise him on our procedures and protocols."

The spa area resembled a gym locker room, albeit upscale to the max, marble lockers, gilt-framed mirrors and rainfall showers with steam-bath functions. Ten women stood in a row, eyes focused on the floor, hands clasped behind their backs. They wore teeny-tiny skirts, skimpy tops, three-inch heels and cut-outs in the most inappropriate places. No jewelry, which Jamie assumed might be a liability during the festivities. And faces heavily made up, way too garish for her taste.

"Good evening, subbies," Colin said. "How is everyone tonight?"

Speaking in murmurs, various versions of 'Fine, Sir,' answered his query.

"Excellent."

A strapping, six-foot tall man walked in, his chest barely contained by the black polo shirt. The submissive coterie stood a little more erect, a few gasped. Talk about stunning: full head of chestnut-brown hair, hypnotic ice-blue eyes and a quirky unbalanced smile that, yeah… made her want to put on some fuck-me pumps and strip to a G-string.

What was wrong with her? Maybe something in the air. Pheromones? Testosterone? Oxytocin?

He marched toward Colin. "Jack said I'd find you here." He held out his hand. "Ian Turner."

Colin shook it. "Welcome. Our staff is getting a little thin. Glad you're here."

"Me too. Amazing club. I'm impressed with what I've seen so far." Ian focused on Jamie's red handcuffs. "Prospective member?"

"Perhaps. This is Jamie Gallagher. She's here for the tour."

"Welcome, little subbie," Ian said. "You're quite beautiful. I'd love to work with you when you're ready."

Jamie gritted her teeth. This was harder than she'd imagined. Two concepts sparred within. The nonnegotiable requirement that men treat her as an equal and the impulse to spread her legs and take it as rough as he could give. And she should have studied up on protocol. She knew certain behaviors were expected of submissives, like kneeling, keeping eyes focused on the floor and not to speak unless spoken to, which was probably her best bet.

COLIN'S JAW TIGHTENED. This was harder than he'd imagined. Ian wasn't doing anything wrong but Colin wasn't sure he could endure guys coming on to Jamie. "Ms. Gallagher will be with me tonight. One step at a time."

"Of course," Ian said. "I'm here when she's ready."

Colin gritted his teeth. *Over my very much still alive and ass-kicking body.* "You up to inspecting the submissives before we let them out on the floor?"

"It would be my pleasure."

Colin faced the row of submissives like a drill sergeant addressing his platoon. He recognized Alyssa, the prospective member he'd recently interviewed.

"Dr. Thayer, happy to see you're still here. How are you?"

She raised her azure eyes to meet his. "Sir, the club has definitely been exceeding my expectations."

"Excellent. I'm glad you're enjoying yourself. Eyes down."

He scanned the remaining lineup. "I believe Sally, Candace, and Marcie are ready to be assigned Doms tonight." He moved closer to the women. "Step forward, please." Three females complied, still in protocol. "Have them report to me when you're done inspecting them and you can take the rest out for a spin. All the Masters will be glad to work with newbies."

"Sounds like a plan," Ian said.

"Have you had a chance to meet the other Masters?"

"I believe I have. You're the last."

Colin secured Jamie's leather clad wrist in his hand. "We normally have ten Masters on staff each night so there should be plenty of help. Watch out for Sam, he's a serious sadist and we only give him clients looking for that kind of attention."

"Understood," Ian said. "I've met him and know his appetites."

"His clientele is well established so we mostly leave him alone."

"Got it."

Jamie twitched in his grip and Colin squeezed her wrist. "I'll wait at the bar. Send my three submissives out when you've finished the inspection."

"Will do."

Colin whisked Jamie out of there and settled her on a bar stool. "You okay?"

"Honestly? It's difficult watching women play this role and men doing whatever they want."

"Men are leashed too, and regardless of gender the standard is mutual consent. Willing participants who know it's just a game. I promise to spare you the tough stuff. I try to be tolerant of others' proclivities."

Jamie inhaled and exhaled, slowly. "Me too. To each his own. Still, I'd rather not look at it. It's hard to comprehend why people find torture arousing."

Colin had no intention of talking this to death. "How about a drink?"

"I'm on duty, so probably not."

"Just one, to take the edge off. You're a tad tense."

Ya think? "Maybe a sip."

"Name your poison."

"Scotch and water."

Colin crooked a finger toward the bartender. She approached, dressed in a skin-tight black leather tank top. Even she had well-toned biceps, her lips tinted a vibrant red to match her nails. "Master Colin. Good to see you."

"This is Jamie Gallagher. She's here for the newcomer's tour." He pivoted toward Jamie. "This is Lisa, Jack's submissive."

Jamie had difficulty accepting Lisa in a submissive role. She could probably kick anybody's ass in a nanosecond.

Lisa leaned her elbows on the bar, squishing her ample breasts together. "You'll love working with Colin. He's one of our most popular Doms."

Of course he is. "Well, I'm flattered he's taken an interest in me."

"What can I get you guys?"

"Scotch and water for both of us." Colin squeezed Jamie's hand as Lisa moved away to pour their drinks. "All good?"

"Stop worrying about me. I'm a big girl."

Colin smirked. "If you say so."

"I do."

"Enjoy," Lisa said, placing the tumblers in front of them.

"Thanks," Colin said, and Lisa jiggled her tits, raised both hands in the air and danced toward a group of fully nude patrons.

Jamie nursed the icy cocktail, hoping it would calm her roiling gut. She eyed Colin over the rim of the glass. He said, "I feel bad. I don't think I prepared you enough for what you're about to behold."

"I'll take responsibility." Jamie placed her drink on the crystalline bar top. "I thought I knew what went on in these places. I doubt seeing it in the flesh is something you can ever prepare for."

"That might be true." Colin twirled his glass on the glossy countertop a few times, then downed it.

"Whoa. I know you're stressed. But take it easy." Jamie hesitated before adding, "I find Lisa a puzzlement. She doesn't appear to have a submissive bone in her body."

Colin grinned. "Just because a woman, or a man, chooses to be submissive in a sexual experience doesn't mean it carries over into other parts of their lives. Many sexual submissives are quite dominant in their careers, CEOs, CFOs, cops, politicians. Often, powerful people want something different in their sex life. They prefer to surrender to someone."

"Really? You don't."

"I'm not everybody."

"You sure aren't, Mister MacKenzie."

Chapter 28

J amie rested her forearms on the bar, studying her red
handcuffs. She picked at the fur, then stroked it. Type A
submissives? Then probably quite a few FBI personnel
lived this life. Hmm.

"What's going on in that pretty little head of yours?" Colin asked.

She opened her mouth twice, as if to answer, yet remained mute.
Finally, Colin said, "Finish your drink and let's take a stroll. I've
got your attention and I fully intend to capitalize on it." Jamie
swallowed a large gulp but left the drink unfinished. Colin picked
her up by the waist and returned her to the floor, then slipped his
index finger through one manacle and towed her forward.

They skirted the throng of grinding bodies on the dance floor and
drilled deeper into the club's enigmatic bowels. Someone called
Colin's name and they faced a black man wearing the club shirt.
Shorter than Colin, he had a wrestler's dense body, a diamond-
grilled smile, and white buzzcut. Jamie's first thought was those
grills could be dangerous on a person's sensitive parts. He sported
twin silver hoops in one ear. He slapped Colin on the shoulder
and his other hand held a leather leash attached to a metal-
studded collar surrounding a petite brunette's neck. Jamie recognized the woman from the submissive lineup. Alyssa?

"Grayson," Colin said, "how's the new subbie doing tonight? Working her hard?"

Jamie watched the woman's face for some sign as to how she fared. She couldn't overcome the need to rescue these women. She tried to wrap her head around this notion of submissiveness and just when she thought she kinda-sorta-maybe understood, something nixed it. A leash felt wrong. Jamie could never imagine agreeing to that behavior. Never-ever.

"Just getting started. We're off to the medical room for roleplay. I fully intend to examine my patient quite thoroughly. And using the paddle liberally if she doesn't comply," Grayson said, his voice threatening. "Although, I might just spank her for fun."

Again, Jamie scrutinized the woman's expression, but couldn't gauge her state of mind. She didn't appear frightened.

Colin put his arm around Jamie's shoulder. It grounded her.

"New subbie?" Grayson said, raking his eyes over Jamie's body. "Permission to touch?"

"Easy," Colin scolded. "This is her first time and I don't want to scare her off."

"Gotcha. A real beauty. Can't wait to get my hands on her." Grayson addressed the leashed woman. "Let's go, pet, we've got work to do. I'm dying to see your ass flaming red when I'm done." He tugged the leash, disappearing into a darkened labyrinth where a musical sound – mystical, like Gregorian chants – oddly echoed.

"Permission to touch?" Jamie said too loudly. "What the fuck?"

"Easy, darling. Remember you're playing a part. Don't freak out on me. All Dominants can touch a sub without their permission. If they're in the company of another Dom then he or she must give permission."

Jamie gave a dirty look. "And what does it mean if the Dom says yes?"

"It means exactly like it sounds. He can put his hand anywhere he wants."

"And you would do that to a woman?"

Colin placed two fingers on Jamie's lips. "Not now. We'll discuss this later. You need to keep quiet if we're going to actually pull this off."

The three submissives from the spa area approached Colin. The redhead said, "Permission to speak, Master?"

"Permission granted."

"We're ready for you, Sir."

"Excellent. Follow me." Colin led the trio toward the club's rear, Jamie tucked into his side. A cozy arrangement of oversized throne-like chairs trimmed in purple velvet held a group of members. Masters, mostly men as evidenced by the club polo shirt, and one woman in a short black leather miniskirt, matching knee-high boots and a red satin vest with the club logo, her enormous breasts barely contained in a leather bra. She slapped a riding crop on her thigh in a tantric rhythm. "Slave position," Colin ordered. The trio sunk silently to the ground. "Good evening, Masters." A round of greetings acknowledged his presence. "I have three submissives who are ready for play. I believe you've read each of their files and understand their needs, wants, and limits."

All nodded. Jamie remembered Colin explaining each submissive's handcuffs displayed a range of charms indicating the behaviors they willingly engaged in: intercourse, certain degrees of pain, flogging or whipping and a host of other lascivious activities. She scanned the handcuffs on display yet couldn't remember if Colin indicated what color meant what. The raven-haired woman wore several charms, one red. Jamie figured it signified something severe… like extreme pain.

"I'll take Marcie," one Master said, standing. "Come here, pet." The redhead obeyed and knelt before him, eyes glued to the floor.

"That's a good girl," he said. He placed his hand on top of her scalp. "Stand," he commanded and she complied. "Eyes on me." Again, she obeyed and he fastened her handcuffs together in front. "Let's find a restraining bench."

She remained silent and he steered her into the crowd.

This behavior repeated itself as Colin assigned the remaining two submissives to club Doms. One marched his submissive off to the Arabian tent display and the other to roleplay in an office suite. Jamie figured they'd be playing some boss/secretary scene, which could be viewed as sexual harassment, or worse, in the real world. The law enforcement side of her brain remained lit, about to explode.

When had sex gotten so complicated? Why couldn't two people simply let nature take its course? Simple as the birds and bees. In the back of a muscle car. A nooner in a fancy hotel suite. Sixty-nine after a long night of wining, dining, dirty dancing. No bells and whistles in the form of handcuffs, blindfolds, chains and floggers.

"Let's finish the tour," Colin said, dragging her from thoughts that might give her a stroke.

Jamie peeked into lighted display windows, where women, and the occasional male submissive, were spanked, flogged or paddled. She saw Marcie getting examined in the medical suite, her legs spread-eagle for everyone's viewing. Despite her entire upbringing with the Gallaghers telling her all of this was very, very wrong, the rest of her body wasn't complying. A throbbing between her legs, a pounding rhythm making her somewhat lightheaded.

Did her mother, being a hooker, possess a genetic component? Jaime had a strong suspicion the apple didn't fall from the tree.

Lisa, the bartender, approached. "Master Colin, there's a situation in the dungeon. Code E. Jack needs you to respond right away."

"Put her in the pen," he said to Lisa and before Jamie could respond, Colin vanished into the maddening crowd.

Panic stabbed Jamie's chest. The son-of-a-bitch left her. Just like that. When she'd told him not to. "Lisa, take me to Colin. Now."

"No way can you go into the dungeon. Colin said to park you in the submissives' pen."

Jamie fled toward the back of the building, pushing sweating, writhing bodies out of her way. A sign identified the dungeon. RESTRICTED ACCESS. She turned the golden knob. It didn't give. She pounded on the door. Shit. She pounded again. No response. Someone grabbed her by both upper arms.

"Never defy a Master," Lisa said.

"You're making a huge mistake. I'm a fucking FBI agent."

"I don't care. That doesn't matter here." She tugged Jamie backwards toward the bar.

Making a scene would be the complete opposite of Jamie staying undercover. No other alternative but to acquiesce for the moment.

"Wait here," Lisa said, opening a small gate where about a dozen women and two men sat. Before returning to the bar, she attempted to buckle one of Jamie's manacles to a ring on a bar bolted to the ground, along with the others.

Jamie wrenched her arm from Lisa's vice-like grip. "Don't make me hurt you."

"You sure won't last long," Lisa said and left.

Teeth clenched, Jamie surveyed the surroundings. Each submissive hung their head, no one spoke. The cocktail bar filled the right side of the area and to her left a burly Dom was whipping a tiny woman, her wrists and ankles bound to a large wooden X. Her bare back and bottom were in full sight, her breasts pressed against the dark wood. The snap of the whip startled Jamie. The woman shrieked. Welts marked her skin but the man kept on lashing her.

Jamie's heart rate spiked. The woman couldn't be enjoying this. *Stop*.

The next lash drew blood and Jamie gasped in sympathy. Horror.

She jumped over the small metal fence and ran to the woman.

Chapter 29

J amie grabbed the man's wrist, halting the whipping. She wrenched his hand behind his back and thrust a foot into the back of his knee. He fell, landing on his stomach. She kneed him in the back, resting all her weight on him, then forced one arm behind his back. "Enough! You're hurting her."

He glared over his shoulder. "She likes it."

"The thing about pain?" Jamie twisted his arm harder, *harder*. "It's equal opportunity."

A crowd formed as Jamie called the man a piece of shit and let go. The stout man struggled to stand, but when he did, he towered over her. His black leather, studded vest proved too small for him, his large gut taking center stage. Sweat trickled down his shaven head, his scraggy gray beard collecting the droplets. He landed one hand on her shoulder, the other held the lash. "On your knees, subbie," he ordered. "You've interfered with a scene. The punishment for your infraction will be delivered immediately and harshly."

The realization of what she'd done hit like a fifty-pound dumbbell. The rules stated if someone interfered in a scene, the Dom could levy a punishment of his choice. Zach's words resounded in her brain: *There are punishments for breaking the rules and take my word, it's something you want to avoid.*

What an idiot. If she was gonna be a rule breaker, she should've picked one that wouldn't result in her getting *whipped*. Oh God. She'd royally fucked up. Yet the woman had screamed bloody murder and Jamie's reflexes kicked in. What now? She'd have to face her punishment or blow her cover.

People pushed through the crowd: Jack, Lisa and… Colin.

"Problem?" Jack said.

"Yes, this submissive fucked up my scene."

"Let's take a beat here, Xavier. She's a newbie."

"I don't care. She knows the rules and must submit to me for whatever punishment I see fit." He gave a small snap to the whip in his hand. Jamie flinched.

"She's my responsibility," Colin interjected. "I'll take her punishment."

"What?" Jamie declared. "No way. It's my mistake."

Colin pulled Jamie to the side and muttered, "What the hell? You knew not to interfere in a scene."

"Well, you never should have disappeared. I'm sworn to protect you. You put me in an untenable position."

"Code E is a potentially life-threatening situation. You are here to protect me, but my job is to protect the members. Which is exactly what I did."

"Your safety comes first. No exceptions."

"This is bad. No way am I letting Xavier have at you. He's a brutal sadist and not something I would ever allow you to endure. Just do as I say."

"Yes, Sir. You're the Dom."

"Sarcasm isn't appreciated."

Colin stood nose-to-nose with Xavier. "You're bi. Get your satisfaction whipping me. I submit."

Xavier studied Colin's face before saying, "I'm not about to whip the club's most popular Dom. I want her."

Jack intervened. "I won't allow you to punish a newcomer. She's an innocent and would be scarred not only physically but mentally. She's not a masochist. You must respect her status." Xavier didn't respond. "Perhaps we can take this into my office and come up with a compromise."

"Fine," Xavier said. "I must attend to my subbie first." He marched toward the woman still strapped to the cross, laid his whip on a nearby rack, and unshackled her, wrapping her in a blanket and carrying her off to a brown leather loveseat. Jamie watched as he cuddled her, offering water and fruit.

Jamie frowned. Why was he being gentle with her after he'd been so brutal?

She felt someone grasp her hand and pull her forward. Colin. He followed Jack into his office, Lisa trailed.

"I'm sorry," Colin said to Jack. "It's my fault. I shouldn't have left her."

"I probably should have stayed with her," Lisa added.

Jack pinched the bridge of his nose. "It's unfortunate, but I'm sure we can resolve this without anyone getting whipped. I'll offer Xavier a year of free dues. That should mollify him."

"What happened in the dungeon?" Jack said.

Colin rubbed his forehead. "Winston again. He still has difficulty understanding a safe word means no."

"He was already on probation so it's time for him to get the boot. See? All good. It's a wash." Jack smiled. "I'm sorry, Jamie. I wish your experience had been more positive."

"We should go," Colin said.

"I think that's wise. I'll handle it from here." Jack rose and took Jamie's hands, removing the fluffy red handcuffs. He stuffed them in the pocket of his black pants. "Take good care of my friend, Special Agent Gallagher."

"I will and again, a thousand apologies."

"All is forgiven. Now go, you two."

COLIN SAT beside Jamie in the backseat as his driver maneuvered the car onto Old Montauk Highway. What a clusterfuck. Jamie would never forgive him for forcing her to leave him unprotected, then putting her in this dilemma. And he deserved her wrath. How pissed was she, or how traumatized? He was afraid to ask. Afraid to find out. The silence between them suffocated, like toxic gas. He leaned forward, his head in his hands and breathed out slowly. A hand rubbed his back, yet he couldn't see her face in the darkened car.

"Can we forgive each other?" she whispered.

"Forgive you? I'm the one who fucked up."

"True, you never should have left me and don't do it again. Even if someone else is in danger."

"Easier said. I get it, though. I shouldn't have put you in that situation."

An interlude of quietness filled the space between them. Not awkward or stifling. Sobering.

Finally, she said, "Mistakes happen when agents get personally involved in a case. First thing they taught us at Quantico."

Colin sighed and slumped back into the seat. No way would he ever convince Jamie to try anything kinky in the bedroom after this debacle. She probably wanted to run from him, and even though her job required she remain, she might call in a replacement and flee the minute her feet hit the ground.

"It's hard to accept people get off that way. I mean, the welts, the blood, the pain…"

"Whipping is sort of an art form at the club. Some guys are masters at it. The lash can caress, elicit a glow, stimulate in ways we can't appreciate."

"But drawing blood doesn't make sense. It's perverted."

"I know, I don't find it a turn-on."

"Have you ever whipped anyone?"

"Flogging is more my style. It's fun, and it's playful. Pain isn't my game."

"And spanking? You do that too?"

"Now, that's really fun. It's popular at the club and even with women outside the club."

Jamie's phone rang. "Matt, what's up?" A pause. "Nothing? You've lost him?" More silence. "I'll let him know. We have one more day at the club before we take off for Telluride. Maybe you'll have a tag on him by then." She ended the call.

"Nothing?" Colin said.

"No. Planchet managed to fall off the radar again. He's slick."

Colin sighed. "And, there's no way we're going to the club tomorrow."

"I can do it. I promise to be a good girl next time. A good little subbie."

Colin touched her cheek. "Somehow, I doubt it. I'll take the night off. Honestly, I need a break. Somehow, seeing the club through your eyes changed everything tonight. In some ways, I guess I've become immune to some of these behaviors. I'm not sure that's okay anymore."

Jamie huddled closer and took his hand. "Let's forget about it. We're getting distracted from the case. My focus needs to be on keeping you safe and finding this bomb fiend."

Colin pressed his cheek into her hair and closed his eyes. Maybe he'd get a second chance. A second chance to let Jamie know… he was falling in love. With her. Hopelessly and forever.

Chapter 30

The car garaged, Colin and Jamie said goodnight to James. They walked past the posted guards and entered the seaside mansion through the front door. Jamie threw her coat on the couch and sat heavily. "This time, *I* need a drink. A stiff one."

Colin laughed. "At your service, little subbie. You've earned it." He moved behind the bar and selected two glasses from the mirrored shelving. "Scotch?"

"Yes. Neat, please."

"Neat *and* stiff. Awesome."

She watched Colin pour three fingers of Macallan into cut-crystal glasses. She slipped off her heels, shimmied sideways and put her bare feet on the chaise end of the couch. She wiggled her toes, focusing on her crimson toenails, one of the few female rituals she always indulged in, although no one had seen them in... well, forever.

Colin handed her the drink and sat beside her. They sipped at the same time. "Mmm. Excellent," she said.

"I was hoping we could start over. Pretend this night never happened."

"It's fine. I don't hold it against you and I hope you won't against me."

"Done."

"You don't have to take tomorrow off."

"I want to. I think some rebooting is required. Daniel and Steve walked away. Maybe it's time."

Her wide eyes made him smile. He put a hand up. "I don't think I could go totally vanilla. I'm always going to be bossy in the bedroom."

Jamie sipped her drink. "That doesn't sound too terrible." Truthfully, she hated when a man asked for direction. Some women probably liked it but she'd rather have the guy in control, a guy who knew how to pleasure a woman. Something she'd never openly admitted to herself before.

"You think you might be interested in trying new things? Maybe some kink?"

"Maybe. Not everything at the club was unacceptable."

Colin sat up and faced her. "I knew it. I thought you were getting into some of it. What did you find intriguing?"

Now Jamie put her hand up. "I'm not ready to admit anything yet. But I do have some thinking to do."

"I'll take that as a win, for now."

They talked about local politics and the state of current world affairs, finished their drinks and headed off to their respective rooms. "Good night," Colin said, his hand on the bedroom doorknob. "Maybe we'll catch a movie tomorrow, get some lunch out. I'd like to pretend we're two normal people spending a Saturday together."

"Sounds nice. Night." And she disappeared into her room.

Colin decided he needed a shower and let the warm jets pummel his body, washing the tension from his muscles. He wiped the mist from the mirror and rubbed his chin, his five o'clock shadow well into midnight. Teeth brushed, he fingered his wet hair and slid beneath the gray sheets. His mind whirred, recounting the night's events. Yeah, a total clusterfuck, but maybe he'd escaped unscathed. He wanted Jamie. Wanted her bad. Maybe, just maybe, she'd come around. And he wanted to make her climax. Hard and often.

JAMIE SHED HER CLOTHING, strewing them across the bedside chair. She threw her shoes and one pounded the wall. What a night. She'd screwed up and probably trashed Colin's reputation at the club. It sounded like he'd forgiven her and even had him rethinking his membership there. She hadn't seen that coming.

She ran a brush through her hair, studying her reflection in the bathroom mirror. The fancy demi-bra Colin bought her to wear with the evening gown made her breasts alluring. She placed a hand under each cup and squeezed, deepening her cleavage. Her blood thrummed, thinking of Colin in the next room. No denying the club aroused her carnal instincts. She wished she'd brought her vibrator. Of course, packing it in front of Colin would have been entirely inappropriate. Still.

Sitting on the bedside, she sighed, running her fingers over the pale yellow quilt. She fell backward landing on the mountain of pillows and stared at the ceiling. Did she dare? Talk about inappropriate, this would be about as naughty as one could get. The ceiling fan whirled, yet did nothing to cool her burning desire.

She gave two sharp raps on his door.

"Come," he said.

Well, she hoped so. If Alyx and Laura were any testament to the quality of their lovers, she might have the best night of her life.

She pushed the door open and met semi-darkness. A hint of moonlight from the large window cast a shimmery glow over the bedchamber. The stars twinkled in the cobalt sky. Colin lay under the covers, his bare chest exposed, hands behind his head. Clad in her underwear, she took a few steps toward the foot of the bed.

"I'm naked here," Colin whispered.

"I hope so."

"Is that the bra I bought you?"

"Guilty."

"You look incredibly sexy in it."

"Thank you, Sir." She cast her eyes downward like a submissive.

"And I bet you look even sexier without it."

Glancing up, just enough light revealed the quirk in his smile. She offered, "I... I couldn't sleep."

"Me either."

"Maybe we need to relieve stress."

"Then come over here and feel my Zen." He crooked his finger then patted the sheets with both hands.

She padded over to the side of the bed. Colin sat up and grabbed her waist. The heat of his touch seared her flesh. He yanked her onto the bed beside him and slung one leg over her thighs, his erection pressed into her belly. "We really going to do this?"

"I think we are."

"Birth control?"

"Covered. And I always get tested after I stop seeing someone."

"We get tested regularly at the club."

He covered her mouth with his, their tongues entwining in a long, slow union. He caressed the side of her face and plundered her mouth again. Her chest rose and pressed into his, her hand grasping his neck to bring him closer. She wedged a leg between his thighs and forced him onto his back and covered him with her body.

"Fancy move, darling. But your flirting with danger. I'm a Dominant and there'll be no topping from the bottom." He kissed her deeply, thoroughly. Her mouth all pink and wet, swollen from his kisses. What would they feel like around his cock? If she knew the dark things he wanted to do to her she'd run screaming. He could play at vanilla sex but he wanted more. His needs demanded to be sated. "Just to be clear, the Dominant is the top and the submissive is the bottom. The top is in control and the bottom submits."

"Yes."

"So, you want to play?"

"Affirmative."

"Here are the rules. If I give an order your response will be, Yes, Sir."

"Okay."

"Nope. Try again."

"I mean, yes... yes, Sir."

"Better." He ran a finger across the top of her lacy bra. He blew his warm breath on her neck, then pressed his lips against her skin. His hands grasped her buttocks and squeezed, then slipped underneath the soft beige satin. He massaged the flesh and it warmed under his touch. "I've wanted you since I first set eyes on you in that damned shop."

She splayed her hands on his chest and pushed back. "What? When I made a total ass of myself? You found that attractive?"

Her long hair draped his shoulders and he reached up and smoothed it down her back. "I was enchanted."

Colin's hands slid up her spine and released the clasp securing her bra. He dragged the straps down her shoulders, ever so slowly, his fingertips making her skin tingle. Pressing her onto the mattress again, he threw the lacy garment over his shoulder. He cupped one breast in his hand and she moaned.

Colin inhaled Jamie's intoxicating scent, like something warm and sweet just out of the oven. He nibbled her neck and she giggled, curling into him. His lips found a taut nipple and he laved it in rhythmic strokes. She pressed her breast against his lips, urging him to take more. More, more. He sucked hard and she slung a leg over him, hugging him closer.

Nose-to-nose, he whispered, "If you think this is going to be like a date with your vibrator, you're in for a disappointment. Sex is not a race. I intend to take my time."

"Promises, promises." Her warm breath tickled his chin.

He nipped her lower lip, then retreated. "I consider it more of a threat."

"Do your worst, Sir. I can take it." She draped her arms around his neck.

A laugh rumbled through his chest. "Oh darling. You're being brave, but don't poke the bear."

"I'm an FBI agent. I like living dangerously."

"Be careful what you wish for, my dear. I'm a professional."

She kissed him hard and he responded, probing her mouth with his tongue. He wanted to explore every inch of her, stimulate each erogenous zone, find every sensitive spot. Give her more pleasure than any human being deserved.

He knelt between her knees and removed her panties, landing them on the floor, then planted her heels on either side of him. "God, you are so beautiful. Your body is magnificent and I'm going to plunder all of it. Take what I want. Take, take, take. And you will submit."

"I will… Sir," she said in a breathy whisper.

He stroked her thighs, his hands drifting down her calves. "You know what a safe word is?"

"Yes." He hovered over her, his hair falling into those sexy blue eyes. She wanted his hands everywhere. She wanted her mouth on his dick.

"Pick one."

She considered her choice. "Red."

Colin secured her wrists in his strong grip and pinned them against the mattress. "So, if I make you uncomfortable or hurt you, you say your safe word and everything stops. Got it?"

"Yes, Sir."

"Good. Are you good with oral sex?"

"Yes, Sir. Good with, and good at, too."

"Anal?"

"Oh… Sir. Never done it."

"Well, that's down the line. We'll do some exploring and you let me know how it feels." His fingers groped her vagina and she gasped. "Easy, darling. We're just getting started."

Chapter 31

Colin's Dom persona roared to life, like a feral animal after a too-long hibernation. He'd love to give her an order and watch her try to disobey. He'd enjoy paddling her sweet round ass. But for now, go *slow*.

He raised one hand over her head, anchoring it to the pillow. Then the other, clasping her wrists in one man-sized hand.

"Hey," she said.

"I'm going to give you your first lesson about being a submissive. I know you're interested."

"How?"

"Do not speak without permission. You are to stay silent, obedient. I tell you what to do and you serve me."

"You can't do whatever you want. I mean—"

"Either use your safe word or do exactly as I say."

Jamie's heart thudded wildly. If she agreed, and she already had, she realized he held all the power. The idea of Colin taking what he wanted heated her skin. Her insides coiled tighter and tighter. She'd never felt such desire, and so desired.

"If you don't obey then I will redden that pretty ass of yours."

Oh no. Years of not buckling to a man warred with the bewildering need to obey. And yet the thought of a spanking made her wet… *wetter.* Pain and pleasure. Who knew it would be such a turn-on? She'd always seen herself as strong, confident. Why did he have this effect on her?

Her hands still pinned above her head, he took her mouth hard, retreated, then dropped his head to the curve of her neck. Velvety lips and the scratch of his beard awakened a flutter deep in her belly. A sharp nip on her lower lip, his tongue plunged inside and he sucked her tongue into his mouth. His kisses were skilled, experienced, overwhelming. The ache of longing burned low in her belly. His fingers circled a nipple, rolling the peak. It bunched and arousal spiked her core. Fire, flesh on flesh, the unknowable sea.

He pushed her breast upward so he could take it into his mouth, then bit down carefully on her nipple. The pain sizzled right to her clit. His tongue hot and wet, his breath cool on her wet flesh. Her back arched, pushing her nipple upward. Each touch a spark of sensation. Beauty, terror. An involuntary clench inside.

"I'm going to finger fuck you until you come." He pushed a finger into her vagina, hard and fast. He added another finger. The intensity frightening. Her legs quivered.

He rolled onto her, his weight flattening her to the bed, and released his grasp on her wrists. Nudging her legs further apart with his knees, he slid down and settled his lips between her thighs. With one finger he stroked between her labia then back up to circle her clit. His fingers never slowed, never increased. Never touched the nub, where the craving was most intense. Her hips lifted, urging him on.

He raised his head. "You can't make me go faster, in fact, you can't do anything at all."

She buried her hands in his thick hair as his tongue continued to probe her wet folds. "Oh God."

Colin's fingers slid in and out, massaging, probing. So wet. He decided he'd tortured her long enough and knew she was struggling to delay her orgasm. Even though he'd convinced her he was in control, the truth was the submissive held the power, one word and he'd be done. He didn't want to push her too far. "Now, baby. Come for me."

She bore down on his hand, her thighs quivering, and shrieked, "Jesus Christ!"

He milked her spasms, drawing out her orgasm, as she said in the rawest of whispers, "Oh Jesus, straight to hell."

Colin pulled his hand away and grasped her hand, settling it on her stomach. "Not sure Jesus had anything to do with that." He smirked, then leaned in for another kiss. Jamie's panting breaths tickled his lips and he laughed. "Sort of like you just finished a marathon."

"Amazing."

"Well, catch your breath darling, we're only partway through this journey."

"What? I'm shot, I can't do that again."

"You will. I will get you there."

"No way…"

He placed his fingers on her lips. "Are you arguing with your Dom?"

Jamie's eyes grew wide. "Ah…no. I don't think…"

"You're over-thinking. You've given me control and I intend to use it until you come again." Jamie's lips tightened as she struggled to keep silent. He went on, "You're not as vanilla as you appear."

He knelt between her thighs and massaged her clit with two fingers and focused on her dark jade eyes. "Hold on to the headboard. I'm going to take you hard." He circled the head of his dick around her swollen nub, probing slowly, then deeper. He slammed into her. Jamie moaned, her hands gripping the brass spindles over her head. He pulled out and rammed in again, picking up the pace into a pounding rhythm. He lay atop her warm flesh and slid his hands under her ass. "You feel fantastic, baby," he murmured, his speed increasing. She squirmed under him, writhing in rhythm with his thrusts.

Jamie couldn't believe she wanted it again. Her excitement increased, the tension building to that magnificent crest, desperate for release. His fingers slid over her clit, making her jolt. Her hips convulsed, and another moan escaped. His merciless cock never slowed. Too much. The torment on her clit, him deep inside, threatened to send her over the edge.

"Now," he growled. And then he pressed deep, and she could feel his cock jerking as they came together. He slid in and out slowly, drawing out the waves of pleasure.

They lay still for an extended moment, then he rolled off and pulled her close, tucking her head under his chin. His fingers ran up and down her spine then settled on her shoulder. "You okay, little subbie?"

"I might have seen the face of God," she murmured.

He kissed the top of her head. "Well, I was in heaven right there with you."

"I've never felt anything like that. I didn't know, I just didn't know."

Chapter 32

J amie woke, disoriented. Her cheek rested on the hollow of a man's shoulder, nice and muscular. Her arm lay across his broad chest, her leg tucked between his thighs. She opened her eyes to meet Colin's bright blue orbs. *Egad. She'd slept with him.*

"Morning," he said. "Did you sleep well?"

"Possibly. You?"

"Like a baby. For a few hours, I forgot an old friend is trying to kill me. I won't lie, it was fucking awesome." His fingertips touched her cheek, drifting toward her lips. He parted them with his thumb. "I love these lips. I love every inch of you."

Well, at least he didn't say he loved her. "Last night was fun. You've got mad skills, mister."

Colin chuckled. "Lots more to explore." He snuggled closer, his erection pressing against her belly.

Now she worried. Colin had every intention of continuing this relationship and she got the distinct impression he was looking for something serious. But she wasn't interested in a relationship. How to handle this? She could blurt it out now, yet that seemed rude. He'd been wonderful to her, and the sex? The best ever. Except she still must serve as his bodyguard.

However, with the case stalled she needed a conference with Rob and Matt. This couldn't go on indefinitely.

She took his hand, lacing her fingers through his. "Colin, last night was great, really great, but still a mistake. I allowed myself to be vulnerable, something I rarely do and if my boss found out I'd be in serious trouble."

Colin narrowed his eyes. "I don't get it. Alyx had sex with Daniel and that seemed fine with your boss."

"Because it was her assignment and I have to admit it was unorthodox. I'm surprised the Bureau condoned it."

"That's because Rob knows——" Colin released her hand and lay on his back, resting a forearm across his mouth.

Jamie propped herself up on one elbow and her hand landed on the soft dark hair on his chest. "What were you going to say? Rob knows what?"

His hand migrated to his forehead. "Not what… who."

"Spill."

"I probably shouldn't say anything." He moved his arm off his brow and turned toward her.

"You started something. Finish."

Colin inhaled and exhaled slowly. "Rob and Jack are friends."

"Jack, from the club?"

"Yeah, they were in the Marines together and did the club circuit in Tampa when they first got out, when they were in college."

"Rob is a Dom?"

"Yeah, I know he told Alyx."

"So, you knew him all along?"

"It's more like I know *of* him."

"Does he play at the club?"

"No, he has a submissive who lives with him. She's an ADA in Nassau County."

Now, Jamie rolled onto her back, her hands on her mouth. Holy shit. Were Doms everywhere? Daniel, Steve, Colin, and now Rob? How about Matt... although he did joke about joining the club to impress his wife. But he seemed too sweet, and a few times on the job she got the distinct feeling *she* had more balls.

Colin placed his warm hand on her shoulder and turned her toward him. "I don't think Rob is the problem. I think it's you. Haven't you been in other relationships?"

"Not anything serious."

"No one in D.C.?"

"There was someone. He was a lobbyist for the NSF. Let's just call him a friend with benefits."

"Why aren't you interested in something more serious?"

She huffed. "I don't have time for a relationship. Too many people need to be saved. My job is my marriage." She paused. "And I seem to recall you saying work was your mistress when we officially met. I got the distinct impression you weren't interested in a serious relationship either."

"Maybe I've changed my mind. Maybe *you* changed my mind."

"That's absurd. You don't even know me."

"Alyx, Laura, and Molly are married with kids. Even Matt, doesn't he have a wife and two kids?"

"You don't understand. It's different for me." Jamie pulled back the covers and sat on the bedside. Colin grabbed her arm but she wrenched away, retrieving her underwear off the floor. She donned the panties, the bra dangling from her hand, arms sheltering her bare breasts.

"Let's not ruin this. It was great, but a one-time thing. I'm still on the job and I promise not to take advantage of you again." She strode out of his room.

COLIN POUNDED one fist on the mattress. Damn. He'd pushed her too hard and too fast. However, she was right, he often flaunted the fact that he wasn't interest in a serious relationship. Much to his mother's dismay. But what was she afraid of? He thought all women wanted a husband and perhaps kids, too. At least most... He'd started out that way, yet his heart had been broken twice and finally he abandoned the idea of meeting someone compatible. Now, he guarded himself, his heart. His sanity. Except Jamie treated him differently. She didn't care about his money. She challenged him at every turn. So many things seemed different. He was sure he was in love with her. Could he convince her that she could love him back?

He showered and dressed and headed downstairs, stopping to view the roiling ocean pounding the shore. "Exactly how I feel," he said to the sea. He clasped his hands behind his neck and squeezed his arms over his ears, then moved to the kitchen. "Shit."

Would Jamie still want to go to lunch and see a movie? Maybe she'd called Rob and asked to be removed from the case. If she had, he'd be crestfallen.

He filled the coffeemaker with fresh grinds and water and pushed the start button, then retrieved milk from the fridge. Setting out two mugs, a spoon and sugar, he leaned on the cold stone counter and sighed.

"Don't be mad. Please, don't." He hadn't heard her enter. All fresh-faced and dewy, dressed in skinny jeans and a pale blue sweater. He wanted to force her into his arms and kiss her until she couldn't remember her name.

"I'm not mad. I'm disappointed."

"Oh God, that's worse." She came close and took his hand, her eyes searching his. "I didn't mean for this to happen. I'm sorry."

"I'm grown. My eyes were wide open."

"Good, then let's compartmentalize this for now. I don't regret sleeping with you."

"Then you'll keep the door open? We can see where this goes after the case is solved?"

"A window… maybe."

PANIC KNOTTED JAMIE'S GUT. How had she gotten herself into this? No way could Colin be in love, not with her. They'd only known each other a few days and she was not a believer in love at first sight. In fact, she didn't think love was something one could count on. True, her parents seemed crazy for each other after thirty years of marriage, but she was convinced that was an anomaly. The divorce rate in America was astronomical. Plus, her genetics probably reduced her odds. Her biological mother couldn't handle a relationship and kids. There was that proverbial apple again, lying at the foot of an ugly gnarled tree.

Colin handed her a steaming mug of coffee. "Thanks."

"You still up for lunch and a movie?"

"Sure."

"We'll head back to the city tonight. The *helo* is scheduled for five."

Her phone rang. "Mom?"

"Jamie, it's your father, he's had a heart attack. We're at the hospital."

"Oh my God, no. How is he?"

"They're doing tests now. We should know something soon."

"What happened?"

"I was in the kitchen and heard a thump upstairs. I found him on the floor in the bathroom. He wasn't breathing. I called 911 and did CPR until they arrived. We revived him."

"Oh, Mom. I'll jump on the first plane."

"All right, darling. See you soon."

"What is it?" Colin said.

"My dad. He's had a heart attack. I need to go. I can call Rob and get someone to replace me."

"I'll take you. I have a plane."

"You have a helicopter *and* a plane?"

"Are we going to do the spoiled rich guy thing again?"

Jamie shook her head. "No. I'm sorry."

"I'll make the arrangements. We can be on our way in an hour. Go pack."

Chapter 33

Colin dumped the freshly made coffee in the sink and hurried to his room to pack an overnight bag. He called and cancelled the helicopter and scheduled the flight to Lake Placid. Returning to the kitchen, he placed his packed bag on a kitchen stool and stashed the mugs and cutlery in the dishwasher, dumping the coffee grinds in the garbage. She snuck up on him again.

"I called Rob and told him what happened. He said everything was status quo and as long as you were with me, I'm technically still on the job. With an unexpected change in routine like this, it's unlikely the perp would be able to target you on such short notice. Plus, we'll be in another locale."

"Fine by me." Colin leaned his butt against the counter and crossed his arms over his chest. "Were you planning on asking Rob to take you off the case? You know, because of our indiscretion?"

"I did consider it. But no. It was my error and it doesn't excuse me from completing my assignment."

Colin's throat constricted. He was just *an assignment*. Well, what did he expect? He was the one turning this into something else. It was his fault things were uncomfortable. And he was determined to change that. This assignment would have a happily-ever-after. What? He kinda scared himself. When had he become *that guy?* Yet he couldn't deny that this formidable special agent had stolen his heart with no hope of getting it back.

"Ready?" Jamie said, pulling him from his fairytale musings.

"Yes." Colin exited the kitchen and Jamie trailed.

"Great. I'll let my mom know."

"The itinerary says we'll arrive at noon. A car will be waiting for us at the Lake Placid airport." He opened the coat closet and retrieved their coats. Jamie was close enough to touch.

She placed a hand on his arm. "Thank you for this, Colin. It means the world to me."

"Glad I can help." He kissed the top of her head, then helped her into her jacket. "Let's go."

James sat in the Range Rover out front and they traveled the twenty minutes to Gabreski Airport in Westhampton Beach. After napping during most of the smooth flight, they landed in Lake Placid on time and a waiting attendant handed over keys to a white Tahoe. "The vehicle has been inspected by your advance security team. It's clean."

"Thanks," Colin said.

They found Jamie's mother in the hospital waiting room, a man and woman bookending her on the green plastic seats.

"Mom." Jamie ran and threw herself into Sally Gallagher's arms, inhaling the familiar baby powder scent. They held each other at arm's length. "How is he?"

"In surgery. They're replacing two valves. We hope to hear something soon."

"How long has he been in surgery?"

"About two hours. They said it could take up to four, depending."

The man and woman embraced her. He said, "Glad you got here so fast. Getting out of New York City can be a challenge."

Jamie pulled Colin into the family circle. "Luckily, I have a friend with a private jet." Everyone gave Colin weary smiles. "This is Colin MacKenzie. Colin, this is my Aunt Jessica and my Uncle Marcus, and my mom, Sally."

Her mom, aunt, and uncle shook Colin's hand. Uncle Marcus said, "Thank you so much, Mr. MacKenzie. It means a lot to have Jamie here."

"I'm grateful I could be of service."

Colin's head spun. He'd gone from lover, to *assignment*, to friend, in under four hours. He didn't know what to think. Maybe he should just stop thinking.

The waiting party settled into seats, Jamie next to her mother, their fingers laced together.

College hockey broadcasted on the small waiting room TV. With all the crazy shit going on he'd momentarily forgotten the Giants were in the playoffs. He and Steve were huge Giants fans and often watched the games together in the days before Steve met Laura. He should call Steve and see how Laura was doing. She was likely getting impatient, and jealous, now that Alyx delivered. He should call Daniel too. They were probably home by now and sleep deprived with the arrival of their son. Colin hadn't thought much about having kids in recent years. In high school, he and Steve would muse about marriage. Their wives would be best friends and their kids too. Then they sort of fell off the marriage wagon after a string of disappointing relationships. They rationalized the whole Dom-thing didn't translate into anything long-term. And then Steve met Laura and now… well, Colin could see himself with Jamie and those nostalgic imaginings might actually come true. Who'd-a-thunk?

"You a hockey fan?" Marcus said.

"Nope. Football."

"Yeah, me too."

"Who's your team," Marcus said.

"The Giants, you?"

"To the death," Marcus said. "The last few seasons haven't been great. But this year might be a comeback."

"Fingers crossed."

A couple walked in behind a small boy on crutches. Not the temporary kind like when a bone breaks, the permanent kind necessary with a disability, his gait awkward, his legs twisted. He tripped and fell on his hands and knees, his crutches splayed beside him. Jamie ran to the boy's aid before anyone else. She picked him up and righted him, offering his crutches. Once stabilized she said, "You okay, little man?"

"Comes with the territory."

"You sure? Nothing hurts?"

"Nah, I fall down all the time. I bounce well." He pushed his dark-rimmed glasses up his nose. Jamie's face brightened and she ruffled his hair.

"Thank you," his mother said. "You're very kind."

Jamie placed both hands on his shoulders. "No problem. Glad to help. He's one tough dude. You must be very proud."

"We are."

Jamie returned to her seat and Colin sat in awe. No doubt Jamie had a compulsion to help others. Maybe an irrational one due to her rough start in life. He hadn't given much thought to her admissions about her terrible childhood, before the Gallaghers came along. There were probably psychological repercussions. Abandoned by her mother, not knowing who her father was... and he recalled her disabled brother. This kid most likely hit that sore spot. Her little brother died and although her father assured

Jamie he'd been placed in a loving family, she still probably felt like she'd abandoned him.

A man in scrubs entered the waiting room. Jamie's family stood as he approached. "Mr. Gallagher did well. No complications. He should be home in a few days."

Jamie's mother threw her arms around the doctor. "Thank you. Thank you so much."

The doctor patted her back. "He's one lucky guy. Everyone did their job, including you and the EMTs. If you hadn't given him CPR, we'd have a very different outcome."

"Can we see him?" Jessica said.

"Yes. I'll send a nurse out as soon as he's out of recovery. Within the hour."

"Thank you," Marcus said.

The doctor exited and the waiting party exhaled a collective sigh of relief.

Jamie chewed on a fingernail. "Thank God," she uttered. "I don't know what I would have done if he didn't make it." Colin wanted to take her in his arms to comfort her. Instead, Marcus did.

"He's going to be fine. He'll be back on the slopes before you know it," Marcus said.

"Yeah," Jessica said. "Can't keep that man off the mountain."

Skiing. Colin thought of his upcoming trip with his parents. Would he need to cancel it? Would Jamie come? With her father ill she might need to stay by his side.

Chapter 34

The bedside monitor beeped steadily, the neon-green graph writhing in rhythm. Mr. Gallagher appeared in peaceful slumber. Colin held back while Jamie approached from the left, her mother on the right. Jamie took his hand in hers. "Daddy?" she whispered.

Colin recalled Jamie saying her adopted father sported red hair like hers—now lightened by a spate of silver, and that there'd been an instant connection. Mr. Gallagher's eyelids fluttered open. A few seconds passed before he recognized his daughter.

"Sweetheart," he muttered. "What are you doing here?"

"Daddy, you had a heart attack. I came as soon as I heard." She leaned in and kissed his cheek."

"But you have work. You shouldn't have traipsed all the way up here. I'm fine."

His wife said, "Well, you weren't fine a few hours ago. You scared us half to death."

"Sally, my darling, hard to keep an old coot like me down. I'm made of tough stuff." Sally Gallagher frowned but didn't dispute her husband's claim. "We'll be back on the slopes soon, right, Jamie?"

"Let's hope," Jamie said.

John Gallagher surveyed the room. "Called in the troops, I see." He focused on Colin. "And who's this strapping young man?" He eyed Jamie. "Something I should know?"

"He's a friend. Dad, this is Colin MacKenzie."

"Nice to meet you, Mr. Gallagher," Colin said, coming closer. "Jamie's told me a lot about you."

"Has she now? All good, I hope."

"The best."

"Mr. MacKenzie has a private jet and flew Jamie up here," Sally Gallagher said. "That was very nice of him."

"That it was." John Gallagher frowned. "Aren't you the guy on the news? The one whose place of business nearly got blown up? And then at your residence?"

"Accurate," Colin said.

John Gallagher asked Jamie, "You on the case?"

"Yes. I'm responsible for Colin's safety until we catch the guy."

Since John Gallagher was also in law enforcement he was likely interested in the case from that perspective. "Bodyguard duty? I thought you left D.C. to get away from that gig."

"Sometimes you don't get a say, right, Daddy? You have to follow orders."

And... he was back to being an assignment. Emotional whiplash.

After some polite banter and expressions of relief, John Gallagher dozed off and Colin approached Jamie. "Can we talk outside for a minute?"

"Of course." She followed Colin into the hallway.

"If I have to cancel our ski trip, I will. I'll have to make a few phone calls."

"Oh, I almost forgot. Um, I don't know what to do. I could ask the Bureau to send someone in my place."

"Jamie, I don't want someone in your place. I'm happy to cancel or postpone. Whatever you think best."

Jamie paced, nibbling on a finger. She stopped and leaned her back against the white-tiled wall. "If he's stable, I'd consider leaving. I hate to disappoint your parents."

"They can handle it and even go on their own if they want. We could catch up in a day or two."

"It's only Saturday, can we wait until tomorrow?"

"Sure."

JOHN GALLAGHER CATNAPPED MOST of the afternoon, his family at his bedside. The nurse came in several times to check on him, as did the doctor before he left for the day. He finally woke to eat his dinner. Jamie cut the chicken into small pieces and buttered his roll. She poured cola into a Styrofoam cup and added ice. "You're not going to feed me," her father told her. "I have some dignity left."

Jamie smiled and Colin's heart swelled at her love for her father. If he'd died, he could only imagination how devastated she'd be. It would rock her foundation and he was glad he didn't have to witness that.

"What about you all? Have you eaten anything?" John Gallagher said, forking a piece of chicken. Nobody responded and he said, "Go feed yourselves. I don't need anyone fainting from hunger. Now go!" He flicked his hand at them. The posse headed for the door, when Mr. Gallagher added, "Except you, Mr. MacKenzie. I'd like to have a word with you. He'll meet you in the cafeteria."

An uncomfortable silence permeated the room. Colin agreed, "Go ahead. Order me anything, Jamie."

Alone with Mr. Gallagher, he watched him take a few bites of dinner before putting down his silverware and taking a sip of cola. "Sit," he said and Colin settled into the bedside chair. His clear green eyes held Colin's gaze. "You're in love with my daughter."

Colin's eyebrows hiked up. "Excuse me?"

"Nothing wrong with your hearing, son, is there?"

"Ah… no…"

"I can see it all over your face."

Colin continued to stammer. "I've only known her a few days…"

"Makes no matter. I knew I was in love with Sally the second I laid eyes on her. At the State Fair that day. And then her pies sealed the deal. I knew I was going to marry that woman."

Colin's throat constricted. He was unprepared for this conversation with Jamie's father. And he had the distinct impression Mr. Gallagher was adept at interrogation, and truth would be his only alternative. "She's not interested in a relationship."

"Of course she isn't. She's terrified. Never had a serious boyfriend. She may look like a tough cookie on the outside, but inside she's a wounded bird. Are you familiar with her beginnings?"

"She mentioned a few things."

"She was found in a crappy motel room with her eighteen-month-old brother. The baby suffered from cerebral palsy. There was only a small amount of spoiled milk in the refrigerator. She went out in a thunderstorm to buy milk to feed him and two police officers spotted her. Her mother was out turning tricks and she was alone with the baby. She wasn't even five and weighed less than thirty pounds. Hadn't been to school."

Colin's heart twisted as he pictured a tiny, frail, Jamie in some sordid motel minding her little brother, then venturing out on a stormy night to get milk. "That's horrible. I can't imagine anyone treating a child like that."

"Me either. She bounced around in the foster care system until we found her. She was nine and I knew she was mine the moment I saw her. That beautiful red hair... and she had spunk. When we met her, she walked right up to me, barely as tall as my belt buckle and said, Why do you want to be my daddy?" John Gallagher's face lit up with the memory and Colin could sense how much he loved Jamie.

Colin smiled. "And what did you say?"

"I knelt so we were eye-to-eye and told her I loved Sally and she loved me, and we took care of each other, but we needed more love in our lives. I told her I wanted to love and take care of her."

Colin could hardly swallow past the lump in his throat. Finally, he said, "What did she say?"

Again, John Gallagher smiled, a twinkle in his watery eyes. "She studied my face for a long time, then Sally's. She wrapped her small hand around my index finger and said, Okay, let's go."

Colin's eyes welled and he clenched them closed to stop the tears. He couldn't utter a single syllable.

"I don't think the feelings of abandonment ever leave someone who's been traumatized at such a fragile age, so she's still compensating by being the best at everything she does. First in her class pretty much everywhere. Won an Olympic gold medal, went to the Naval Academy. The list is too long. She *over*compensates, afraid if she isn't perfect, she'll be abandoned, unloved. Her mother and I have tried hard to make her understand she is loved and valued even when she's not perfect, but it's a hard sell. She's hard-wired that way and doesn't even know she's doing it. She's had plenty of therapy but all the therapy in the world won't erase that."

"I get it, sir. Totally."

"So, son, here's the deal. You hang in there, be patient. I wooed Sally for six months before she finally went out with me. Only fools rush in and I don't take you for a fool."

"Honestly, that was my plan, sir. As soon as this horrible situation is resolved, and hopefully I'm still alive, I have faith she'll come around."

"Good. This heart attack has made me worry. My girl needs a nest, a foundation. Her mother and I won't always be here."

"I understand."

"I'm holding you to your word. Now go get something to eat."

"Yes, sir," Colin said. He stood and Mr. Gallagher held out his hand. Colin shook it.

"I like you, Mr. MacKenzie and I have the distinct impression you know how to close a deal."

"I do. But Jamie is so much more."

"That she is."

Chapter 35

Jamie spied Colin across the dining room and waved. He took the empty seat beside her where a cheeseburger and fries awaited. "What did Daddy want?"

"Just curious about the case. Making sure you're all right." Colin shoved two fries into his mouth. He hadn't eaten anything since the few sips of coffee that morning and was starving. He bit into his burger.

"It's not too cold, is it?" Jamie said.

"It's fine. I didn't realize I was so hungry. I'd eat it cold and still be happy."

"Really? That's all Daddy wanted?"

"Yup. I think he was checking up on his little girl with an objective observer. He's very protective of you." Everyone else was half-way through their food and it didn't take Colin long to catch up. "Have you decided about our plans for tomorrow?"

"What plans?" Jessica said.

Jamie answered, "Colin is taking his parents on a ski trip for their anniversary."

"Oh, that's lovely," Sally Gallagher said. "Where?"

"Telluride," Jamie said.

Colin chewed and swallowed, taking a sip of water. "It sounded like a good idea until all this bombing stuff happened. I was going to cancel but then they sighted a guy they think might be involved in Telluride and I agreed to act as bait."

"Colin!" Jamie exclaimed. "We're not supposed to discuss the case."

"Oops, forgot. But we're in safe company, right?"

"Yes, but still…"

"Bait?" Marcus said. "The FBI does stuff like that?"

"No," Jamie said. "No one has agreed to let Colin be bait. We were still debating him even going to Telluride, but then Dad got sick and we're here. I haven't been in touch with the Bureau since this morning." She glanced at her phone. "I should probably check in. Excuse me." With her usual confident gait, she exited to the hallway.

JAMIE CONFERRED with Matt and all agreed to follow through on the ski trip to Telluride. They weren't using the word *bait* as they didn't plan on dangling Colin out anywhere unprotected. Rob and Matt, along with a contingent of local FBI personnel were on their way there now. Matt said everyone at the office was sending good wishes for her dad and pressed Jamie on whether she was up to the task. She assured him she was. "What about the attorney? Anything new on him?"

"He's in the Cayman Islands. Sounds suspect and we've sent a team down to find him."

"You said the lawyer took advantage of the Planchets."

"Looks that way. As I said, the dad was terminally ill and when he realized they were so deep in debt and they'd lost the company at auction, he killed himself. I think the sons might be out for revenge. Only they think Colin was behind this, that's why they've targeted him. If we could only get them to understand it was the lawyer and Colin had nothing to do with it."

"Agreed."

"On that note, Rob and I have decided to release details to the media. If we plaster the guy's picture over the airwaves and social media, we might get a hit. You okay with that?"

"I guess so. Not sure Colin wants it blasted all over the place but it really might move things along. I know he wants to give the impression that he's not running scared."

"Yeah, but these guys are so tech-savvy, I'm reasonably sure they can track him without much effort. I'd expect them to be right around the corner at every turn. However, if we could find them and explain that Colin isn't the culprit maybe we could stop them. Anyway, the ski trip is a go. We'll sweep his place before you get there and it's unlikely they could bomb the mountain, so we'll be on the lookout for the brothers in case they have some other tricks up their sleeves."

JAMIE DIDN'T RETURN to the cafeteria so Colin and her family made their way to Mr. Gallagher's room. The nurse was checking vitals again, completely charmed by her patient, praising him for delivering her new granddaughter in the backseat of the family car recently. Jamie arrived a few minutes later and the clan engaged in upbeat conversation and no one would suspect they'd suffered a near tragedy.

John Gallagher scrubbed his face with his large hands. "I'm beat, so I think you should all go home so I can rest."

"Are you sure, darling? I'm happy to stay," Sally Gallagher said.

"Nope, you all go. I'll see you tomorrow."

"We'll stay at the house tonight and stop by before we leave tomorrow," Jamie said.

John Gallagher's gaze narrowed. "You need to get back to work. And make sure you take good care of this man. I like him." Jamie peered at Colin. What had he really been talking about with her father? She tilted her head and squinted one eye at Colin, but his face gave no hint.

The family levied their kisses and goodbyes but as they exited, John Gallagher called Jamie back. "I need a minute with my girl."

"We'll wait in the lobby," Sally Gallagher said, and they left Jamie with her father.

He patted the bed and Jamie climbed up. He clasped her hand in both of his. "That boy is in love with you."

"Colin? That's ridiculous, Daddy. We've only known each other a few days. And this is work."

"It's written all over him."

"Oh my God. Is that what you talked to him about?"

"That's neither here nor there. I'm telling you, he's in love. With you."

"It's a lovely thought, but this isn't that. It's probably rescue-syndrome. I did save his life and we both know how that happens. How many women have thrown themselves at you after a rescue?"

"That's because I'm hot for an old guy. They can't help themselves."

"Yeah, you're lucky Mom puts up with that crap."

Her father squeezed her hand tightly. "I know you find it difficult to trust, but your mother and I won't always be around. You need a family of your own."

Jamie shook her head. "Daddy, I don't want—"

"Don't give me that crap about not wanting a family. You had a shitty start, but you know what a good family is and you'll make a good wife and mother."

"I can't. I have too much work to do. My work is my passion, to save as many people as I can for as long as I can. That's what I'm good at."

"I think you should give this guy a chance. I'm an excellent judge of character. He's a good man."

Jamie tugged her hand free and stood. "I can't talk about this anymore. I promise to think about what you said, but right now I have a case to solve and a target to protect."

John Gallagher frowned. "He's not a target. He's a man."

Jamie knew her father was right about Colin being a good man. And even though she logged him as a target in her brain, in her heart he was becoming so much more. But he would not be a target of her affections. No man would.

Chapter 36

Marcus and Jessica bid their farewells and Colin escorted Jamie and her mother to the white Tahoe as Sally Gallagher had arrived via ambulance, unwilling to leave her husband's side. They'd agreed to spend the night at her parents' house.

Jamie buckled her seat belt. "Just giving you a heads-up. We're releasing details of the case along with the Planchet brothers' pictures. So be prepared for a media circus."

"Shit," Colin said. "I was hoping to avoid that. Not sure my clients will be happy about the prospect of my imminent demise."

"It's on the news already so get over it. Circulating the suspects' pictures can't hurt."

"I guess." Colin exhaled forcefully.

They entered the driveway of a two-story gray colonial with navy-blue shutters and a detached two-car garage. A pair of deputies exited their parked cruiser. "Jamie, good to see you again. Sorry it's under bad circumstances. How's your pops?"

"Paul, so great to see you too." They hugged. "He's good for another hundred thousand miles."

"Super news. The house, garage and property are clear. We'll keep surveillance until you're gone."

"Thanks, we're leaving tomorrow morning." Paul tipped his hat and returned to his patrol car.

"High school boyfriend," Sally Gallagher whispered to Colin. "I think he broke her heart."

Colin frowned, but didn't comment. He carried both bags into the house, a veritable temple of garage sale antiques with a distinct nod to down-home goodness.

"Long day," Sally Gallagher said. She hung her royal-blue parka in the coat closet, then held out her hand for Colin's and Jamie's coats. "I'm going to make tea. Anybody want a cup?" She grabbed the kettle and filled it with water, then switched on the gas burner.

"No thanks," Jamie said.

"I think I need something stronger," Colin said.

"Help yourself. Jamie will show you the liquor options. I'm going up to change."

Jamie opened the double doors on a wooden buffet cabinet. "What's your poison?"

"Scotch if you have it."

She pulled out a bottle of Dewar's and two glasses and carried them to the kitchen island. "Rocks?"

"Please. And a splash or two of water." Colin leaned against the counter.

She filled the glasses with ice cubes, poured about three-fingers, then topped them off with water from the fridge.

"Thanks," Colin said, taking a sip. "Glad your dad is okay."

"Yeah. I don't know what I would've done if this had turned out differently." Jamie rubbed her temples then took a drink.

Colin wished he could share the conversation he had with John Gallagher, hoping to persuade Jamie to give him a chance, yet he didn't dare. As if reading his mind, Jamie said, "I know Daddy was pressuring you to pursue a relationship with me. I told him I wasn't interested. This health scare has him off-balance. He's not thinking straight."

"You seemed pretty enthusiastic when we were in bed last night."

"Ha-ha. I told you not to read into it."

The tea kettle whistled and Sally Gallagher appeared in the kitchen, her footsteps silenced by fuzzy slippers. "I heard nothing," she swore, making the sign of the cross.

Jamie stared at her mother who averted her gaze. "I made a mistake, Mom. Please don't tell Dad."

Friend, assignment, lover, mistake. Colin couldn't keep up and his temper flared. Maybe this was futile and he needed to rethink. He wasn't a doormat.

"I wouldn't dream of saying anything to upset your dad right now," Sally Gallagher said. She poured hot water into a mug and added a pyramidal tea bag from the canister atop the fridge. "I'm taking my tea upstairs. You can settle Colin into the guest bedroom... or wherever."

"*Mom.*"

"Lighten up, Jamie, I'm teasing. You're a fully grown woman and can do whatever you want. It wouldn't hurt you to loosen up and let your hair down once in a while."

"Mom!"

"Good night, Colin. Oh, and there's pie if you're interested." She pointed to a glass-covered dish on the counter alongside the refrigerator.

"Thank you, Mrs. Gallagher."

Jamie's phone rang. "Matt, what's up?" She listened, a frown marring her face. "Shit. Not good. We can't charge him now, which could've flushed Dave Planchet out and we could explain that Colin's not guilty." Silence again. "Okay, see you tomorrow."

She scrutinized Colin's face and he braced himself for bad news. "Your lawyer killed himself."

Colin blanched, but didn't respond.

"They closed in on him in the hotel but he had a gun. Bullet in the head. Dead at the scene."

Sally Gallagher gasped. "Oh Lord."

"Jesus," Colin said. "I can't believe it. I had lunch with him a few days ago, just before he headed out on vacation. I had no clue what was going on."

"I'm sorry. I know he was a friend," Jamie said.

"It's not that, I wanted to confront him. Ask him why he did it? Didn't I pay him enough?"

"There's no excuse for greed. People fall victim to it all the time. Although they're not victims, they do it by choice."

Colin dragged his hands down his face. "I guess. I'll never understand why people treat each other so terribly."

"Night," Sally said. "I'm sorry, Colin." She touched his forearm before heading to the stairs.

Jamie approached Colin, placing both palms on his firm chest. "I'm sure this whole thing is turning you inside out. It's horrible when people deceive you, someone you trusted, a friend."

Colin's eyes bored into her. "I'm just so conflicted. I love him and I hate him. He must have gotten himself into so much trouble and he saw no way out. I would have helped him."

"That's what everyone who is touched by suicide says. But that's about them, not the victim... wasn't I a good enough mother, father, sister, brother... friend? You can't blame yourself."

"Not that easy."

"I know." She dropped her hands. "How about some pie?" She walked to the counter and removed the cake-dish cover. "Lucky you. It's her triple berry delight, the one that earned a blue ribbon at the state fair. It's delish."

Colin squeezed the bridge of his nose. "Sold. I guess it will just take time, but right now I feel pretty shitty."

"Pie is joy, go for it." Jamie cut two slices and rested them on small black-and-white polka dot plates and secured two forks from the drawer. She carried them to the living room coffee table, Colin brought the drinks. They positioned themselves on the couch and Jamie flicked on the TV. "Not much on Saturday nights. Anything you want to watch?"

"Anything but the Hallmark Channel." Colin winked. Although maybe that would be a *good* idea. Maybe Jamie was more of a romantic than she admitted to herself. Good God, he was going over the edge.

Jamie narrowed her eyes. "Am I ever going to hear the end of that?"

"No chance. And I don't get it. You like romance on TV but not in real life?"

"Don't take it personally, Colin. You're a great guy but I don't picture myself in a long-term relationship."

"You forgot hot."

"What?"

"You said I was hot the other night, I'm holding onto that. Maybe my hotness will wear you down." He wagged his eyebrows.

Jamie punched him in the arm and laughed. "You're an ass."

"Ouch," he said, feigning injury and rubbing the offended spot.

Jamie scrolled through the channels, then resorted to the DVR to check recordings. They settled on *Last Week Tonight* with John Oliver as he spewed his weekly rant on the sad state of the country. Exhaustion hit and as the credits rolled, she announced, "I'm shot. Let's go to bed."

Colin's eyes widened, but before he said what she knew they were both thinking, she added, "Alone."

"Grinch."

She clicked off the television and returned the plates to the kitchen, stacking them in the dishwasher. Colin placed his empty glass on the counter and she put the glasses in with the dishes. They grabbed their bags and Jamie shut off the lights and they climbed the stairs. Jamie opened a door and ushered Colin inside. He dropped his bag on the red, white and blue quilt and faced Jamie. "Night, Agent Gallagher."

"Night." She closed the door and leaned her back against the sturdy wood. She sighed. His hotness *was* wearing her down. But she couldn't imagine herself in a relationship with Colin. He was a fucking billionaire. The thought terrified her, she'd be a total misfit. And yet Laura managed it just fine. No one would ever suspect her wealth and Steve seemed like a guy with simple tastes, as did Laura.

Entering her room, she stripped out of her clothes and tossed them on the chair in the corner. Her eyes landed on her bulletin board covered in citations, blue ribbons and medals. Over-achiever much? Her father's words resounded in her head. *Family of your own. You had a shitty start but you'll make a good wife and mother. He's a good man. Good man. Good man.*

She zipped open her duffle and retrieved her toiletry bag and PJs, or rather the oversized tee she slept in, then dropped the bag on the floor. She donned the shirt and trod toward the bathroom, settling her make-up case on the counter, she pulled out her toothbrush.

Foam bubbled over her lips and she reminded herself Colin was a job and she needed to nix the feelings she feared were blooming, like a victorious crocus pushing through the snow. Her father continued to speak to her. *He's not a target. He's a man.*

In bed, she pulled the pink quilted coverlet up to her chin. Smiling at the frilly pink-and-white striped lamp shade, she extinguished the bedside lamp. Her mother tried to make her a girly-girl yet it hadn't stuck. She closed her eyes and images of being in bed with Colin accelerated her pulse. At this rate she'd never get the sleep she so desperately required.

His hands massaging her breasts, pinching her nipples. His mouth between her legs. The weight of him pressing her into the mattress. Her cheeks burned. Her body coiled tighter and tighter.

He was next door… She slapped her cheek. *Stop thinking about him.* Except it was hopeless and eventually she drifted off. In a reverie, wrapped inside Colin's strong arms, protecting her from the wide ugly world. And then he whispered the most extraordinary words: *You waited all this time because you were waiting for me.*

Chapter 37

Colin woke to his alarm at 7:00 a.m. Considering the recent chain of events, he'd slept fairly well and yet he yearned to be back in his normal life, the gym, work, and nobody trying to kill him or his family. And yet he couldn't imagine Jamie being gone from his life. He'd never lived with a girlfriend. Senior year he and Kaitlyn rented an apartment, but she bolted before moving in, sticking him with a rent payment he wasn't sure he could afford. He and Dave Planchet sold their app but the contracts weren't signed and no money had hit his account. Something could always go wrong at the last minute. He wasn't the type to overextend himself financially, but he was impatient to move in with Kaitlyn and his judgment had been blinded by love.

He never got the full story, yet a friend reported she'd had some kind of breakdown. She'd always been anxiety prone, a bit OCD, but he'd sloughed it off as growing pains. He hadn't talked her into anything too kinky in the bedroom but he'd hoped once they had privacy, he could've convinced her to be more adventurous. He loved her and would've taken care of her, eased her insecurities. She could've counted on him to hold her up whenever she needed him. He wasn't even sure she'd graduated.

Now? He figured he'd dodged a bullet.

Showered and dressed, he repacked his bag and surveyed the stars-and-striped bedroom. Jamie's home was just that… homey. His heart surged, thankful the Gallaghers rescued Jamie from foster care. He couldn't imagine how much more damage there would've been if they hadn't. And yet she'd turned out competent, intelligent, and brave, until it came to a relationship. Perhaps the damage was permanent. He hoped not.

He inhaled the savory aroma of bacon as he entered the kitchen. Mrs. Gallagher cooked scrambled eggs and bacon while Jamie manned the toaster, her back to him.

"Good morning, Colin," Sally Gallagher said. "Did you sleep well?"

"Morning. I did, thank you, although I have a sudden urge to go to a parade."

Sally Gallagher smiled. "It was a trend back in the 80s. I keep reminding myself it's time to redecorate but it always seems to get pushed to the back burner."

Jamie dropped two pieces of toast on a dessert plate and turned, placing it alongside the butter dish. "Morning," she said. Her smile changed the temperature in the room. Each room. Every time. Colin wondered if Jamie had any idea how attractive she was. Those years in a uniform probably skewed her perception. Most would say she was a ten but he considered her a solid eleven-plus.

"Morning," he said. "Ready to hit the slopes?"

"I'm looking forward to it. We need to stop and see Dad before we go."

"Can I serve you?" Sally Gallagher said, offering the pan of eggs.

"Sure." Colin held out a plate from the stack next to the stove and Sally shoveled a healthy portion and added four slices of bacon.

Jamie placed two pieces of buttered toast alongside as the toaster popped, announcing two more slices in the queue.

"I could get used to this," Colin said.

"You have a maid," Jamie said.

"She's not a maid, she's more of a housekeeper and I'm gone before she arrives."

They carried their plates to the table and Jamie offered Colin orange juice. "It's fresh squeezed. My mom got a juicer for Christmas."

Sally chuckled. "I wanted it so I could make one of those healthy green drinks." She wrinkled her nose. "Haven't found a recipe I can stomach yet."

"The orange juice is delicious. You can tell the difference." Changing the subject, Colin said to Jamie, "The plane is still scheduled for our departure tomorrow at noon. I spoke to my parents and they're ready to go. We'll meet them at LaGuardia."

"Great, let's not forget my ski gear in the garage."

"Point me in the right direction and I'll load it into the car." The conversation drifted to Jamie's father and their collective relief that he'd escaped with his life.

They finished breakfast and Colin helped clear the table and load the dishwasher as Sally washed and Jamie dried the pots. Jamie escorted Colin to the garage. With the frigid January temps, they should have grabbed their coats. Jamie pumped up and down on her toes, her hands wedged in her armpits, wisps of warm air snaking through the ether as she exhaled. Colin lifted the garage door and stopped short. "Holy shit. Is this your dad's?"

Colin circled the Aston Martin, running his gloved fingers over the pristine green paint.

"It's mine. My parents gave it to me when I graduated the Naval Academy."

He'd returned to where Jamie stood. "It's a real beauty. Do you have any idea how much it's worth?"

"No, and I don't care."

Colin winced at his inappropriate comment. Of course the monetary value meant nothing to Jamie. "Do you ever drive it?"

"When I'm home, which isn't often. I'd never take it to the city."

"Understood. But you could keep it at my beach house. It would be fun to drive out east."

"Let's just load my ski stuff into the Tahoe."

Colin tightened his lips and followed orders.

ALONE WITH HER MOTHER, Jamie asked, "Have you spoken to Dad this morning?"

"I tried but they said he was sleeping. I'll follow you and Colin over there."

"You think it's okay for me to leave? I feel like I'm going on vacation while Dad is sidelined in the hospital."

"You're working, Jamie. It's not a pleasure trip."

Jamie settled onto a kitchen stool and rested her elbows on the countertop, her chin in her hands. "I guess."

"And speaking of pleasure, I think you need to give Colin a chance. I see the way you are around him."

"God, Mom, not you too." Jamie covered her face with her hands. She exhaled forcefully then crossed her arms in front of her. "What's with you two? You're trying to marry me off. It's annoying."

"I was talking pleasure, not marriage. That part comes before marriage."

"Mom."

"I don't know what your father said, but it's obvious to me Colin has feelings for you and just as importantly, you have feelings for him." Sally Gallagher leaned over the counter, her face only a foot from Jamie's. "Love doesn't often come around twice."

"And when did you become psychic?"

"It's obvious. Even Jessica and Marcus noticed."

"What?" Jamie huffed, hanging her head in her hands again. "Oh my God," she muttered.

"What are you afraid of?"

"Oh, I don't know… abandonment? Abuse? Alcoholism? The list is endless. Besides, my job isn't conducive to a relationship. Can you picture me a wife and mother?"

"Bullshit. And yes, I can."

Sally reached out and secured Jamie's hands in hers. She rubbed the backs with her thumbs. "Sweetheart, I understand your trepidation. What happened when you were a child was terrible. But you've had time to heal those wounds, to trust people. Now you need to learn how to lean on someone once in a while. To let someone catch you when you fall, instead of being so afraid to fall that you never let go, never take a chance, never allow yourself to be vulnerable." Her mother's words pricked the iceberg in her chest and she held her breath to ease the stabbing pain. "Oh sweetie, I'm not saying this to hurt you. You're the most adventurous, competent, intelligent woman I know. Why not be adventurous in love?"

Jamie's words couldn't maneuver past the giant frog in her throat. A frog that threatened to suffocate her. She inhaled slowly and let the breath out even slower.

"I hear you, Mom. I promise I'll think about everything you and Dad said."

Sally Gallagher squeezed Jamie's hands and released them. She rounded the counter and took Jamie into her arms. "I only want what's best for you." She kissed the side of Jamie's cheek and stepped back, holding Jamie at arm's length. "I love you, darling. So much."

"I know." Jamie studied her mother a moment longer, and then the door opened and Colin's frame filled the space.

"Ready?" he said.

COLIN HAD the distinct impression he'd walked in on something he shouldn't have. Too late now.

"Yup, let's go," Jamie said. She grabbed their coats from the closet and offered Colin his. He helped with hers, before donning his own.

"Go on without me, I'll be right behind you," Sally said.

Colin seized both duffels and held the door for Jamie. They buckled into the Tahoe and exited the driveway. Colin wasn't sure he should venture into sensitive territory again. Seemed like everyone was dumping on Jamie lately. "Everything okay?"

Jamie didn't answer and he worried, it was obvious she was upset.

"Yes, just concerned about my dad." Jamie dropped her chin to her chest and fiddled with the zipper clasp on her jacket.

"Understandable. We can return in a flash if necessary."

"That's sweet of you, Colin, but we're losing focus. Your safety is my main concern and I feel like I've been slacking. I promise to get my head back in the game."

He glanced at her downturned face, wanting to hold her hand, to embrace her, all of her. "Don't give it another thought. I've never felt safer than when I'm with you." Colin's forehead wrinkled at his words. Words he'd never said to another human being.

Jamie placed a hand on his knee and he peered down, hesitant to touch it. He couldn't resist and covered it with his own. He wanted to tell her he loved her, he needed her and couldn't bear the thought of her walking out of his life.

He wanted to yell it at the top of the highest mountain. And he just might. Soon.

Chapter 38

J amie's father appeared on the mend and even rather chipper, joking about how his formidable prowess and six-pack abs would have him back to normal faster than anyone on record. Jamie and her mother narrowed their eyes at each other. The man was a legend in his own mind.

They said their goodbyes again, and after a short flight later they'd returned to Colin's penthouse. Jamie unpacked her meager belongings and dropped down on the bed in her room, her eyes fixed to the stucco ceiling. She was glad to be home. *Egad.* She'd just called Colin's place *home.* A slip of the tongue. Yeah, she could never be at home in this outrageously huge and luxurious apartment. Right?

"Jamie," Colin called from downstairs. "Should I order a pizza?"

She jumped up and ran to the railing. Colin stood with his hands on his hips, dressed in well-worn jeans and a tattered white tee. He looked absolutely edible. His hotness eating away at her resolve. "Fine by me."

"What do you want on it?"

"Just cheese unless you want something more."

"I want something more but not on my pizza." He winked.

231

"Colin…"

"Okay, naked pizza it is."

Geez. Don't say naked, Colin. He smiled so wide she wanted to jump him right there and rip his clothes off. Her face heated and she hoped she was far enough away that he didn't notice. She retreated to her room and slipped into yoga pants and her gray NYU sweatshirt. Hmm, she either needed to do some laundry or stop by her apartment to gather more clothes. That's if Colin even knew where the washer and dryer were. She laughed aloud. Probably not.

The door buzzer announced a visitor who turned out to be James, pizza, and one of her favorite IPAs in hand. Colin thanked him and told him to take the rest of the night off and return in time for their 10 a.m. flight to Telluride.

Colin's phone rang and he chatted with his mom, while Jamie dished out pizza and poured beer into two frosty mugs from the freezer. They ate at the breakfast bar, Colin inhaling his first slice in the time it took her to chew and swallow two bites. "Hungry?"

"Starving."

"There was food on the plane, why didn't you eat something?

"I don't know, I felt kind of queasy but better now. Probably stress."

Jamie smiled as Colin grabbed another piece. "This is really good for takeout," she said. "Still pretty crispy."

"I think the place is only a block away. Not enough time to get soggy." Colin gobbled more pizza as if it was his last meal. "You all ready for the trip? Do you need anything?"

"I should probably either do laundry or stop by my apartment to get more clothes."

Colin swigged more beer. "We don't have enough time to stop at your place tomorrow."

"Where's your washer and dryer?"

Colin narrowed his eyes. "Like I know?"

Of course…

"We'll buy you new clothes when we get there." Colin downed the last half of his beer.

Was his stomach a bottomless pit?

"And don't even think of telling me *no*."

Colin glanced at her, her mouth open. She recovered and said, "Colin, you are not going to buy me any more clothing."

He put down his pizza and faced her, one arm on the counter, the other atop the chair back. "I mean it, Jamie. Don't piss me off about this or I might have to spank you."

Jamie's eyelashes went as high as they could go, but she remained silent… and *obedient?* A tingle sizzled between her legs. No denying his dominant tone, her heart rate accelerated. She shoved pizza in her mouth and gulped beer. It did nothing to cool her insides.

"Good girl," he said. "However, I would have thoroughly enjoyed spanking your adorable ass." His blue eyes shimmered with an eerie light, his gaze imploring her to take her clothes off and kneel in front of him. *Egad.* There was that submissive thing again. She wanted him to throw her on the bed, tie her up and do evil things. Heat continued to flush her cheeks and she could do nothing about it. Surely Colin saw her reaction.

His blue orbs burned into her, like two flaming stars searing the night sky. "You want to play, don't you? You want me to spank you."

Oh God. Yes! Yes, she did, but… How much more of an idiot could she be? She gave him this whole speech about last time being a mistake and promised herself she'd never go there again. Now, all she wanted was him to… Oh God.

She didn't answer. Colin grabbed her shoulders and made her face him. "You're aroused, I can see it."

Jamie bit her lip before she said something she'd regret. But would she? The sex was incredible last time but it was totally vanilla. What would it be like to venture into the darkness? The unknown?

Their eyes searched each other and she swore he could see into her soul. Read her mind. He knew what she wanted even if she didn't, and was perfectly capable of giving it to her. She'd never felt so desired, the draw irresistible, the need so great.

Colin took both her hands and brought them to his lips. His warm breath caressed the backs of her hands. He kissed each fingertip, then slipped a hand between her thighs. She quivered as his fingertips pressed against her crotch. "You're wet, all the way through your clothing."

She broke their gaze, her eyes focused on his hand wedged between her legs. He nudged her chin up with his knuckle. "Say it. Say you want me to make love to you. To show you how much more there is to sex. To test your limits. To bring you pleasure you've never experienced."

COLIN'S DICK THROBBED. He wanted Jamie in his playroom but he needed to go slow. Not yet. Not to worry, his bedroom hid plenty of secrets to amp the excitement. The restraints were hidden behind the headboard and under the foot of the mattress. He had plenty of toys in his portable toy-bag in the playroom, ready for an unexpected field trip. He hadn't played outside the club in months, maybe a year. The toys were all new, wrapped in their sanitary wrappers. You never used a toy twice and he always left them as a parting gift.

"I'm waiting, little subbie. And a Dom doesn't like waiting."

Jamie's lips parted and he wanted to seal them with his, to thrust his tongue into her mouth and his dick into her moistness.

"Ah… yes, I want you to make love to me."

"Try again." He held her wrists tightly in his.

"Yes, yes, Sir. I want to play."

"Better."

"I will tell you what you want and I won't go further than you can take. If you think you're getting close to red, say yellow, and I'll know you're reaching your limit. If I question you and you're good, say green."

Jamie flashed a small smile and he thought fear showed in her eyes, except no, it was arousal, excitement, *submission*.

He stored the pizza in the fridge along with the remaining beer. Snatching her waist, he hoisted her off the chair and slung her over his shoulder. Jamie squealed. "Quiet, little subbie." He swatted her backside and she yelped again. "Ah, disobedient. Now you're really going to feel my paddle."

Chapter 39

Colin tossed Jamie onto his king-sized bed, her wish fulfilled. He used his phone to mute the overhead lights and music filled the room, a band Jamie didn't recognize, sultry, romantic, sexy. "Who is this?"

"Enigma."

The beat primal, the lyrics haunting, beguiling.

"Be right back." He disappeared, quickly returning with a black leather satchel. Her interest piqued, what was in there?

He stripped off his white tee and unbuckled his jeans but left them on. His bare chest, dark hair dusting his pecs and surrounding his nipples made her hands twitch with the urge to touch him.

"You remember the rules?"

"Yes, Sir." Her arms surrounded her chest, ankles crossed.

"Safe word again?"

"Red, Sir."

"Good girl." His arms clasped over his chest made his biceps bulge. Jamie had never experienced sex with a man of his well-toned musculature, like magazine pictures she'd seen of the Sexiest Man Alive. She was glad she was prostrate or she might swoon. "Let's get you into protocol. Stand."

Jamie scooched to the bedside, afraid her legs had melted and she'd tumble to the floor. She stood before Colin, his presence commanding, authoritative, *big*.

He stepped closer, eroticism radiating off his body like a lava flow threatening to consume her. She cast her eyes downward.

With a finger he chucked her chin, then tugged a lock of her hair. "I can't decide which of your features is the most magnificent. Your gleaming auburn hair, forest green eyes, incredible body... I love every inch of you." He punctuated his remarks by running his fingers through her hair, a kiss on her eyelid, hands drifting over her shoulders and down her arms. His piercing gaze never wavered.

Jamie dropped her chin and focused on her bare feet. She wasn't being submissive, just *humble*. No one had ever said anything like that to her. Never, ever. Something about the way he looked at her... or rather looked into her. She noticed it when they weren't doing anything in particular... in the car, watching TV, drinking coffee. It should make her uncomfortable but it didn't, it felt good, endearing, loving. She gave him a sidelong look.

He smirked. "Remember, I give the commands and you obey. If you need to speak you must ask permission."

COLIN ACHED to fill his hands with her full breasts, to wrap those legs around his waist and pound into her, a jackhammer inside her, until neither could remember their name. "Time to lose the clothes. Leave your underwear on. I'll remove them at my leisure."

Jamie pulled her sweatshirt over her head and threw it behind her. Next came her yoga pants.

"Put your hands behind you. Lace your fingers together." Jamie complied and Colin commanded, "On your knees." She glanced up. "Eyes down. Slave position." Jamie scowled. "It's just a position, you're not a slave, you're a sub."

Jamie sank to the floor in one fluid move, her butt resting on her heels. God, she was so beautiful like this. "Don't move. Eyes down. There are consequences for disobedience." Colin chuckled. "Oh right, you've already been disobedient. You need a good spanking."

Colin fisted her hair, forcing her gaze upward. He wanted to take her now and chastised himself – *Slow down, buddy* – his erection nudging him onward. He needed some restraint, although the leather restraints would be on her.

He released her and sat on the bedside. "Stand." Jamie instantly complied, keeping her hands behind her and eyes on the floor. She was good at this and his heart swelled with affection. He clutched her upper arm and landed her belly-down over his thighs. She gasped. The excitement of a new subbie always thrilled him, except Jamie wasn't just a sub, she was more, so much more, and he prayed he'd deliver the goods.

He slipped his hand under the flimsy satin material, stroking her firm cheeks, massaging, warming, before he delivered the real heat. His fingers slid down her crack, touching the most forbidden place, her dark star. He could sense her holding her breath. "Breathe, darling. Don't want you passing out on me."

Slipping her panties down, he tugged them off her feet and tossed them aside. His other hand held her neck against his calf, her panting breaths warming his skin. "Hands on the floor. Brace yourself, sweetheart."

COLIN'S VOICE WAS LEVEL. Firm. No anger, just instruction. He caressed her bare bottom with his hand, soothing, calming.

She couldn't believe she was actually doing this. Wasn't this perverted?

He hit her ass with a loud whack and she yelped, followed by a vehement, "Ouch."

"Quiet," he said. "Ouch isn't a safeword." He rubbed the spot to bring the blood to the surface. "Breathe through the burn, baby." He smacked her harder, two more times. Zings of pleasure shot to her groin. Like he flipped a light switch. He'd said he would tell her what she wanted and wouldn't go further than she could take, yet she wasn't sure. Another slap and she lifted her hands off the carpet and gripped his calf, her mouth pressed against his skin to stifle a screech.

"Easy, baby, hands back on the floor." She instantly complied, her need to please greater than anything she'd felt before. Stinging spanks rained over her burning skin. The pain morphed into roiling hot pulses, driving her higher. The melting started in the pit of her stomach. Her clit swelled, throbbed, her need for relief searing her insides. She needed to come but he'd been adamant she couldn't until he allowed it. She wanted to beg him. Touch, release. Touch. He massaged her stinging bottom, the spanking returned to stroking. "Well, done, darling. I know that was hard. I'm giving you a reward for enduring your first spanking." He pulled her thighs apart and plunged a finger into her wet folds. She lost control. The volume of her moan startled even her. She was never noisy during sex.

He rubbed her clit with two fingers, deeply probing the sensitive spot behind her pubic bone. She writhed on his lap, clutching his ankle with both hands to anchor herself. Her body twisted in rhythm with the strokes of his fingers. *Oh God.*

"I give you permission to come, love. Let go."

She detonated, every cell and nerve shaking with pleasure. Stars streamed through her vision, and she feared he was right, she might pass out. He left his fingers inside her, still pressing against her clit, drawing out her orgasm for an endless cascade of interludes.

She choked on a sob, her breath trapped in her chest with no chance of escape. Her body shook. What was happening? The sensation of relinquishing control was like opening a fist and feeling the blood flow back into cramped fingers.

And then the dam broke. The flood came.

Colin stiffened, her scream more of a keening shriek, like a small animal being tortured. He gripped Jamie's sobbing body and sat her on his lap, brushing away the river of tears.

"Jamie, what's wrong? You may speak freely. Did I go past your limit?"

Uncontrollable cries continued, an earthquake of unending shivers and shakes. He gripped her shoulders. "Jamie, talk to me. Tell me what you're feeling. Please." He hugged her to his chest, stroking her hair tenderly. Her hot tears wet his chest.

She whispered into his pecs. "I-I…" Another sob.

He wrenched backward and studied her. "What? Tell me?"

"I've never done that before."

"I know. You told me you'd never tried spanking. I thought you'd like it."

Jamie placed a hand on his chest and regarded him through wet lashes. "Not the spanking… the crying. I don't understand. I've never cried before. I'm not just talking about after sex. I mean I've never cried in my entire life."

Colin's eyes narrowed. "That's impossible. Everyone cries."

"Not me."

"Not even as a child, or baby?"

"If I did, I have no memory."

Colin sighed. "How can that be? It's a human reflex. I'm a grown man and I still cry when I watch *Field of Dreams* with my dad."

"I…" Another crying hiccup. "It might be a reflex for babies but when you get smacked so hard you fly across the room every time you cry your body learns crying is not productive. I never knew what piece of furniture I'd hit."

"This happened when you were young, when you were with your birth mother?"

"Yes, and the occasional stray she brought home. None of those men were what I'd call stand-up guys."

"Oh, Jamie, you were a child. It's unforgiveable. Did any of them sexually abuse you?"

"No, although while I was in foster care some pimply-faced twerp got handsy with me. He told his parents the black eye was from football practice."

Colin dragged a hand down his face. He didn't know what to do next, which unnerved him. He always knew his next chess move.

"Jamie, I've experienced this many times. Pain often serves as a catalyst to release buried emotions as a result of abuse or sexual trauma."

"Really?"

"Absolutely. It happens often at the club and is a sign of progress. Venting buried emotional pain is vital to being healthy and allowing yourself to be vulnerable. Children are vulnerable, as they should be, but when they are taught not to trust the people who are entrusted with keeping them safe, their view of the world distorts. The same during sex, the vulnerability you need to have great sex is essential. You must trust your partner."

Jamie wiped away her tears. She sniffed and he offered her a tissue. "Thanks, Dr. Freud."

"You're welcome, little subbie." Colin kissed her nose and then found her mouth, all salty and warm. His erection grew larger.

Jamie sat erect, and looked him right in the eye. "I have something to say." She swallowed hard then licked her lips. "You freed me from a prison I didn't know I was in. It was like I was trapped inside a cement straight-jacket. You've been chiseling away at it all week, and then my mom and dad delivered another crashing blow. I could feel the tiny chips falling away. And now you've breached the wall, spoken the secret language."

He hugged her tightly, inhaling her sweet scent. "I promise I'll always keep you safe. I'll protect you."

"I know," she whispered.

His chin rested on her head. "We're done for tonight. You're too upset."

Jamie pulled back, wrenching herself free. "No, I don't want to stop. Now that you're in, I want you all the way."

Colin shook his head. "I don't know. You're in a fragile state. I won't risk it."

Chapter 40

All Masters dealt with women's fears, inhibitions, and insecurities, especially victims of sexual trauma. But Jamie wasn't in that head space, it was more like... he was loathe to name it. She exuded confidence, bravery, sensibility, certainly not a fragile butterfly that needed to be handled with tender care. Now that the tsunami had receded and the storm passed, maybe he should accept her word. He desperately and for the first time in ages wanted to make love rather than just fuck. There was more time for fun and games later, at least he hoped.

"Don't make me beg," she said.

Colin managed a smile. "Normally, a Dom would be pleased if a submissive begged."

Jamie smiled, then covered his face with kisses, wrapping her hands around his neck, the last kiss spiked with extra passion, their tongues dancing an erotic jig. *Maybe...*

"Have your way with me, Sir. I'm yours to ravage."

Colin mocked a frown. "Careful, darling, you're topping from the bottom."

"I'd say you should spank me for my insolence again, but I think once a night is sufficient."

Colin chuckled. He brushed Jamie's hair off her face, her green eyes ablaze. "You ever play with restraints?"

"No, Sir."

"Let's start there. I want your body open and available for my use."

THE CRYING JAG TERRIFIED JAMIE, but the after-effect left her aglow. Being alone in bed with Colin didn't hurt either. Until now it was as if she'd lived a black and white life. She considered sex a biological function, like eating and sleeping. She recalled Colin's shock when she confessed she could orgasm with a vibrator in under two minutes. *Egad.*

Colin pushed her back against the headboard, centering her on the gray sheets. "Ready?"

"Yes, Sir." Jamie folded her hands in her lap, eyes down.

"That bra needs to go."

Jamie reached for the fastener yet Colin clasped her wrists and placed them palms-down on her thighs. "Did I tell you to remove it?"

"But I thought…" Jamie bit her lip and lowered her eyes again. "No, Sir."

"Good girl. We're in protocol. You only do what I tell you. Understood?"

"Yes. Yes, Sir."

"And remember your safe words. Yellow to slow down and red if you need to stop."

"Yes, Sir."

Colin pulled her down the bed, legs out straight, head on the pillow and straddled her, sitting on her thighs. A stomach-quivering warning slithered through her. He placed his forearms on the sides of her head and plundered her mouth. His kisses intensified and he moved his hands behind her and released the hooks on her bra. Such a multi-tasker, him. He slipped the flimsy garment off her shoulders and down her arms (at least she hadn't been wearing her sports bra), then draped it over the headboard. His hands cupped her breasts. He squeezed and her nipples hardened. He brushed his knuckles over her cheek and the expression of worry vanished.

"THESE ARE SO MAGNIFICENT. Your nipples are like tiny rosebuds, pink and hard. Waiting to be plucked. I could play with them all night." He kissed her again, the traces of saltiness gone. In fact, she tasted sweet, so damn sweet.

He leaned toward the left side of the filigreed brass headboard and fished out the leather restraints. "I'm going to tie you down. If you get uncomfortable say yellow."

Jamie nodded, kept silent. Colin buckled her wrist into the leather strap, not too tight that she couldn't slip out if she wanted. He pulled the lash, stretching her arm over her head and tied it to the headboard. "You can hold on to the headboard if you need to."

He repeated the motion with the other hand, then leaned back, his ass on her thighs again. "You're beautiful like this." Jamie grinned, her eyes twinkled. So far, so good.

He bent over and suckled a nipple, holding both firm tits. He massaged the lonely one, rolling the nub between his thumb and forefinger. Jamie gasped, then let out an extended, dramatic sigh. "Don't forget to breathe, darling. We've only just begun."

He leapt off the bed and jerked the foot restraints from the crack between the mattress and box spring. He spread her legs wide and her eyes followed his every move. Slipping one slender ankle into the soft leather strap he pulled the buckle tight and laced it through the clasp, then secured the other ankle. "Still good?"

Jamie nodded.

"Use your words, little subbie. I want no miscommunication." Honesty and open communication were a Dom's duty.

"Yes, Sir, green all the way," she whispered. "But when do I get to touch you?"

"No baby, not this time." He wanted her to stay in position while he touched her. Doing what he wanted.

"But you should get a turn."

"Oh sweetie, my turn comes from pleasing you."

"I don't get it. Guys aren't like that. It's mostly about them."

"Again, you haven't been with the right man."

"I don't get it."

"You will and you're going to get it good." Recognition dawned on her face. He placed two fingers on her lips. "Shush. Enough talking."

A sudden image of Jamie in tears, sobbing in his arms, made him flinch. But he reminded himself she was brave and confident, the opposite of a submissive in everyday life. He hoped he could reconcile the two, allow her to give up control in bed and set her free. He wanted in, all the way in.

His erection begged to be freed so he stood, unzipped his jeans and stepped out, following with his boxer-briefs. He reflexively grabbed his cock and squeezed. *Down boy, we're pacing ourselves here.* Well, not *down*, on pause.

JAMIE FOCUSED on Colin's massive dick, his winter-blue eyes amused as her lids heaved upward. Her faced flamed, again. How many times could a person blush in one day before having a stroke? She wanted to grab his cock and wrap her lips around it, but she was trapped, she had no control, spread eagle, lashed to the bed.

Jamie lied to Colin when he asked about her sexual fantasies. Well, she hadn't truly lied. The occasional thought of bondage and other kink proved fleeting contemplations, nothing she would ever act on. And now here she was and the anticipation of what would happen next jolted her libido. Egad. She'd already survived one explosive orgasm and had never been multi-orgasmic. One and done… that's if she was lucky. But she'd orgasmed twice with Colin last time and he threatened more.

Colin rummaged in his toy bag but Jamie couldn't see what he removed. What instrument of torture was he planning on using? He kept the mysterious item from sight and tucked it under the pillow, then knelt between her knees and shoved a pillow under her ass, the rush of cool air confirming she was utterly exposed. *Oh God.* "Mine to touch," he said, his eyes examining her most intimate place. He leaned over and nibbled her neck. She moaned, urgent, needy. "Close your eyes. I want you to just feel, concentrate on the feelings, not the actions." His warm breath tickled her ear canal and she shivered. He rolled onto his side, his head resting on his bent elbow, and brushed his fingers over her collarbone and between her breasts, then his hand crept over her stomach, like tiny butterflies parading across her sensitive skin. A rip current of fast-moving thoughts swept her away from logic, and normalcy, out into a roiling sea of desire. A delicious thrill seared her arteries.

When she giggled, he said, "Ticklish, little subbie?"

Oh no, had she made a mistake? Jamie never thought a man would be happy if his partner laughed during sex. But Colin was different and he did call this *play*. He didn't sound angry. "Yes, Sir."

"Good. That means we're having fun."

She ached to have her hands on him yet all she could do was drink in his handsome countenance: the sharp stern angle of his jaw and the firm line of his mouth, his wicked, sexy smile, which she witnessed many times when he wasn't even trying. The sight of him always erupted in a delicious thrill, like when she first saw him in the coffee shop or first thing in the morning.

"Now close those pretty green peepers or I'll resort to a blindfold."

What? A blindfold? That never occurred to her. Better than another spanking. But he was taking her sight away. She already couldn't move. Two down: touch and sight, only three senses left. Well, not entirely, he could still touch *her*. She closed her eyes, her body humming with longing, her swollen, bare clit making urgent demands. A shiver shook her. Not like before, when she'd cried like a fucking baby. A shiver of delight. With every brush of his fingertips, the temperature in the room went up another degree. Her heart did somersaults in her chest.

"I'm going to learn what you like, what you don't like, and then mix everything up until your busy little brain shuts down."

As he pressed his chest against her, she could feel the thump of his heart, a pounding rhythm sending champagne-like bubbles through her.

Chapter 41

Colin's fingers arrived at their destination, slick with arousal. Jamie spasmed and he'd barely touched her swollen clit. He spread her open, one finger stroking the engorged nub, then through her wet folds before pressing onward, hot velvet wrapped around his finger. He wanted his mouth on her.

Jamie gave a husky moan. Fuck, she was adorable. "You do not have permission to come, baby. I'm in control."

He probed deeper, alternating between rubbing her clit and exploring her sweet wetness. Her hips arched upward, demanding more. He withdrew his fingers and she groaned.

"Please," she begged.

He stopped her whimper with his mouth. His kiss deepened. His tongue took possession, nibbling her lips, biting, nipping, then he took her lips again. He retreated, surveying her face, eyes shut tightly. *Good little subbie.*

"Please, Colin. I can't hold out any longer."

He slapped the side of her thigh. "No talking. I'm the boss and you do as I say. And how do you address me, little subbie?"

"Sorry, Sir. Yes, Sir."

"Don't make me drag out a gag too." Jamie inhaled sharply. That got her attention. But he didn't want to push her too far. Not this time.

"Breathe, baby." Her panting breaths excited him. She was so close but she needed discipline to reach the mind-blowing climax he intended to give her. He took her chin between his fingers and steadied her. "You can do this. And trust me, giving up control will set you free."

Jamie stilled, the stress in her body lessened. Not for long, however. He reached under the mattress and slipped the tiny gadget onto his thumb. It whirred to life. He kissed her again, then knelt between her legs and spread her open with two fingers, his thumb nestled against the side of her clit. He moved the tiny vibe on top and thrust two fingers into her wetness. His penetrating fingers intruded and retreated. She was soaking wet, threatening to send him over the cliff.

Jamie shrieked and writhed under his touch, her moans escalated. She yanked on the restraints, trying to lift her knees. His smile hurt his face, she was so beautiful like this, at the edge and waiting for him to allow her release. It was time.

SWEAT BROKE out on Jamie's skin. Her muscles grew taut, her thighs trembled. Her hips jerked, pushing upward. Demanding more. So close. She whimpered. He kissed her, rough, deep, invasive. And now that vibrating thing hurtled her skyward. Was she about to have an out-of-body experience? How much longer would Colin keep her restrained… physically and emotionally? Phantom wings in her chest yearned to be free. To fly the vivid azure sky, soar into the puffy silver clouds, barreling toward the sun.

She struggled to stay silent, but wasn't successful. Moans and whimpers escaped her lips no matter how hard she tried to suppress them. Tugging on the restraints she desperately wanted to touch him. He wrapped an iron hand around her wrist, his body alongside her. The heat radiating off his flesh stoking the fire between her legs.

His vibrating thumb pressed hard against her clit, he thrust two fingers inside her, then three, the merciless rhythm unrelenting. She was about to lose control. What punishment would she suffer?

"Okay, baby, it's time... let go." He pressed the vibrator against her clit, the pounding rhythm of his fingers shoving her off the precipice. The wave crested and took her out to sea, riding the waves into oblivion.

She gasped for air, her chest heaving, her pulse dancing. *Oh God.*

COLIN TOSSED the tiny vibrator onto the floor then settled his hand on her stomach, caressing her overheated flesh. "Nicely, done, darling." His palm pressed against her sternum. He leaned in and pecked her cheek, her nose, ending at her lips, and kissed her tenderly. His arm rested on her breasts, soft cushions he could fall asleep on. "You may speak, little subbie."

"Oh God, that was amazing, Sir."

"I'm glad. You were incredible. Watching you come is the most beautiful thing I've ever seen."

"What was that vibrating thing? It's nothing like a rabbit."

"My little secret. Besides a vibrator is always better in the hands of a man." He nibbled a breast and licked the areola, then bit down. Time to take her arousal up a notch. He sucked the peak against the roof of his mouth.

Jamie wheezed and tugged on the restraints in an attempt to

curve into him. "Not yet darling, we're only halfway there." Her saucer eyes bespoke her uncertainty. "Speak, darling."

"Colin, I don't think I could have another orgasm."

"Trust me, you will."

He rose and released her feet from bondage, then pushed her knees up and spread them wide. He kissed the sensitive skin on her inner thighs and blew his breath on her exposed labia. Jamie writhed and wiggled. He probed her with his tongue and she groaned. He continued his ministrations, sucking, his tongue swirled around her clit. Jamie pressed herself against his mouth, demanding more and he was greedy to comply. His mouth closed over her and sucked.

Jamie screamed. "Oh God."

JAMIE'S BODY pulsated with longing, her breasts swollen, nipples throbbing. She felt drunk. He had amazing lips, firm, yet so soft. Hot and wet. She wanted to fondle his hair but the restraints nixed that. He inserted two fingers, sliding them in and out with slow torturous movements. His tongue worked her up and up, higher and higher. She couldn't believe she was going to come again. He continued his assault on her vagina, the combination of tongue and fingers lit her up like a supernova.

Everything stopped and he barked, "Not yet. Eyes on me."

She lifted her head off the pillow, yanking at the arm restraints. "What? I can't, I'm too close."

"Yes, you can. Pull it back. You can control it." Colin tilted his head, his dark brows drawing together. "You do not have permission to come, baby." He shoved his hands under her ass and pinched her reddened skin.

"Ouch," she screeched. But she knew it wouldn't gain her a reprieve. Not a safe word. She considered, yellow, or red, but she didn't want it to stop. She wanted more, needed more.

Jamie bit her lip and stopped squirming. She clamped down and squeezed hard. Colin resumed his relentless licking, massaging, probing. *Oh God.* She was back at the apex in a nanosecond. His tongue rubbed firmly. Fresh waves of pleasure threatened her undoing, hanging on the cliff of a third orgasm. Hanging on by her fingertips.

Colin sucked again and then shoved a wet finger in her ass. What the hell? The *pop-pop-pop* hit her like opening endless champagne bottles. "Up you come, darling." Colin released her from the arm restraints, gripped her waist and turned her over, positioning her on her hands and knees. He slid his fingers into her puffy labia, then eased his cock in an inch, then penetrated her with one decisive thrust. Jamie moaned. "Easy, babe." His fingers tormented and he teased her clit and she clamped down hard around his shaft.

He pressed in and out a few times. "Now," he said, "brace yourself, darling." He continued thrusting his cock into her, deeper, harder, faster. Her arms gave out, dropping her onto her elbows, her cheek pressed into the pillow. She grasped onto the headboard to avoid banging her head against the unforgiving cold brass. She came in a rolling hard orgasm, or perhaps it was a continuation of the last one. Time shifted differently, a kaleidoscope of thrills. Shockwaves here, shockwaves there. Something pinching every bit of her flesh, everywhere.

He increased to a hard, pounding rhythm, his powerful hands rocking her forward then yanking her back onto his shaft. The sounds of slapping flesh filled the room. He wrapped strong hands around her hips, forcing himself deeper. A tremor surged within her, sizzling up her spine. Shudders wracked her body.

COLIN TRAPPED her against his cock and growled, his release explosive, mind-blowing. He hadn't explained this to Jamie, but holding his own orgasm back for as long as he could enhanced his climax as well. A few more gentle thrusts and he pulled out. He leaned onto her back and she collapsed under his weight. He covered her with his body, grasping both her hands and trapping them over her head. He kissed her ear and inhaled her musky scent. In a husky voice, she said, "Permission to speak, Sir?"

"We're out of protocol, do as you wish." He basked in the softness of her body a minute longer then rolled off her and wrapped her in his arms, holding her close. She laid her head on his shoulder, her palm against his chest. She gently tugged at the hairs on his chest, then kissed his neck. Her emerald eyes studied him, then her gaze dropped. He leaned forward and nuzzled her cheek.

"I never knew sex could be that good, or creative. I'm... ah... I don't have words."

He squeezed her hand and sucked on a finger. "You don't have to say anything. Your body did plenty of talking." Their eyes met and Colin's heart melted. She'd given herself over to him, and her orgasms were the most precious gift a man could receive. He cupped her cheek, trailing his thumb over her swollen lips.

"What did you do to my ass? I've never experienced that."

"Anal play is lots of fun. Lots of nerves there. We have so much more to explore. I still have plenty of tricks in my repertoire." He winked.

"O*kay*." But she wasn't so sure. The last guy she dated insisted no one go near anybody's asshole and she heartily agreed. But she trusted Colin to show her pleasures she'd never imagined and they were off to an innovative start. "But I still don't get it. I want to give you pleasure too."

"Soon. I can't deny the pleasure of having your lips on my cock is something I'm looking forward to." He ran his fingers through her tussled mane. "By the way, you make lots of adorable little sounds when you make love."

Jamie rolled onto her back and laid her forearm over her eyes. "Oh God," she said. "I never considered myself noisy in the bedroom." She peeked one eye out.

Colin laughed and took her arm off her face. "I like it. You're very responsive."

Jamie's eyes grew heavy. Contentment swept over her like hot fudge softening vanilla ice cream. Although nothing vanilla had occurred. And she loved hot fudge.

Chapter 42

Jamie woke with Colin wrapped around her. This time she knew whose thigh lay across her pelvis and whose bicep had wedged under her chin. Colin puffed soft breaths against her ear and she struggled not to giggle—ticklish... again.

The bedside clock glared at her: 8:37 a.m. Egads. They needed to hustle to make their flight. Her phone rang and she glanced at it. Matt was Facetiming her. "Shit." Still in bed with Colin and probably looking like it. She threw the covers off and fled from his bed, grabbed her sweatshirt off the floor. Her pinky toe slammed into the bed frame. A few seconds elapsed where the pain sped toward her brain. "Shit. Fuck." She hopped on one foot, rubbing the offended digit then donned her sweatshirt. She ran her fingers through her tangled hair and tied it into a makeshift bun. The phone screamed at her. She prayed she didn't have racoon eyes, hoping the water-proof mascara kept its promise.

Colin sat up, his hair tousled. "Are you running?"

"No, it's Matt Facetiming me." She picked up the phone. "Be quiet."

"Yes, ma'am." Colin smirked and put his fingers against his luscious lips.

Jamie hit the red button. "Hey, Matt, what's up?"

Matt narrowed his eyes. "Did I wake you?"

"Ah, sort of… heading to the shower."

"Looks like you had a rough night."

Just spit it out. Walk of shame. She glanced at Colin, his head tilted, eyes gigantic. She wrinkled her nose. "Uh… I'm processing a lot right now. What's up?"

"Everything is in place. Rob and I are on site, the locals have been alerted, including the ski patrol. We searched the house and the woods and the locals are keeping guard. We're expecting you around one."

"Perfect. Any sightings of the Planchets?"

"We're continually running facial recognition and have alerts set up for their credit cards, but they're either gone or keeping a low profile."

Jamie sunk onto the bedside chair. "I'm worried they've been there too long and have had plenty of time to prepare."

"We've also set up alerts at the local hardware and other stores that might sell anything needed for bomb-making."

"Yeah, but there's a good chance they'd bring what they needed with them."

"True."

"Still no hit on what they might be driving?"

"Nada. But something popped up. We've been researching the brothers' social media and found them on some incel sites. Some pretty nasty rhetoric about how the government owes them sex. And there's a reference to an old girlfriend named Kaitlyn, someone from college. We're trying to track her down."

"Incel rants are seriously disturbing. Do you think there's any connection to Colin?"

"If they have any idea that Colin's a member of an elite sex club, one that would never allow their entry, it might be more motive to take the guy out."

"True. Thanks Matt, will give you a heads-up when we're close."

"Roger that."

The call ended and Colin's face deflated. "Honestly, Jamie, I've had a few hours to forget someone is trying to kill me. Now, it's back. I can feel the boogie man breathing down my neck."

"Don't worry. We'll catch them and at the very least we'll keep you and your parents safe."

"I'll take you at your word." Colin rose and wrapped his muscular arms around her, his nakedness enshrouding her in a loving embrace. "Thanks for last night. You are amazing."

Jamie still couldn't believe she'd climbed a fucking emotional mountain a few hours ago and made it to the other side. And that she'd cried like a baby. She'd never felt like she fit in, as if she was from Mars or Venus, probably Pluto, actually, which had been ostracized. Her whole life she'd guarded herself, her heart. And now she'd left it vulnerable. Given up control, allowing someone else to take charge.

Their hug melted away, yet Colin's gaze kept her trapped. His voice throaty, he asked, "You sure you're all right?"

"Everything's great. I feel great, maybe a little sore."

"Then a good time was had by all."

COLIN WANTED to tell her he loved her, but he was walking a tightrope. The first time having sex with Jamie was wonderful, but in the daylight she'd put a negative spin on it. He wasn't risking that again. He'd let things lie and hope what Jamie said last night stuck. Her admission that she wanted 'all the way in' made his heart glow. He couldn't imagine going on without her. For once, his heart was in charge, leaving his brain and his dick in the dust. And like that famous quote went, 'the heart wants what the heart wants'.

Showered, dressed and packed, Colin met Jamie in the kitchen having checked with James to make sure all their gear was stowed and ready to go.

"Want me to make coffee?" Jamie asked.

"Not necessary. There's refreshments and food on the plane."

"Oooh, la-di-da."

Colin took her into his arms. "Are you making fun of me again?"

"Me? Never," she said, batting her eyelashes.

"Good, because it will earn you another spanking." A flush crept up her face. He added, "A bit of punishment and a whole lot of fun."

JAMIE HAD a difficult time admitting the spanking had been hot, and the key to unlocking her secret heart. The whole night raged at star-like temps and she wanted to do it again. Soon. "Luckily, we'll be staying with your parents so you'll have to behave."

"It's not me I'm worried about."

"What? I can behave. I'll be a perfect angel."

"There's nothing to stop me from sneaking into your room at night."

Her breath caught at his words. "Colin, everyone will have eyes on that house. This has to stop until I'm off the case."

"And then?"

"I don't know. I need to think about what happened last night."

"Perhaps you need to shut off that thinking part for a while and let your other parts have free rein. You think too much." His smoky voice, easy smile and steely-blue gaze sent a trail of tingles down her spine, heating her insides and making a full stop at her clit.

Jamie slapped both hands on his chest, then pushed back. "We better get a move on." She grabbed her navy-blue parka off the chair yet Colin seized it and held it out for her. She slipped her arms in and zipped it up.

Colin retrieved his ski jacket from the closet and donned it, then escorted Jamie into the waiting SUV.

COLIN CALLED HIS MOM. "On our way," she said. "Traffic isn't bad. We should be there in about a half-hour."

"Great, see you soon."

"Is Agent Gallagher with you?"

"She is."

Jamie leaned in and said, "Hi, Mrs. MacKenzie."

"Oh, hello, Agent Gallagher. Keeping an eye on my son?"

"Taking very good care of him. Staying close."

Colin raised his eyebrows, but kept his mouth shut. Jamie punched him in the arm.

"You have your FBI tail?" he asked his mother.

"Yes, they're driving us. The house in Telluride has been searched and secured and a new team of agents will be taking over when we get there. I do hope it's not too intrusive. I don't want to be looking over my shoulder the whole vacation. Are you sure we should be following through on this?"

Colin wouldn't dare mention to his mother that he might be

helping the FBI by tempting the Planchets to make another attempt on his life. She'd freak and he wondered why he was handling this as well as he was. No doubt, Jamie had a lot to do with it. Keeping him calm and… *distracted.*

They arrived at LaGuardia airport with about twenty minutes to spare. Not that it mattered, the plane's itinerary revolved around his schedule, not the airport's. Colin often thought if he had to tighten his budget for some unfortunate reason, the private plane would be the last to go. No security, flexible scheduling, and parking fifty yards from the tarmac was a luxury he'd fight to keep. In this case, he was indeed a spoiled rich guy.

James and the airport personnel loaded their paraphernalia onto the plane. The pilot and copilot introduced themselves and checked IDs, his parents already on board. Jamie embarked first, her tight little ass guarded by denim. He almost touched her, thinking her ass was his to claim but pulled his itchy fingers back at the last second. Keeping his hands off Jamie would be more difficult than he thought. Jamie hesitated on the top step and all his efforts came undone. His face hit her ass. Jamie glanced over her shoulder and frowned.

"Sorry, accident."

"It's a felony to lie to the FBI." She patted his head.

"I'll never let you put cuffs on me. They're only for you."

"Shush," she said. "Your parents are here."

"I brought handcuffs with me. I plan to sneak into your bed tonight and ravage you."

"No way. And remember I have a weapon."

"So do I…"

Chapter 43

J amie took the seat opposite Mrs. MacKenzie, a shiny russet table between them. As his mother sipped coffee, Colin slid in beside Jamie, across from his dad. Mr. MacKenzie munched on a Danish. Jamie ran a hand over the soft ivory leather cushions, surveying the taupe motif. What a luxurious way to travel.

A flight attendant approached and placed a well-manicured hand on Colin's shoulder. "Good morning, Mr. MacKenzie, so nice to see you again. Can I pour you coffee?"

"Yes, Greta, thank you."

"And you, ma'am?" the attendant said to Jamie.

Colin's eyes focused on his phone. "This is Agent Jamie Gallagher. She's my bodyguard. She takes her coffee the same as I do."

"Yes, sir. We have plenty of food, Agent Gallagher. There are egg sandwiches, a bakery tray and fresh fruit. Everything organic. Non-GMO."

"Just coffee, please."

"And for you, sir?"

"Same."

Jamie bristled, first at Colin's businesslike introduction, then at Greta as she sashayed her cute little butt down the aisle, enhanced by her short, hip-hugging gray skirt. This must be her full-time job as she appeared comfortable around Colin. The plane rose into the azure sky and Jamie gazed out the small window, fashioning the wisps of clouds into animate objects. Tension accelerated her pulse. Jesus Christ. Was she jealous of the flirty little flight attendant? She considered this carefully. Yes, yes she was. Absolutely. What was wrong with her? This was an emotion she'd never experienced before. Never ever. And she considered it absurd. They weren't even dating. Although they *had* been together for a week straight. If the average date was around four hours or so – she did the math in her head – a week was a hundred sixty-eight hours, divided by four, that's roughly forty-two dates. Hmmm, that could be considered a relationship.

Colin cleared his throat and Jamie turned her head. Greta held out a china mug of aromatic coffee. "Smells delicious," Jamie said. She accepted the steaming brew with two hands. "Thank you."

Jamie read on her e-reader most of the way, making the four-hour-and-twenty-minute ride fly by. Colin perused emails and messages while his parents reclined their seats and dozed. The plane landed at Telluride Regional Airport several minutes early.

Five men in dark suits awaited as they disembarked. The crew unloaded their gear and transferred it to the waiting Suburban. Jamie half expected Matt but she guessed he was waiting for them at the chalet. The brisk air under the wide blue sky filled her lungs. She closed her eyes, lifted her chin skyward and inhaled through her nose, exhaling slowly. Little pricks of frost tickled her nostrils. Most people thought her crazy, but she loved winter and skiing in weather like this was her idea of perfection. The elevation would take some adjusting to and she was glad they hadn't planned to hit the slopes this afternoon.

The ride to the chalet took under twenty minutes and Jamie spotted Matt and Rob near the front door. Several uniformed police officers were stationed at the corners of the house and the driveway. Jamie and Colin exited the vehicle while the driver and his partner unloaded suitcases and ski equipment. Jamie approached her fellow agents.

COLIN TRAILED Jamie when his phone pinged a voicemail message. Hmm, not too many people left voicemails these days, the caller identified as *Unknown*. He rarely entertained a number not in his contacts and would normally delete such a message, but for now at least, times had radically changed. He placed the phone to his ear. *"Colin, old buddy. Don't try to trace this call, it's impossible. I know you're fucking that sweet-ass little Feeb. She isn't going to save you. Your days are numbered and you'll never see me coming. You owe me and you'll pay."*

His gut knotted and queasiness churned the coffee in his stomach. The voice made it real. Not only was someone out to kill him, the pathological murderer was his old friend Dave. He replayed the message, each word a tiny dagger pricking his gooseflesh. He didn't know what to do. If Matt or Rob heard it, it could fuck up Jamie's career. Sure, Alyx and Daniel messed around but that was sort of her assignment, and Steve and Laura hooked up yet they worked together and had equal status. Colin wasn't sure Jamie would be given the same latitude based on her assignment. He could play the message for Jamie except if she didn't share it with her boss and her partner it might be considered withholding evidence. He didn't want to put her in a tough spot. Since Dave said the call was untraceable, he'd take him at his word. Dave was a computer genius and could hack anything. In college, he told Colin he'd gotten in trouble with law enforcement several times for breaking through government firewalls. The NSA attempted to recruit him to test security protocols.

He had to share this message with the FBI. It wasn't just his life at stake, but his parents. He'd message Dave back, tell him the truth. Arrange a meet and end this debacle. He tucked his phone into his pocket.

"COLIN," Jamie called out. He walked to greet Matt and Rob. "What's the matter? You look upset."

"Nah, all good. Just checking in with the office. Some clients are getting twitchy. Need to make a few calls once we're settled." He shook hands with Rob Scarborough and Matt.

Rob said, "We're doing everything in our power to keep you and your family safe, Mr. MacKenzie. We've got local authorities on scene and ski patrol has been alerted. We doubt the perp could manage a bomb anywhere on the mountain or in the ski lodge and of course, your lodging is secure."

"Thank you, Agent Scarborough, and you too, Matt. Jamie's kept me up to speed. I know you're working hard to catch this guy."

"We'll stay on site. I'll let you all settle in. Enjoy your vacation."

Colin's parents were already inside and Jamie and Colin joined them. "This is gorgeous," Mrs. MacKenzie said. "Thank you so much, darling." She kissed Colin on the cheek and hugged him. "You're the best, son."

Mr. MacKenzie slapped Colin's back. "That you are."

They shrugged out of their ski parkas and Colin collected them and hung them in the closet. With the bags already placed upstairs and the ski gear lined up on the rack near the door, the MacKenzies marched upstairs to unpack and settle in. Jamie turned to Colin, her hand on his arm. "Something's bothering you."

"No, I'm fine. Seeing Rob and Matt brings this all home again." Colin ran his fingers through his dark, wavy hair. "I need this to be over."

"I know." She rubbed his back. "Let's hope Planchet gets bold and stupid. We've got enough trained personnel to bag his ass."

"I can say a lot of things about Dave, but stupid isn't one of them."

Jamie massaged the back of her neck. She gazed into Colin's blue eyes. "Is there any other reason why he might be targeting you? Aside from the business aspect. This could be more personal."

Colin sunk onto the brown leather sofa and hung his head in his hands. "Maybe…"

Jamie sat beside him. "Tell me."

"Dave and I were roommates in the dorm from the first day. We got along great even though we were quite different. He was on the shy side, the typical nerd, but he had a good heart and was anxious to meet new people. He begged me to show him the ropes, how to talk to girls, go on a date, stuff like that. I was pretty sure he was a virgin." The lines between Colin's eyes scrunched together.

Jamie placed a hand on his knee. "Go on."

"We hung out a lot and he was getting more relaxed around women. He'd had a few dates but nothing came of it. He called me his wing man." Colin sighed. "We eventually moved off campus and senior year Dave started hanging around this girl, Kaitlyn, from his physics class and he intended to ask her out. One day, I was in the Commons when I bumped into her. She'd partied with us plenty and I thought her pretty and smart, easy to be around. We drank coffee and wound up talking for several hours. She made me laugh. I didn't think much about it until one afternoon she showed up at our apartment. Dave wasn't home. A few drinks later, we wound up in bed. I should never have done it because I knew Dave liked her, but then she told me I was the reason she hung around Dave. She wanted to be with me. I still shouldn't have done it, but I did."

Jamie stayed silent and Colin continued. "He came home and found us in bed together. He was pissed." Colin pressed his folded hands to his mouth and closed his eyes. "I thought he'd forgiven me. Now, maybe the truth is he'd spent his entire life planning my death. A spectacular death, it seems. I feel awful. I never meant to hurt him. And the business aspect isn't even my fault, it's my lawyer's. If I could only talk to him, maybe I could make it up to him." And he would tonight, the second he got to his room. Alone.

"Have you ever heard from Kaitlyn?"

"No. I lost track."

"Planchet mentioned her name on one of the sites."

"Fuck, that's not good. Do you think she's in danger?"

Jamie rubbed her temples. "Perhaps. We're trying to locate her now and this certainly adds another motive." Jamie leaned back against the couch and propped her legs onto the coffee table. "You steal his girl and then his business. Makes for some pretty bad blood. He's an incel."

"A what?"

"Incels are involuntary celibates. They define themselves as unable to find a romantic or sexual partner, despite desiring one. A state they call inceldom. Online forums showcase misanthropy, resentment, self-pity, misogyny and racism. They have a sense of entitlement to sex and endorse violence against sexually active people. It's a male supremacist ecosystem and basically a hate group."

"Are you fucking kidding me? That's a real thing?"

"They even go so far as believing sex is a God-given right and the government should provide them sexual partners."

"Jesus Christ, what's this world coming to?"

Jamie laughed. "If Dave is one, and he knew you worked at a sex club and had more sex than he could ever hope for, that might induce some rage."

Colin shook his head. "I'm fucked then. If he's one of these... *incels*... then it sounds like there's nothing I can do to appease him."

Colin's phone burned a hole in his pocket. The angel and devil on his shoulder arguing over whether to show Jamie the message from Dave. He cracked his knuckles and leaned back against the couch. Jamie patted his knee. "Let it all go for now. Let's unpack and make plans for dinner." She stood and held out her hand. Colin took it and let her tow him upstairs.

They picked adjacent bedrooms and stowed their things, Jamie returning to his room. Colin said, "Do you have enough clothes? We could go shopping."

"I don't know. I'm going to see if they have a washer and dryer first." Jamie set out on her hunt and Colin sat in the corner chair. *Fuck. This was turning into another clusterfuck.*

Chapter 44

The MacKenzie clan and Jamie enjoyed a candlelit dinner at the Chop House, security personnel guarding the restaurant's front and back doors. Colin invited Rob and Matt yet they politely declined.

Jamie felt underdressed, wearing her jeans and white sweater. Colin insisted the dress was casual, but even a pair of dressy black pants would have made her feel more in-tune with the clientele. Most women, including Mrs. MacKenzie, wore dresses, although a few sported black slacks with a ski sweater... and expensive jewelry was on full display. Never much of a jewelry enthusiast, Jamie didn't own a single piece that couldn't be bought at Target.

She perused the menu, eyes wide. Fifty-nine dollars for the New York strip steak? She imagined she'd have to get used to this if she intended on spending more time with Colin. Most guys she dated were agreeable to splitting the check but she doubted Colin would ever allow that.

Colin and his dad ordered the strip steak, medium-rare, while Mrs. MacKenzie chose the Colorado Striped Bass, and Jamie the Pan Seared Muscovy Duck. They shared the Tuna Tataki and the Cheese and Charcuterie Board for appetizers along with a cabernet Colin selected from the sommelier. The restaurant was also touted as a wine bar and Jamie couldn't conceive of how much the wine might cost.

Friendly chatter and a few laughs later they returned to the chalet. Jamie spoke briefly with Rob and Matt, who were about to check into the nearby motel. Nothing new on the case. The plan was to get to the slopes around 10 a.m., as Mrs. MacKenzie insisted on not rising before the sun. "After all, this is a vacation," she said. The MacKenzies turned in for the night and Jamie kicked off her shoes and sat on the couch, her bare feet atop the coffee table.

Colin said, "I think I'll head up to bed. I'm exhausted."

Jamie arched her eyebrows. "Perhaps because you kept us awake until the wee hours with all your shenanigans."

"I didn't hear any complaints from my submissive."

That word still grated her nerves, but she loved playing the part. And it was just that, role-playing for hot sex. Totally worth it. Especially since Colin never expected her to be that way in the other aspects of her life. "Well, *I'm* not tired." However, she was still a bit sore and a night off would be good. She wanted to be in top form the next time they played.

"I'll make it up to you. Promise." He bent down and kissed her lightly on the lips. "Night, see you in the morning." He trod up the stairs like someone carrying a hundred-pound weight.

COLIN STRIPPED and turned on the shower, hoping the scalding water would ease the knot between his shoulders. However, he had knots everywhere: stomach, head, even his biceps were tense. What he really wanted to do was punch something. He sat down heavily on the bed, phone in hand. He retrieved the message from Dave and typed: *It was my lawyer that screwed you, I had no idea. Why don't you face me like a man? We could work this out instead of you trying to kill me and my family. I'll make amends.*" He didn't mention Kaitlyn because… well, there was no way to make amends for that. He waited for a response.

Several minutes ticked by. Nothing. He entered the shower, much like his own, water jets pummeling him from every direction. A seat and handheld attachment were also featured, and he envisioned Jamie in the throes of passion while he made her come with just the force of the water.

The showerhead doused his hair with delectable warm water, streaming down his back. He turned and the hot rivulets wet his face. He scrubbed it with both hands, running his fingers through drenched hair. He sighed and placed both hands on the wall as the water attempted to wash away his troubles, the message from Dave eating at him like maggots. And Jamie knew something was bothering him and she'd probably misinterpreted his sullen mood as a reflection of their blossoming relationship. Withholding Dave's threat made things worse. Maybe he should ditch his phone. That would be a giant pain in the ass, yet it might make it impossible for the FBI to find the damned message. Now he was being a real idiot. *Everything* lived in the cloud and the FBI certainly had people with the expertise to find it.

Maybe they were doing it right now. Had they been monitoring his phone all along? Didn't they need permission? His head was about to explode. Nothing more he could do about it tonight and so he fell into bed with a giant headache. For now, he and his parents were safe with protection inside and outside the chalet. If Dave didn't message him back, he'd tell Jamie first thing in the morning.

Sleep… he prayed for sleep.

JAMIE DAWDLED ON THE COUCH, nibbling on a fingernail. Huh, what could have put Colin in such a crappy mood? The total opposite of their amazing night and easy morning. He seemed fine until they got off the plane. Maybe it was a business call. Nervous clients could definitely be cause for worry. She'd asked him several times and he'd been unwilling to share. Nothing left to do tonight. She switched off the lights and peeked through the blinds, six officers posted out front in the frigid weather.

Lingering at Colin's door, she was sorely tempted to check on him. Maybe he needed some alone time. She entered her room, folded her jeans and sweater and tucked them inside a dresser drawer, then deposited her black pumps on the closet floor, her underwear followed. Donning her oversized tee-shirt with the FBI logo, she grabbed her toiletry bag and headed for the bathroom. She washed her face and brushed her hair, studying her reflection. In the course of a week, she'd become a new person. Never could she have imagined a man like Colin entering her life. And now, hmm… she couldn't imagine losing him. At the same time, she found it difficult to believe Colin could be interested in her over the long haul. He lived in an entirely different world. Money, status, an influential career, he moved in circles she didn't navigate. Maybe this was a game he was playing. And the club… how would that play out? If they were together, she could never reconcile him still having sex at the club, even if it was sort of his job. Seriously, a job that meant having sex with people? *Egad.* Never ever.

She slipped between the sheets and rolled onto her side, her hands tucked beneath the pillow. The full moon lit the night sky, so bright, beautiful and she wanted to instead crawl into bed with the handsome billionaire.

STILL NO RESPONSE FROM DAVE, Colin spread organic almond butter on a toasted English muffin and his mom poured coffee. He'd stocked the refrigerator with foodstuffs so they could have a leisurely morning. Rarely a breakfast eater, he often indulged on vacation. He took his coffee and plate to the kitchen table and sat opposite his dad, who scoffed down eggs and bacon.

"Have I mentioned how much I like bacon?" Mr. MacKenzie said, shoving an entire piece into his mouth. He followed it with a bite of toast and washed it down with coffee.

"Pretty much every day of my life," Colin said. He smiled. His mother rubbed her husband's back, then leaned over and kissed his cheek. His parents were so happy. Growing up, they had the occasional verbal spat, never an out-and-out fight. When his mom got on one of her health kicks, his father got testy. But mostly, he ignored her until the phase passed, supplementing his diet with forbidden items on the sly.

Jamie entered the kitchen dressed in dark blue ski pants and her perennial white sweater. He wanted to buy her some clothes. Maybe he'd surprise her, although it would probably piss her off.

"Morning," she said. "Did everyone sleep well?"

Mrs. MacKenzie chimed in, "Like the dead." She paused as her husband gave her a squinty look. "Oh, I'm sorry, everyone. I guess it's a good thing we can forget for a little while."

"No worries, Mom," Colin said, then pivoted to Jamie. "Had some sweet dreams, you?"

"None that I can remember," she said. Or rather, none that she could talk about in mixed company.

Jamie sauntered over to the coffee pot and filled a mug. He couldn't keep his eyes off her perky ass and chastised himself for sleeping alone. He'd wanted her next to him last night. Not for sex, for… comfort. She was his safe port in this fucked up storm.

"You brought in breakfast stuff?"

"Yeah, I figured we'd treat ourselves since we're on vacation."

Jamie perused a tray of donuts and other baked confections. "Don't mind if I do." She selected a cinnamon roll and brought her breakfast to the kitchen table, taking the open seat next to Colin.

Colin checked the weather app. "Looks like a good day, temps around twenty-six, but sunny all day and not much wind."

"Perfect skiing weather," Jamie sad.

"Just so you know, I'm only good for about four hours," Mrs. MacKenzie said. "I figure two hours, then lunch, then two more hours. I like skiing but I'm not a huge fan of freezing my butt off."

"Sounds perfect," Colin's dad said. "We're getting to be old farts." He grabbed his wife's hand and kissed it. "At least we haven't deteriorated to the point of talking about all our physical ailments." He winked at his wife.

"Tell me, at my book club it sometimes takes a half-hour to get to the book discussion. Everyone needs to report on their health status."

They ate leisurely, chatting about their hopes for the next election when Colin said, "Let's get a move-on. Don't bother to clean up, I have housekeeping coming in. I'll tell James to warm up the car. Can everyone be ready in ten?"

Agreements nodded, they suited up as James loaded their skis, boots and poles into the car. Colin came close and zipped Jamie's matching navy-blue parka. "Ready for some fun?" he said, trying to convince himself as well. He tweaked her nose, garnering a sideways glance from his mother.

He'd tell Jamie about the message soon. Definitely before lunch.

Chapter 45

The trip to the lodge zipped by and they were met by Matt and Rob, who fitted Colin with a tracker and introduced them to the captain of the ski patrol, Josh Gremmel. "Morning, Mr. MacKenzie," he said, extending his hand. He turned to Jamie, "Agent Gallagher, pleasure." They shook hands. Jamie's Glock was secured in a shoulder holster inside her ski parka and her secondary weapon strapped to her calf. No one liked wearing a shoulder harness because it inhibited getting your hand on your weapon quickly, especially if you had to maneuver around a breast. But it was the best she could manage. Wearing it on her waist wasn't viable. Skiing with a weapon (or two) proved a challenge.

"All members of the ski patrol have been alerted to your presence and we've distributed your photo for visual reference. I'll include a description of your clothing now that I've seen it. The same goes for you, Agent Gallagher." Josh crooked his forefinger and two figures wearing red and black uniforms approached. "We have two of our most experienced skiers assigned to follow you throughout the day." He turned to the petite blonde beside him. "This is Alice Washington." She nodded. "And this is Brian McCarthy." He also nodded. "They're instructed to have eyes on you at all times. And we have additional members assigned to your parents." He crooked his finger a second time and introduced Colin's parents' shadows.

"Thank you," Jamie said. "No one is armed, correct?"

"Correct," Josh said. "We're not attached to law enforcement. This is for observation only. We are in contact with each other through our earpieces and can respond if needed. We also have EMTs available. Hopefully, there will be no need for them."

"Speaking of which," Rob said. He handed Jamie her earpiece—an invisible two-way micro Bluetooth headset. "You can reach everybody, all agents and the ski patrol."

"Roger that," Jamie said, slipping the little nub into her ear and pulling down her yellow North Face beanie.

"I guess we're all set. Have fun," Rob said.

They grabbed their skis and headed for the chairlift to Ute Park. Jamie grimaced. Ute Park consisted of both beginner and intermediate runs. It would be littered with newbies and lots of kids. Dangerous for a double black diamond skier, the odds of running over someone entirely likely. At least it wasn't the Meadows, bodies strewn everywhere as skiers rotated through classes with instructors who have the patience of saints.

Obviously sensing her disdain, Colin said, "Just a few runs to warm up, and they have some cool jumps. Then we'll head over to Gold Hill."

"You're the tour director." Jamie lowered her goggles and adjusted the strap over her hat. The wind minimal, she left her face exposed.

They took a few runs and nobody died. Jamie considered that a win. Colin told his parents he and Jamie were heading over to the expert trails and everyone agreed to meet back at the lodge around one for lunch.

Jamie chatted with Alice on the lift. She'd done two tours in Iraq as a sniper in the Marines. She'd enlisted right after earning her

MSW, much to her parents' dismay. Jamie thought being a social worker an odd choice for a former Marine. She shared her attendance at the Naval Academy before entering the FBI and even mentioned being an Olympian for skiing and shooting. She didn't mention the gold medal and Alice didn't ask. It felt like they could be friends. Alice counseled victims of PTSD.

The brisk air filled her lungs, tiny ice crystals in her nostrils making her sneeze. A flawless day, and she couldn't imagine being anywhere better. She surveyed the majestic white peaks, the acres of pristine snow icing them like cake frosting, only accessible by snowmobile, or snow cat. If only this were a real vacation and Colin wasn't in fear for his life. As was she. They needed this to be over. She wondered if Dave Planchet was in the vicinity. He could make himself invisible through technology, but his physical imprint would be more difficult to conceal. Of course, he could hide behind goggles and a ski mask, which didn't make the prospect of identifying him easy.

They descended the lift and Colin stood alongside. "Ready?"

"Let's do this."

They took several runs, Alice and Brian close on their heels. Jamie was happy she still had her 'ski legs'. She hadn't hit the slopes once this year, still determined to spend some time with her dad as soon as he mended.

Colin skied expertly and on the next run, she challenged him to a race.

"You sure, little subbie," Colin said. "I'll beat your ass." Jamie blanched, hoping nobody, including Alice and Brian overheard.

She leaned in. "Don't call me that in public."

Colin adjusted his goggles. "You want a head start?"

Jamie was a little annoyed at his comment and decided to take the offer instead of answering. She planted her poles and pushed off, leaving Colin in the powder. The conditions were ideal and she maxed out her speed, reaching the bottom in what she guessed would be record time. She gazed up the mountain... searching the vast expanse. Empty. No Colin, no Alice, no Brian.

THAT LITTLE MINX, she cheated, grabbing a pretty good lead. Damn. He planted his poles, ready to push off, when someone grabbed him from behind and shoved a sweet-smelling cloth in his face. He held his breath to avoid breathing in what he assumed was something bad. Unable to hold out any longer, he inhaled and fell into a dark abyss, his body like lead, his legs giving out, unable to support him.

JAMIE YELLED INTO HER MIC. "Alice? Brian? Where's Colin?" Silence. Rob said, "Jamie, what's wrong?"

"Colin and I were racing down the mountain but when I arrived at the bottom, he wasn't with me. Check the tracker." *Oh God. She'd lost him.* No way Planchet could snatch him off the top of a double black diamond trail. Even if he did, he'd have to get him off the mountain and if he made it down with Colin, they'd spot him in a nanosecond. It didn't make sense. What had she missed?

Matt reported, "The tracker says he's at the top of the mountain. Ten feet to the west."

"No sign of my guys?" Josh Gremmel asked.

"No, I'm taking the lift up again, I'll report back ASAP." This time the ride up was interminable. Jamie scoured the mountain in search of Colin and the attending ski patrol personnel. Nothing. Getting off the lift she saw two groups of people gathered around prone bodies. She muscled her way into one, announcing her FBI status. Alice, out cold. She knelt and felt for a pulse. She was breathing, alive. She scrambled to the second crowd, Brian too, unconscious but alive. "Rob," she said, "Alice and Brian are here but they're unconscious. I don't see any injuries so not sure what happened. Could be drugged."

"Josh and the EMTs are on their way."

"What's the tracker saying about Colin's whereabouts?"

"It still says ten feet away, to the left."

"Roger that," she said. Jamie walked left and found it on the ground. "Shit, it's here. Someone must have removed it."

"Shit, is right," Matt said.

Rob ordered, "Wait for the emergency personnel to arrive, then meet me back at the ski patrol office. I've alerted everyone to the situation."

Queasiness roiled Jamie's gut. How could they haul a six-foot male in ski gear off the mountain? The Planchet brothers were scrawny guys.

Josh Gremmel jumped off his snowmobile and approached, surveying the insentient bodies of Alice and Brian. The EMTs assessed their patients then reported to Josh. "No injuries we can see. Their vitals are normal, a little sluggish. My guess is there's some sedative involved. I smell something sweet, maybe chloroform."

Josh, goggles atop his hat, rubbed the back of his neck. "Transport them to the hospital. Keep me apprised of their status." He faced Jamie. "How could he possibly have been spirited off the mountain? The only way off is down. And we would have spotted him."

"I thought it was a pretty tight circle of surveillance," Rob said into their earpieces.

"What about up?" Jamie asked Josh. "Is there any way they could have taken him up the mountain?"

Josh studied her, then his eyes traveled upward. "Maybe. There are cabins up there. They are private residences and you can only get there by cat or snowmobile. None of which are quiet means of transportation. Plus, Mr. MacKenzie isn't a small guy, hauling him up the slope unconscious would be a challenge."

Jamie pinched the bridge of her nose. "What if they had a sled? Like the ones you use to transport injured skiers."

"The forest is pretty dense here. Could easily hide snowmobiles and a sled."

"Do you have a map of what's up there? How many cabins?"

"Back in the office." Jamie skied down, almost beating Josh on his snowmobile.

They entered the ski patrol office where Rob, Matt and a contingent of agents and ski patrollers crowded the diminutive space. Josh fumbled through his desk drawer, laying out a map on the surface.

What could she say to Rob? She'd bungled her assignment. She'd fucked up. But it wasn't her career she was worried about. *Oh God. Colin, where are you?*

Chapter 46

Colin's head pounded, had he been on a bender? Wait, wait. No, he wasn't drunk, was he? The confusing moments expired. He'd been abducted! Determined to beat Jamie down the mountain, he'd lowered his goggles, planted his poles, when arms encircled his chest and that cloying rag covered his nose. His stomach queasy, his cheek on some flat surface, he forced his eyes open. He was tied to a chair, his hands bound, his feet lashed to the chair legs. Restrained, and not in the fun way.

The room was out of focus, like looking through a fogged lens. Dizziness swarmed him, his equilibrium compromised. He couldn't stand if he tried. As his vision slowly and stubbornly cleared, he scanned the room without raising his head. A log cabin, a fireplace, a shabby plaid couch. Two men spoke quietly, their words unintelligible. A brunette in a heap beside the fireplace. Face bruised and swollen, her clothing tattered and soiled. Could it be… Kaitlyn?

He wriggled his hands, seeking escape. No chance, the ropes too tight, his fingers numb. His ski boots were gone, wool socks his only barrier to the cold. His back ached and he struggled upright, his head a fifty-pound kettle bell. He swallowed hard, forcing back the bile in his throat.

"Princess is awake," a male voice said. The man stood in front of Colin, the giant brass belt buckle with the initial D the first thing Colin saw. He pulled out a chair, the wood scraping the planked flooring and sat. Colin cringed. Dave Planchet's beady dark eyes met his. Colin always thought his eyes were too close together, which gave him a sinister look. The years hadn't been good to Dave, his face was completely wrinkled, and dark circles surrounded his eyes like bad bruising. His hairline had receded and what was left hung too long and stringy, like a character out of *The Hobbit*.

"Finally, I have you right where I want you." Another figure appeared, taking the opposite seat. Noah.

"Dave, I messaged you back explaining the circumstances. I was hoping to have a sit-down with you, to make this right."

"Too late, buddy. I'm bankrupt and in so much debt there's no way out. It killed my father. We couldn't pay his medical bills. We couldn't afford treatment. I hold you responsible for his death."

Colin rolled his shoulders hoping to relieve the strain of his hands tied behind his back. "How about you untie me and we talk about this like civilized human beings?"

Dave Planchet huffed, his brother, Noah, guffawed. "A civilized human being wouldn't have stolen my company out from under me."

"It wasn't me, it was my lawyer."

Dave slapped Colin across the face. Blood seeped into his mouth, his lip split. "Bullshit. Your lawyer works for you. He wouldn't do anything without your approval."

Colin licked blood off his swollen lip. "I didn't think so, but the FBI confirmed otherwise. You could have called me instead of trying to blow up my workplace and then my residence. And is that Kaitlyn over there?"

Dave beamed, a front tooth missing. "Icing on the cake. I thought you'd pay more if it included her life."

"Then she's alive?"

"A little worse for the wear, but she's hanging on. Probably waiting for her knight in shining armor to rescue her." Dave grinned and Colin knew his former roommate and friend was too far gone. There'd be no redemption for Dave Planchet, or his brother.

"What the fuck is wrong with you, Dave?"

Dave made a fist and Colin braced himself for Dave's wrath. He closed his eyes and steadied his jaw. He needed to calm down, making Dave angry wouldn't help remedy the situation. Dave's fist plowed into his nose. The force sent Colin backward. The chair tipped and he landed on the floor, his hands crushed under the impact. The blow sent his pulse all jittery, blood poured down his cheeks, spilling into his ears. Shit, was his nose broken? The pain wasn't as bad as he thought it would be, having never taken a punch in the face before. Swelling made it difficult to breathe and he inhaled through his mouth, gasping for air.

"Dave, take it easy," Noah said, his hand on his arm. "If we kill him the whole plan falls apart."

Dave reached down and righted the chair, landing it with such force that Colin groaned, pain zinging his bones as if he'd been tased. The room whirled around him in a tornado of fire and wood. The smell of smoke nauseated him and he feared he'd vomit. Blood gushed over his bloated lips, and onto the table, forming a puddle. Could you bleed to death from a broken nose?

JAMIE PACED THE SMALL OFFICE, her heart in her throat. They needed a plan. Josh pointed to a spot on the map. "There's only one cabin at the crest of that trail. There's no way to get there without a cat or snowmobile. You'd never be able to approach without being seen, or more aptly, heard. They're noisy suckers."

Jamie rubbed her forehead. Rob and Matt stood nearby. How to get there? But then… "What about a helo?"

Everyone frowned. And then Matt said, "You want to helicopter in?"

Jamie ignored him, and shifted toward Josh. "Is that possible?"

"We have Heli-Trax. They take people up. Do you have any experience?"

"She's a world class skier. Won an Olympic medal—skiing and shooting, she's also an HRT certified sniper. And she's got the balls to go with all that," Rob said.

How in the hell did he know that?

Rob smirked. "It's on your background check. I know you don't like to talk about it."

Jamie let his assessment of her skills go. "How fast can you get me up?" she asked Josh.

"Wait a second," Matt interjected. "Helicopters are major-league noisy."

Josh countered with, "It's our busy season. If these guys have been up there for a least a day they know we have choppers up there all the time. It probably wouldn't arouse suspicion."

To Jamie, he said, "They're on site and a pilot is on standby in the event we have to airlift someone who's critical. Probably within fifteen minutes."

Matt faced Jamie. "How are you going to pull this off? There are two of them. They're armed and dangerous and probably crazy. Plus, you'd have to jump out of a helicopter with your ski gear and carry a Remington 700. Sounds too dangerous to me." He turned to Rob. "How about backing me up here?"

"I can do this," Jamie said, matter of fact. "I'm the only one here who can."

Rob exhaled slowly. "Jamie is extraordinary, and resourceful. Our only other option is to wait it out and I'm not happy with that prospect. We all know the more time that elapses for any kidnapping, the greater the chances the victim dies."

"Besides," she explained to Matt, "you don't jump out, they land you. You just have to keep your eye on those rotors."

"I don't like it," Matt said. "They'll hear you coming."

"Not if we land her up high enough," Josh explained. "It will just look like routine surveillance. We do it all the time."

Josh continued. "It won't be a marked trail. You good in deep powder?"

"Not a problem."

"I'll make the call."

The ski patrol hooked her up: backpack, water, hand warmers, granola bars, flares, duct tape, snowshoes, shovel, hiking boots and their good wishes. The helicopter landed at the bottom of the mountain, a crowd forming, expecting a show. They loaded her skis into the side compartment, and Jamie climbed aboard. She tucked the radio earbud into her ear beneath her hat. "I'll keep you posted," she told Rob.

"Stay safe," Matt said. "My kid's birthday is next weekend and I'll expect you there."

Jamie smiled. "Count on it."

In a rare expression of friendship, Rob leaned in and whispered in her ear, "I'm counting on you, Agent Gallagher. Bring our guy home in good shape." He squeezed her gloved hand.

"I will, sir."

"LOOK, Dave, I promise to make this right. Name your price. I'll pay it. My lawyer killed himself. That should give you some satisfaction." Confessing that his attorney had offed himself would probably not help the situation. He didn't think anything but money would appease Dave's ire.

"You don't have enough money to pay for my father's death. You can't bring him back. Besides, the FBI won't let me off after I tried to kill you, twice, plus our little slut, Kaitlyn."

"Not if you let her go. We can figure this all out. I'll give you enough money to live a great life, you and Noah. And with your skills you can disappear on some desert island. Find peace and comfort."

Noah turned Dave's chair toward him, grabbing his upper arms. "Bro, this was the plan. We get a big payout and disappear. MacKenzie's got clout, he can make this happen. Fuck the Feds. He transfers the money, we escape, and live happily ever after. All the booze and women we can buy."

Dave shook his head. "It won't be easy to duck the Feds. And that little bitch agent won't let go until she finds us. She's in love with MacKenzie."

Colin had no idea how Planchet had come to such a conclusion. How could he possibly have seen them together enough to deduce that? Even Colin didn't presume... He hoped, but by no means was it a given. Jamie must be freaking out. She prided herself on getting the job done, and now she'd be on a death mission, doing anything necessary to save him.

Something told him this wouldn't end well.

Chapter 47

Arriving at the landing spot near the mountain's crest, Jamie stepped out of the helo and clamped on her skis. Backpack donned, snowshoes strapped to her pack and a Remington 700 sniper rifle slung across her chest, she accepted her poles from the copilot. He yelled over the whir of rotors, "Call when you need a pickup. We're ten minutes out."

Jamie gave a thumbs up.

"The cabin is about three miles in. Stay to the left. There's smoke coming from the chimney so keep your eye on that."

"Will do."

"Good luck, Agent Gallagher. We're rooting for you."

The helo lifted off, creating mini white tornadoes, as Jamie ventured into the thick forest. Like skiing the Glades at Killington. Ski or die. And sometimes ski *and* die. The sun was casting yellow shafts of light, piercing the throng of pine trees.

The temps plummeted along with the sun, the adrenaline surging into her muscles a temporary deterrent to frostbite. She got into rhythm, thighs pumping, tips up. Faster, faster! Shoulders leading the way. She mused over her plan, covert approach mandatory.

Catching them off guard, paramount. They weren't trained professionals when it came to guns, which she hoped gave her a much-needed advantage. Smoke trailed skyward as she closed in on the cabin. She stopped about twenty yards out, hidden behind a large tree trunk, dropping her poles and slipping her backpack off her shoulders. She crouched and unpacked her hiking boots, then sat and switched out her ski boots. Three weapons in her cache, she doubled-checked the rifle, unhitching the safety, her Glock still in her shoulder harness and her tertiary weapon secured against her calf. She unzipped her parka to have easy access to her Glock.

Now or never.

She kept low, darting from tree to tree, until she got in range of the cabin. Muted light emanated through a grimy double hung, nine-paned window with primitive wooden boards as shutters. Inside, the animated shapes of three humans took shape. She crouched behind a diminutive pine tree, the rifle sight providing a close-up: Colin strapped to a chair, his face bloodied, and two men sitting at the small wooden table alongside him. The man with his back to her pounded the table, screaming words she couldn't comprehend. Colin's injuries twisted her heart, then her stomach. In moments like these, the temptation to break all the rules and kill the perpetrator fought with her training and sense of morality. Her job wasn't to pass judgment but apprehend and turn the suspect over to the courts.

One man stood and walked toward the right side of the cabin. The door opened and Jamie recognized him, Noah, Dave Planchet's brother. Only ten feet away. He grabbed logs from the woodpile, stacking them in his arms. Jamie zipped the duct tape and handcuffs into her pocket.

Focus. Get him. Focus.

A snow-burdened branch overhead snapped, plunging into the deep powder. Noah twisted at the waist, clutching wood to his chest, feral eyes searching the forest. Jamie slinked backward, her spine rigid, her arm clutching the rifle to her side. She held her breath, praying he hadn't seen her. If he did, she'd be forced to shoot him and then everything would spiral into hell.

Wolves howled in the distance. She waited, her breathing shallow, her pulse speeding, and waited some more. Should she risk it, come from behind? Utilizing surprise, she still might get the jump on him. Except maybe not.

Jamie peeked around the tree trunk. Noah had returned to his task, grabbing another log. She chucked the rifle over her shoulder and sprinted. He pivoted. Dropping his burden, logs fell in soft snow. Her gloved fist plowed through air. His mouth expanded into a gaping O. The start of a scream. *Crack, crunch.* Blood spurted. Three-quarters of her hand inexplicably buried inside his mouth. His vocal cords vibrating against her knuckles.

His scream stifled, he bit into her glove. With savage strength, she extricated her hand along with two bloody teeth. She pressed her palm against his bloodstained lips and trapped his neck in the vice of her elbow. Squeezing. With. All. Her. Might. He writhed, tugging on her arm to free himself. She kept the pressure on until he stopped struggling and collapsed, his knees furrowed into the snow-covered ground. She handcuffed him behind his back, and duct-taped him to a tree, slapping a strip over his swollen lips.

She approached the door – left ajar – and glimpsed inside. Colin saw her but his expression didn't sound an alarm.

"If you want to make amends, I'm listening," Dave Planchet said.

"Name your price," Colin said.

"Twenty mill."

"Done. I'll have the money transferred immediately."

"How you gonna do that from here?"

"I assume you have an offshore account. Give me the number and a phone and it's done."

Dave Planchet rose and paced. He faced Colin and hesitated, then untied his hands. "Okay, I'm giving you a chance for all of us to walk out of here alive." He paused. "How do I know you don't have the Feds on alert?"

"What does it matter? They can't stop the transfer."

"Then how do we get out of here?"

Jamie stepped inside. "I have a helicopter on standby." Her peripheral vision spotted an unconscious woman curled into the fetal position alongside the fireplace. Who?

She aimed her rifle at Planchet. He wheeled on her, reaching for the gun on the table. "Don't," she said. "FBI. On your knees or you'll be dead before you touch it." Jamie realized Colin was too close and her rifle too powerful, the bullet would easily go through Planchet and hit Colin.

Planchet picked up his revolver and aimed it at Jamie.

"Drop it," she said. "You'll never make it out alive. We've got fifteen agents surrounding this place. No chance of escape unless I allow it."

Planchet fixated on the door. "Where's Noah? Did you kill him?"

"No. He's tied up outside. Alive." She left out the part about the knuckle sandwich. Her finger on the trigger, she gritted her teeth. A hair more pressure and the suspect would be dead, unfortunately maybe Colin too. If only Colin would duck. She shifted her eyes slightly to the left, hoping he'd get her meaning.

Planchet's hand shook. Anger, fear? Maybe both. Should she take the shot? Colin sat tall in the chair, her eye-flick hadn't translated. Her adrenaline spiked, her heart jackhammered. Somehow her hand remained steady, her eye on the target through the scope. "It's over, Dave. Either surrender or take my offer for a one-way ticket to the morgue. Those are your options. I know Mr. MacKenzie wants to do right by you." Keep him talking and thinking, essential. The longer she could distract him, the more likely he'd calm down. A peaceful resolution—

Dave's gun exploded, the round hitting her left shoulder. She spun, knocked to the floor. A bullet from her rifle pierced the ceiling. Stars shattered her vision. Pain sizzled her insides like an electric current zapping boiling water.

COLIN FREED HIS ANKLES, jumped up and knocked Planchet to the ground. They wrestled, grappling for Dave's pistol. Colin's stamina remained low, his body achy, epinephrine reserves depleted. He heard Jamie moan and yell, "You motherfucker!" Dave pinned Colin to the floorboards and punched him in the face again. Stabbing pains stung his eye, stealing all breath from his lungs. The revolver slid across the floor, smacking the wall.

Dave lunged for Jamie, snatching the rifle from her wounded arm. He stood and aimed the barrel at her. "Cunt," he said. "We almost hit the sweet spot, until you arrived."

Colin scrambled toward the wall and grabbed Dave's weapon. His back against plaster, he aimed and fired. The bullet pierced the stone above the fireplace mantel. Dave turned toward Colin, Jamie grabbed Dave's ankle, tumbling him forward, landing atop Colin. The rifle pinned between them. Colin shoved him off with an elbow to the chin. Dave still gripped the weapon in both hands. Colin kicked the rifle, snapping Dave's head back against the floor. The weapon skidded to the far wall and slammed into the door jamb.

Colin searched for the pistol, unsure if he could beat Dave to the rifle. Dave had the same idea and they grappled for the ivory-handled gun. A shot rang out. Dave collapsed on top of Colin. Neither moved.

Jesus fucking Christ.

Jamie screamed, "Colin!"

Colin heaved Dave aside and pushed himself upright, leaning his head against the wall, his legs splayed in front of him. Dave lay on his back, blood drenching his flannel shirt. Eyes wide shut. Colin crawled to Kaitlyn and eased her onto her back. "Oh God, Kaitlyn!" She groaned and her eyes fluttered open. Colin carefully removed the tape over her mouth and released her bound hands and feet. He rested her head in his lap. "How bad?" he asked.

Kaitlyn's bloated lips stuck together and it took a second for her to speak. "I think my ankle is broken. I fell when trying to make a run for it. He was waiting in my apartment when I got home from work."

"Horrible. I'm so sorry." Colin pushed the tangled dark tresses off her face and wiped the tears from her cheek.

Kaitlyn whispered, "Dave's crazy. What happened to him?"

"It's a long story but it's over now."

"I thought I was dead."

"Me too."

JAMIE PRESSED two fingers against Planchet's neck. No pulse. She regarded Colin. "Nice shot, mister. You ever shoot a gun before?"

"Yeah, no. Not a fan."

"I hear you. But you have potential."

"Pure luck. Maybe angels."

Jamie opened her jacket and checked for a bullet hole. The slug pierced her upper shoulder, a lot of blood, yet she was pretty sure it hadn't hit bone. She took off her hat and stuffed it inside her jacket to apply pressure.

"You hit?" Colin inquired.

"Grazed my shoulder. I'll survive." Jamie knelt beside Kaitlyn. "I take it this is the old girlfriend?"

"Kaitlyn," Colin said. "This is Special Agent Jamie Gallagher. She's been on the case and acting in the capacity of bodyguard. We'd both be dead if it wasn't for her."

"Thank God for you, Agent Gallagher," Kaitlyn murmured.

"What about you?" Jamie asked Colin. She put a hand on the side of his head. He'd taken a serious beating. "I think your pretty-boy face may be in jeopardy."

Colin rested his hand atop hers. "Will you still want to hang with me if I'm ugly?"

"Your face isn't why I like you." She smiled, then dropped her hand.

Colin winced. "I think my nose is broken."

"Distinct possibility." Jamie stood and withdrew her service revolver. "I need to check on the brother, hopefully he hasn't died from hypothermia."

Colin rested Kaitlyn on the plaid couch and followed Jamie outside, his socked feet crunching the crusty snow. Jamie aimed her Glock at the restrained subject. Noah stared at her, eyeballs nearly popping out of his head. "Noah Planchet you're under arrest for attempted murder. You have the right to remain silent. Anything you say can be used against you. You have the right to lawyer up—"

Noah screamed under the tape. Jamie reached down and ripped it off.

"You bitch, did you kill my brother?" He spat, the slimy wad hitting her cheek.

She wiped the scum away with the back of her hand. "Unfortunately, yes. I gave him a way out but the idiot didn't take it."

Jamie cut the tape binding Noah to the tree, yanked him to his feet and marched him into the cabin. Colin forced him into the rickety wooden chair and tied him to it. Jamie realized her earpiece had dislodged and located it under the table. She put it in and heard Rob yelling, "Jamie, report in. What's happening?" She heard Rob tell Matt, "Get the helo up!"

"Hi Rob. All good, both of us are a little banged up. Dave Planchet is dead. You'll need a way to remove the body. I have the brother in custody."

"Jesus, you kept me hanging, I feared the worst."

"There's another victim. The former girlfriend, Kaitlyn, they abducted her and brought her along for additional incentive. She's not critical but requires medical attention. Now get us out of here."

"Roger that."

Colin shrugged off his jacket and tucked it under Kaitlyn's head. He rose and surrounded Jamie in a hug, whispering, "Thought I'd lost you." He kissed the top of her head.

"Me too," she said. "I'm so sorry. I fucked up and almost got you killed."

Colin pulled back, his eyes bloodshot and puffy. It wrenched her heart. He'd gotten hurt because she'd left him unguarded.

"It wasn't your fault."

"Yes, it was. I should never have left your side. I got sloppy, I deserve to be disciplined. I just hope it doesn't cost me my job."

Colin sighed, running his fingers through his hair. "Listen, Jamie, there's something I have to tell you."

Jamie's eyes narrowed. "What?"

"Planchet called me yesterday. He left a voicemail threatening to kill me."

"Are you fucking kidding me? When did you get it?"

"It must have come in while we were on the plane. It pinged when we arrived at the chalet. You were talking to Rob and Matt."

"Why didn't you tell me?"

"I meant to last night and then again this morning. I messaged him back, offering to meet and clear this all up. I figured my parents and I were safe for the moment, with FBI protection. I worried that if Matt or Rob heard the message you'd be in trouble."

"Why, what did it say?"

"That he knew we were sleeping together. I panicked, then realized that withholding just made it worse."

"You were worried about my career? What about your life? And your parents'?" Jamie paced, then faced him. "That's why you were in such a crappy mood last night."

"The longer I kept if from you the worse it got."

"That's unforgivable, Colin. It could have been a break, we could have traced the call."

"Dave said the call was untraceable and I took him at his word. He can hide anything. Even from the cloud."

"Jesus. I'm furious. With *you*."

"I know. But we're both alive."

"Don't be so sure. I might kill you."

"Are you going to tell your boss?"

"Of course."

"I'll defend you. I'll tell Rob I used poor judgment. My ego got in the way. Thought I could handle it on my own."

Jamie shook her head and strode to the cabin door, the frigid night air made her shiver. All's well that ends well. Right? But, but... *fuck.*

Chapter 48

Two helicopters alit and Jamie, Colin, and Kaitlyn clambered into one. Two members of the ski patrol loaded the corpse into the metal Stokes basket on the second helo along with Noah Planchet. The pilot of their aircraft said, "We've been instructed to transport everyone to the hospital. Agent Scarborough is awaiting your arrival."

In under ten minutes, they made it to Adirondack Medical Center, Jamie, Colin and Kaitlyn were delivered to the Emergency Room and Dave Planchet's body to the coroner's office. Noah was transported to a local detention site awaiting extradition to New York.

Rob and Matt paced the waiting room like two expectant fathers. "Hey," Jamie said, supporting her injured arm. Rob and Matt ran to her. "You guys look like shit," she said. "When's the last time you slept?"

Rob exhaled loudly, shaking his head. "You scared the crap out of us." He studied Jamie's shoulder. "You've been shot? I thought you said you were just a little banged up."

"That's a lot of blood," Matt said.

"I don't think it's too bad, I'll get it checked out."

Matt gave Colin a visual inspection. "You look like you went a few rounds with the heavyweight champ and lost."

Colin struggled to say, "It seems the other guy fared worse."

"Colin shot him," Jamie said.

Rob frowned at Colin. "How'd that happen?"

Jamie answered. "I had the suspect at gunpoint, trying to get him to surrender. The motherfucker shot me. Colin tackled him and got his gun. The suspect took my rifle and aimed it at me. Colin fought Dave to the suspect's weapon and in the struggle he shot Dave. He saved my life."

"You around guns much?" Rob inquired.

"Never touched one before and hope I never do again."

Matt and Rob exchanged shocked glances.

"I suppose I'll be under review for my substandard performance," Jamie said.

"You leave that to me. I don't see a problem. We'll take statements and I'll make a report to Merryl."

"Who's Merryl?" Colin asked.

Jamie kept her eyes on Rob. "Rob's boss."

"Colin," someone yelled. His mother rushed toward him. "Oh, baby," she said. "You're hurt." She placed a hand on his cheek. "Have they checked you out?"

"Not yet, Mom."

"I want to talk to the doctor immediately."

Mr. MacKenzie put both hands on his wife's shoulders. "Easy, Carol. He's going to be fine."

A nurse escorted Colin into an examination room. "Did you win or lose?" she said.

"The other guy's dead."

The nurse's eyebrows arched. "Oh, I'm sorry. That was seriously inappropriate of me."

"He had it coming."

The doctor confirmed Colin's broken nose and closed his gashes with surgical glue. Not much to be done for the black eye, nearly swollen shut. Ice, some R&R and a prescription for pain medication and Colin was released. He still hadn't seen his reflection in a mirror and put it off a little longer.

He exited the treatment room and witnessed Jamie being wheeled toward him on a gurney. His heart twisted, seeing her injured hurt more than a broken nose and ten black eyes. They rolled her into a nearby bay and Colin followed. He stood at her bedside and took her hand. "Hey, how are you doing?"

"I think I dodged a bullet, mostly. The doctor ordered an MRI to make sure there was no serious injury. I should hear something soon."

Dr. Garcia entered on cue. "MRI looks good. Some torn cartilage, a little soft tissue damage but tendons, bones and muscle all intact." He instructed the nurse to fit Jamie for a sling, instructing her not to use the affected appendage for a few days. No stitches, some surgical glue to keep the edges smooth and an assurance there would be minimal scarring. The medical personnel left, leaving Colin alone with Jamie.

"Thankfully, it's my left arm," she said.

Colin smiled. "I want to kiss you right now but my lips are on the injured-reserve list for the time being."

Jamie squeezed his hand. "Thank you for saving my ass... for everything."

"My pleasure, I covet that adorable ass." Colin raised her hand to his cheek, her touch a salve that eased his pain. "Let's head home and we can lick each other's wounds… figuratively, not literally, that would be gross."

Jamie pulled her hand away and focused on the window behind him. "I need to go home, Colin. The assignment is over and I need some time. It's been fun and you're a great guy, but…"

"Stop," Colin said too loudly. "Don't say another word. I can't listen to any of your bullshit about walking out of my life."

"Colin, I want to go home. I need some space. We'll talk in a few days."

"Don't do this to me, Jamie. This has been the worst day of my life and you leaving will put it on a whole other level."

"I'm sorry, Colin, I'm not doing this to hurt you, I'm doing this to save you. I'm not the girl for you. I live in an alternate universe. Our lives are nothing alike. It was fun and you're a super guy. I even enjoyed being a fancy lady that night." She beamed. "You'll find someone to make you happy. Someone from your world."

"I don't want anyone else. I want you. I'm in love with you. I have been since the first day we met. That day in the coffee shop I wanted to scoop you into my arms and take you home."

"Now you're waxing poetic again, like characters in a movie."

"Well, this is *my* movie and I want you in the starring role. You can't deny our compatibility. Under the worst conditions for a relationship, we've had fun, you kept me calm and sane. I want you by my side always." Jamie tightened her lips, the ones he desperately wanted to kiss. He couldn't stop himself. "I know you feel the same way. What are you afraid of?"

Jamie inhaled deeply, her ire apparent. "I'm not afraid of anything. I already told you that."

"What about the other night? You told me you'd finally let me in and you wanted me all the way in. Why the change of heart? Was that a lie? Were you playing me?"

Jamie clasped her hands together, squeezing and releasing, her head down. "I-I guess it was the heat of the moment. I do care for you, and I hope we can still be friends."

"I don't want to be friends. I want more and I thought you did too." Her sad green eyes tore at his gut.

"Look, Colin, I don't want to be a wife and mother. I'm not cut out for that life."

"That's crap and you know it. In fact, everyone knows it. Ask your parents or Alyx and Laura. They'll tell you the truth."

"Darling, there you are." Carol MacKenzie marched in, her husband in tow. She scrutinized Jamie. "And how are you? In a lot of pain?"

"I'm fine, a little bruised. Nothing permanent."

"Thank God," she said. "And thank you for rescuing my son. I can never repay you."

"Just doing my job, and the truth is he saved me," Jamie said.

Jamie's declaration stabbed him in the heart. There he was again, an assignment. His anger flared. "I don't understand," his mother said.

"Not now, Mom." Because he knew the real truth. If Jamie hadn't found him, he'd definitely be dead. She'd helicoptered in alone. No one else could have gotten to him. And now that he knew about all this Incel stuff, he understood Dave had deeper scars than he knew. He never would have let him go. He'd have taken the money, killed him, then disappeared into a life he'd hacked for himself and his brother.

"I'm heading home, Mom. You guys stay and enjoy the rest of the week."

"We don't have to stay. I could take care of you. Or you could come home and convalesce?"

"Thanks, but no, Mom. I need to re-group and solitude is required. I intend to sleep for a week. Then, I look forward to getting back to work. I'm just glad this nightmare is over."

"Me too, darling. Rest up and I'll keep checking on you. If you need me, I'll be there in a flash."

Colin kissed his mother goodbye and hugged his dad. "Glad you're safe, son," his dad said, slapping him on the back.

Colin turned to Jamie. "If you need a ride home, the jet is available. Let me know."

"Not necessary, I'll travel back with Matt and Rob."

He studied her face, unable to break eye contact. This was all fucked up. He wanted her home. They could eat chicken soup and nap all day, he'd even watch the Hallmark channel. He didn't care what they did as long as they did it together. And forever. Maybe she just needed some time, as she'd claimed. But he feared she was running scared and would burrow into her tiny nest and never come out. He hoped the Bureau wouldn't reprimand her for losing sight of him. He thought of calling Rob, but he had no influence with the FBI, as it should be.

His head hurt, inside and out. And he agreed with Jamie on one thing, he needed to go home too. He faced Jamie, wishing he could hold her hand again. "Thank you, Agent Gallagher. I am forever in your debt. I wish you nothing but the best." He shoved his hands in his pockets and walked away.

He checked on Kaitlyn who had her ankle casted. The FBI agreed to transport her parents to her bedside, their arrival imminent. They caught up with each other's lives, Kaitlyn apologizing for her unforgivable disappearance. She confessed that she suffered from bipolar disease and had improved with treatment. They bid each other a fond farewell.

He dialed James and instructed him to gather his belongings and ready the jet.

MR. MACKENZIE STOOD at the foot of Jamie's gurney. "That's it? I thought you two had something going on. Something good."

Mrs. MacKenzie picked up where her husband left off. "Jamie, you must know Colin is in love with you. I knew it the first time I saw you two together, at the Gala that night. I think you feel the same way."

Jamie threw her head back against the pillow. Her parents and now Colin's parents… why did everyone keep lecturing her, telling her how she felt? It was exhausting. She closed her eyes and inhaled deeply, exhaling, breathing in a meditative way. She was so tired, and Colin was right, she intended to sleep forever. No poison apple required.

Chapter 49

Aboard the jet, Colin swapped out his bloody sweater for a new one James brought. Greta fawned over him, wrapping ice in a towel and placing it on his puffed-up face. "What else can I get you, Mr. MacKenzie?"

"Nothing, I just need to rest."

"Of course," she said. She reclined the seat he was in and covered him with a warm blanket. He slept most of the way and James herded him into the car and drove him home. James stowed his ski paraphernalia in the garage and brought his luggage upstairs. Jennifer, his housekeeper, had been by and his mail was stacked on the breakfast bar. He leafed through it, finding nothing important.

"Anything else I can do for you, sir?"

"No. And thanks for all your hard work and attention to detail this week. It's taken a toll on all of us. Take the rest of the week off. Take a vacation on me. It's the least I can do other than make sure there's a sizable bonus in your next check."

"Not necessary, sir. I'm always glad to be of service."

"I insist. Take some time off. I'm not going anywhere for a while."

"My wife is pregnant and a getaway would be awesome."

Colin studied James' features. "Can I ask you something personal?"

"Of course, sir."

"Do you like being married?" Colin glanced at his feet then looked up. "I know that's a ridiculous question."

James smiled. "Not at all, sir. Sometimes I still can't believe I found the love of my life. I was a confirmed bachelor. When I joined the Marines, I planned on making it my career. I'm definitely one of those alpha personalities and didn't think domestic life would suit me. Then I met Reese and my whole world exploded. I couldn't imagine life without her."

"Is this your first kid?"

"Yeah." James shoved his hands in his trouser pockets. "Never thought I'd be a father either. Now, I can't wait to meet the little bugger."

Colin grabbed the side of James' arm and squeezed. "I'm happy for you. Now go take that vacation. What do they call it? A babymoon?"

"Very good, sir, never thought you, or I, would know that. My mother-in-law has been coaching me every now and again."

Colin laughed. Both Jamie's parents and his were rooting for Jamie and him to enter the kingdom of happily-ever-after. Maybe he should garner their help.

"May I ask you a question, sir?"

"Sure. Shoot."

"Will we be seeing Agent Gallagher again?"

"Debatable. Right now, I'd say no. I think she's walking away."

"I'm sorry to hear that, I liked her and I think you did too. Maybe even a little more than me?"

James departed and Colin climbed the stairs to his room, a shower mandatory. James left his bloody sweater in a plastic bag on his bed. That sweater was going in the trash. He never wanted to see it again. He discarded his clothes, leaving them on the floor and headed toward the bathroom. He flicked the light on, yet kept his eyes down. He stood before the mirror, bracing himself on the cold marble. *Gird your loins, buddy.* He raised his chin, an inch at a time, his eyes closed until he faced the glass. He opened his eye, one still swollen shut. Bile rose in his throat, if he had anything in his stomach he'd vomit. *Mother fucker.* The full spectrum of the rainbow ornamented his face. His nose was twice its size. His eye resembled cooked meat, charred even, with a corona of red and blue splotches. He pried his eye lid open about a quarter inch, the white completely red. His stomach twisted again. He examined his lip, the cut was closed but it still felt like his mouth was taped shut.

JAMIE BOARDED a commercial flight with Matt and Rob, sitting in the seat between them. "We'll escort you home and take your statement, then leave you to rest. Let me know when you're ready to come back to work," Rob said.

Jamie twiddled her thumbs, unable to respond. The image of staring into the barrel of her own rifle, death imminent, still sent her adrenaline all wacky. She'd sworn to protect Colin and then let down her guard. She wished she'd get a do-over, yet life rarely offered those. And in law enforcement, pretty much never. Maybe she should focus on the outcome. She and Colin both survived and the perp would never be a threat to anyone ever again.

Matt put a hand on hers and squeezed. "Glad you're safe. And heli-skiing into that remote location was a game-changer. We'd never have been able to get to him without your special skillset."

Jamie squeezed the back of her neck. "I wouldn't have had to if I'd been doing my job. I never should've let him out of my sight."

Rob and Matt didn't respond and she knew what they were thinking. She fucked up and then been forced to clean up her mess. Luckily, they got a positive outcome. The universe slingshot a miracle in her direction. It easily could have gone the other way.

"Listen," she said. "There's something I need to tell you. Colin got a call that went to voicemail just before we arrived at the chalet. It was Dave Planchet and he threatened Colin. He never told me about the message."

"Why not?" Matt said.

"Because Planchet said he knew Colin and I were sleeping together. Colin worried that I might face disciplinary action so he kept it from me."

Rob stayed mute. Jamie's pulse spiked. Why had she put her entire career in jeopardy for a man? A man she'd never see again.

"I say it's water under the bridge. The case has been resolved. No need to dredge up any shit. Besides, you're not the first one to step in it. Lots of us have."

Jamie's jaw dropped. "Understood, sir."

She dozed through most of the flight, and soon was in her apartment. Matt made coffee and they drank caffeine to keep them all focused. Matt recorded her accounting of the incident on his phone, Rob prompting her for clarification as needed. It took about an hour and upon their departure she crawled into bed, probably before they'd pulled away from the curb.

Her sleep proved fitful, replaying the disturbing incident, often without the positive outcome. She woke in a cold sweat several times, awakened by her own screams. She even reached for Colin, desperate to have his strong arms around her, and hers comforting him: safe now, out of harm's way, they'd always protect each other. He'd actually said those words to her and she knew he meant every one. She walked to the kitchen for a glass of water. Her whole body ached.

This special type of misery endured for several days, sleeping, watching terrible TV, not eating much. She hadn't showered since her first day home. Colin called four times, she'd dismissed each attempted contact. He didn't leave a message. She didn't want him out of her life. She liked him. A lot. But she couldn't slip into his twenty-four-karat golden life. Never ever. She chuckled, remembering him buying the evening gown and dressing her in diamonds. How ridiculous, and yet the whole night had been Cinderella magic all the way. And the debacle at the St. Andrew's club? She'd screwed up and Colin offered to take a whipping in her stead. One she totally had coming.

Noon. She should eat something. Coffee and peanut butter toast her only sustenance for days now. She nosed into the refrigerator. Not much food. She should venture out to the market. That would require a shower. She planned on returning to work next week, it was time to get her life back.

The buzzer announced a visitor. Ugh. She pressed the call button. "Yes?"

"Let me in," her mother said.

Shit. She hit the button again and opened the apartment door as footsteps neared. Her mother towed a small suitcase, her arms laden with groceries. "When can you afford an apartment with an elevator?"

"Mom," Jamie said, taking the provisions from her. She'd discarded the sling yesterday. "What are you doing here?"

"Colin called me. He's worried about you. You haven't been answering his calls. Are you not talking to him?"

Jamie placed the foodstuffs on her tiny kitchen counter, her back to her mother. "It was an assignment and it's over." She huffed. "It's complicated, Mom."

"Bullshit. Anything worth anything is *complicated*. Period. Welcome to life!"

Jamie rested her palms on the counter behind her and faced her mother. "You don't understand."

"Bullshit twice. And you look like it too. When's the last time you showered?"

"I was about to when you showed up."

Sally Gallagher opened the refrigerator and gasped. The contents consisted of orange juice, three apples, which were at the end of their shelf life, two slices left in a loaf of pumpernickel bread and some jars of jelly and salad dressing. "Jesus, what are you living on, moldy air?"

"Nope. Mostly coffee and peanut butter toast."

Sally grabbed Jamie's shoulders and turned her around, marching her into the bathroom. She rotated the knobs, testing the water temperature with her hand and adjusting the shower spray. "Get cleaned up and I'll fix you a sandwich. Then we'll talk." Sally Gallagher moved toward the door, her hand on the doorknob. She glanced over her shoulder. "And don't make me call your father because I will. I told him I could handle this on my own, but he'll be here in a flash if you don't get your shit together." She shut the door behind her.

What was this, a fucking intervention? Who the hell did Colin think he was? Calling her parents? Way over the line.

Jamie stripped and focused on her shoulder wound in the vanity mirror, running her fingertips over the scab. Mostly healed. She made wide circles with her arm, no pain. Maybe she'd go to the gym tomorrow, build up her endurance after being a slug for nearly a week.

Toweled dry, her hair untangled, she slipped into jeans and one of her old navy tees.

Her phone rang. Colin. She hesitated, then declined the call.

Chapter 50

Colin threw his phone on the couch. "Damn it, Jamie, pick up." She was probably pissed he'd called her parents. Now that he considered it, he'd be pissed if someone called his mother on him. His judgment was off, desperate to see Jamie again. He'd probably made things worse. She needed time and his impatience wasn't helping.

He slumped on the couch and switched on the TV, depositing his phone on the side table. The clock announced 12:42 p.m. He should probably eat something. He closed his eyes, hands over his chest, ankles crossed. Some reporter on cable news was quoting stock market figures. He did need to get back to work. Monday, for sure. The front door opened and somebody punched in the entry code.

Panic seized him. If this was a home invasion how would he protect himself?

Footsteps. He peered over the back of the couch. Jennifer. She gasped, her mittened hand over her mouth, the other held bags of groceries. "Mr. MacKenzie," she finally said. "I'm so sorry, I thought you were still on vacation."

Colin sat up, his back against the arm rest. "Things didn't go quite as expected."

"I saw it on the news but I figured you'd stay and chill out for a while." She deposited the groceries on the center island. She removed her coat, hat, and mittens, and approached, her eyes wide. "Oh God, your face."

"Gruesome, huh?" She should have seen it a week ago. "Good thing my face isn't my fortune or I'd be bankrupt."

"How are you doing?"

"Honestly, I don't know."

Jennifer leaned her hands on the couch back. "I'm so sorry, sir. At least they got the guys. That should be a relief."

"Yeah, I thought I'd be back to normal once the culprits were caught." Colin pinched the bridge of his nose, hoping to squelch the pounding in his head. "Did you bring food? I haven't been eating much."

"Oh, yes. I'll fix you something."

"Thanks." The swelling in his lips had vanished and his eye too, although it was still a cacophony of colors, including the blood-shot eyeball.

His phone rang and his heart thudded. He glanced at the screen and his excitement deflated. "Hi, Mom."

"Darling, how are you feeling?"

"Much better. I plan to get back to work on Monday."

"We're home and I wanted to thank you again for the lovely trip, not counting the first day of course. Although I do rejoice over the fact that you and Jamie are alive."

"I was glad to do it, Mom. Happy Anniversary, again."

"Have you heard from Jamie?"

"I haven't. She's moved on, I'm afraid. Getting back to work will be good. Back to my routine, my old life. I'll forget about her." Total lie. Hadn't he called her mother for help? He rubbed his forehead. He needed to pull himself out of this hole he'd fallen into voluntarily, and maybe he'd dug it, too. Withdrawing from life, unable to see his future. Shit. He sounded suicidal. Enough of the pity party. *Pull yourself up by your bootstraps and start being You again.*

JAMIE GOBBLED the roast beef sandwich, chips, and pickles, like a starving waif. Her mother watched, chin in her hand, elbow on the table. Her mother sighed and sipped iced tea. Jamie swigged her own. She leaned back in the chair and blotted her mouth with a paper napkin.

"I have some things to say," her mother said. "Don't interrupt me." Jamie crossed her arms over her chest. Her mother pointed her index finger making tiny circles. "And don't give me that defensive posture either."

Jamie uncrossed her arms and laid her hands on her thighs. "Doesn't look like I have a choice."

"If you want me out of your hair then shut up and listen." Jamie pressed her lips together. "Good." Sally Gallagher took a large gulp of tea. "Everybody sees it but you. That man is in love with you. You should give him a chance. Leave the past behind. The darkness of the world you were born into shouldn't define you any longer. Wasn't it Nietzsche who said, *"when you gaze long into an abyss, the abyss will gaze back into you"*? You walked out of the darkness, don't let it have any power over you. He also said, *"whoever fights with monsters should see to it he does not become a monster in the process... emptiness eventually causes a shift in consciousness, which you no longer have the autonomy to walk away from"*. I know you fight monsters at work but leave them there. Come home to someone who loves you, who will comfort you. I know you think you can take care of yourself, and you can, but it's nice to have someone say 'let me do this for you, don't worry, I'm here and I'll protect you'."

Jamie raised her hand like a grade-schooler, unable to remain silent.

"Go ahead," her mother said.

"First, I can't believe you're quoting Nietzsche to me. And I'm afraid I do love Colin, but I don't fit into his world of celebrities, designer clothes, money, multiple homes and Lamborghinis, it's too much and I'll make a fool of myself trying to keep up with snooty gossip."

Sally shook her head. "There's that word *afraid* again. And I get the distinct impression Colin doesn't give a hoot about that frou-frou shit. You're highly educated, super accomplished and smarter than most. Just be yourself, that's who Colin loves."

Jamie hung her head in her hands. Her phone pinged an incoming message from Laura: *It's a girl. Born at 6:12 a.m., 8 lbs. 21 inches. She's beautiful. We named her Quinn. Come visit. At NY Presbyterian. Will be here through tomorrow…* followed by the kiss emoji.

Jamie grinned. "Laura delivered her baby. A girl, they named her Quinn." She texted Laura: *Congratulations. So happy for you both. Will come by tomorrow…* followed by the kiss and the party emojis.

She observed the deep lines between her mother's eyes, the wrinkled brow. "Are you done?"

"Yes. Lecture over, but Colin deserves a phone call. It would be better if you met in person though."

"I already told him how I feel, he just won't accept it."

"No, you didn't tell him how you actually, really, truly feel. You made some rash judgments and reacted poorly. I mean your honest feelings. You owe him that much."

Her mother stayed the night and they watched Turner Classic movies where an old Betty Davis flick brought a tear to their eyes. She gave her mother the bed and slept on the pull-out couch. The following morning, she called an Uber to take her mother to the airport. A Baby Gap was just a few blocks from her apartment and she stopped to pick up a gift, selecting a cozy pink sweater with matching hat and booties, along with a furry pink teddy bear. Who was she? Not a pink person, that's for sure. Everything about her was upside down, she had no idea who she was anymore.

She hopped the subway en route to NY Presbyterian. The room was crowded, maybe she should have waited and visited Laura and Steve at home. Alyx embraced her, Daniel cradled his newborn son in his arms, crowned in a teddy bear hat complete with ears. The baby was even more beautiful than the first time she saw him and she ran a thumb over his perfect pink cheek. Daniel blew a kiss. "Good to see you, Jamie."

"Hey," Molly said. "How are you?" Her husband Sam's arm around Molly's waist, his other hand tethered to their three-year-old daughter, Justice.

Jamie hugged Molly and Sam, then knelt to greet Justice. "Hi, aren't you getting big," she said. Justice wedged herself between Sam's legs, clutching his thighs tightly, her back to Jamie. Sam rubbed her curly dark mop. "She's a little shy."

Molly added, "Maybe if we saw you more, she'd be hugging and kissing you."

Jamie stood. "Promise, I'll come by soon." She walked to Laura's bedside and presented Laura with her gift and a kiss on her cheek. "Congratulations. I'm so happy for you both."

"How's your shoulder? Heard you had a challenging assignment."

"I'll say. Luckily, it turned out okay."

Steve Moretti stood on the opposite side of the bed, his daughter in his arms.

"Can't believe I have a daughter. I want to give her the moon. Keep her safe always." He paused. "When did I turn into such a sap?"

"I don't know, but it's freaking me out," said a male voice. Everyone turned.

Colin.

Chapter 51

Colin filled the doorway, a huge bouquet of flowers clutched to his chest. He wore khaki pants, a white button-down shirt and a blue blazer, his wool coat draped over his arm.

"Eww, that face," Steve said.

Colin smiled, but warned, "No cracks about the other guy, I've endured all the Mike Tyson jokes I can stand." Hugs and kisses were levied and Colin added his congratulations. He'd never met Molly and Sam, so introductions were made. He offered Laura the flowers with a peck on her cheek, then held Quinn. "Hey, gorgeous, welcome aboard." He stroked the side of her cheek with his knuckle.

Jamie melted. *Oh God.* What terrible luck. She should have thought this out, the chances of him being here entirely too probable.

Colin returned Quinn to her father's arms as the visitors cooed and coddled the new entrant on the world's stage.

Jamie moved to the foot of the bed, allowing others to fuss over Laura and the newborn.

Colin came up behind her and whispered, "Good to see you, Agent Gallagher." The warmth of his breath near her ear sent a delicious shiver down her spine.

She turned toward him. "Enough with the Agent Gallagher. It's Jamie."

"Okay, *Jamie*. How's the shoulder?"

Jamie rubbed her temple and inhaled deeply. She needed to say something to Colin, but what? This wasn't the time or place for a heart-to-heart. "The shoulder's fine." She lifted her chin. "Colin, we need to talk. I can't do it here, today. I need a little more time. I promise to call. Maybe we can meet for coffee?"

He shoved his hands into his trouser pockets. "I'd like that. Let me know when and where and I'll be there."

She touched his face, so very tenderly, running her fingertips over his eyelids and lips. "Looks a lot better, much pain?"

"No, feels better than it looks. Going back to work Monday. Being the boss, I'm hoping everyone will ignore the sight of me and have their work faces on. I can't take much more of the running commentary."

Jamie focused on his steel-blue eyes. "I can't tell you how sorry I am. I fucked up royally."

He grabbed her wrist and squeezed. "Enough. I don't want to hear any of that shit again. Move on, I have."

She inhaled slowly and exhaled. "You're right. I need to let it go. Getting back to work should help."

Colin loosened his grip on her wrist and laced his fingers through hers. "There weren't any repercussions, were there?"

She held her breath at Colin's touch. Would she ever be in a place where she could forget it? "No, Merryl called me and commended me on a job well done, so I guess I'm still in good standing."

"Excellent. If the Bureau can forgive you, you should forgive yourself. I'm not in the law enforcement business but I imagine no operation is without risk. It's how you adapt and manage the situation when things go awry that matters."

"Wise words from a spoiled rich boy." She smiled. There was no denying Colin could ease her out of her worst mood. She owed him a conversation, an expression of her true feelings. Maybe Monday morning, before they went back to work. At the coffee shop where they met. "I'll call you tomorrow and we'll make a plan."

Colin smiled, then released her hand. The loss of his touch left her feeling bereft. "I'm already there."

COLIN'S CHEST swelled with relief. *Maybe... just maybe...* Seeing Jamie brought all his feelings to the surface again, not that he'd been able to submerge them much. When she touched his face, he resisted the urge to take her in his arms and whisk her away.

He'd promised to travel to Long Island to visit his parents, so he excused himself and drove the fifty miles to their house. The traffic was light for a Saturday afternoon and he found the ride enjoyable for a change.

His parents were overjoyed at his arrival. His mom made Chicken Parmesan, which she knew was his favorite, despite it breaking all her diet rules. Even with her best effort it could never compare to the Morettis'. He missed his days eating with Steve's big Italian family. Yeah, he wanted a family like that, of his own.

Sunday dragged on, waiting for Jamie to call. What if she didn't? Should he call her, or was this the final brush-off? He couldn't bear the thought. Well then, he'd show up at her apartment and demand she talk to him. He knew she loved him, he just didn't know how to make her see it. The usual accoutrements to flatter a woman: flowers, fancy restaurants, expensive wines, would be wasted on her. When they'd first met, she blurted out she could climax with her vibrator in a few minutes. He wondered if he'd convinced her sex was so much more than that. Her way was like eating fast food. It got the job done but there wasn't as much joy in it. Their time in bed had been so much more, like a five-course dinner eaten leisurely, savoring each bite, basking in the candlelight and romantic music. Damn. He was getting a hard-on.

The sun set and his impatience got the best of him. He considered a drink but feared his frustration would translate into a hangover on his first day back to work. Remote in hand, he trolled the channels for a distraction. He hit the Hallmark channel where the credits rolled and a couple kissed chastely in a field. Moving on.

His front door opened unexpectedly. He sat up abruptly wondering, for the second time this week, who was invading his home. It couldn't be Jennifer, too late, and Sunday. Her day off.

Jamie stood in his living room dressed in jeans and a jade sweater he never saw before. "Hey," she said. She stepped closer and slipped out of her navy parka and draped it over the nearby chair. Her long auburn locks hung loosely over her shoulders, gleaming under the dimmed light over her head. He leaped over the back of the couch and faced her. "How did you get in?"

"I have the codes, remember? You should probably change them."

"I will," he murmured, yet he was thankful he hadn't. His heart thudded harder than if a criminal *was* burglarizing his home.

"Why are you here? I thought we'd meet tomorrow."

"I couldn't wait till tomorrow. We need to talk. I need this anxiety to be over."

Oh God. This was it. She'd tell him to fuck off. He pressed his hands into fists, the urge to punch something straining his resolve.

JAMIE GATHERED HER NERVE, although it wasn't necessary. Standing in front of Colin eased her insecurities, ones she didn't know she possessed until she'd let Colin in… into her life, into her heart, and into her… well, other parts of her body. She longed to take him in her arms and love him. She wanted more incredible sex, yet more than that, she wanted his arms around her, his shelter in a storm, she wanted everything he could give. And she'd give all of herself in return. She'd navigate his world and she'd be clear about how much of a fancy lady she could be. She laughed and Colin studied her, his eyes scrunched together.

"I love you," she said. "I'm ready."

———

COLIN PICKED Jamie up and twirled her in an affectionate hug. He squeezed her so hard, she probably couldn't breathe. He returned her to the ground and… just loved her. Their eyes met and he kissed her, and kissed her, and kissed her until he was breathless.

He held her at arm's length. "I love you too, more than I thought one human being could love another. And fancy isn't a requirement. I'll take you just the way you are. You're the first woman I've met who doesn't treat me differently for my money. You're willing to challenge me at every turn. I see things differently because of you."

"No one has ever, ever said those things to me. And by the way, the private jet doesn't suck."

Colin laughed.

"And the sex is incredible. I won't mind a lifetime of that."

Colin embraced her enthusiasm, his body aflame. He wanted her naked, in his arms, to ravage her until she couldn't remember her name. He grabbed her hand and led her to the couch. They sat alongside each other and he held both her hands. "I have a confession to make." Jamie's eyes narrowed. "Remember the first time you were here? You needed to search my apartment, but we never finished because we found the bomb in my closet."

"Okay…"

"There's one more room. It's to the right of my bedroom, at the end of the hall."

"I did think that odd. The hallway leading to a dead end."

"I have a playroom."

Jamie's gaze widened. "You mean like at the club? With *equipment*?"

"Yeah. I can't remember the last time I used it. Do you want to see it?"

Jamie was breathless, like the first time they'd met and not because of the passionate kiss… kissing, or his exceptional good looks, which aptly defined the oft-used cliché, breathtaking. And now he wanted to most likely play, in a real BDSM room. *Egad.*

"It's not a dungeon, is it?"

Chapter 52

Colin led Jamie upstairs, her hand in his, navigating right at the landing. He pushed the hidden panel near the ceiling and a door-sized wall swung out. His hand found the switch and half-moon wall sconces cast the room in a low sultry light. He pulled Jamie into his side, his arm around her waist. "Ready?"

"As I'll ever be."

"Your shoulder okay?"

"Yes, Sir."

He pushed her forward, both hands on her shoulders. "I want you to take some time. Explore. Get comfortable." He sidled up alongside her and coaxed her chin toward him. "Not too comfortable because I have lots of surprises." He knew some paraphernalia might be off-putting, although he didn't indulge in stuff he found creepy. No ball gags, no masks, no whips, just a soft deerskin flogger, which most women loved.

"Well, at least it's not a medieval dungeon."

"Take a walk around. Touch anything you want. I'll give you five minutes. When I return, I expect you naked, in the slave position."

"Yes, Sir."

Jamie's heart still beat at a rabid staccato. Not fear. Excitement. The thrill of playing this game with Colin. She studied his dark cobalt eyes, fire igniting between her legs. Colin grasped her chin, tilting it up. His firm lips took charge, his tongue dancing with hers, her need to touch him desperate.

"Good girl," he said. "Back in five."

JAMIE REMOVED her shoes and tossed them into a corner. She skirted the perimeter of the chamber, her fingers trailing the maroon walls to anchor her, to confirm reality: she was in a room and not at heaven's gate. At the far end, a massive platform bed waited, the restraints visible, not like the secret ones in Colin's bedroom. To the side, a restraining bench. Her hands caressed the soft brown leather, then picked up the brass buckle on one of the leg restraints. She pictured herself strapped there, unable to resist whatever Colin planned to do to her. At his mercy like last time, submitting, obeying, concepts that had never made their way into her sex life until she met Colin. She still couldn't understand how she found this sexual interaction so hot, yet she damned sure did, and she wanted more. Then another helping, please. And another.

More, more, more.

Next to the spanking bench stood a tall wooden X, leather straps attached to the four ends. She guessed this was where floggings went down. Would Colin do this tonight? She did know she'd never engage in whipping and Colin assured her that wasn't in his repertoire. The debacle at the club invaded her psyche. That poor woman with red stripes on her back, and the burly sadist slashing the whip, again and again. Her screams not a deterrent. Yet apparently the woman was into it, and Jamie's attempt at rescuing her sent the club into a frenzy of a different kind. Sigh.

She sat on the soft-as-a-cloud mattress, covered only by a black silk sheet, topped with matching pillows. Worried five minutes had elapsed, she pulled her green sweater over her head, folded it and placed it on a huge leather recliner in the room's center. It seemed out of character in the, dare she say it... erotica lair, and she wondered what it was for. Facing two large wooden cabinets, she opened the first to discover an array of ropes, fur-lined hand-cuffs, and a variety of implements resembling her rabbit vibrator. She shut the cabinet doors and skipped the next one. The element of shock amplified and distorted sensations, reactions, mindset. Everything.

Time to get ready.

Her jeans and underwear added to the pile her sweater had begun, and she knelt at the foot of the bed, resting on her feet, palms upright on her thighs. If her heart kept pounding so errati-cally, she feared she'd faint.

There he stood.

Bare-chested, charcoal grey pajama pants hanging low on his hips, the cut of his muscles forming a V pointing toward his obvious erection. She dropped her gaze, focusing on the burgundy carpet.

His naked toes touched her knees. "Good girl," he said. "So beau-tiful like this."

Her lips parted to respond, but she tightened them and remained silent. His feet vanished from view and she glanced up and saw him removing her clothing pile and tucking it into a drawer under one of the cabinets. He pivoted toward her and she held her breath and closed her eyes. Kneeling, he said, "Eyes on me, darling."

She opened her eyes ever so slowly, his gaze dark and dangerous, hungry.

"You're in protocol, you remember the rules?"

"Yes, Sir."

"What's your safeword?"

"Red, and yellow if I'm getting uncomfortable. Green means full steam ahead."

"Excellent." He slipped his fingers between her legs and she gasped. "Easy, babe, we're just getting started. Jamie bit her lip to stifle a moan. "You're so responsive, so wet. I like that." He snatched a kiss from her.

"We'll begin with a flogging." He helped her up by her wrists and led her to the St. Andrew's Cross and pressed her back against the wood. "I will use a flogger. It's made of supple leather and only provides stimulation, perhaps a little pain. No marks." He ran his hands over her shoulders and breasts, her nipples erect, then secured one wrist in the leather strap, followed by the other, slipping a finger inside the soft fur to ensure they weren't too tight. He massaged a breast and suckled the nipple. A soft moan escaped her perfect lips. He kissed her neck, inhaling her intoxicating scent and she giggled, leaning her head into his cheek. "Green?" he said.

"Yes, Sir, all I see is green, green, green."

HE SANK TO HIS KNEES, spreading her legs and shackled each ankle to the cross. Two fingers penetrated her and he gazed up. Silent and obedient. Perfect. His fingers moved in and out in a slow rhythm, her vagina clenched around him. Way too soon for an orgasm, so he backed off.

He lingered before her, the leather implement in hand. "I'll start slow, then increase the intensity. If it's too much, use a safeword."

"Yes, Sir," she whispered.

He draped the knotted lashes over her breasts, then down her belly, zigzagging her thighs and back to her shoulders. The fronds creeped over her flesh, across her neck and down to her breasts again. He stepped back and flicked his wrist, delivering the first blow. Jamie clasped the arm restraints and he noticed she was holding her breath. "Breathe, baby, relax. Lean into it."

He quickened the pace, the gentle lashings landing on her breasts, belly and thighs. He increased the force and Jamie writhed and wiggled to escape the wrath of the flogger, except no reprieve from his ministrations came.

She blurted, "Please, Sir, I can't take much more."

"Is it too painful? Use your safe word."

"*No*. I need release, it's too much and I need to come."

"Not yet, darling. Control." He dropped the flogger and closed in on her, pressing his chest against her soft breasts. He laced his fingers through hers and kissed her. Her lips hot, wet and soon to be nice and swollen.

"Such sweet torture, and so much more to come." He unbuckled the restraints and massaged her wrists to ensure the blood flowed freely, then moved her to the spanking bench.

"This will be an erotic spanking, not a punishment, yet it will still redden your adorable ass." He kissed her again, then manhandled her forward. "Lie down, chin on the rest." He guided her down and wrapped her wrists around the handles, buckling them, continuing with her ankles. He tightened the strap around her waist. He debated using a paddle, but remembering her struggle from the prior spanking, decided to save it for another time. He ran his hands down her spine, over her buttocks and massaged the flesh. He rubbed the knot between her shoulders away. He kept at it, massaging her flesh until she melted into the leather.

"Brace yourself, babe. Hold on to the handles." His voice held the steely edge of command and her insides turned to mush, the tension between her legs unbearable. "I'll deliver ten spanks, I want you to count."

JAMIE'S MUSCLES tensed in protest, yet she wanted this, wanted it badly. Every nerve came to attention, already on high alert after the flogging. Colin was right, she found it electrifying, a heady cocktail.

His hand landed on her left buttock and she yelped. Her heart pounded.

"I didn't hear you."

"One," she murmured.

He dealt a second slap.

She squealed and gave a breathy, "Two."

"Breathe, baby, breathe through the burn."

He levied nine blows and then it happened.

Oh God. Fuck me. God. Jesus.

Chapter 53

"Now, what shall we do about that? You lost control. But since you just had a spanking and orgasmed, we must stop. Another spanking wouldn't exactly be a punishment." In truth, Colin had no desire to punish Jamie. Ever.

"I'm sorry, Sir. I tried to hold back."

"With more discipline you'll learn. The longer you can suppress the climax, the more intense it will be." Releasing the restraints, he eased Jamie off the bench and carried her over to the bed, laying her down, her head on a satin pillow. He didn't want to push her too far, there'd be plenty of time for exploration. Anal plugs, hot dripping wax... yet maybe... a spreader bar and a blindfold?

"I'm restraining your hands," he said, sliding one slender wrist into the fur-lined manacle. He tightened the buckle, ensuring it wasn't too unforgiving, then secured her other hand. He hovered over her, both hands on the side of her head, his knees straddling her pelvis. "You okay?"

"Green, Sir."

HE BENT down and kissed her, hard and deep. Jamie moaned into his mouth, her arousal rising too fast again. He rose and opened a cabinet, the one she hadn't investigated. *Oh God.*

Returning to the bed, he laid a metal bar with manacles at both ends beside her right leg. Her head came off the pillow, trying to identify the apparatus. Colin stepped out of his pants and kicked them sideways. He arrived near the headboard and rested his hands on his hips. Jamie focused on his immense erection. She still couldn't understand how she could take it all, but his cock inside her felt incredible, like it filled a giant hole in her soul.

"Houston, we have a problem," Colin said.

"What?" she said, lifting her gaze to those smoldering sapphire eyes.

"Excuse me, little subbie?"

"I mean, what, Sir?"

"That's better. I will blindfold you. You're a curious kitten and I want you focused on feeling, not seeing. You're too distracted."

A blindfold? Made sense, in a crazy way.

He sat beside her, the mattress sinking with his weight. "Lift your head," he commanded. She complied and he wrapped a soft, silky black scarf around her head, securing it. The mattress rose and anticipation zinged every nerve.

He spread her legs wide and attached one ankle to the bar, closing the clasp, then secured the other. He stretched the bar wider forcing her legs apart, leaving her exposed and vulnerable. *Oh God.* He touched her, resting his palm over her vagina, the heat threatening her undoing. *Control. Hold on tight.* She gripped the arm restraints, her fingernails cutting into her palms.

"This will keep you open to me. I can do whatever I want."

Oh God. And she wanted it all, every last bit.

THE OVERHEAD LIGHTING covered Jamie in a soft glow, her glistening wetness urging him on. He'd chastised Jamie for losing control, yet he wasn't so far away himself. His balls tightened at the thought of being inside her. Pounding hard, until they both screamed their release. Two fingers penetrated her wet folds and he massaged her clit with his thumb. Jamie moaned.

"Quiet," he barked. "Control, baby."

He added a third finger, probing deep, curling his fingers toward the sensitive spot right behind her pelvic bone. He withdrew and pinched her clit. Jamie gasped, yanking the restraints, lashing her arms over her head.

"Do you want to come?" he asked.

"Oh God, yes. Please."

"Just call me Sir." He smiled in satisfaction.

"Yes, Sir, please, I'm begging."

He lifted the bar off the bed, and probed her vagina, an unhurried and steady tempo spiraling her higher. He dipped one wet finger into her ass, in and out, then pressed his thumb against her clit.

"Come for me, baby. Let go." He bent down and circled her clit with his tongue, his hand still on the bar. Her pelvis pushed against his mouth as he continued the pressure on the swollen nub.

THE HEAT of Colin's mouth sent her body aquiver. Her nerves cried for release and she shrieked right along with them. The tension unbearable, her whole center clamped down, the tidal wave of pleasure washing her toward oblivion. Everything went white beneath the blindfold and then an eruption of stars bombarded her head. The sensation like nothing she'd felt before, dynamite popping inside an all-consuming fire.

"Oh, Colin," she moaned, her breath difficult to catch. "Jesus."

He knelt between her legs and deftly removed the spreader bar. "There you are with the God references again." He chuckled. "We're not done yet."

"Colin, no, I can't take anymore."

"You will, little subbie."

He pushed her knees apart, grabbed his dick and circled it in her wetness. One thrust and he was in, filling her, taking away what little breath she had. She made a sound she didn't recognize and clutched the restraints tethering her to the bed. His chest melded with hers, pushing her into the mattress. His hands grasped hers as the relentless pounding continued, taking her higher and higher. A pyre burned deep in her belly, her back arched for more. *Jesus*. She didn't think she could orgasm again yet there she was, at the crest looking into the bottomless abyss of fireworks, diving into unending, carnal bliss.

COLIN'S RESOLVE VANISHED, unable to hold out any longer. "Again, baby, come."

He pressed his lips against hers, the kiss deep, as deep as his cock felt inside her. His lips retreated, giving them both air. He reached up and stripped off the blindfold so he could look into her eyes when they both came. Jamie screeched, her chin arching up, her knees like a vice around him. Her insides convulsed and he growled, his release imminent. He poured himself into her in uncontrolled fury, the feeling indescribable, a dazzling splendor he never wanted to end. She quivered beneath him and he savored the aftershocks that rolled over them in tandem waves.

He kissed her again, each gasping for breath until they lay nose-to-nose, matching smiles signaling satisfaction, happiness. Love?

He released her hands from the restraints and she circled him in an embrace. Spent, he collapsed atop her softness, nibbling her neck, her ear, then rested his head on her shoulder. Her fingernails traced up and down his back, her palms following in their tracks.

"Yes," she whispered, answering her own unspoken question. "I love you."

"I know," he said. "Finally."

They rested for several minutes yet he feared if he lingered longer, he'd crush her. He hoisted himself, went to the bathroom and grabbed a warm washcloth from the wall cabinet and cleaned her, then wrapped her in a blanket from the adjacent cabinet and settled into the recliner, positioning her on his lap. He reached into the side cabinet and withdrew a water bottle. "Hydrate," he ordered.

Jamie drank half the bottle and handed it back. "Wow," she exclaimed. "That was fucking amazing. I think I'm ready to be your slave."

"Well," he said, pulling her against his chest. "That's a one-eighty from a week ago."

"Tell me," she said. She shifted toward him, her hand on his chest. Her finger pushed on a nipple. They sat there tangled together.

"We both need sleep," Colin said. "Back to work in the morning. But one more thing we need to discuss."

He carried her back to his room, freed her from the subbie blanket and tucked her into bed. He settled beside her and opened his bedside drawer, retrieving the black velvet case. He hid it under the covers and slipped his arm under her neck, pulling her into his shoulder. Her soft green eyes scanned his face, her smile like a Cheshire cat. "You know," he said, "there's a custom in the Dom/sub relationship called collaring." Jamie's brow wrinkled. "The Dom puts a collar around his sub and locks the padlock. It symbolizes a relationship, the Dom claims the sub as his own and states he is taking full responsibility, or ownership, of the submissive. The sub agrees to give herself freely. They release their body, heart and mind to each other, unconditionally, to do with as they please."

Jamie sat up, her hand on his chest. "Collared? Like a pet?"

"No, and pet is a common term of affection at the club that I don't use anymore. Sounds demeaning."

Jamie hesitated. "My first reaction is no way, but on the other hand it's similar to a friendship or engagement ring."

"Exactly." Colin sat up beside her. "I want to collar you." He plucked the hidden package from the covers and placed it between them.

"We could pretend this is a collar until we pick out a ring."

"Aren't we moving kind of fast?"

"Not for me. I'd marry you yesterday."

"You don't know what I want. I don't know what I want. I've never thought much about marriage or a wedding. I'm not sure wife and mother is in the cards." She hesitated. "Until now. Maybe people do change. I feel like a completely different person from when we first bumped into each other. Was that just a week ago?"

Colin glanced at the bedside clock. "Eight days, and about seventeen hours."

Jamie smirked. "You're ridiculous."

"Guilty." He took both her hands in his. "I will give you whatever life you want. I'd like to have kids, but it's not a deal breaker. As long as I have you, I couldn't expect anything more."

"What about the club? Will you still go there and work with the subs? Be a dungeon monitor?"

"I'll never play at the club again. I don't want to be with anyone but you. We could still go to parties there if you want. There are private rooms available for play, but we have everything we could want right here."

"I'm not comfortable asking you to give up anything, but the thought of you having sex with anyone else is a deal breaker for me."

"Agreed. One hundred percent. So?" he said, lifting the pendant from its resting place.

Jamie studied the dazzling diamond solitaire. It didn't look anything like a collar, which eased her angst. Yet it symbolized exactly how she felt. She would give herself fully to this amazing man. Soulmate wasn't something she believed in, yet loving Colin nudged her belief system. She couldn't imagine life without him.

"Yes," she said. "I give myself freely. I release my body, heart and mind to you, Colin MacKenzie, unconditionally, to do with as you please."

"You'll marry me?"

"I will." She'd never imagined those words ever crossing her lips.

"You've made me the happiest man in the world." Colin opened the clasp on the necklace and reached for her neck.

Jamie put both hands on his wrists. "But I want the same vow from you."

"I do," he said. "I promise to protect and love you always. To give myself freely, to commit my body, heart and mind to you, Jamie Gallagher, unconditionally, to do with as you please."

Jamie smiled. "All right, then. Collar me, Sir." She tucked her long locks to one side, giving Colin unfettered access to her neck. He closed the clasp and centered his grandmother's diamond in the hollow of her neck, then leaned in to kiss her. Jamie put a hand on his chest, stopping him.

"One more thing, Mister," she said. Colin frowned. "You stated you'd give yourself freely to me to do with as I wish, right?" She touched her neck, the gemstone between her fingers.

"Yes."

"Good, then when do I get to give you pleasure? I want your cock in my mouth."

Colin's eyes bored into her. "Hmm, topping me already? That didn't take long."

"I like playing submissive, it's hot. But sometimes I want to please you."

"Giving you pleasure gives me immense satisfaction, but I'm willing to hand over the reins once in a while."

"Good, then it's my turn tomorrow."

"Yes, ma'am. I'm yours to do with as you wish."

Jamie dropped her hand from his rock-hard chest and they kissed, long, gentle, unhurried. They had all the time in the world. She'd opened her heart and given it to Colin to guard and he had done the same.

They snuggled beneath the covers, her body curved into his, her leg over his thighs. But this time when she woke, she'd know intimately – on an almost metaphysical level – the body she hugged. Tomorrow and every day for the rest of her new life.

Epilogue

Three months later

Jamie had left her tiny apartment and moved her meager belongings into Colin's penthouse two months ago.

It was a leisurely Saturday morning at the beach house. They'd slept late, did a quick workout in their home gym and passed the afternoon with Colin watching a PGA tournament on the giant TV and Jamie reading the newest New York Times top seller.

Jamie stood on the deck in an emerald green cocktail dress and silver three-inch heels. She'd gotten better at managing the tricky footwear. She inhaled the salty ocean breeze. Spring was approaching, she couldn't wait to sun herself on the white sand and dive into the roiling sea.

He came up behind her, and his arms circled her neck, his gold cufflinks reflecting the bright sunshine. "I love you in this dress."

"You say that about everything I wear." She turned her head and gazed into his ocean-blue eyes. "And what I don't wear…"

"Guilty."

The MacKenzies insisted on throwing an engagement party. Her parents, helping with the celebration, had already arrived and they'd be returning with Jamie and Colin to their Manhattan apartment. Her parents reported her future in-laws were welcoming and excellent hosts and showed genuine excitement at the prospect of melding families.

Jamie and Colin sat in the backseat of the Range Rover, James behind the wheel so they could enjoy the night without worrying about a DUI. Waning sunlight reflected a tiny beam from her engagement ring. She stared at the three-carat diamond with smaller ones circling it and smiled. She'd tried talking Colin into something smaller, but lost the battle. She had to admit, it was a beautiful expression of his love and she needed to learn to stop balking about his compulsion to buy her things and just say thank you.

Her wardrobe had nearly doubled and she reluctantly admitted having a housekeeper didn't suck either. She often worked long hours and sometimes a case took everything out of her. But Colin was always waiting for her with a drink, a hot bath, and a hug. Every time his incredibly muscular arms tightened around her, she melted, all the tension drained from her body. Being near Colin was her joy and even with this opulent housing, the complete opposite of her childhood homestead, she felt at home —like she belonged. Here. Fitting snugly into each bright room, shadowy corner, every nook and cranny. The temperature was warm for an April day on Long Island and Jamie feasted her eyes on the beds of tulips and daffodils along the roadway, the crocuses already asleep until next spring.

The crowd welcomed them with hoots and hollers, then a parade of kisses and hugs. Laura and Alyx attended with their husbands, leaving the babes behind with the nannies. They heartily expressed their thrill at being childless for the evening. Steve Moretti's parents attended and Jamie understood why Colin found them so endearing. Alyx's mother-in-law also appeared and Jamie mused that all three men – Doms – had such wonderful families and were the progeny of strong women with important careers. They'd managed to raise incredible sons, which bolstered Jamie's confidence that she could have a demanding career and still raise a kickass kid.

Rob Scarborough and Matt chatted in a corner, Rob's arm around a petite blonde, who Jamie now understood was his submissive. Matt's wife, Jillian, intertwined her hand with his as she sipped a martini. Others came from her office as well as a contingent from Colin's.

Drinks and hors d'oeuvres were passed, conversation animated, and dinner served. Colin whispered in Jamie's ear as he forked a piece of prime rib. "This is damn good food. My mother may not cook well, but when it comes to hiring a caterer, she's an expert."

Food was cleared in anticipation of dessert, a giant faux wedding cake sans bride and groom—replaced by two fondant hearts standing side-by-side, a brilliant sparkler flaming behind them. Jamie cut the cake, Colin's hand on hers. Applause filled the air and guests clinked their glasses, demanding a smooch. The engaged couple complied and then Colin whispered in her ear, "Can't wait to get you all to myself tonight."

"My parents will be there."

"Well, then you'll have to be very, very quiet."

"You know I'm not so good at that."

"Hmm, I don't usually resort to a gag but we might have to make an exception tonight."

Jamie slapped his chest. "You're evil."

Colin smirked. "Guilty again, Agent Gallagher. But no handcuffs on me. They're only for you." Cake was passed and champagne flowed.

Jamie went in search of Alyx and Laura, wondering how motherhood was treating them, Colin in tow. She found them in the kitchen talking with her mom and her mother-in-law-to-be.

Daniel and Steve completed the circle around the center island, smiling as the women lamented about the good and bad of managing an infant.

"Well," Colin's mother said to Jamie's mom, "we didn't have live-in nannies like people do nowadays. We had to make do with family and friends and the occasional teen." Eyes lowered at Mrs. MacKenzie's assessment.

Jamie defended her friends. "You also didn't have careers as demanding as ours."

Mrs. MacKenzie huffed. "Well, I'll give you that. A college professor can't hold a candle to what you do."

Changing the subject, Jamie said, "Didn't you invite Molly and her husband?"

"We did," her mother answered. "They said they might be late but I didn't imagine this late."

Alyx offered, "Maybe I should give her a call. Perhaps her daughter got sick or the sitter didn't show." She fished her phone from her jacket pocket. It rang, startling her. She frowned at the screen.

"Who is it?" Daniel asked.

"Unknown caller."

"Don't answer."

Alyx pressed the green button. "Hello? Yes, this is Alyx Taylor." Her face contorted. "There's been an accident," she announced, covering her mouth with one hand. She mumbled through her fingers.

Alyx laid her phone on the table and pressed the speaker button. "This is Detective Sergeant John Wixted. I'm at the scene of an accident. The female appears to be federal agent Molly Masterson. You're her emergency contact."

"Yes, is she hurt?"

"She's unconscious, no visible injuries other than a bump on the head. Vitals stable, breathing on her own. One male dead at the scene."

"Oh God," Alyx exclaimed. Tears welled and slid down her cheeks. "Sam's dead?"

"Yes, ma'am. Sorry for your loss."

Steve chimed in, "John, Steve Moretti here."

"Hey, Moretti. What can I do for you?"

"Tell us what happened. Alyx is also a federal agent, in fact there are several agents here with us."

"Your wife?"

"Yes."

"Gotcha. It appears they were traveling east on Northern State Parkway before the entrance onto 347. As you know, it's a limited access road. Apparently, a tractor trailer entered illegally and hit an overpass, rolling over onto the agent's car. It's crushed. A miracle anyone survived."

"And the driver?" Alyx inquired.

"Also deceased."

Daniel spoke. "Detective Wixted, this is Dr. Daniel Taylor. I'm Alyx's husband. What hospital are you taking her to?"

"Stony Brook. They're leaving now."

"Thank you," he said.

"You have my number, Agent Taylor," Sergeant Wixted said, "I'll inform you regarding further developments and if you require additional information don't hesitate to call."

"Thank you, Sergeant, we're on our way," Alyx said. Silence shrouded the room, the reality of Sam's demise a crushing weight almost too great to bear. "At least Justice is home safe." Alyx rubbed her temples, plucking a tissue from the nearby box to mop her face.

"I can't believe it," Jamie said. She could barely choke out the words. She grabbed Colin's hands, and squeezed. "We need to be there for Molly."

"Of course," he said. "I'll tell James." He exited the kitchen.

"I'll call Lydia," Laura told Steve. "Get the car."

"I'll call our nanny," Daniel said to Alyx. "Meet me in the car."

Jamie kissed and hugged her mother, then Colin's mother. "Please make our excuses," she said. "And thank you both, it was a beautiful party."

"Of course, dears, hurry off," Colin's mother said. "Drive safe and let us know how Molly is doing."

"I will."

"Sally, I'll send a car to take you both back to the city. We'll meet you there later. You have the entry code, right?" Colin said.

"Yes, thank you, Colin."

Jamie exited the back door and nestled in next to Colin. She rested her head on his shoulder, his arm circling her shoulders. Jamie hiccupped a sob, and the torrent raged. Tears and snot covered her face. Colin handed her a handkerchief and she wiped the wetness away.

"Oh, baby," Colin said, rubbing her back. "I'm so sorry."

"I can't imagine how horrible this is for Molly. How do you go on after something like this?" Another sob wracked her body.

"I know, it's terrifying to think your reason for living can be snatched from you in a split second."

Jamie gazed up into Colin's face, his compassionate smile warming her shattered soul. "If that ever happened to us…"

"Don't," he said. "It won't." He kissed the top of her head. "We'll always be together."

"You can't know that."

"I do. I know it in my heart. We'll lead a long happy life and walk into the great beyond together."

"That's absurd. There are no promises in life."

"Yes, there are, and I promise to be with you forever. That's my vision and I'm sticking to it."

"You're crazy, but I love you. I think I'll go with your vision."

"I love you," he said and bent his head, finding her lips.

She never knew it could be like this, his strength, his optimism and his love soothed her. She could believe the happily-ever-after fairytale with her handsome billionaire. Never in her wildest dreams had she envisioned this life, a life that gave her hope, confidence and a reason for living. She hadn't thought she needed that, but now? "I love you too, so much, with everything I have. And more."

She kissed him again, his muscular arms like a collar around her heart. No one could unlock it, break it. Never ever.

The End

Kendra Greenwood

Kendra Greenwood has always been a storyteller. She often told stories to her kids at bedtime in lieu of reading to them. A serious daydreamer, she used to think it the complete opposite of her education and work in the sciences, but now realizes scientists are the ultimate daydreamers. Fantasy has always been an escape for Kendra. Weaving a thrilling romantic tale around her favorite TV and film characters, her favorite way to fall asleep at night. Eventually she wrote them down and found a place to share her stories.

Kendra grew up on the beaches of Long Island's bucolic east end, but recently relocated to Virginia. When she's not writing you can find her in the kitchen whipping up something scrumptious or in the studio fusing glass into decorative dishes.

Follow her on:
Twitter @k51greenwood
Facebook Kendra Greenwood
Email kendra51greenwood@gmail.com

Don't miss these exciting titles by Kendra Greenwood and Blushing Books!

Steel and Desire Series
UnSub
UnBound
Unguarded
Unsaddened

Blushing Books

Blushing Books is the oldest eBook publisher on the web. We've been running websites that publish steamy romance and erotica since 1999, and we have been selling eBooks since 2003. We have free and promotional offerings that change weekly, so please do visit us at http://www.blushingbooks.com/free.

Blushing Books Newsletter

Please join the Blushing Books newsletter
to receive updates & special promotional offers.
You can also join by using your mobile phone:
Just text **BLUSHING** to 22828.

Every month, one new sign up via text messaging will receive a
$25.00 Amazon gift card, so sign up today!